AN UNEXPECTED
HERO

RHETT C.
BRUNO

JAIME
CASTLE

aethonbooks.com

To all the authors who allowed us to use their names in this book, and even those who didn't.

—RCB & JC

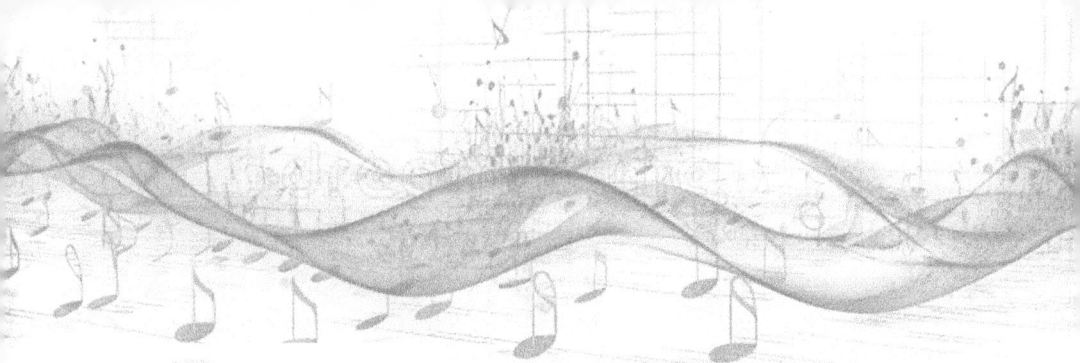

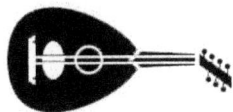

I s there anything more exciting than the rush that comes from standing on a stage, guitar strapped over your shoulder, microphone in hand, getting ready to make some suburban MILFs go crazy?

Because that was me. Right now. Danny Kendrick, star of the stage at the Heart-Shaped Box. A prism of clearance-sale lights blazed behind me. This was my domain. I was in complete control.

Being the sole source of entertainment for these poor ladies was a responsibility I took very seriously. Even on a Friday night, there wasn't much to do in Willistown, unless you were the kind of person who rented out motels by the hour.

This was my time.

After all, someone had to care for them.

One more sip of beer, and it would be time to launch into my kickass rendition of "American Woman," Lenny Kravitz's version, of course, complete with my attempt at the obligatory guitar solo.

I try to sneak in a Danny original or two from my short-lived touring days, but nobody wants them. Just the classics. So, it wasn't my dream gig of being a rockstar, but it was paying work, which is better than most musicians get.

I'd primed the crowd with a few slow jams. Got the seats wet, so to speak. Now let's make them gush.

The only thing throwing off my game tonight was the fact that the table up front—normally reserved for the Friday-night-soccer-mom-crew and smokin' hot Trish with the blonde pixie hairdo—had instead been stolen by a brood of bikers who'd been there since four, chugging dark beers like water. The drunker they got, the louder they got. The louder they got, the less attention I received from Trish and her friends at the back.

Though I'd complained to the Box's owner, Jerry, his only response was to remind me that they were spending more money than I was making.

Thanks, Jerry.

Needless to say, the motor-straddlers hadn't been impressed with my first cover of "Making Love Out of Nothing at All" by Air Supply. And then they'd soured even more when I followed it up with "Who Will Save Your Soul?" by Jewel. Things got damned near dangerous when I launched into "Don't Speak" by No Doubt.

I mean, if you don't think Jewel and Gwen Stefani are hot, do you really even get to call yourself a man of the '90s?

"Hey, asshole, don't you know anything harder than these girlie tunes?"

I looked down at the biker who'd spoken. He was a beefy sort of fella, with eyes that could literally watch both doors at once. Reminded me of the kind of guy whose cousin got pregnant in high school and no one knew who the father was, if you catch my drift. He had a jet-black beard and mustache that looked like an overgrown hedge, bugs and all.

I wasn't particularly thrilled with being heckled, so I decided to do something about it. The confidence I'd gained from the few beers I'd already thrown back helped.

"Wait for it, my man," I said mid-song. "It's coming up next."

"Yeah, better be." The biker turned to his friends and muttered something that produced uproarious laughter.

My face went hot. To hell with this. I stopped the song, held up my pint of beer that also cost more than I'd make tonight, and toasted everyone in the crowd. "Welcome to Friday night fun, ladies!"

The moms all went wild. They knew me. I was safe. They liked safe. They could come, flirt, get wasted, and tell themselves they "still had it" even though they were all on the downward slope toward Early Bird Specials and AARP memberships.

It wasn't my old days of playing big clubs and tall stages, but I'd done this enough to know that *Girls Night Out* was just code for "does alcohol make me forget about the boring-doofus-accountant waiting for me at home?"

I settled my eyes on the jeering biker and leaned forward with a grin. "This next tune is for my new best pal in the whole wide world. Er, what's your name again?"

The biker scowled. "Kurt."

"Burt! How 'bout a big round of applause for my pal Burt?"

He tried to correct me, but no one could hear him over the whooping ladies.

"Burt requested I play something 'harder'," I said. "Now, Burt, if that's what you want, it's possible one of your hairy pals there can help you out. But this isn't that kind of show."

I probably shouldn't have said that, but I was floating on quite the buzz. Besides, even though Kurt clenched his fists, the guys sitting with him howled in laughter, so the joke clearly landed.

What the hell. You only live once, right?

Time to get playing.

I fingerpicked an A chord. I sucked at fingerpicking, but Trish loved it. *Wink-wink.* The stage monitors squealed, feeding back as I stepped a bit too close to one. I ignored it. I'm a professional. Sharp hisses sounded behind me, and fog filled the stage while a few of the bargain-bin lights whirred.

The first tinny notes spun out of the *economical* speakers, and I sucked in a breath, then grinned at Kurt. "*My love, there's only you—*"

"SONUVABITCH!" Kurt sprang up, his wooden chair rocketing behind him and into the soccer moms' table.

My adoring fans screamed in half-drunken horror.

I staggered back a few steps as Kurt rushed the stage. "What— you don't like 'Endless Love' either? But it's Diana Ross!"

That was as far as I got before Kurt's beefy, hair-laden fist collided with my face in a chorus of sickening crunches.

I soared across the stage. I'd like to say I looked like a trained dancer as my boot slipped and I stumbled off the lip. Usually, I prided myself on my impeccable balance but, you know, beer. Graceful I was not. I slipped or tripped or both. It happened so fast, all I could see were the words blinking on the screen of an arcade machine: *An Unexpected Hero.*

My head smashed into the video game, cracking the monitor. My poor guitar—a Gibson Songwriter I'd spent a lot of money on— crunched beneath me, and the beer glass someone had carelessly left sitting by the video game's joystick shattered. Who leaves an almost full beer unattended? It's sacrilege! Warm, sticky IPA splattered all over and inside of the machine. Bright lines of pain radiated through my skull, then spread all over. This was what I imagined being struck by lightning was like.

The room became a glittering carousel. There was Trish. Bye, Trish! Oh, hey, Kurt. There's Trish again.

I blinked and something new appeared before my eyes, flickering as electricity continued surging through my veins. A square? A holo-gram? Was it the arcade cabinet?

I thought I'd felt pain already, but I was wrong. Agony wrenched my insides and then came *real* pain. Lots and lots of real pain.

And then blackness.

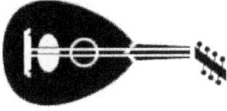

2

"**U**ghhhhh..."

It wasn't elegant, but it was the only sound I could make when I started coming to. My face throbbed.

I swore.

My face... That's my money-maker. Sure, I could sing—kinda— but my face...

I reached for my should-be-busted nose even before opening my had-to-be-swollen eyes. I let out a sigh of relief. Fortunately, everything seemed to be where it was supposed to be.

"Worthless bard. All you do is drink and pass out," someone said.

"Kurt?" I mumbled, voice coming out slurred and pained.

Didn't sound like Kurt, though. I risked opening one of my eyes, expecting the bright rainbow-lit bar to be excruciating. But the light was dim. And flickering. Like it wasn't really light at all.

I peeled open my other eye, sitting up slowly. The stench of spilled beer was overwhelming. That was appropriate, considering what'd happened. What wasn't appropriate was that I appeared to be sitting in it.

And it smelled old and stale. How long had I been out? My pants were soaked with—

A pair of rough hands hoisted me off the floor.

"Kurt—wait... wait a second—"

Not only did it not sound like Kurt, it didn't look like him either. An old geezer wearing a leather apron and a stern expression got in my face. He had frizzy muttonchops that curled into a mustache. His yellow teeth were caked in food, and I nearly retched at the smell that accompanied his words.

"Every night, it's the same damn thing. You waltz in, try to sing, then get drunk and keel over in a heap. I'm sick of it." He took a step back and his face softened as if he'd instantly calmed. He brushed me off like I was a kid who'd fallen in the dirt. "And you haven't paid your tab in ages, Daniil."

"My tab?" I blinked, trying to clear the stars from my vision. "Who's Daniil?"

The man shook his head. "So drunk you don't even remember your own damn name. You need help, boy." He steered me back to a stool. "Try and stay upright for the next few minutes. I'm gonna get you some work."

"Work?"

Seemed that in my confusion, repeating words had become my only form of communication.

The man threw up his wrinkled hands and wandered across the bar, leaving me on a wobbly stool. After a few seconds, I regained composure enough to survey my surroundings. I wasn't sure where I was, but I knew, without a doubt, it was not the Heart-Shaped Box.

The flickering light I'd previously noted came from a stone fireplace and some candles on wooden tables. Also, the floor and walls were rough stone, no sheetrock or paint. No neon lights missing letters. No mirrored back wall. It looked like the place hadn't been cleaned since the dawn of time. The tables were filled with folks dressed straight out of a renaissance fair, only dirtier, and smellier.

Oh, the smell.

You know when you flip open a garbage can that's too full and has been left out in the hot sun? It smelled like that. Everywhere.

"Where the hell am I?"

The words had barely left my mouth when a light blue square materialized in front of my eyes. A hologram? Or a floating touch screen? The juxtaposition of the old-timey world around me and something that better belonged on an episode of *Star Trek* had my mind whirling.

Within the light blue field, words appeared...

PART ONE

AN UNEXPECTED HERO.
PART I: Gags, Hags, and Filthy Rags, Oh My!

CURRENT LOCATION:
Tavern

NEW OBJECTIVE:
Convince the braugs to let you sing for them.

REWARD:
Food

The screen, since I guess that's what it was, wasn't opaque. Not exactly. It took up a good chunk of my vision, though. However, I could see the rest of the place through it. Superimposed over everything and staying directly in front of my face, even as I turned, the box projected as if from my eyes.

Bizarre. Did everyone see this? I glanced around. No one seemed to pay me any mind at all.

My head still ached from the punch and then the slam into the video game. Was this a symptom of a concussion? Or had I had more beers than I'd realized? Sometimes that happened when I got in the zone.

I looked at the words again...

An Unexpected Hero? Wasn't that the name of the arcade machine?

I glanced around for Trish and the other moms. Apart from a semi-attractive redhead doling out drinks from table to table and wearing what looked like an Oktoberfest barmaid's cosplay outfit, everyone was old and of the male persuasion.

Maybe I was dead. Maybe I'd spilled my brains all over that

machine and this was the afterlife. It was a far cry from any kind of heaven or hell I'd been lectured on as a kid in Sunday school. Eternity in a tavern. Solid. At least if I was dead, the suburban housewives would be talking about my final performance forever.

But I didn't *feel* dead. And I'd had enough bad hangovers in my time to be pretty confident about what I thought death would feel like.

A new message flashed across the weird hologram in front of my face.

CURRENT HEALTH: 70% (Drunken Impairment)

That was true. No one is one hundred percent after three or more Guinnesses. Or is it Guinessi? And how did this thing know what my health was? I'd never considered my health state in percentages before.

Maybe Kurt had socked me into a coma, and this was some sort of weird new healing technique that combined virtual reality with therapeutics. Hadn't I read an article about that somewhere? But where?

Ugh.

Thinking made my head hurt.

The guy who wasn't Kurt ambled back over, rubbing his hands together. What was this guy's problem? Could he see the hologram and read that I was drunk?

I hadn't even asked the question out loud, but the screen promptly issued a written response.

No. I am present only for you, Danny Boy.

It flashed again as the guy stopped in front of me. He suddenly became... highlighted? Literally. A thin aura of whitish-blue light surrounded him, not unlike the color of the screen itself.

NAME: Rarmir
OCCUPATION: Tavern Owner
RACE: Wellick (male)

What the hell is a wellick?

Again, I hadn't spoken out loud, but the screen answered.

Wellicks are a humanoid race that make up much of the world. They differ only slightly from your kind—mostly below the waist— so you will blend in. Until you take your pants off.

Can I continue now?

I blinked, then shook my head. So, the screen could answer my direct thoughts?

Hey, what do you mean until I take my pants off?

You'll see.

I groaned. Okay, I had questions and needed answers. I tried a simple one.

Have you got a name?

No.

Where am I?

A tavern. Hence, the Tavern Owner.

I meant location.

CURRENT LOCATION (EXPANDED):
Tavern. Town of Nahal. Kingdom of Pyruun.

Kingdom? What the actual hell? I guess I shouldn't ask what planet I'm on, huh? Because obviously, I've cracked.

I swear the screen sighed.

If you continue asking such silly questions, we'll never get anywhere.

I'm... sorry?

Very good. Now, where was I? Ah, yes...

RARMIR'S SPECIAL ABILITIES: Master brewer, spirits distiller, facial hair to die for.
WEAPONS: Oaken Club

He has a club?

I didn't get an answer, because the Tavern Owner—Rarmir, or whatever his name was—started babbling at me. Listening to him made my head hurt even more. But one thing was for certain, he couldn't see the screen. Nobody would act so normally if their own profile stood in midair before them. He just talked right through it.

"All right, I had a talk with them, but it's gonna be up to you to win them over," Rarmir said, deep chasms creasing his brow. "They're a rough lot, no doubt. If I was you, I'd put on my best performance tonight or they're liable to beat you senseless."

I kind of wanted to vomit all over him just to see his reaction. Honestly, it wouldn't be hard with how I felt.

"What are you talking about?" I asked.

Rarmir grunted. "I don't put up with your antics because it's funny. I keep you around to entertain my guests. There ain't much in way of entertainment 'round these parts—and you barely do that. But enough's enough, Daniil. You're gonna earn your keep tonight. Now get your skinny rump over there and strike up a conversation with their leader. See if you can't get him to hire you proper. Who knows, you might even make enough to settle your tab here."

He pointed to a group behind me that I hadn't noticed before. Which was shocking since they were louder than a flock of elephants. *Flock?* That can't be right.

A group of elephants is commonly called a herd or, less commonly, a parade.

Hmmm. Thanks?

"C'mon. Move!" Rarmir shouted before waddling away like a penguin.

I didn't feel very much like doing anything except possibly going to sleep. For a really, really long time. But, I was pretty sure if I wasn't dead, I was already asleep and having one of the weirdest, most vivid dreams of my life.

What was in that beer?

It's ale—or more specifically, a stout—which consists of roasted barley, malted barley, hops, yeast, and water.

This is gonna get old.

As I stood and approached the crowd of ruffians, butterflies unfurled in my stomach. Something I didn't think happened in dreams. A mix of men and women, each one was fiercer than the last.

They looked like they'd just raided a Burlington Coat Factory. Or an S&M shop, all furs and leathers.

The screen flashed again.

BRAUGS: A surly, barbarous folk from the far north. When they aren't battling, they are anxious for good food, drink, and amusement. These warriors are most sought after as hired guards and mercenaries, as their natural size and innate Rage give them extraordinary strength and unparalleled melee skills.

They are not likely to be kind to you.

Gee, thanks. That's helpful.

Look at me, being sarcastic to a floating box like a moron.

**You're welcome. Go talk to the braugs.
That is your current quest.**

Quest? Am I a knight here?

Hardly.

I heaved a sigh. My head still throbbed like a tiny dwarf was working a hammer and anvil inside of my skull. But what the hell? I'd play along and see how far into the weird this nightmare took me.

Standing, I glanced down for the first time. I wore a ruffled shirt that had once been white but now appeared permanently stained tan from sweat and alcohol.

The puffy shirt from Seinfeld. *Classic.*

"I don't wanna be a pirate!"

You know Seinfeld?

The screen didn't respond. Holy crap. I *was* going crazy.

I shook my head and continued examining my clothing. My pants weren't really pants at all. What'd they call those things? Breeches? Capris? All I knew was they certainly weren't comfortable. They ended just above my ankles and were coarse and itchy.

The screen's warning repeated in my mind. What did it mean the wellicks were only different if I took my pants off?

I considered peering beneath the fabric to see if anything had changed before thinking better of exposing myself in a room full of strangers.

Instead, I continued examining my clothing. But that was it, other than simple leather shoes that covered my feet.

Not exactly GQ material here, slick.

"Oy!" Rarmir barked.

I turned back to the bar to find him scowling and pointing at something behind me.

"Don't forget your lute, you numbskull."

I followed his finger to the instrument on the sticky, worn bar. I didn't even know what exactly a lute was. Some sort of woodwind instrument, except this thing had strings like a guitar.

That's a flute, not a lute.

Thanks, WikiAnswers. Well, I know how to play a guitar. How hard can it be?

It's your lie. Tell it how you want to.

I huffed, then picked up the lute. It was old and used, but it held a certain _charm_.

The crowd of braugs I was apparently meant to entertain tore through a table of unappetizing food Rarmir must've laid out for them earlier. None used any utensils; just dirty, nasty hands, all greasy and wet.

Suddenly, I noticed my bladder overflowing with all that beer. Was there a bathroom in this bar?

Tavern.

Whatever, you dumb screen.

I took a breath and wondered if I could hold it for roughly an hour. Probably not.

I really have to do this, huh?

Yes.

I sighed again.

Awesome.

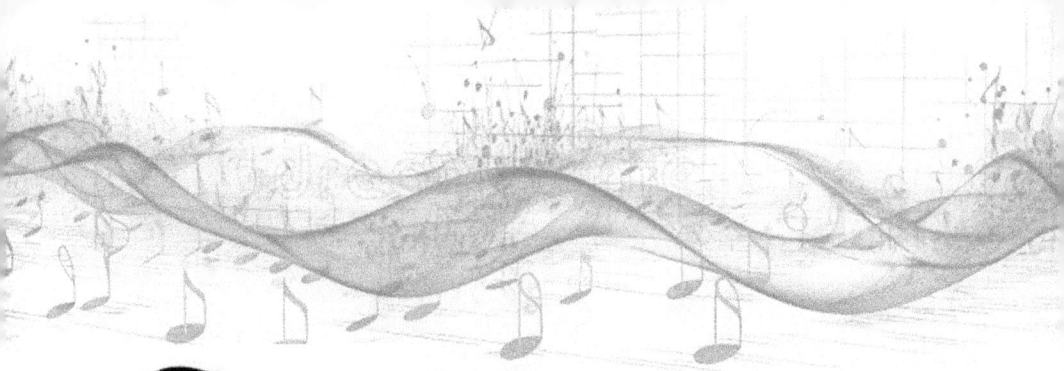

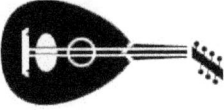

3

It was easy enough to pick out the braugs' leader. He was the largest of the bunch and double-fisted a couple of huge tankards of ale. The frothy, golden liquid sloshed all over a huge, black, gangly beard hanging from a head that was a scar-flecked cueball.

He looked... familiar.

Kurt? No. That's not possible. Is it?

The screen that popped up in response was much smaller than before, only large enough to fit one word that reeked of derision.

Nope.

It then highlighted the giant of a man just as it had Rarmir the Tavern Owner...

NAME: *Curr*
OCCUPATION: *Sellsword*
RACE: *Braug (male)*
SPECIAL ABILITIES: *Melee Weapon Combat bonus with all 2-*
Handed weapons, Tarton's Rage, Hardened Skin
WEAPONS: *Steel Dual-Edged Battle Axe*

Braug is a race?

Of course it is, you racist.

The big man scowled as I neared. Sensing his hostility, I decided to go for the friendly approach, especially since my head still throbbed, and the last thing I needed was another beating.

"Hi."

The braug—Curr, if the screen could be believed—gawked, appraising me up and down.

"What in Tarton's Tusks are you?"

Tarton was the name of an ancient—

Not now! I thought as authoritatively as I could manage. Thankfully, it worked, and the screen disappeared. Now I could take in the whole of the colossus with clear vision.

"Can you speak?" Curr asked.

"Uh... hi, I'm Danny."

"You are Daniil? The bard?" The braug slammed his tankard down on the table, spilling a fair bit of its contents in the process. He belched and I could taste it on the air in front of me.

I fought back the sensation to gag when he leaned forward.

"Before you speak," he growled, "I would like you to know that I am tired, hungry, and thirsty. So, if you have business with me, then spit it out or I might run you through for mild amusement."

I glanced at the massive two-handed battle axe leaning against his table and almost rolled my eyes.

Tell me you've got a small dick without telling me you've got a small dick.

He doesn't have a small dick.

"Uh, Rarmir said I might provide some entertainment for you." Then I quickly added, "I sing," so no one got the wrong idea.

Curr belched again. His eyes continued to rove over me, obviously sizing me up.

"You dance too?" one of the braugs shouted.

I ignored him.

"That lute of yours any good?" Curr asked, flicking my instrument. The strings rang out discordantly.

I held it up in front of me. "Sure is."

I hope...

Curr turned to his other party members. "Listen up, you worth-less scum. This boy here is going to sing for us."

Boy? Geez, dude. I'm in my late 20s.

Braugs can live for upwards of three hundred years. You are, to him, in fact, a child.

Three hundred years?

Either way, I wasn't some stupid kid. Just wasn't a good idea to argue with people who looked like they'd killed five people before my alarm went off. And since this big beast of a man reminded me a bit of Biker Kurt, playing nice seemed my smartest option.

I unconsciously raised my palm to the spot on my face where there should have been a dent the size of Kurt's fist.

Roars of laughter broke out along with a few taunts. Just like being back at the Heart-Shaped Box.

Not quite. The braugs will kill you if you don't entertain them.

Yeah, I kinda got that impression. Thanks for stating the obvious.

I returned my attention to the lead braug. "Allow me to entertain you and your brave war party, sir."

"Curr," he said.

"Excuse me?"

"You mispronounced my name. It is Curr, not 'Sir'. Hard 'C' sound. Do not botch it again."

This had to be a bad dream. Dreams did have a tendency to mirror real life, to echo reality in a way that stirred up joys and terrors. That had to be what this was. Someone dragged my drunken, injured ass back home to my bed. Or left me curled up on the floor of the bar, more likely.

I exhaled and tried to smile. "Of course, Curr."

Curr nodded. "All right, bard. You sing and amuse us."

I glanced at the table of food and my stomach growled, despite how gross it looked. Damn, I was seriously hungry for some reason. Did getting walloped in the face make you famished?

Before I could give it any more thought, the screen flashed again.

OBJECTIVE COMPLETED:
You have been hired by the braug leader, Curr.

REWARD:
Speechcraft!

You have gained +1 in Speechcraft. You silver-tongued devil, you.

Your Speechcraft is now 9.

I'd rather have food. You can't eat 'Speechcraft,' last I checked.

NEW OBJECTIVE:
Successfully entertain braugs.

REWARD:
Coin... orrrrr fooooooooooooooood.

Wiseass.

I stepped back and away from Curr. The tavern had a simple wooden stage adjacent to the fireplace, which I believe might've been called a hearth in these oldy times. There were no lights. No fog machines. And as I gave the room one last once-over, I decided there was definitely no Trish. I strode over, and after one very small step, mounted the platform that passed for a stage. If Curr stood, I was pretty sure I would still be shorter than him by a full head.

So close to the fire, the air felt hot and humid. Doubly so with all these hairy monsters exhaling their booze-laden breath into the already noxious tavern air. They were also either wholly blitzed out of their skulls or partially unconscious.

I took a quick gander at my lute. Maybe they'd be too drunk to care about what I sang. A spasm gripped my gut. What in the world was I going to sing? I hadn't been able to stomach playing any of my originals since my band broke up. And I couldn't very well trot out my sterling interpretation of "Semi-Charmed Life" by Third Eye Blind, could I? They'd cut me to pieces and probably eat me for dinner.

I placed my hand on the fretboard. One thing was immediately clear: this wasn't a guitar. The shape was all wrong and there were a lot more strings. I swore. I might have been damn good with a six-string, but with this? I wasn't even sure what to do.

Would you like to access your Catalog of Songs?

Wow, your timing is impeccable. That's a thing? You could have let me know earlier.

Well, would you?

Of course!

Four song titles I didn't recognize appeared before my eyes. None of them were by the Red Hot Chili Peppers, that was for sure. How was I supposed to sing any if I didn't know the words?

Curr abruptly cleared his throat, and I snapped back to the moment. Panicking, I picked one at random.

That one. "Stones, Bones, and Crones."

Call me crazy, but rhymes really get me. As soon as I thought it, a warm sensation flooded my body like I'd just taken a shot of good whiskey.

I mindlessly started plucking the strings and the words and melody to a raunchy tune about a virgin dwarf who suddenly found himself in a pickle involving a pair of old succubi came streaming out of my mouth. I had no idea who'd written the song, or how I'd known how it was sung, but I had to give them credit for the lyrics.

What's more, I was seriously surprised by how good I sounded. Don't misunderstand, I wasn't *good*. But at least the chords sounded like chords.

The last note rang out. I took a breath, feeling pretty damned stoked about the performance. I'd also never known so many things could rhyme with *rock*.

Unfortunately, the crowd of braugs didn't share my sentiment.

"What in Tarton's Tusks is a succubi?" one of them in the back called out.

"Uh..." I paused. Good question.

OBJECTIVE FAILED.
Would you like to try again?

I frowned. Clearly my skills were above the cultural education of this particular group. Then I saw Curr waving me over and I felt another gut spasm. I stepped down from the stage, my knees wobbling.

"Yes, sir?" I said.

Curr growled. "Are you braindead? I told you it is pronounced with a hard C." He waved a dismissive hand. "Listen. You are far from good. You have a bland voice."

"Bland! We used to tour with—"

He belched. A whiff of it shut me right up.

"And your playing is marginal at best," he continued.

Marginal. That's a pretty big word for a—

He belched again.

"My fellows here are getting restless..."

I gestured toward his crew. "Some of them are actually asleep."

Curr nodded. "And trust me, that is not a good thing for you."

He leaned closer, and I wrinkled my nose. The guy stank like he hadn't washed his undercarriage for at least a month.

"Now, you are going to play a wedding tune for Fargus and Vulna over there. They were just betrothed after we slaughtered a group of trolls."

"They got engaged after killing trolls?" I asked.

Wait, there are trolls here?

And not the internet kind!

Curr stared at me blankly. "Can you think of a better time for prenuptials than covered in the entrails of those foul creatures?"

I could think of at least five thousand better times but instead, I said, "Uh, not really."

"Right. So, you get up there and dedicate your next song to them. And make it good or else things are liable to get... broken."

"Broken?" I gulped.

Curr nodded once, then pointed back to the platform.

I returned to my singing spot, grateful to finally inhale through my nose without wanting to retch from Curr's stench.

The screen appeared once I was in place, repeating its last message.

OBJECTIVE FAILED.
Would you like to try again?

Duh, obviously. What's the other choice? Death?

This time, the screen remained conspicuously quiet.

Unsure what else to do, I turned to look at the... uh, happy couple. Though he was seated, Fargus looked like he stood at least seven feet tall and nearly half that wide. Where his eyebrows should have been was a long scar. He was also missing an ear—which might've been good for me.

And Vulna... I shuddered. She too had scars that scored her face, as if some wicked claw had raked its way down her cheek. Huge jowls hung below her jawline, and her hands, which now gripped both a tankard of ale and a leg of some kind of barely cooked meat, looked as though they could easily handle the massive broadsword slung over the chair behind her.

No wonder the braugs drank so much. They had to pass out just to be able to stand the sights and smells of one another.

Without thinking, I took a deep breath—instantly regretting it—and muttered, "Here goes nothing." Then I spoke up. "This next tune is dedicated to Fargus and Vulna, who are celebrating a very happy day."

The entire room came alive with hoots and howls. Tankards crashed into the tabletops and boots pounded the floor. Ale spattered onto gnarled wooden planks, yet nobody gave a damn.

Uh-oh.

My half-asleep crowd was now completely awake and alert, and all staring right at me.

You don't happen to have one about weddings or troll-killing or... anything remotely helpful?

The screen flashed.

No.

I stared down at my lute, sliding my fingers along the neck. How hard could it be to string a few lines together and play a simple melody?

It looks like you're about to improvise.

Would you like me to initiate suicide now?

Gee, thanks for the vote of confidence. I can do this.

Good luck.

I took another long inhale and started to strum as best I could, then raised my voice to cover the dissonant sound.

"There once was a fighter named Fargus,
As mighty as any has dared
He trod where the shadows loomed longest
And killed when others were scared..."

The screen flashed.

You almost rhymed.

You have gained +1 in Singing.

Your Singing is now 14.

A round of cheers rang out.

See? In. The. Zone.

If only Trish were around to hear it.

The braugs listened intently now, so I took another breath and continued.

"But alas, mighty Fargus was single,
For never throughout the whole land,
Could he find someone with which to mingle,
With whom he could walk hand-in-hand..."

Now the cheers turned to playful mockery aimed at poor, lonely Fargus. For a moment, I thought the big man might've taken offense, but instead, a tear broke free from his eye as he downed his tankard and slammed it back on the table.

"'Tis true! There weren't none who could be my equal. None! And aye, I was lonely as shite, ye scurrilous dogs!"

The room erupted in laughter. I chuckled nervously with them as I strummed and prepared for the next verse. Then they all turned back toward the stage.

"Then one fine day, mighty Fargus,
Gazed upon a true... beauty."

I swallowed. The words in my head were becoming muddled, fear of screwing up flooding through it. Somehow, my playing became even worse but kept on.

"With hair like gold and lips like sugar?"

The words were coming out like questions now.

"Fargus knew he'd at last found his... booty."

A few guffaws broke out at this, but the rest of the crowd started murmuring among themselves. Vulna frowned in my direction. I probably should've ended the song there, but stupid me, I kept going.

"'I am Fargus,' said the strong mighty braug
'I kill and pillage with ease.
I promise to love and to cherish you.
And never give you a disease.'"

Crap. Where did that come from? I glanced out at the crowd. Fargus stared down at his crotch with a quizzical expression on his gnarled face.

No turning back now.

"'The woman before you needs no man,
Here stands the one they call Vulna,
I swing swords and axes with glee.
Last night I ripped out a man's...

Oh. My. God. What in the world rhymed with Vulna?

"'... ulna!'"

Muttering broke out all over the room.

"What in Tarton's name is an ulna?" someone roared from the audience. "Is that like a cock?"

I stopped playing and hurriedly pointed to my arm. "It's a bone, actually. Right here."

More murmurs. My skin crawled. I should've said vulva. But men don't have them. And you can't pull them out, can you?

I, uh. Don't think they liked it.

Gee, thanks!

I panicked worse than ever. Sweat poured down my back, pooling in my underwear. It was then that I realized I wasn't wearing underwear.

Vulna looked none too pleased with the song. Fargus was still peering at his crotch and talking to it, apparently.

"Should'a been a cock," someone else said. "That would'a been a much better thing to rip off."

Someone else laughed at that.

My throat felt dry. "No, it couldn't have been that. It doesn't rhyme, you see—"

Stop talking.

Curr eyed me, then got to his feet a bit unsteadily. He held up one hand to quiet the room, walked over, and wrapped one of his beefy paws around my shoulders. I was right. He still towered over me. Small victory in the light of certain death.

"I think I speak for everyone when I say... Tarton's Tusks, that was terrible!"

His arm tightened around me, and I wanted nothing more than to be very far away from this tavern, dream or not.

"Since our bard friend here has introduced us all to the word 'ulna,'" Curr said, "I think it only appropriate that we see how easily one rips out. And possibly some other bones of his as well."

"Now, hang on a sec..." I complained.

With perfect timing, the screen added:

OBJECTIVE FAILED.
Would you like to try again?

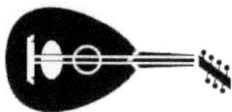

4

"Wait, wait, wait!" I took a moment—which was all I had—and gathered myself. I tried to pull my arm away from Curr in hopes of preserving it a bit longer, but he had a grip like the Jaws of Life.

"I meant no disrespect. Really," I said. "After all, I thought as braugs, you guys would appreciate the violence. Am I right?"

Curr still squeezed my arm like a stress ball, glaring down at me. He'd have made Andre the Giant look like a green bean.

"We do appreciate violence," he said. "And Vulna can certainly tear a man apart with ease. But the manner of your song left us feeling a little like we had been disrespected. We do not like being disrespected."

"Rip off his arms, Curr!" Fargus roared.

I did my best impression of a puppy dog begging not to get kicked—or in this case, have my bones extracted. And here I thought getting punched by Kurt had been bad.

By some stroke of luck or fortune, Curr raised his other hand. "Now, now... perhaps we are a bit hasty with that decision."

"Thank you. Thank you," I said. "I was only trying to entertain, like you asked. I meant no disrespect."

Curr frowned. "With a performance like that? You would fail to procure a job serenading the deaf."

Well, that was cruel.

It was also true.

"It was an especially awful series of notes there at the end," Curr continued. "Do you not understand keys and scales?"

"Look, I'm kind of new at this," I argued.

That was the truth. I still didn't even know where I was or what I was doing there. Not to mention I had no idea how to properly play a lute, which made inventing a song to sing along with all the more difficult. However, I knew one thing from my career as a performer: don't piss off the locals.

Curr pointed to my lute. "Looks like you have been in possession of that for some time."

I followed his gaze to the well-worn instrument. It had a small hole like Willy Nelson's guitar, and most of the paint had worn off.

"I... uh... got it secondhand."

"You what?"

"Used," I explained. "It was used when I got it."

"By someone better than you, no doubt."

Just then, my stomach rumbled so loudly, even Curr noticed.

He squinted. "When is the last time you partook of a meal?"

"Uh..."

The screen flashed.

Three days.

Three days? What the actual—?

Almost Four.

I sighed. "It's been a while, apparently."

"And yet you had enough coin for a drink?" Curr said. He got even closer to me, which was like being downwind of a port-a-potty. "Perhaps you should have spent that meager earning on a leg of lamb. Or lute lessons."

"Oof. I can't stand the taste of lamb," I said without thinking.

"Don't like lamb?" Fargus snatched the meat from his fiancée's hand and threw it at me. The leg of lamb hit my left arm and bounced to the floor. "You want to eat, little man? There's your meal."

I looked down at the meat on the gross tavern floor. It was already covered in dirt and God knows what else, given the lack of cleanliness of the entire room.

Curr pointed. "You hit him in his ulna!"

At that, the whole crew of braugs broke out in a fit, slamming tables and shoving one another.

When it all settled down, Curr said, "That will be our payment for your... services tonight. I suggest you accept that small token, because Fargus gets upset when people take advantage of his generosity. And I know you would not want to do that."

I nodded. "Of course, of course." I bent and picked up the already gnawed upon leg of lamb using my index finger and thumb.

ITEMS OBTAINED:
Leg of lamb ("cooked" sort of), origin questionable, two small flies.

I peered closer. There really were two flies on it, battling for meat. I shooed them away, but they just flew for a second and returned to duking it out.

Fargus chuckled. "Aye, take a bite. I'm sure you'll find it as delicious as we did."

I swallowed hard. "Oh, I'm not so hungry at the moment."

Then my stomach betrayed me again, launching into a digestive orchestration that managed to silence the entire room until they were all staring at me with judgmental glares.

I had no choice.

I steeled myself and brought the leg to my lips. Closing my eyes —not sure why—I bit into it and nearly heaved. The only thing keeping me going was the threat of dismemberment if I didn't manage to choke this down.

What kind of sick dream is this? Maybe I am dead.

You're not dead.

So, I'm dreaming?

No response. Of course.

"Oh, it's just lovely, thank you," I said to Fargus as I forced it down my throat.

HUNGER: 30%
You're not going to last much longer without more food.

"Well, I guess I'll be going now," I said through clenched teeth. "You all have a lovely night."

"Not so fast," Curr said.

My stomach was already reeling, and I just wanted to get away so I could vomit in peace. "What now?"

He extended his massive hand. "The lute. I am afraid we have a duty to render it... dead. There is no way, in good conscience, I can let you go back out into the world, torturing people with what you call music. Hand it over."

"Really? But it didn't do anything wrong."

"It could be used as a weapon of torture in your hands." Curr's fingers closed over the instrument's neck, and he snatched it away from me. Even if I tried, it's not like I could've stopped him.

"Take your meal and go," he said. "I suggest you do not try to play for braugs again. It is only because we have had our fill of killing that you are even walking out of here with your life."

I started backing away slowly, fearful my guts were going to turn inside out at any moment.

Curr raised the lute before the crowd. "And now..." He smushed it between his hands, crunching it into shards. "The threat is over."

Fists slammed on the tables, and braugs clasped arms in victory.

That was now my second instrument destroyed lately.

He wasn't even wearing gloves. I'm not sure why I worried about him getting a splinter as he removed his hands and the pieces tumbled to the floor. Then he picked up a couple of them and handed them out to be used as toothpicks.

I hurried away, the leg of lamb still dangling in one hand. Behind me, the braugs celebrated jovially.

Rarmir scowled at me as I passed. "Another man might've lost his life there tonight. You're a damned fool, Daniil."

"Danny," I said. "It's Danny."

Rarmir waved me off. "Out of my establishment. I don't need angry braugs asking me why I put up with the likes of a talentless bard in my place. Especially one who tries to fleece my customers out of their hard-won coin. Now get."

He stabbed his finger at the door.

I didn't need to be told twice. I'd learned long ago to feel the tide of a crowd turning. I missed Trish and her trophy-wife friends. They appreciated me at least.

"I'm not talentless," I said as I found the exit—a big, chunky wooden door—and pushed out. No knob to turn or anything.

It was dark outside, the moon covered by thick clouds. The only illumination came from torches here and there. I was on some sort of cobbled street, the silhouettes of low structures in every direction. No bright Taco Bell sign where I could get some late-night grub. Not like I even had the couple of bucks for that.

The screen popped up.

CURRENT LOCATION:
Nahal, Main Street.

I made it three steps before leaning on the tavern wall and gagging. I expected my stomach to empty all over Main Street, which in reality wasn't much more than a muddy track, but nothing came out.

Lightning flashed overhead.

Great. Now it's gonna rain.

Imminently.

The only saving grace was, as the first few drops fell, I was able to wash out my mouth and spit the bad taste to the side of the road. That relief soon turned to worry. It was cold and the rain was even colder.

Helluva way to end the night. Would be nice if I had a map.

I'm sorry. I'm not a GPS.

Fantastically unhelpful.

I examined the street. To my right, it was dark. To my left, even darker. Fog billowed in the distance regardless of which direction I chose. So, taking a right turn, I wandered aimlessly down the street.

The stone and wood buildings clustered on either side of the street started to thin out. It looked like a set from *Game of Thrones* as I passed all manner of shops and market stalls, each one closed for the night. Save for a few houses atop a hill to my left, the only place with lights on—so to speak—was the tavern behind me and a small inn at the edge of town. Too bad I had no money. I would have to find somewhere safe and, hopefully, dry to sleep.

As luck would have it, I spotted a stable attached to the inn on the northern side—okay, fine, who was I kidding? I had no idea which direction north was, or if there even was a north in this weird-ass world.

I paused, waiting for the screen to inform me of the cardinal directions, but when no response came, I made my way to the stable.

An overhang would shield me from the rain and elements, and there was a pile of hay in one corner I could curl up in. Despite the weirdness of whatever was going on, maybe falling asleep, buried in some soft hay, would make things right. Maybe I'd wake up, safe and sound back in the real world.

At least for now, rest would be grand. And I had no doubt the stable would smell better than those unwashed braugs.

It's now pouring.

Master of the obvious. Because I couldn't possibly extrapolate that valuable piece of information from my soaked clothes.

Two horses turned toward me and whinnied softly.

"Sorry about this, guys," I said. "I'm just here for the night while I figure out what the heck is going on."

I half-expected the horses to talk back, but they simply snorted and turned away.

The clouds had all but blotted out the moon now, and the blackness grew so thick, I was forced to feel around with my foot once under the covering. Locating a tall hay bale, I settled in. It wasn't the Tempur-Pedic mattress I still owed two grand on, but it was pretty comfy.

I shifted this way and that until I had most of the support I needed and then leaned back. For a moment, I considered trying the lamb again, but couldn't stomach it. I held on to it anyway, knowing if I woke up hungry enough, I might then have the courage to eat it.

Overhead, the pitter-patter of rain drummed along the roof. I was asleep before I even knew what was happening.

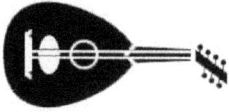

5

Something tickled my subconscious. And not like that one time Trish tied me up and used a feather to tickle me either. This was more... alarming.

Okay, fine, that *was* a dream. Trish and I never hooked up, much to my chagrin. The worst part? I really thought the other night was going to be *the* night. But then... Kurt.

The titillation at hand turned out to be a noise that was out of time with the natural rhythm of rainfall still peppering the roof. I couldn't quite place it at first. Then, after a few seconds awake, I realized it seemed almost like someone chewing on something.

Gross, smacking, slurping, wet sounds.

My eyes popped open. A fleeting hope passed through me that I was awakening from a bad dream by someone in the Heart-Shaped Box chomping on bar-nuts and back in my world. Or better yet, my bed. My home. Somewhere familiar.

Except, that would be weird if someone was eating in my bed. Okay, I'd prefer the bar.

As ever, my luck continued to fail me. I was in a bar*n*. With an N. At some point in the night, I'd covered myself with some of the hay to ward off the chill. I glanced around, eyes blurry, brain hazy. Oh, it was just something gnawing on my arm.

Wait—what?

I shot bolt upward and saw the huddled form of... something bent over my arm.

The leg of lamb!

It was still tight in my grip. Even as my mind reconciled with the situation, that sloppy sucking sound and loud munching magnified. And someone's cold, clammy hand held my arm firmly in place.

What the hell has my arm?

A pale blue screen popped up, reminding me that the screen existed and clearly had pertinent information for me.

HAG.

Dick.

No. You're looking at a hag.

She was highlighted in blue...

NAME: Unknown
OCCUPATION: Hag
RACE: Unknown (Female... probably)
SPECIAL ABILITIES: Unknown, and you probably don't want to know.
WEAPONS: Same as above

What the hell is a hag?

I asked all this while watching the haggard-looking thing and feeling its disgusting drool all over my hand and forearm.

HAGS: Magical, sentient creatures who typically appear as wizened old crones. Thriving—or trying to—they normally inhabit areas just on the edge of civilization. Though not a requirement to be old and ugly, they normally are. Most hags are able to cast spells and work various forms of sorcery from middling to great effect.

I jerked my arm free, pulling the leg of lamb away also.

"Noooooo," a voice moaned, sounding physically pained.

I guess now might be a good time to remind you that you're unarmed, and relatively scrawny.

Too bad your sarcasm is utterly worthless in a fight.

Would you like to try sweet-talking the hag?

I'd like to try wringing your neck.

I was interrupted by the sight of the hag spinning toward me. Instinctively, I scrambled backward like a crab into the inn's exterior wall.

"Who are you?" I stammered.

Having apparently ventured outside of the "highlighting zone," the blue glow vanished, replaced by a putrid green light illuminating the small space around us. Likewise, the effect washed over the visage of a horribly disfigured crone dressed in layers of filthy rags. Her face looked like an old, withered map where warts and pock-marks stood as landmarks, but her golden eyes sparkled despite her grim appearance.

"I am Phlegm. And I am hungry." She jabbed at the leg of lamb with one crooked finger. "I have traveled for many days without sustenance. Give me that so I may feast."

I raised the leg of lamb. It looked utterly pathetic, and yet...

"This is literally all that I have in this world," I told her.

Phlegm cocked her head. "What path in life would grant a man naught but a leg of animal flesh to make his way upon it?"

I tried to come up with a witty retort, but the truth was, I had no idea. I was still trying to figure out why I was even in this world.

"I was a... bard," I stammered. "From a faraway land. I, uh... I played and sang songs. I'm sorry, did you say your name was Phlegm?"

At that, what passed for eyebrows rose on Phlegm's face. She stood and licked her horribly chapped lips, an act that made my stomach lurch. Had I said something wrong?

"A faraway land, you say?" she asked.

"Uh. Yeah." Though my response was reluctant with her towering over me, I nodded.

"A bard?" Her head cocked.

"A musician and singer."

"You lie to me," she snapped. "Bards have instruments. You have none. Who would call themselves a bard and yet have no simple thing with which to make music?"

"True enough," I said. "But I *was* a bard. Just not a very good one, apparently."

"Tell me more," Phlegm demanded.

"I... hmmm. Well, my lute was destroyed earlier this evening— last night?—by a crazed group of drunken braugs who smelled worse than this stable. They didn't appreciate my... style of music."

The screen flashed.

NEW OBJECTIVE:
Make a bargain with the hag.

REWARD: ???

I frowned, which I'd been doing a lot lately.

How the hell do I do that?

Hey, I can't give you all the answers.

I'd settle for a few.

Phlegm cackled. "A bard so bad that his instrument got destroyed by mindless barbarians. That is indeed a conundrum for you." Her eyes flitted toward the leg of lamb. "And yet, you still manage to possess an item of great value to me."

"This thing?" I held up the meat, chunks of its flesh hanging by strands.

"I have not eaten for many days," the hag repeated.

"That makes two of us." I wasn't counting what little I'd choked down earlier against my will.

"Give it here," Phlegm said. "I will gladly devour it."

I regarded the leg of lamb. It was revolting, but it was still mine. Sooner or later, I'd have to eat something. Just that thought alone nearly called back the puke.

"I have to keep it for myself," I said. Then, softer, added, "Not that I'm looking forward to it."

"You are young," she replied. "Too young, some would say. You can survive without much. But I require more. Give it here."

She lurched for me, but I drew back. Oh, and guess what? She reeked. Par for the course. Not like the raw sewage stench of Curr, mind you. More like that sort of rotting plant life by ponds and creeks. Like something had died recently and hadn't been washed away completely. What was it about this world that everything stank in equally offensive ways?

I really have to make a bargain with this creature?

Yup. Enjoy yourself, kid.

What if she wants my... body?

Not even she is that desperate.

I swallowed. Nothing ever came easy. Our eyes met, and I was instantly reminded of the time when I was a kid and my mother brought me to visit Gram in the retirement home. Food fragments hung about her lips and chin. Some kind of eye goop trickled down —that might've been infected. Her hair was matted with muck.

As my gaze passed across Phlegm's warts, an idea came to me. Bargaining was a two-way street.

"You ask me to give you the only source of food I have," I said. "What would you offer in return?"

Phlegm's eyes lit up. "Would you make a bargain with this old woman? Would you give her a meal in exchange for something that you desire or require?"

I hesitated. This had to be played right or else I'd fail another objective. And I wasn't sure I'd always receive a second chance.

"I suppose it would depend," I said, dangling the temptation before her in the form of a rotted carcass.

After a moment of silence, Phlegm clapped. It scared the hell out of me. I think I even jumped. "Let us do it. Let us strike a bargain. And then I will feast, and you may return to your slumber."

I smiled like a gameshow host. "What would you offer me for this *glorious* leg of lamb?"

I held the lamb high, feeling like an idiot. Phlegm stared at it, saliva already dripping from her mouth. I noticed the meat had a sickly green slime on it and couldn't decide if it was from Phlegm or just the natural spoiling process doing its thing. Either way, there was no way I was gonna eat something so disgusting. The fact that it looked appealing to anyone, even her, was beyond me.

"A bard with no instrument is no bard at all," Phlegm said. "For my part, I will replace the lute that was destroyed earlier this evening."

I tried desperately to recall anything I knew about bards. They seemed kind of lame. I guess that meant I sounded kind of lame.

After a moment, I said, "It's not only the instrument that makes a bard, but an ability to weave a tapestry of words and songs and woo an audience with them."

Phlegm cackled again. "So, you doubt your abilities as well?"

I heard Curr's voice in my head again, telling me how awful I was in no uncertain terms.

"Let's just say that I can admit they may not exactly be my strongest attribute at the moment."

Phlegm frowned. "You ask a steep price for that sliver of meat."

"Sliver? There's so much juicy meat here." I swallowed back a gag. "More than enough to sustain you for several days. That alone would be worth the price."

"You strike a fine deal, young bard. Woo them, you shall."

Phlegm's hands waved in front of me, then almost seemed to dance as she spoke in low tones, muttering some sort of phrase three times before finally speaking to me again.

"Give me the leg of lamb and desire shall come to fruition before the sun sets once more."

I scoffed. "That's it? You expect me to hand this over without seeing anything in exchange?"

Phlegm spat a gob of mucus at me, which fortunately missed. "Foolish man. You think I can make something appear out of thin air when I am so weakened with hunger? Even one such as I cannot perform so grand a feat. But believe what I tell you—what you seek shall be yours. Even now, the gods conspire to deliver it into your hands. The instrument will find you."

"And my... singing?"

What really sucked was my whole life I'd believed myself to be a fine singer. Even paid the bulk of my bills doing so. My band opened for some pretty big acts back in the day. I don't know what happened, but here, I sounded like a hog being run over by a tractor.

In Willistown, crooning some old cover-tunes was enough for my usual crowd of cougars. I was young, virile, and had nice hair too. Maybe they just didn't care what I sounded like. No. That wasn't true. This place was just getting to me.

Phlegm extended an open palm and wagged her spindly, twisted fingers. They reminded me of a tree branch in the dead of winter. A piece of loose skin stretched between two of them like a duck's foot.

"First, the lamb," she said.

I reluctantly handed the food over, and Phlegm snatched it away before I could change my mind. She fell upon it like a ravenous wolf. For the next several minutes, my ears were assaulted by the gruesome sounds of Phlegm the Hag devouring the leg. When she was full, when I thought she was finally done, she broke open the bone and sucked at the marrow from the bottom, tucking whatever scraps were left away in her cloak.

I covered my mouth with my arm, dry heaving, and regretting losing my bargaining chip before guaranteeing she'd fulfill her promises. "Okay, I kept my end of the bargain."

"You have indeed." Her face was freshly slick with animal grease, the green light that continued to illuminate the barn enhancing the oily gloss.

"Ugh, and here I am, fresh out of wet-naps."

Phlegm clearly had no clue what I was referring to. Martha Stewart would've soiled herself if she ever saw this.

Once again, the hag waved her hand and muttered some sort of incantation into the night air. She reached into the depths of her rags and produced a small vial of liquid as green as the light surrounding us.

"When—and only when—the first part of your bargain finds its way to you, drink this," she said, offering it to me.

I took it like it was a sample of her urine and held it up to the meager light. It seemed to pulse with some sort of energy.

ITEM OBTAINED:
Vial of Musical Aptitude.

Maybe now you won't suck.

"You want me to drink this?" I asked, incredulous.

Phlegm cocked her head and stared at me. "You ask stupid questions. Of course, you must drink it. How else will you become that which you desire? The potion will give you the skill that you seek. But *only* when you have received the first part."

"The instrument you promised," I said. "What will happen if I drink it before then?"

"Bad things," she said in a more than ominous tone.

"Okay, so when I get that, then I drink the potion."

Phlegm smiled and revealed rows of sharpened teeth. "Yesssssss. First the one, then the other. And finally, the third."

"The third?"

"Everything happens in threes," Phlegm said. "It is the way—the only way—of the gods. Magic once given returns thrice. Gratitude is that which is sought. Goodness imparted does likewise. You have helped an old woman on this night, and so we have struck a bargain."

OBJECTIVE COMPLETED:
You have made a bargain with the hag.

You have gained +1 in Bartering.

Your Bartering is now 6.

That might not have been the best idea.

But you said...

If I said to jump off a cliff, would you?

NEW OBJECTIVE:
Procure a new instrument.

REWARD:
A new instrument

No crap.

"Okay then," I said to Phlegm, frustrated. "Before tomorrow night. That's what you said, isn't it?"

She nodded. "Before the sun sets once more."

"Are those different things?"

"Before the sun sets once more," she repeated. "It will be as I foretold. Then the second. And then—"

"The third. Yeah, I got that part. But what is the third? How will I know?"

Phlegm continued wearing that putrid smile. I swore I would have nightmares about those crooked tooth-daggers until my death bed.

"All things in three," she said. "Three is the way. The only way for those like me. And you will discover it soon enough when you search within." She licked her lips and rose, her rags whispering around her ankles. "And now, I will continue on my way, having been sated by your bargain."

"Really? But it's pouring outside."

Are you inviting her to spend the night?

I panicked as Phlegm turned, hoping she hadn't taken it that way.

"I mind not the storm that rages. As the meat of that lamb gave me strength, so too does the wrath of nature." She glanced back over her shoulder. "Good fortune to you, young man. And remember the three."

With that, she stepped out into the stormy night. I blinked once and she was gone, along with the eldritch green light that she'd somehow produced.

I raised the small vial to my eye-line. Remarkably, unlike every-thing else in this Godforsaken—or gods forsaken, it seemed—world, it was utterly clean.

"Hi, I'm here for my drug test," I muttered to myself. "Got my sample right here."

I shook the bottle, and it tumbled out of my hand and clattered in the dirt. I swore and swept it up, thankful I wasn't on hard ground.

Was I insane for even considering drinking anything given to me by a strange hag? Imagine trusting a vial from some random hobo back home. Hello, accidental overdose.

Sighing, I tucked it into my pocket. It wasn't like I'd lost anything of any value, and who knew what Phlegm might've done to me had I denied her. Maybe would have turned me into lunch with those teeth...

I shuddered before turning over to try and get back to sleep. Then I rolled onto my back, worried something else might sneak up on me. Sleep would not come easy.

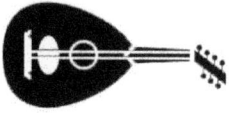

6

Sleep came easier than expected. I must've been more exhausted than I'd realized.

Chirping birds and a brilliant blue sky greeted me when I awoke just after dawn. It would've been a nice start to the morning, if not for a sudden urge in the pit of my stomach leaning me over to one side where I vomited everywhere.

Ugh. I felt like crap. At least I'd only puked. Getting the runs in a place that didn't look like they knew what toilet paper was would have been much, much worse. That damnable blue box splattered itself across my tear-smeared vision.

CURRENT HEALTH: 65% (Food Poisoning)

Good job. You ate rancid food. Your belly is less empty, but you are sick. You're lucky you only had a bite. The effect should wear off shortly.

Seems about right. I knew that leg of lamb wasn't good.

What clued you in?

Yeah, well you weren't exactly offering filet mignon last night.

Correction. Fargus wasn't offering filet mignon.

Whatever. Listen up, you worthless box. I'm starving and I have no money. So, if you have any ideas on how to correct that situation, you could go ahead and share them. Because, you know, I'm in some weird world, with absolutely nothing except for some vial of green goo, that I apparently have to wait to drink.

The screen didn't respond.

Figured.

And what about Phlegm? She was as hideous as a sixty-something Karen full of Botox and Bud Light. Old and weak—food poisoning might kill her. Then again, maybe not. She seemed more accustomed to working with... I dunno... sickness? It didn't make any sense, but I figured if she was traipsing about the town dressed in a schmatte, she might not really care about whether or not the lamb was rotten.

Me on the other hand... My mouth tasted like butt. I needed to rinse.

There's a puddle over there.

I'm not drinking out of a puddle. What am I, an animal?

Well, you did just sleep in a stable.

I'll survive until I can find something in a mug or glass or even a horn.

Suit yourself.

THIRST LEVEL: Parched

I felt awful and was uneasy about my meeting with the hag. Hell, maybe it wasn't the leg of lamb, after all. Maybe just being so close to Phlegm had poisoned me somehow?

I said food poisoning, not hag poisoning.

Yeah, yeah. Okay. I get it. Hey, 68%? I'm not drunk anymore. That should count for something, right?

I don't make the rules.

That got me thinking about something Phlegm had said. The gods were preparing to help me.

How many gods exist here?

Pyruun citizens worship many gods and goddesses, including, but not limited to Ludos, God of War, Fre, the Goddess of Light and Shadow, Baruu, God of Summer's Flame, Wokaaner, God of the Emptiness and Void, and Prakuma, the Goddess of Death.

Is that all?

Not remotely.

Shall I continue?

No, that's okay.

I felt pretty dumb, conversing with whatever this thing was in my own head, but I had to admit, it was nice to have company in such a bizarre place. Still hoped to snap out of this and find myself back in Willistown, except more and more, I was losing faith it would happen. I can't remember ever sleeping while dreaming, not to mention the myriad other things I'd experienced over the past twenty-four hours.

I'd been so distracted with the screen, I kind of forgot I was walking. Back on the main road, I came across a set of small footprints that led off into the wild woods on the... western(?) periphery of the town. The hazy peaks of several mountains rose in the distance, and I got the sense that if I followed the tracks, they would eventually bring me to them.

No doubt, the footprints belonged to Phlegm. I could tell by the way they dragged like some zombie from the *Walking Dead*. Though there were other, more pressing matters to attend to at the moment.

NEW OBJECTIVE:
Obtain food.

REWARD:
Food. Duh.

I sighed.

You don't actually have to tell me that. Believe it or not, I'm pretty good at figuring out when I need to eat.

And I currently wasn't hungry. My stomach was still knotted from the food poisoning.

You'll feel better, and then return to being starving.

I said I know how it works.

I gradually lumbered back to the center of Nahal, taking my time since that seemed to be all I was in control of. And wouldn't you know it, as my feet sloshed across the wet mud of what seemed like the town center, the screen was right.

CURRENT HEALTH: 70%
Effects from food poisoning have worn off.

You are starving.

I was, indeed.

Nausea was promptly replaced by a hunger pang. Sensations in this world sure did progress aggressively.

Townsfolk went about their daily chores, all dressed in medieval-style clothing. One of which was a baker carrying his goods down the path, and he seemed like a potential opportunity.

I fell into step with him, noting his obvious girth. Eating well had apparently never been an issue for him. He had a white beard, and flour dusted across his face and apron. Then I realized his beard was actually red, and was just also coated in flour.

In an instant, he began glowing that blue-white glow...

NAME: Mork
OCCUPATION: Baker
RACE: Wellick
SPECIAL ABILITIES: Cream pastries that'll make you cream.
WEAPONS: Probably a rolling pin.

That's gross. Besides, they can't be that good.

BET.

I gave Mork the baker a cheery greeting. "Hello!"

The man looked me up and down and I could tell he wasn't impressed. Couldn't blame him either. I wasn't all that much to look at, especially not after sleeping on hay and puking everywhere.

"I got nothing to give ye, beggar," he said. "Now leave me be."

I pretended to be shocked.

"A beggar? Me? No, good sir, I would implore you not to think of me as such. I am a bard, gifted with the skill of spinning yarns and singing tunes to entertain the masses."

May as well embrace the role I was playing, I figured.

Mork studied me again. "Masses? Pfft. Where's yer instrument then... *bard*?"

Balls.

"I, uh, was regrettably waylaid last eve and it was destroyed by the sort of hooligans one would hope never to find themselves in the company of. Alas, I am left with my voice alone."

The baker grunted. "Fine. Why don't'cha sing me a ditty, then, and perhaps, if it's any good, I'll throw ye a few crusts as thanks."

"A man can hardly sustain themselves upon mere crusts, my good sir. A few coins may well be a better option."

Mork shook his head. "I have scant few meself. Why d'ya think I'm selling this lot? Are me loaves not good enough for the likes of ye? C'mon now, give me a tune as we plod."

"Very well."

The prospect of only being paid in crusts did little for my pride, but the gnawing in my stomach was content with the proposal.

I cleared my throat.

Oh, man. You're not really going to try improvising again, are you?

I'll do better today.

No doubt. It would be hard to envision a worse performance than last night.

You know, you could offer up some helpful advice every now and again.

You're right. Don't suck. How's that?

Unreal. I took a breath and started singing.

"*On the road one fine morning*
Strolled a baker and a bard
The smell of fresh bread
The taste of warm lard—"

"I don't use any lard in me recipes," Mork the baker interrupted. "Well, except perhaps in the sweets and confections. But me bread don't have none."

"It's not customary to interrupt when one is singing," I said.

"Well, it's a stupid song. Sing something else."

Would you like to access your Catalog of Songs?

"No, shut up."

"What'd ye say to me?" the baker said, stopping mid-step.

Frustration got the best of me, and I didn't realize I'd answered the screen out loud.

"Not you," I said, bowing. Why the hell was I bowing? "I wasn't talking to you."

"Then who was ye talking to? Only me here, lad. Now if ye can't be cordial, I—"

"No, no. Seriously. Okay. Fine. A new song? Here we go."

I took a deep breath and started again.

"Do you know the muffin man
the muffin man, the muffin man
Do you know the muffin man
who lives on Dreury Lane."

I continued as one would expect until the song was done.

"So, what do you think?" I asked.

Mork sighed. "Weren't the rousing ditty I had in mind. Was looking for something, I dunno, more heroic? Of places far off and heroes long lost? Besides, this is Main Street, not whatever you called it. This is boring stuff yer singing about."

"That song's actually about a serial killer, I'll have you know. Nothing more exciting than that."

"Serial what now? Alright, alright. The song was boring, but your voice was... not bad. Wasn't good neither. Ye sure yer a bard?"

I thought my advice was helpful. Did you not understand it?

Shut up and bring up the catalog.

Ya think?

The same six songs appeared in front of my eyes. One popped out at me and it sure as hell wasn't the one I'd sung last night.

That one.

As I was about to sing a song called *T'was Morn in the Eve*, the baker said, "Know what? How about a dance instead. Ye dance, right?"

"Well, not re—"

"Dance nice for me and I'll give ye a whole pastry. How's that sound?"

"Dance?" I asked with trepidation. I've never danced before in my life. I didn't even go to prom in high school.

You heard the man. Dance, monkey.

I'm not a stripper. I'm not just going to dance because some dude tells me to.

Oh. Silly me. I thought you were hungry?

And that, folks, is how bad life choices are made.

HUNGER LEVEL: Dangerous

Dangerous?

You haven't eaten properly in days, Danny. This is how the world works. Perhaps a Snickers bar?

I started to ask if they really had those here, but Mork the baker was getting restless.

"Ye gonna entertain me, or should I continue me delivery?" he asked. "These boxes are getting heavy."

"Got anything with cream inside?"

Hahahaha.

"Ye'll get what ye get and ye'll like it," Mork said.

"Alright, okay. Dance..."

I thought of the only dance I could. In my head, I sang the *Macarena* and began the steps.

Both hands out. Then flipped them. Crossed my arms. I felt

like an idiot. Absolutely must've looked like one too. When I got to the part where I shook my hips, the baker had had enough.

"Stop, stop, stop!" he said. "I'll give ye something to eat just to get ye to stop."

He set the boxes down, reached into one, and tossed something glossy and sugar-coated at me, mumbling about "the worst bard he'd ever seen" as he retrieved his goods and left me standing there in the middle of the street with a few of Nahal's citizens staring at me in abject horror.

ITEM OBTAINED:
Pastry.

If it tastes weird, don't worry. The baker has cats.

I tore a chunk free and started eating it. Then I called after him, "Thank you for your patronage, my good sir. I wish you well."

OBJECTIVE COMPLETED:
You've found food. It was sugary, sweet, and the cat hair was
fibrous. Be careful. Diabetes exists here too.

CURRENT HEALTH: 82%

HUNGER LEVEL: Acceptable

The pastry was soft, warm, and doughy. Different from breakfast desserts back in my world, and somehow better. More wholesome. It filled my stomach as I delved deeper into the town center. Then I worried it really did have cat hair in it and that was what was so filling.

As good as it was, it wouldn't be enough to sustain me for very long.

NEW OBJECTIVE:
Obtain a heartier meal.

REWARD:
Food. Duh.

A hearty meal. Right. Like some meat—but *not* lamb. Something solid. Protein. That sort of thing.

Question was, how?

The screen offered no advice, but it didn't need to, the answer obvious. With money of course! No matter the world, money talked. I wasn't sure if barding paid well—it sure as hell didn't back at the Heart-Shaped Box—but I needed to earn somehow.

I thought about Phlegm again and the bargain we'd struck. Before the end of the day, or before the sun sets once more—as she'd put it—she'd promised a replacement for my instrument. Did I tell her it had to be a lute? A guitar would be even better.

Crap. It better not be a huge harp that I'd have to lug around everywhere.

That would be pretty funny.

Yeah, for you, maybe.

I wandered down the town's main thoroughfare. Colorful triangular flags hung from strings draped between buildings that were surprisingly well built, considering they didn't have power tools or machines. The place was sort of bustling. I mean, it wasn't Times Square or anything, but for a podunk town like this? It was lively.

A hand-carved sign with an anvil swung above one building, and the screen told me it was a Blacksmith. Another had what looked like a needle and thread—apparently a Tailor. There was an Apothecary.

Maybe they had some good drugs that would snap me out of this whole ordeal.

Then I heard a commotion and spotted a band of entertainers performing for the early morning passersby.

TROUBADOURS:
Wellick, dwarf, and halfling.

Wellick... huh. That was what the tavern owner was. And Mork. This woman looked just like a human.

I guess I'm just a wellick here.

You'll pass until you—

Take off my pants. I know!

The wellick lady was a bit of an acrobat, flipping and cart-wheeling around, while the stout dwarf lifted heavy items to show off how strong he was—and yes, he had a legendary beard. The curly-haired halfling played a small pipe of some type.

That's *a flute.*

A fellow bard, huh?

No lute, though.

The small crowd gathered around them didn't seem all that impressed. Surely, it was nothing compared to my ravishing rendition of "The Muffin Man." The troubadours looked anxious that their show wasn't winning anyone over. Sadly, I understood the feeling well.

The halfling inched his way toward me.

"Don't like the music?" he asked. "How about a magic trick?"

"I'm not really the *magic trick* kind of guy," I told him.

"Aww, just a small one?"

The halfling got uncomfortably close, so I took a small step back and felt something solid slam into me. Or rather, I slammed into something solid.

A strong hand squeezed my shoulder.

"Well, well, well... it is you again."

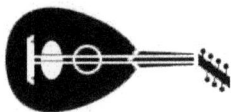

7

M y body was turned around despite my desire not to, until I faced a hulking man.

Oh, balls.

Not just any man. Curr the braug, bald and bearded, scary and tattooed in his fine leather armor. And now, his massive axe was strapped on his back in a... what do they call it? A sheath? A scabbard?

Either works.

I immediately tried to back up as I stammered, "Good morning, sir, er... Curr."

"Better," the braug said. "I see you managed to find someplace to hole up last night."

I ran a hand through my hair, brushing out bits of hay. "Well, yes. Yes, I did. I can be quite resourceful, and street smart."

Curr looked over my head, which wasn't hard for him to do. I could tell he was eyeing the troubadours.

"You know he was trying to pickpocket you, right?" he said loudly.

"He... what? Him? No, he was trying to show me a magic trick."

Curr let out a barking laugh. "Aye. The trick would have been when you got home and found your purse-strings cut."

I glanced back at the halfling, who stared at Curr like he'd just swallowed curdled milk.

"Well," I said. "Joke's on him. I don't have a home or a purse."

"Right," Curr said. "No job anymore either, huh?" He didn't let me respond. "And the leg of lamb that Fargus gifted you with?"

"Oh, just the best. Delicious. An exquisite meal. Far more generous than I probably deserved after my offenses to you fine folks last night, for which I am eternally sorry. I meant no such harm, I assure you."

"You did not really eat that, did you?" Curr asked.

"I—well." I looked down at the cobbled street. "No."

Curr laughed again. Who was this good-natured man who'd replaced that grump from last evening? "Good thing! Probably would have killed someone as puny as you."

Oh. Same guy.

He must've noticed a change in my demeanor.

"I am just having a bit of fun teasing you. Surely you are not so sensitive."

I glanced around, searching for an out. The troubadours had apparently given up after Curr called out the halfling loud enough for onlookers to hear. They were starting to pack up their cart.

"Speaking of Fargus and Vulna," I said in what might have been the worst segue ever, "where are they and the others in your company?"

Curr shrugged. "I do not know. Our quest was completed, and so we have gone our separate ways after our final celebration."

"Oh..."

I couldn't keep from considering what that kind of relationship looked like.

"Speak your mind," Curr said.

"It just seemed you and the others were awful close to just... part ways."

"Bonds are forged in battle, but I knew them barely a fortnight. That is simply the way of us sellswords. Suits me just fine. I am more accustomed to my own company anyway. However, oftentimes, the enemies we face are such that they require more brawn than brains to deal with. So that is what I put together: a company of simple-minded yet strong fighters."

"You put the company together?"

Curr squinted. "You seem surprised by that fact. I sincerely hope for your sake you are not about to say something stupid."

Careful. He's starting to like you.

"Not at all, I just thought that you were all—"

"Senseless duddards given to bloodlust?" Curr nodded. "Yes, I know. And as such, most people think us incapable of possessing even a modicum of intelligence. But there are more things in this world that can be accomplished without violence than with it, so I try to engage my intellect more than most of my folk."

I decided to ply his ego a bit. "You do seem very wise."

Curr grunted. "With my intellect, I also have a rather well-developed lack of tolerance for obsequious behavior. My axe is swift to deal with such transgressions."

The screen flashed.

Oops. Your attempt at persuasion failed.

Do you have an off button?

Trust me, you don't want to shut me off.

I held up my hands to Curr. "Again, I meant no offense."

Curr fixed me with a steady glare. "Tell me, bard, what is that accent of yours?"

Accent? He was the one with the accent. It was something like Russian, but also maybe Native American? There was a bit of haughtiness to it also, like a royal from England, but maybe that was just his love for obscure words. Honestly, I couldn't describe it if I tried.

"What is the farthest you have been from this town?" he continued. "Three leagues? Ten? More?"

I didn't even know what a league was.

A league is a difficult unit of measurement to define. Historically, 7,500 feet to 15,000 feet, it is now widely accepted as three miles.

Good question. "Not far." It was the truth, after all. I still had no clue why I'd ended up here.

"No wonder you are so pathetic," Curr said.

"I'm not pathetic," I said, gaining a little courage. "I'll have you know, I played in a band—"

He clapped me on the shoulder. "Forgive me, I meant no offense by it." He gave me a knowing glare, repeating my own words.

"Pathetic is just not the word I would've chosen to describe me," I said.

"Ah, do tell. What would the lowly bard say of himself?"

I chose to ignore the question. "I may not have the most well-traveled itinerary, but I—"

"Do not really have a good singing voice either." Curr grinned. "Or even an instrument that you can play to try to scrape up some work."

"No thanks to you."

Curr chuckled. "You made the mistake of trying to con us out of our hard-won gold. I know you realize that you are not the best bard that has ever strummed a lute."

"Hey, I was hungry and had to try to earn a meal." I sighed. "Yes, perhaps I'm not the greatest. Maybe my voice isn't exactly... mellifluous—"

"What does that mean?"

I slapped my knee. "Ah! Did I stump the intellectual?"

Curr's features darkened. "Just tell me what it means before I stomp you into mushed bard."

I swallowed hard. "A flowing, soothing quality to it... like honey."

He stuck out his tongue in disgust. "Never liked honey. Too sweet for my taste."

"Anyway." I was starting to get annoyed. "I was able to do a lot more last night when I had my lute. You remember that, right? Before you crushed it? Now I can't even play."

"You could not really play it last night either."

"You know what? I don't really have to take this kind of abuse—"

"Relax, friend! You were lucky Fargus chose not to rip you into tiny pieces after comparing his betrothed with a bone. I was doing you a favor. Your lute instead of your skull."

"Doesn't he understand? That's the point. I make rhymes. Not everything does so easily, but you try regardless. And oftentimes, you have to come up with them on the fly."

"You chose the occupation, did you not?" he asked.

I ground my teeth.

I didn't choose any of this.

The screen flashed.

HUNGER: *Your tummy will start growling soon.*

OBJECTIVE UPDATED:
Convince Curr to buy you a meal.

Now, how the heck am I supposed to do that? Curr demolished my lute last night for trying that very thing! Now you want me to do it again? What—the rancid meat and food poisoning wasn't punishment enough?

You need more meat.

Hah. That's what she said.

If I wasn't so frustrated, I might have smirked at that.

No, I need to figure out what the hell is going on here! Like, why I'm here in the first place and all that. Y'know, the important stuff.

Feeling a stare, I looked up. Curr watched me curiously. I must've checked out there for a few moments while arguing internally with the screen and hadn't yet responded to his question about choosing this life.

"Sure, I did," I lied. "But that doesn't make it any easier. You have to do your best with what you have and hope the audience likes it."

"And do you have a lot of fans of your work?" Curr asked. "Followers?"

I considered how best to answer that. Before the Heart-Shaped Box, I had a pretty decent career. Though that was then...

"I am... tolerated."

Curr chuckled again. "Tolerated? Why would anyone aspire to be tolerated? Who cares what people think of you?"

"Well, I kind of have to care." I crossed my arms. "Imagine if I simply stopped caring and went around singing whatever I wanted to? Or said things that offended my audience? I'd have to be a capable fighter to deal with that. And trust me when I tell you, I am no fighter."

"I trust you. You could barely hold the lute aloft last night. I do not struggle to imagine what you would look like wielding a sword."

"Once again, thanks." This conversation was doing great things for my ego. Subject change time. "So, where will you go now?"

Curr rolled his shoulders. "Back to the tavern. I am hungry and need sustenance."

Here's your chance. Don't blow it.

"Yeah, I'm starved too," I said. "And given that you destroyed my only means of earning money, I'll probably go hungry."

"My sincerest apologies."

"That's it?" I asked. "That's all you've got for destroying my livelihood? *Sorry?*"

He blinked at me, then offered a slight nod, as if the idea of me even questioning that was illogical.

"How about a consolation gift?" I said. "Maybe a hearty meal at the tavern? I could use a good one. I've only had last night's solitary bite of lamb in days."

Curr pointed at my tunic. "You have breadcrumbs on the front of your tunic." My face went red. Curr crossed his ridiculously muscled arms. "Is it your custom to lie as much as it seems? That is a very dangerous hobby to pursue. Especially to someone twice your size."

"Look, Curr, I only want fair compensation for you destroying my livelihood. A meal won't cost you too much. And as you've already noted, I'm half your size. How much could I possibly eat? Besides, I am something of a decent conversationalist, and now that you're alone..."

I let the statement hang in the air, hoping he was as smart as he perceived himself to be.

He took a breath and then exhaled. "Indeed, you certainly are better at conversing than you are at singing."

"Thank you. Wait—"

Curr pointed over his shoulder. "I will provide you a meal, but then we must part. I do not intend to take on a new partnership so soon after my last one dissolved."

"Hey, I'm good with a one-meal stand. Relationships aren't my thing."

RHETT C. BRUNO & JAIME CASTLE

Curr's brow furrowed. "I have no idea what any of that means."
"Forget it. I'll explain later."

OBJECTIVE COMPLETED:
You have convinced Curr to buy you a meal.

You have gained +1 in Speechcraft.

Your Speechcraft is now 10.

NEW OBJECTIVE:
Discover the nature of Curr's next quest.

REWARD:
The feeling of a job well done.

So demanding. I complete one task and get another before I even have time to enjoy the fruits of my labor.

Okay, precious. And you should really eat something more than fruit... Enjoy the meal.

I don't like you.

70

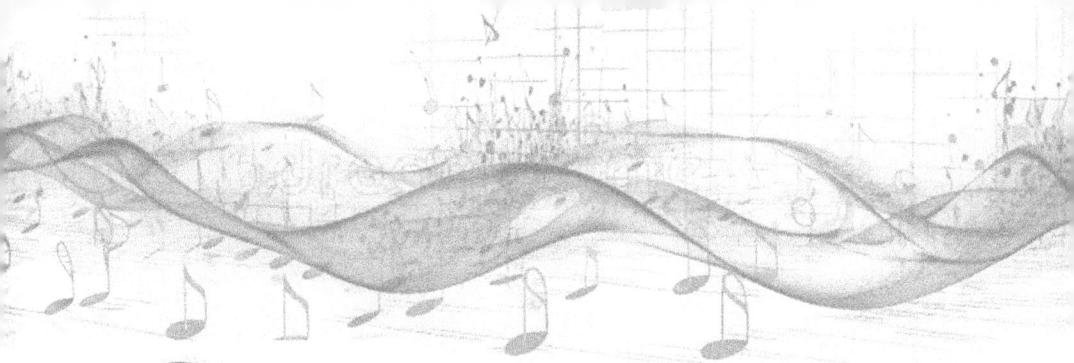

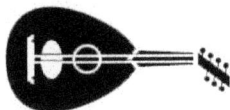

8

I fell into step beside Curr, which was more difficult to do than it sounds, given that his stride was double mine. Certainly wasn't about to complain, not when I'd managed to win him over with my charm.

Wow. You're delusional and clueless.

I did my best to ignore the thing floating in front of my eyes and followed Curr into the tavern. There were already a few souls drinking away whatever lives they had. The hearth glowed with old embers, nobody caring to get it roaring again so early in the morning.

As much as I enjoyed a good lager, I'd never understood the need to drink before noon. Then again, at the moment, I didn't care who was around and what they did. I just wanted something decent to eat and to forget the nightmare of the lamb. Maybe afterward, I could while away the hours until Phlegm's bargain came to fruition.

I wondered if I needed to be anywhere in particular for it to happen. She didn't say so. I mean, what good was magic if it required all these rules to make it work? I decided to just go on about my day and hope the hag would take care of the rest.

"Oh, no," came a voice from the bar. I turned to see Rarmir throwing his towel down and stalking toward us. "What part of 'get lost' hadn't I made clear?"

I began to respond when Curr stepped between us. "Take heart, my friend. This one is my guest."

Rarmir looked between us, muttered a curse, and stomped away.

"You truly are not liked here," Curr remarked.

"I noticed."

We seated ourselves at a table, and Curr ordered us two big bowls of stew. With water.

"Water, huh?" I asked.

"Did you want something more?"

"Me? No. I just figured—"

"Stereotypes are hurtful," Curr said. "Try to be more tolerant."

The front door swinging open stole the response out of my mouth. In strolled the pickpocketing troubadours. Maybe they felt like they deserved more praise and affection from the townsfolk, I don't know, but they looked pissed and apparently decided to head to the tavern to blow off some steam.

Loudly, they took their seats a few tables away from us. They ordered several draughts of ale that lasted only seconds.

The halfling, in particular, was in a sour mood.

Serves him right for trying to rob me.

Of nothing.

I rolled my eyes.

The halfling was a jerk, lambasting the tavern staff, telling them they moved too slow to be good at their jobs. He even flicked a few coins across the floor and ordered them to pick them up if they wanted their pay.

Curr observed the commotion and shook his head. "It is too early in the day for that sort of behavior." He glanced at me. "Gives bards a bad reputation, huh...?"

It was then I realized he'd forgotten my name.

"Danny," I told him. "And, psh, he's no... *bard*. Just a clown with a pipe."

Curr leaned back and let out a full belly laugh.

"A clown with a pipe! Ha ha, fine joke!" He turned toward the halfling and then back to me. "Your assessment is accurate. He does resemble a clown! Red hair and all!"

The halfling heard all of this and scowled. My stomach lurched.

The screen flashed.

Oh crap.

NEW OBJECTIVE:
Convince the halfling that you didn't insult him. Between us, he definitely looks like a clown.

The halfling made a show of downing the rest of his ale, then hopped off his seat and stormed toward us. Curr ignored him until he was only three feet away.

NAME: *Garvis Wittleman*
OCCUPATION: *Thief*
RACE: *Halfling (Male)*
SPECIAL ABILITIES: *Sneaky, quick with hands, can conceal weapons. Has a vicious knee-strike.*
WEAPONS: *Unknown... mysterious!*

So, I was right. He isn't a bard.

Want a cookie?

Does that count as a meal?

You'll spoil your appetite.

"What did you just say?" the halfling, Garvis, demanded, pulling me back to the present.

Curr took a small sip of his water, smacked his lips, and said, "Well met!"

The halfling's face scrunched up like tin foil. "What did you just say when you were laughing?"

"It was not I who said it," Curr informed Garvis. "It was my friend here. He suggested you resembled a clown with a pipe. Clever."

"You?" Garvis appraised me. "You have the nerve to call *me* a clown? You look like you slept in a barn."

Curr let out a barking laugh and slapped the table. "He did! He did in fact do that very thing. Look at the straw still in his hair!"

"Thanks, Curr," I muttered.

As small as Garvis was, he looked angry enough to battle ten men. Plus, he happened to be built like a small barrel.

I cleared my throat. "I said it was amazing how fast you put that ale *down*. My friend here must have misunderstood."

Not bad. Not bad at all. Not good either. But not bad.

Garvis looked somewhat placated by the lie. The screen started to flash again, then curiously, disappeared. Curr nearly spat out his water, as if I'd retold the joke again.

"No, no. Your memory fails you, Danny. I clearly recall you saying he favored the appearance of a clown with a pipe. I found it an entertaining observation." He grinned at the halfling. "I think he means your instrument."

OBJECTIVE FAILED:
You have gained an enemy. A small one, sure. But he's feisty.

OBJECTIVE UPDATED:
Defeat the halfling.

Defeat—what?

I stared at Curr, baffled. He seemed determined to get me killed.

Garvis growled and pulled a dagger from his boot. Curr caught his wrist immediately.

Thank God.

"No weapons. There will be no need for bloodshed here. The proprietors of this fine establishment are decent folk." Curr nodded toward me. "If you have an issue with my friend, then it will be settled with fists."

"Huh?" I said.

Garvis gawked at Curr's massive hand. Curr could have lifted him like a feather, and the halfling knew it.

"All right." He nodded. "That seems fair."

"I don't think—"

"Shhh, Danny," Curr said.

Garvis released the dagger, which Curr caught with his other hand. It may as well have been a sewing needle resting in his over-sized palm.

The halfling pulled his arm back and rubbed his wrist, then pointed at me. "So, I'm a joke to you, is that it? You think you're better because you're tall, Wellick?"

I shook my head. "No, I—"

"Well, let's see if you change your mind when I get done stomping your brains out."

I held up my hands, palms out. "There's no need for this. I apologize for insulting you."

"No." Garvis shook his head rather violently, his curly red mop waggling. "What's said is said. I can't let you insult me in front of my friends over there."

I looked beyond him at the bar where his dwarf and wellick companions barely paid attention to the altercation—as if this were a common occurrence.

"I'm not much of a fighter," I said.

"Then you'd better learn fast." Garvis got Curr's attention. "If he don't fight, I get to stab him to death."

"Obviously," Curr agreed. He then clapped as the bowls of stew arrived. "Ah, time to eat." He pointed at me. "You had better take care of this business if you want that meal I promised. Otherwise, I will be forced to eat yours."

I groaned. "I hate this place."

I started to stand, but the moment I did, the little halfling rushed in and tackled me to the ground. My head knocked against the floor and the few patrons in the tavern exploded in cheers.

Garvis started raining blows down upon me. I turned this way and that, trying my best to avoid the assault, but he was remarkably consistent with his strikes despite the amount he'd imbibed. Quick with his hands, indeed. His little fists landed like tiny hammers, blasting me in the face three times in rapid succession. I tasted blood.

WARNING: If you continue to sustain damage like this, you will die.

Nothing helped the situation like a blue box popping up in my face.

Curr spoke, but my head was ringing. It sounded like, "You had better find a reason to fight, bard. This little one is not going to stop until you are dead."

"Little one?" Garvis spat, turning his attention to Curr.

I took full advantage of his distraction and threw my knee up. It managed to dislodge him. Then I scrambled backward, trying to get to my feet.

Garvis regrouped, pointed at Curr, and said, "You're next, giant!" Then he came at me again, launching a stubby, two-legged kick that bounced off my left knee and hurt like hell. The vicious knee-strike I'd been warned about. Without thinking, I threw my own kick and it caught Garvis squarely in the crotch.

He buckled and moaned from the impact.

I felt a rush of guilt. It felt like kicking a kid. I leaned in. "I'm sorry! I didn't mean to—"

Even as I spoke, the halfling attacked again, catching me by surprise. He landed a punch on my jaw that knocked me back onto the floor.

Out of the corner of my quickly swelling eye, I spotted Curr shaking his head in disapproval as he slurped the stew from his bowl. I vaguely saw him reaching for my meal.

"Y'know, a little help here would be nice!" I called to him.

"He'll get his chance!" Garvis snarled as he tried to pin me again.

I flailed and a lucky elbow bashed him in the side of his head. He staggered, clutching his temple. He was wobbly, and I regained my footing before bringing my hands up.

"Do it now," said Curr simply.

I looked down at my hands and clenched them into fists. This was foreign to me. Most of my life—Kurt excluded—I'd been able to avoid fighting by using my quick wit and willingness to flee. But now...

"Do it."

Taking a deep breath, I delivered a straight shot to the reeling halfling's nose. The impact sent a bolt of pain shooting up my arm, while the effect to Garvis was violent. Blood gushed like a fountain from his nostrils, and the little man's head snapped back. He wobbled, then toppled to the floor where he completely stopped moving.

The tavern erupted in cheers again.

"Did I kill him?" I asked, horrified.

OBJECTIVE COMPLETED:
You have defeated the halfling.

You have gained +1 in Unarmed Combat

Your Unarmed Combat is now 3.

It wasn't pretty, and he was very small. You shouldn't be too proud.

Would you like to loot the body?

I can do that? Everyone will see me rooting through his pockets.

You have an ability to pickpocket.

Would you like to use it?

Uh, I guess?

Try it.

Without knowing what I was doing, I got my hands under the halfling's armpits and hauled him to his feet. I tried to make it look like I was brushing him off as I did so, holding him there for several seconds as his eyes refocused.

Would you like to take the pouch?

Somewhat embarrassed at what I was about to do, I nodded a very slight nod. What happened next was almost unconscious. I leaned against the halfling, and my fingers slipped into his pocket, transferring a small pouch of gold onto my person.

It all happened so fast.

+17gp.

You have gained +1 in Pickpocketing.

Your Pickpocketing is now 9.

Congrats! You're a thief. Your mother would be proud.

I swore under my breath.

A thief?

This is what it's called when you take other people's stuff.

Can I put them back?

No one saw you, dude. Just keep the loot. At least you didn't strip him naked, right?

I was starting to believe the screen didn't have my best interests at heart. Not that Garvis didn't deserve it. He'd tried to do the same to me out on the street. But still, I'd never stolen before.

Aw, you're no longer a virgin.

A tiny bit richer, I steered the halfling back to his comrades and then returned to my table.

"Bravo," Curr said. He kicked out my chair. "Now sit and eat."

He slid what remained of my bowl back to me. The stew looked chunky and unappetizing, but it beat rotten lamb big time. I sat and forced myself to eat a few spoonfuls, then found myself enjoying it.

All the while, I kept a wary eye on Garvis the halfling.

Curr stretched across the table and laid a huge hand on my shoulder. "Do not worry about him. You earned his respect enough that he will leave you alone now."

I took another spoonful of stew. "I've never fought like that before."

Curr nodded. "That is obvious. You punch like a wean."

"Always there to cheer me up."

Curr chuckled. "You did what needed to be done, but it was not very nice to look at. You are lucky the halfling was inebriated. Had he been sober, it might have been a different story."

I rubbed my jaw. "He didn't seem too affected by the booze."

"You will have some bruises and welts, no doubt," Curr continued as if I hadn't spoken. "But that is good!"

"How is that good?"

"They will remain a temporary reminder that you cannot let people walk all over you."

I rubbed my cheek. "I suppose. And girls dig guys with battle scars, right?"

No.

Curr just laughed. "The world cares not a bit for you, friend. You either find a way to make peace with the fact that sometimes violence is necessary, or else you are not going to live long enough to find yourself a new lute."

Wait a second.

Dun. Dun. Dun...

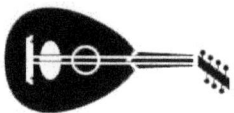

9

"A new lute... Who said I was looking for a new lute?" I asked, trying to keep my voice casual, and not looking up from my stew.

"Is that not what you bards do?" Curr said. "Play instruments and sing songs?"

"Usually. But my lute—"

"Yes, yes, I know. I destroyed it. But all that means is you should be looking to acquire a new one."

I frowned. Did Curr somehow know about my bargain with Phlegm? How could he possibly, though? There was no way. He seemed pretty straightforward. Maybe he really did assume I would be looking to replace my instrument after he broke it.

"Or you could have just not broken the first one," I said.

"Alas, I was fairly drunk myself," he replied. "Not to mention I had just spent days immersed in battle rage. Once more, my apologies."

I eyed him, trying my best to suss out any deceit. Spying none, I decided I was willing to accept that response. Who hasn't been drunk and done something stupid?

"Thing is, I'm a little short on coin to think about buying something new," I said. Sure, I'd just gained seventeen gold from pick-pocketing Garvis—an act I was not very proud of—but that couldn't possibly be enough to buy a lute. Could it?

I wonder what the dollar-to-gold coin ratio is?

Does not compute...

Curr took a big swig of water and motioned for the waitress to bring more.

"There are other ways of procuring items," he said.

My brow lifted.

Did Curr notice me picking the halfling's pockets?

It's possible. Your aptitude using that skill is still low, therefore your actions were somewhat obvious.

Obvious?

You weren't exactly Oliver Twist, champ.

I'm getting sick of you.

"Well, I'm not gonna break into a shop and steal something," I said to Curr. "I'd get arrested, maybe even killed for doing something like that. Right?"

Curr shrugged. "You would likely just lose a hand."

"Just a hand?" I scoffed. "And what value would a lute be to a one-handed man?"

"If that man were you, I am not sure most would notice the difference."

"That stings." I dropped my spoon and leaned back in my chair.

"You should be less sensitive. Besides, you could have easily been killed by the halfling a few moments ago. Somehow you managed to survive that little ordeal."

"I don't know about *easily*," I argued. Then after a few moments of silence, I added, "You think he could've killed me?"

Curr nodded.

Your Luck is fairly high.

Seriously, what does that even mean? How are people ranked here? Are you messing around about all this?

A lesson for another time.

Perhaps once your Intelligence is greater than a 4.

That gave me pause.

Is that low?

Quite.

I know I'd never been the brightest crayon in the box—my grades in high school had proven that—but I'd never considered myself dumb. I was smart enough to make a decent living off my music until my agent screwed me over. Convinced me not to take a deal with a midsize label. Said better would come. Only... it never did.

Then the suits were no longer interested in us when we came crawling back, and my agent was no longer interested in me. My band broke up and we all stopped talking. Goddamn suits.

That was how I wound up stuck with a regular Friday at the Heart-Shaped Box half-a-year back. I was on the precipice of something great and then, wham! All my dreams, washed away in an instant.

"On another day, that little man might have mopped the floor with you." Curr looked around the tavern. "Something this establishment would benefit from."

"Still, there's a bit of a difference between a barroom brawl and shoplifting, don't you think?" I asked, deciding I was hungry enough to quit my mope sesh and return to the stew.

"A fight is a fight. Whether in combat or the battle to achieve a goal."

"Does everything in your world come down to fighting?"

Curr grinned. "On a good day."

"Well, I'm sorry. My life is a bit different. Really different, in fact. There's not much room for fighting in it."

Even as I said it, I felt stupid. We might not battle with swords and shields back in Willistown, but there's always one group arguing with another about some policy or law.

Curr leveled a finger at me. "Do you not sing songs about brave heroes besting vile monsters? Do those stories not involve fighting something or *for* something? A treasure, a princess, a mug of ale even?"

"Well, yes, I suppose so."

"And there is the point. Conflict is the thing that makes people desperate enough to listen to your singing. It is certainly not for your quality. Life without conflict is no life at all. There is nothing that makes a man relish living like being near death."

We were quiet for a bit, listening to clay and pewter banging around the tavern, the few patrons talking and laughing.

"And what if you happen to be terrified of dying?"

"Then get good enough at fighting that you do not fear death," Curr said. "It is a simple solution to a complex problem."

"Yeah. Easy for you to say. Look at the size of you. There's never been a fight you couldn't win."

"You know nothing of my battles," Curr said, sterner than I'd heard him yet.

It made me wonder what trials filled his past, and reminded me he wasn't alone just the night before; he'd been surrounded by fellow braugs.

"That's fair. But you saw how badly I fought earlier." I tried to steer the conversation back to my shortcomings. Which wasn't all that difficult. I had a lot.

His smile returned. "You will improve with every battle. Worry not."

He is correct. Your current Melee Weapon skill is a 9.

A nine?

That didn't sound encouraging.

My old nana was probably an eleven. Ugh.

Information unknown.

"How good is a nine?" I asked Curr, since the screen was a worthless pile of garbage. I wondered if every skill in this world was based on a number system.

"Nine is higher than eight. Lower than ten," he said. That answer didn't reveal whether or not he knew what I was talking about.

He doesn't.

Does he have a... you?

No.

Does anyone here?

Only you. Aren't you just the shiny penny?

But... How do they know what they're good at?

By living. Duh.

So, I don't actually need you?

Psh. You wouldn't be able to live without me.

I wasn't sure if the screen was speaking metaphorically or literally, but I let it go for now. I couldn't help but wonder why I was special enough to get this detailed, play-by-play look at the world around me. It seemed apparent that the screen wasn't ready to answer such deep questions.

"Did the fight injure your head?" Curr asked, likely noticing my faraway stare as I conversed in my head with the screen like a mental case.

"Sorry, just thinking..." I said. "This is all new for me."

He smiled. "Be proud you fought for something, Danny. That is what is important."

"It didn't seem like I had a choice."

"No. You fought to defend your honor. He drew a knife and showed none."

"I guess..." I'd never thought of myself as having any sort of honor. Though after what Kurt did, I can't say it didn't feel good to stand my ground against a hotheaded thug.

"You have a limit which you will not allow yourself to be pushed beyond. And that is a good thing. It is the cowards who never fight for anything that will always break loyalty at the first opportunity. People like that are worthless and gutless and should not even exist."

He spoke as if he had experience with such things. Probably did. He spooned another big helping of stew into his mouth. I hadn't even noticed the bar wench—am I allowed to say that these days?—deliver another bowl.

"Seeing you fight makes me hopeful you are not one of those

scum," he added, a bit of thick brown liquid dribbling down his chin and into his beard.

"I'm not," I responded as quickly as I could.

I'm not, right?

No. You're a thief.

"Words do not carry the same weight as watching you in action," Curr said. He gestured to my bowl of stew. "Eat up."

I helped myself to a few more bites, which by now tasted amazing. The nausea I'd felt after my fight slowly waned as I ate and washed it down with the tepid water.

CURRENT HEALTH: 95%
Looking good, stud. Remember, food is fuel!

I smiled. Ninety-five percent seemed accurate. Better than I'd felt since being here.

Curr, for his part, appeared determined to eat the tavern out of their entire stock. I figured as long as he was buying, what was the problem?

When we were both finished—him long after I'd had my fill—I leaned back and took a breath. "I'm stuffed."

Curr patted his stomach. "With that completed, let us see about procuring you a new lute."

"Really?" I asked. "Why are you helping me now? What happened to the asshole who broke my lute?"

In response, he lifted his mug. "Water, not ale."

"That's it? I was drunk so I did bad things?" It wasn't the first time he'd made that claim, and now, it seemed he was sticking to it.

"Perhaps I see now that you may have the potential to become adequate at your profession."

"Because I didn't die?"

"Because you have heart," he said, tapping his chest.

I went to stand, but he took me by the hand.

"Two things," he said. "One: never refer to me as an 'asshole' again. That is disgusting."

I nodded.

"And two..." He placed a dagger in my open palm. It was the one he'd taken from the halfling and clearly hadn't given back. The blade had a few nicks and a bit of rust at the base.

I didn't close my fingers. "Why would I need this?"

Curr blinked. "Why would you not?"

"I'm not going to stab—"

"It is not the finest blade, but it is small, and you have a lesser chance of hurting yourself with it. Take it."

He forced my hand shut around the grip and once again left me feeling like I had no choice. I guess it couldn't hurt to have something to defend myself with, considering drunken halflings were apt to pull knives on you in this world for just an innocent joke.

WEAPON OBTAINED:
Rusty Old Dagger (Melee Damage 1-3).
It's kind of worthless.
It'll probably break the first time you use it.

"Thanks," I said, awkwardly stowing it in the back of my belt.

"We will have to get you a proper scabbard."

Curr had promised me a meal and that was it. What had him wanting to help me further was beyond my line of reasoning, but I'd been taught never to look a gift horse in the mouth. After all, I was alone here except for the annoying screen.

As we exited the tavern, the wellick and dwarf troubadours gave us—mostly me—a sneering glare. They now sat away from Garvis, at a separate table even. The halfling was almost comatose from the beating and the beers.

Still, he did manage to nod at me. "Thanks for the fight."

I didn't know how to respond to that, so I simply nodded back and followed Curr outside. The bright sunlight made me wince, my eyes soon adjusting. Townsfolk continued to bustle about without caring that a giant of a man and an instrument-less bard stood, gathering their bearings.

"Wait," Curr said, raising a hand.

"Now what?" I groaned.

Curr motioned for me to follow him. "Over there."

He pointed to a small alleyway. Someone had parked a brightly painted wagon in it.

"What's that?" I asked.

"Their wagon," he said. "The halfling learned his lesson, but the others should not support his trade or behave as they did in an upstanding establishment. We must teach them a lesson."

"Wait, what?" Who was this guy, Batman? "What are we gonna do?"

"We are going to make them reap what they have sown."

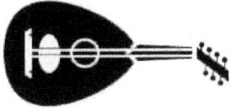

10

Curr only laughed to himself as he hurried toward the wagon. A childish sound coming from such a big fella. I followed, but moving wasn't easy, given how much I'd eaten and the beating I'd endured at the hands of a halfling.

What an embarrassing thing to say. It was like admitting Verne Troyer got the better of me, God rest his soul.

Eventually, I reached the wagon and found Curr already rummaging through it.

"Worthless bunch of junk," he muttered. "I fear they have nothing of value to pillage to show them the error of their thieving ways. Nothing is worse than a man who takes what is not his without fighting for it."

I didn't bother pointing out that that was exactly what he wanted to do. My clash with Garvis was long over. I guess because it was a lesson, it didn't count? I wasn't the one to argue with the giant.

Looking over my shoulder, I expected to see someone eyeballing us. The streets were empty. I suppose everyone was eating or working, being midday.

Would you like to loot the cart?

Do I need your permission?

You are the master of your domain.

Another *Seinfeld* reference. Was the screen trying to tell me something?

No. Stop reading into things.

I couldn't see the value in looting the cart. Especially since Curr had already said there wasn't anything in it. Still, as I peeked inside, I spotted several sheets of music.

"Look," I said, jutting my chin toward the parchment sticking out from below a busted drum. I call it parchment because it wasn't like paper back where I was from. This had a rough quality to it, and frankly, looked a lot more durable than A4 sheets of printer paper.

Curr tugged at his long beard. "Not very valuable. I was hoping they might have a lute, but perhaps those mean something to them. A worthy lesson, Danny!"

Should I take them?

Do you need my permission?

I groaned. If I had to endure this damn screen, I was going to have to learn to not think stupid questions. But really, should I do it? I'd already technically robbed the halfling, though Curr didn't know that, and I certainly wasn't going to tell him after his diatribe about thieves.

"Dispense justice, Danny," Curr said, inviting me to do it.

I reached slowly into the cart, feeling awful the entire way. Then, I clutched the sheets, folded them, and tucked them into my pocket.

You have decided to continue your life of crime.

You are on your way to unlocking the Title Petty Thief.

Actually... just take it...

TITLE UNLOCKED: Petty Thief.

ITEM OBTAINED:
Unidentified Sheet music. Rehearse to add to Catalog of Songs.

Petty Thief. My heart sank. I'd never in a million years considered breaking into someone's station wagon to steal a bunch of papers. Yet, here I was, in this strange world doing just that. The only way to press forward was to imagine this wasn't real. It was just a dream.

And what better way to live a dream than to do precisely the opposite of what I'd do in real life?

I returned my attention to the wagon.

"Where are the horses?" I asked, noting the empty hitch at the front.

Curr shrugged. "Being tended to elsewhere, I would venture. No sense leaving them with the wagon when they could be getting washed and fed."

"I can't believe you were gonna steal a lute for me. Couldn't we just buy one?"

"Now what in Tarton's Tusks is that?" Ignoring me, Curr stuck his head deeper into the rear of the wagon, his own rear sticking up and waggling behind him like a dog searching through a pile of dirt for a bone.

"Hey!" someone shouted.

I turned and spotted the wellick and dwarf emerging from the tavern. They had the halfling propped up between them, and dropped him when they spotted us ransacking their wagon. Garvis splashed face first into the mud, his entire front getting covered.

When he didn't immediately rise, I worried he would suffocate or drown.

However, the life expectancy of the halfling was the least of my current problems.

"Uh, Curr," I said. "I think we've been made."

NEW OBJECTIVE:
Avoid another fight with the troubadours.

REWARD:
Nothing bad happens.

Always with the obvious!

"C'mon!" I nudged Curr, which wasn't exactly easy to do. To him, I probably felt like an annoying fruit fly.

"Huh?" He removed his head from the back of the wagon and followed my gaze to the troubadours charging at us. "Oh, yes."

I started to take off in the other direction, while he did just the opposite. He stepped out of the alley and toward the wellick and dwarf, and his hand shot to the grip of his giant axe.

"What are you doing?"

Despite my shouting, I was ignored. So, I swore under my breath, vaguely wondering if such profanities existed in Pyruun.

Curr came off quite cheery, but he could crack a coconut on his bicep, let alone a man's head. Let alone with a battle axe. Let alone if he was angry.

Oh, man, was I about to see him in action?

The performers stopped dead in their tracks. I think they might've pissed themselves at the sight of the pissed-off braug reaching for his weapon.

"Your duty is to entertain, not steal and abuse good men like Rarmir," Curr pronounced. "The bard, Danny, and I have relieved you of items important to you to show you the error of your ways."

He looked to me. Unsure what to do, I simply waved awkwardly.

"Hey, that's his thing, not ours!" the dwarf yelled, pointing back at Garvis. The halfling muttered his own curses—and I noted they were not the same as mine. At least he was alive. "We're just tryin' to make a livin' the best we know how."

Curr was now stopped in the middle of the street, bouncing his axe shaft against his open palm. "Averting your gaze when your fellow does wrong makes you equally guilty. I do hope you learn from this disagreement and walk away better for it." Curr's fingers tightened around the grip of his axe. "But if you would prefer a fight, that is your choice."

He twisted his neck, and it sounded like firecrackers.

The troubadours looked between him and me, anger reddening their features. Their lips pursed, then they took a step back.

The wellick woman stared daggers at me. "You're lucky you have him with you, *bard*. We ever catch you alone, by Ludos, you're dead meat."

The dwarf ran a thumb across his throat to accentuate her words—as if they needed such emphasis. Then, they both headed away from the tavern, arguing with the mud-covered halfling as they scrambled to haul him to his feet.

OBJECTIVE COMPLETED:
You avoided the fight!

Remember, violence never solves anything—except most disagreements.

I took a deep breath and smoothed out my clothes. "Whew, I thought we were gonna have to take them. Not exactly the way I usually prefer to digest my meals."

"Those two would have been much more formidable than the halfling. If for no other reason but mere size alone. No challenge for me, but better that we do not engage with them with someone as puny as you at my side."

He started walking down Main Street, away from the tavern. I had to run to keep up. "Can we slow down just a bit?"

"Ah, tiny legs. I forgot." He reduced the gap between his steps.

"I don't have tiny legs. I have normal legs. You're the freak here."

Curr stopped. "'Freak' is as bad as 'asshole,' Danny. Do not say it again."

"So what? You're allowed to insult me all you want, but I can't say anything in return?"

Yes.

"Yes," Curr said, trudging forward. "Just be glad we did not have to engage those two."

"Didn't you just tell me that fighting meant everything to you?" I asked.

Curr grunted. "It does not mean *everything*. What did I tell you about fighting for a cause? Fighting for the sake of fighting is mindless. I am not mindless, Danny. Their lesson has been well learned."

"Sorry. It just really seemed like you were trying to provoke the halfling to fight me back there."

"Oh, I was." He guffawed.

"What?" I asked, flabbergasted.

"It was my intention to determine whether you had anything of value within you." He poked me in the heart with a massive extended finger. It felt like a gunshot.

I grasped my chest. "Well, I'm glad I could be entertainment for you."

"As am I. It was quite amusing. Far better than your performance last evening."

It seemed he would never tire of reminding me of that fact.

I groaned. "Have you *never* heard of sarcas—"

The clatter of wagon wheels erupted behind us. I peered over my shoulder. The troubadours' cart careened recklessly toward us, drawn by horses now, and sending any townsfolk in their way scattering.

Now you're in trouble.

"But alas," Curr sighed. "There are times when the gods demand we fight." He ripped his battle axe free from his back and turned, brandishing the weapon. It didn't just hum through the air as it moved; there was a damn breeze.

Instead of slowing to confront us, the troubadours swerved out of the way, scaring more townsfolk before they settled on a direction. With the wellick woman at the reins, the horses galloped past us, spraying up dirt and mud.

"Hey, bard!" she shouted back at me.

I barely had time to bring my hands up or see as I realized one of them had thrown something right at me—a large melon of some sort. It exploded and sent me stumbling.

What happened next was the most embarrassing of all the embarrassing things that had happened since finding myself in this hellhole of a world.

I tripped. Into a well. Flipped right over the low stone wall, and found myself face first in the water, gurgling. As luck would have it— if twisting my ankle could be considered luck—my boot got stuck on the rim, so I didn't sink.

Hm. I guess you didn't avoid the fight entirely.

My hands waved desperately to find something to push off. That was when I saw it, and I nearly stopped breathing. Sitting just above the water, lodged between two broken stones, rested a lute.

No sooner had my fingers closed around it, that I was heaved out of the well and plopped down in front of Curr. He'd lifted me as if I were a child.

Hooves pounded in the distance as the troubadours fled. I could still hear them cackling like old hags.

Hags... Holy crap. Phlegm had come through.

Hags never recant on their end of a bargain. However, not all deals are what they seem.

That same broad smile that Curr seemed to perpetually wear was plastered across his face. "Tarton's Tusk, you should have seen yourself falling!" He burst out laughing, having to sit on the edge of the well just to get a hold of himself.

I stared down at the beautiful new lute in my grip.

OBJECTIVE COMPLETED:
You have discovered a new instrument!

Don't break this one.

I didn't break the last one!

Potato, potahto.

ITEM OBTAINED:
Truly Fine Lute [Unique].

Ancient magic courses through the wood of your newly acquired instrument.

There is no doubt in my mind, this instrument is too good for you. Go ahead, try it.

I gave the strings a strum, and as I did, a jolt of energy filled my hands, spread up to my arms, and farther into my body until the whole of me felt on fire.

Two new songs have been added to your catalog!

When you desire to play them, you'll know the way.

Wow, and it comes with a soundtrack. Groovy, baby.

I was still shocked that the old hag hadn't been a fraud. She'd promised a lute and by some luck, I'd found it in the most unlikely place. Or was it thanks to those pesky troubadours, and she'd done nothing at all?

Who cares? I found a lute in a well!

I swallowed as I analyzed the instrument closer. In the sunlight, its strings shone, and the lacquer gleamed with intricately carved symbols in wood that had that fresh pine smell. It was perfect save for a spot on the headstock where it seemed something was missing. A teardrop-shaped crevasse stood alone as a blemish on an otherwise pristine lute.

"It's amazing," I said under my breath.

For the first time since being in this weird world, I felt... right again. I'd only known one thing my whole life, and that was music. Sure, I wasn't a fighter, or maybe even a thinker, but despite these last few days, I could perform.

Curr shifted to his feet. "Tarton's fortune shines! A new lute. You discovered that in the well?"

Unsure what to even say, I simply nodded.

"Congratulations." Curr clapped me on the back. "You are a bard once more!"

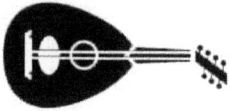

11

A bard.

I think I was still having a hard time accepting the fact. I guess it was no different from what I did back at home, except with a fancier title. If memory served me, in role playing games—not that I knew much about them—the fighters got the glory. Magic users had awesome spells and magic items.

And bards? They made up songs about the triumphs of others. They didn't have adventures of their own, so they sang about everyone else. What was even appealing about singing about someone else's bravery or some other guy's exploits?

But what did I know? I never played any of those games in high school. I was too busy getting laid—or trying to at least...

The brief image of hot Trish flashed through my mind.

Keep dreaming.

The screen was just being the asshat that it was, though that once again begged the question: am I or am I not dreaming? It already told me in no uncertain terms I wasn't dead, but if this wasn't a dream, what the hell was it?

Here was another question: could the screen be trusted? What if I *was* dead and it was lying?

I suddenly became aware that Curr was staring at me funny.

"What?" I snapped.

He shrugged. "I have never seen someone so lost in thought after acquiring their heart's desire. It does not make sense."

"You're telling me."

But he had a point. And until I figured out exactly what was going on, I had to at least make it look like I belonged. If I told Curr the truth, he might think I was crazy. Or worse, some sort of threat to his world to be dispatched by braug violence. If it floated like a duck, weighed the same as a duck, and was made of wood, it got burned.

Even if Curr was friendly at the moment, he had the size and skills to pulverize me into a Danny puddle if he wanted to. Especially if he thought I was some kind of witch or time traveler.

Whoa, was I a time traveler?

To a past that somehow had hags and wellicks? Idiot.

NEW OBJECTIVE:
Continue with the hag's instructions.

Drink from that mysterious vial you received from a total stranger with questionable origins.

Oh! Crap.

I was supposed to drink that now that I'd obtained the lute, wasn't I? She said when the instrument came to me, not a second before. But how long after? Should I do it now, or is there a waiting period? What if I did it wrong?

You'll probably die.

That's not funny.

Not really any other choice but to do it now, since no other instruction was given.

As nonchalantly as I could, I reached inside my pocket for the small vial. It felt warm as I wrapped my fingers around it. I knew it had a stopper that I would have to release. I just hoped I could manage to do so without Curr seeing me.

"Hey, Curr, isn't that one of your friends from the other night?" I pointed behind him.

Smooth.

Curr turned and I jerked my hand out, ripped the stopper off, and sucked down the odd green liquid faster than I'd ever shot tequila before. Then I tossed the empty vial into the well even as Curr turned back with a frown.

"I do not see anybody," Curr said. "What was that?" He peered over the lip of the well.

"A coin," I lied.

"A coin? I am purchasing you meals and you so carelessly throw away gold?"

Why can't anything be easy?

"I—uh, made a wish."

"What kind of a wish?" he asked, eyes narrowing.

"If I told you that, it wouldn't come true now, would it?"

"I have never heard of such a preposterous thing."

You have successfully distracted Curr.
Your talent at being a terrible friend has increased.

I tried to respond, but at that precise moment, the contents of the vial began to burn, scorching their way through my insides. My throat suddenly felt like I'd swallowed a hot coal, nearly causing me to gag or black out. Possibly both. I couldn't tell because, all of a sudden, I started sweating intensely.

"Is it hot out here?" I asked, waving my hand in front of my face and pulling at my collar.

Curr's blurry silhouette swam in front of me almost like he was melting.

"It is quite a fine day," he said. "Are you sure you are okay?"

The screen's words from earlier came to mind...

Hags never recant on their end of a bargain. However, not all deals are what they seem.

Whatever Phlegm had given me was causing this intense pain.

I did warn you.

Oh, my God. Had she poisoned me? I'd been a damned fool to trust someone like her! *"Here, Danny boy, drink this and all your musical dreams will come true."*

Was this what selling your soul to the devil was like? Only an idiot musician would do that. I guess I finally understood.

The ground seemed to rush up to greet me even as I realized I was falling. Curr's strong hands caught me and kept me from crashing to the dirt.

"Tarton's Tusks, I did not believe you had so much to drink."

"I only had wat—" I started to retch and Curr let me drop to the ground.

"Not on me."

I crashed to the street and a weird spasm danced in my gut. Like someone was taking my insides, knotting them up, and twisting them like a pretzel. It felt horrible. I'd had food poisoning a few times before the lamb, but this was a thousand times worse.

"Maybe it's a concussion," I squeezed out, but I don't think they were coherent words. Moaning, I writhed around, vaguely feeling little stones cutting my flesh, hoping that any sort of motion would help dispel the pain and agony. It didn't, and now I was bleeding from my fingertips and arms. My breathing came in sharp spurts, and I barely held on to consciousness. Blackness clawed at the edges of my vision, and spots broke out. They were weird, green, swirling into one another, and the effect made me want to vomit even more.

I bit down and managed to quell the rising tide of bile at the back of my throat. Vomiting probably wasn't the smartest idea. If that green stuff was supposed to help, then I had to make it through the effects of consuming it and possibly emerge on the other side better for it.

Or perhaps I'd just die.

I tasted dirt then and recoiled. Why was my mouth even open? How long was this going to last?

The screen was flashing, but frankly, I couldn't even see what was written on it. Sweat beaded along my hairline and ran into my eyes like I'd just broken a fever. I was even somewhat cooler than from moments before.

Was this the end? Maybe I was being possessed. Like that scene in the *Exorcist*.

Cool, cool. cool.

It was like someone turned out the lights. Total darkness, and then, finally, my vision started to clear. My breathing slowed. I was beginning to feel somewhat like myself again. Only... stronger. My vision grew sharper.

OBJECTIVE COMPLETED:
You have completed the hag's instructions.

Vial of Musical Aptitude Consumed: You have received The Hag's Blessing!

+10 Bonus to Dexterity, Charisma, and Intelligence. +10 Bonus to Instrument Playing, Singing, and Speechcraft.

Wow.

That was some concoction. Phlegm came through again.

You should feel ashamed for doubting her.

"You okay now?" Curr's voice seemed sincere, but I wasn't sure if I could trust him with the truth just yet.

Still, I managed a quick nod. "I certainly hope so."

"That was the most writhing without puking I have ever witnessed," Curr said. "I thought for sure you were going to erupt."

"So did I." I calmed my breathing a bit more and sat up. Using the back of my hand, I wiped the drool from my mouth and chin.

"What happened?" Curr was showcasing genuine concern. Which was nice.

"Must've been a late reaction to the lamb," I lied again.

Keep this up and you could run for president.

The lute lay nearby, propped up against the base of the well. I swear it gleamed a little bit brighter as it lay there, catching the rays from the sun overhead. I looked up, wondering if that sun was even my sun or the distant star of some other planet or world or whatever.

Didn't matter. The lute called to me now, seemingly begging to be played. It truly was a beautiful piece of workmanship. And it was also mine. All mine. *My precious.*

I picked up the instrument and the screen flashed.

Would you like to play your instrument?

You'd like that, wouldn't you, pervert.

Just strum the damn strings.

I positioned my fingers and drew them across the fretboard. Unlike my guitar, it had no metal frets. And unlike with the lute Curr had broken, my fingers instinctively knew exactly where to place themselves. I strummed with my other hand and the melodious notes coming out of the thing surprised even me.

You have gained +1 in Instrument Playing.

Your Instrument Playing is now 16 (+10).

Wow, a 26 in Instrument Playing?

16 (+10).

How is that any different?

Before the screen could answer, Curr said, "Mellifluous." His eyebrows danced a little. "Had you played so well last night, you would not have had need of a new instrument."

He was right. Had the vial made me this much better? I actually felt like a musician again!

I paused, trying to figure out what I should say. "I guess I was just a little tired."

Strumming again, I smirked. Might not have liked the idea of being a bard, but there was something pretty cool about hearing what I could now play on this unfamiliar instrument. I wondered what some Nirvana would sound like from this baby.

But that would have to wait for another time. I stopped playing, rose, and swung the lute over my shoulder by its leather strap.

"What do you think?" I stretched my hands out to my sides.

"Passable," Curr said, shrugging. "I mean, it was leagues beyond your pitiful performance last eve, but so would be the strangulation of kittens."

"Have you ever... strangled kittens?" I wasn't sure I wanted to know the answer.

"Not on purpose." He glanced around, watching a local go by, and scratched his beard. "Well, I suppose it is time for me to move on from this boring small town. I am glad you were able to find a suitable instrument. Perhaps I will see you again playing in the hall of a great king." I started to answer, but he sniffled as I watched him hold in a snicker. "Though I do not think anybody will be alive long enough for you to improve so drastically!"

Then, in a knee-slapping jerk, he let the laugh out.

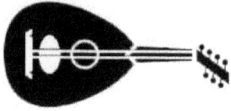

12

"Wait, wait," I said, trying my hardest to keep the panic from my tone.

As much as Curr was infuriating, destroying my lute, getting me into a bar fight, making a thief out of me—okay, fine, maybe he wasn't solely responsible for that—I didn't know anyone else in Pyruun. And I had no idea how long I'd be here.

The thought of leaving this town and heading out into the big, wide world alone was... terrifying.

"You can't just... leave."

He wiped his eyes, finally calming after his last joke. "That was the deal. A meal and new instrument means our pact is complete. Plus, our temporary companionship earned you a brawl and offered you the opportunity to deal justice. You might recall, I am not looking for a new partnership at the moment."

Time to strike up the old Danny Kendrick charm.

"But I can be fine company. You don't want to be all alone, do you?" I smiled, raising an eyebrow.

Curr's face scrunched up. "My apologies, Danny. I do not fancy that kind of partnership either."

"What? Hey. No. I didn't mean that!"

Perhaps if you show him your tits.

Quiet, you!

Maybe it was just my way of dealing with the craziness of it all. Dive in headfirst. I didn't have much to care about back home. Unless you count Trish. She'd been coming to listen to me at the Heart-Shaped Box every Friday night for the last few months, and sure, we'd talked... but there wasn't anything there. Was there?

Mom and Dad had passed years back. Any family left was distant, if I'd even known them. My old friends had moved on to better things or started families of their own.

That kind of hurts to think about.

Oh, don't worry. You'll find love someday.

Are you ever not listening to my thoughts?

I zone out sometimes.

Honestly, life had been a whirlwind over the past couple of years. I went from touring regularly with my band, to being stuck at a dive bar in the ass-end of Willistown. It's been hard for this performer to get his life straight. I do have *some* self-awareness. This was just another storm to weather.

Thing was, did I really want to travel to some foreign land with a braug named Curr?

C'mon. Live a little.

Oh, what the hell. When he grabbed his axe in front of those troubadours, they crapped themselves. He was exactly the sort of friend I'd needed back before Kurt knocked me here. Curr could keep me alive long enough to figure out where the hell I was, and if I'd ever go home.

"I just…" I groaned. "Please let me come along. I'll carry my own weight. I promise."

"You do not weigh much." Curr appraised me, then shook his head. "No, you will only slow me down."

"Not true!" I argued. "I'm fast. I'm small, so I'm light on my feet." I did a little running man move and immediately regretted it.

"You do not even possess a weapon."

"Ah-hah! Still not true!" I pulled out the old rusty dagger Curr had given me that he'd taken from Garvis the halfling.

"That thing would break if I blew on it hard enough."

"You gave it to me!" I argued.

"I did not want it." He scanned me again, head to toe. "I do not think this will work out in my favor."

You're losing him.

How about a little incentive.

NEW OBJECTIVE:
Convince Curr to take you with him on his next quest.

REWARD:
A new weapon and armor.

Curr is undoubtedly going somewhere super cool. Just look at him. He oozes awesome. Convince him to take you with him. If you fail, you die.

Die? Seriously?

We all die eventually.

Curr turned to walk away, and I grabbed him by the arm. A little too aggressively.

He spun so fast toward me, he almost ripped my arm off.

"Relinquish my ulna, this instant!"

I let go of him. "Fine. I'm sorry. Curr, please, don't leave me in this place by myself. I'll die here. Do you want that on your conscience?"

He snatched the dagger from me. "See this?" He pointed to the rusty splotches on the blade. "That is not embellishment. It is rust." He then held it between thumb and forefinger with one hand and the hilt with the other. Applying the minutest pressure, the dagger snapped in two.

WEAPON LOST:
Rusty Old Dagger.

"Great," I said. "Now I have nothing. Do you get off on breaking my stuff or something?"

"Everything you have is just so pathetic."

Ouch.

"Not this!" I tapped on the lute.

He scratched his beard. "Finding that was indeed good fortune."

"Maybe I'm lucky. And you said I had value. That counts for something. And I can carry things for you. Keep you entertained with riveting conversation and song—" I caught myself before I finished the word. "Basically, whatever helps."

Curr stared at me for so long, it became uncomfortable. Then he took a deep breath.

"Fine," he said. "But if you are going to accompany me, you will need to be better armed."

OBJECTIVE COMPLETED:
You convinced Curr to let you join him.

Great job. Now you will travel beside a bloodthirsty braug dead set on killing anything and everything he can.

You have gained +1 in Speechcraft.

Your Speechcraft is now 11.

What about the reward?

Did I say there would be a reward? How about you just be satisfied with not dying. Or be patient...

I returned my focus to Curr. "You'll let me join you?"

Don't act too excited, Danny. Play hard to get.

"Until I change my mind," he said. "There is a Fighters Guild Hall in Balahazia. It has been many moons since I last checked in, and there ought to be plenty of quests worth embarking upon. Perhaps there is an undead plague somewhere and we can join a raid!"

"That sounds, uh, dangerous."

He nodded. "It is. For you."

OBJECTIVE COMPLETED:
You have discovered the nature of Curr's next quest. His next quest is... to find a new quest!

Don't you feel great about yourself? What better way to start your new life than killing mindless, bloodthirsty zombies?

"Maybe I've changed my mind..."

"Nonsense! There should be something you can handle too. First, let us find you a blade worthy of the wilds so you might perhaps stand a chance." Curr slapped me on the back, an action that was beginning to leave me sore. "Way to be bold, my new companion. Glad to see that you did not let that awful fight with the halfling get you down."

"Yeah, well... all that really counts is that I fought, right?"

"Indubitably," Curr said. "Not dying is an added bonus."

NEW PARTY MEMBER ADDED:
Curr the Braug (Level 23)

Aw, you guys are Facebook official now.

You know about Facebook?

Sure. It's where you'd stalk girls you were too afraid to talk to.

Not cool.

I wonder if Trish has posted any new pictures of her labradoodle?

This is borderline creepy, man.

Did you just assume my gender?

Enough.

I was beginning to wonder if I'd just made the biggest mistake of my life. Getting into a fight with a drunk halfling was one thing; battling it out with monsters or undead was another entirely. I wasn't exactly feeling confident about my abilities. I'd nearly gotten my ass handed to me back in the tavern.

Before I could back out, Curr took off down the road, his stride increasing with what appeared to be excitement. Once again, I was forced to jog just to keep up. For someone who claimed to like to work alone, his demeanor sure did change after he agreed to take me on.

What's Balahazia? I asked the screen as we traveled.

BALAHAZIA: A fortified wellick town east of the Masked Mountains. The largest settlement south of Hoarfrost. Home of the Fighters Guild Hall and the Scholars Union, Balahazia is the northernmost trade port in Pyruun.

I winced.

Should I ask what the Masked Mountains are or why the town is fortified?

Do you really want to know?

I sighed. Maybe it was better not knowing. I was already preparing myself for encountering monsters I'd never imagined could be real.

This was a mistake.

You want to be a hero, don't you?

I wasn't planning on it.

You really are a strange human. That's what everyone in this world wants. I'm only trying to get you there faster. In fact:

**NEW OBJECTIVE:
Reach Balahazia safely with your Party.**

> ***REWARD:***
> ***A chance at a new life.***

> ***NEW OBJECTIVE:***
> ***Improve Your Equipment before departing Nahal.***

> ***REWARD:———***

Stop doing that!

"Here we are!" Curr said.

We stood before a long, squat building with a wooden sign that read: **BARITONE'S BLACKSMITH AND BARBERSHOP** hanging from a post.

"Blacksmith and barber?" I asked.

"Finest shave you will ever find yourself on the receiving end of," Curr said, pointing to his freshly shaved dome. "But we do not have time for that."

"Don't worry. I'm fine."

Curr stared at the mop of hair on my head and his lip twisted. "If that is what you believe. Let us see what awaits us."

The clanging of a hammer against an anvil rang out in perfect rhythm, and when we stepped inside, the heat from the forge nearly knocked me sideways. Curr took a deep breath and exhaled.

"There is nothing like the smell of molten steel in the morning," he said.

"It's afternoon," I said.

"Do not correct me."

The hammering stopped at the sound of our voices. A woman who looked much like the building stepped out from behind the stone forge. She was short and stout, with arms like I'd never seen on a lady.

Sexist.

No, I'm... impressed!

Her graying hair was pulled into a ponytail that nearly reached the bottom of her dirty leather apron. Dangerous by fire, but she didn't seem to care. The screen highlighted her as I focused.

NAME: Baritone

That's a woman's name?

Do I need to say it again?

Sorry. Continue.

NAME: Baritone
OCCUPATION: Blacksmith and Barber
RACE: Wellick (female)

SPECIAL ABILITIES: *Weapons crafting and making you look damned good.*
WEAPONS: *Look around you.*

"Not back for another shave so soon, are you?" she asked Curr, her voice deep and raspy. Like her name.

Curr nodded in my direction like I was his red-headed stepchild. "He is in need of a fine sword."

The blacksmith wiped the grime and sweat off her face, then sized me up just like Curr had so many times already, the deep chasms on her forehead deepening.

"And a haircut, too, by the look of him," Baritone added.

"Just the sword this time, thanks," I said.

"Ever used a sword before? You don't look like it."

Are these two related?

I gulped. How the hell was I supposed to answer that? In truth, I'd never swung anything more than a wiffle ball bat. Clearly, this was neither the time nor place to admit that.

"I mean, who hasn't?" It wasn't a lie. It was a question. Not my fault she took it as a response in the affirmative.

Baritone glowered at the instrument on my back. "About the sort of answer I'd expect... from a *bard*."

She spat after that last word. I was guessing my fellow minstrels hadn't done much to make this woman like them over the years.

Baritone turned to Curr. "I've got a short sword he might be able to handle. It's nothing great, but it'll do the job. Where you headed?"

"Pikeman's Trail," Curr said. "Toward Balahazia."

The blacksmith chortled. "Pike's? With the likes of him?" She shook her head and smiled as if it was the funniest thing she'd heard in a long time. "You're better off going alone, friend."

Curr leaned forward, hulking over the blacksmith. "Just because you shaved my head, that does not make us friends. I *am*, however, now his. And I do not appreciate you talking about him like that."

A part of me warmed at the sound of that.

See, I knew you'd find love.

The blacksmith held her ground. "Listen, braug, I ain't afraid of you."

Curr growled. "You should be."

"Lay a finger on me, and you won't make it out of town." Her warning sounded foolish being directed at Curr. At least, it seemed to have done the trick.

"A short sword," Curr spoke. "Get it and let us be on our way."

Baritone nodded. "Fair enough. Need anything else?"

"A scabbard for it."

"Of course. I'm no cheap wench."

"That is yet to be determined," Curr said. He folded his arms and leaned against the wall, looking entirely unhappy with the transaction thus far.

"A short sword?" I asked. "What about one of those big ones that Vulna had? I'd feel much safer with something like that."

Curr did what Curr did best and let out a big belly laugh. He hadn't even breathed again before the blacksmith returned holding a dusty short sword still sheathed in its scabbard.

Curr took it, pulled it free, wiped off the dust, and gave it a few test swings before re-sheathing it and handing it to me.

I hefted it, finding it light enough.

"Not the best-looking sword," he said, glaring at Baritone from the corner of his eyes, "but it will do."

"Won't find a better one for the price," Baritone argued.

"How much?" I asked.

"Twenty gold," Baritone said.

I gulped yet again. Then I pulled Curr aside and said, "So, I'm a little short of coin right now. Only have seventeen. I don't suppose there's any way—"

"You will take thirteen," Curr interrupted me, stepping up to the blacksmith. "Because we both know it is worth not a coin more."

"And what would you know?" the blacksmith asked, raising her nose.

"You think because I am a braug I do not know the value of things?" Curr moved closer. He actually looked pissed. "See, I know weapons. Do you want a presentation?"

Baritone didn't budge, just scratched her chin. She didn't even look pissed, unlike Curr. I got the impression this was just how business was done in Pyruun, like a flea market.

"Fifteen," she conceded. "You strike a hard bargain, braug."

"And an even harder blow," Curr said. "Fifteen will do. Smart choice." He nodded to me, and it took me a few seconds to realize what he meant.

I reached into the pouch I'd stolen from Garvis and handed over what I owed. Baritone took the money with hands rougher than a cheese grater.

The screen flashed.

-15gp.

You have 2gp remaining.

WEAPON OBTAINED:
Iron Short Sword (Melee Damage 3-7)

It's not the size of the weapon. It's how you use it.

Thank you, Garvis, for the generous donation to the Danny Fund.

I wasn't happy about being so close to broke, but... problems for another day.

"It was a pleasure." Baritone pocketed the gold in one of the many pouches strapped to her belt. "Enjoy the sword. I'm sure it won't be long before that blade makes its way back to its home here."

Curr waved me along. "Let us depart. We are through here."

I stayed rooted to the spot. "What's that supposed to mean?" I asked Baritone.

Maybe I was just brave with Curr so close, but I'd grown weary of this lady's condescension, even if she might've been right.

She started chuckling as she returned to the forge and lifted a hammer that I probably couldn't have. "Nothing. Not a thing. You have yourselves a jolly time in the north. I hear it's lovely at this time of year. I'm sure you'll really enjoy it." And then she let loose a hearty laugh that kept going and going even as Curr dragged me out of the shop.

Once back on Main Street, I brushed myself off. "What was that all about?"

"She does not think much of you," Curr said.

"Yeah, I got that part."

"The wild can be dangerous. She thinks you will die."

I raised the short sword like a proud kid who'd just been given a toy lightsaber for Christmas. "But now I have a blade."

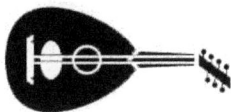

13

"**D**o not cut yourself on that," Curr warned. "It would be a shame to do so before any orcs get their chance."

"Orcs?" I replied.

"Oh, did I not mention the orcs on Pikeman's Trail?" he asked with a smirk.

"I think I would've remembered that. When you say orcs... you mean—"

"Orcs."

ORCS: Mindless reptilian beasts with razor-sharp teeth bigger than their own mouths. Sadly, this often results in them slicing off their own tongues or other appendages. Needless to say, orcs don't participate in some of the sexual activities your kind is so fond of.

Yikes.

"If Pikeman's Trail is so dangerous, how come no one has cleaned it out?" I asked.

"Oh, it is far safer than it used to be. People must reach Balahazia."

I shrugged. "Well, couldn't the government or whatever mount some sort of expedition or campaign to make it completely safe?"

Curr laughed. "A nice thought, my naïve little companion. But orcs and goblins are masters at dissolving into the landscape, hiding in caves and ancient ruins. They never fight a pitched battle. Were we to send a show of force, they would vanish faster than a dwarf at the time of cleansing. And they live for hundreds of years. They can afford to wait forever."

"And we're gonna fight them? When not even an army could?"

"As soon as the soldiers leave, the beasts return. King Shirtaloon VI gave—"

I could barely hold back a snicker. Curr looked perplexed.

"What is so funny?"

"That name. Shirt... a... loon."

"You have a very odd sense of humor," Curr chastised. "It is a strong, royal name, handed down by great and powerful kings."

"Was Pantaloons taken?" This time, a full-on cackle slipped through.

"That is not a name," Curr said matter-of-factly.

"You're right. Just ignore me."

Curr did just that and moved on. "Pyruun gave up focusing its might on this region years ago, ever since the conquering of Hoarfrost." He spoke that last part with a bit of venom in his tone.

HOARFROST: a vast tundra in the far north, extending beyond where any wellick wishes to go. It is rich with the furs of borebears, iron ore, and mercenaries, as these nearly inhospitable, frigid lands are where braugs hail from.

Thank you, screen, for the unrequested information.

Did I mention the king's grandfather, King Shirtaloon IV, also known as Shirtaloon the Monster Slayer, is the one who conquered

*Curr's homeland? By the way, the monsters were the braugs...
Maybe be more thoughtful.*

I gulped and made a note to myself to try and be more careful with things I said out loud concerning a world I should probably know more about. I had my irritating screen after all.

"It just seems foolish?" I said to Curr, moving on. "Shouldn't making all roads to a port city like Balahazia safe be kind of crucial?"

"Ship access has made the old roads less significant," Curr said. "It is much faster to transport ore to support the war that way."

War?

Pyruun has been at war in the east with the Assiri for decades. It's quite a big deal. Don't look stupid.

"Oh, right. The war," I said aloud. "That makes sense."

You are a master wordsmith.

"I know more than a few songs about it," I added.

"Please, do not sing them," Curr said. "The king still sends soldiers on occasion, but only when enough complaints are made at court. Truly, that is more often as of late. If the local magistrates could merely stop their bickering long enough to set a permanent emplacement there, perhaps we could be free of dangers in the woods. Even so, I am still not convinced it would ever be truly safe."

"The mountains," I realized.

Curr nodded. "The foothills and mountains. The orcs and goblins know them like no others. They can use them to hide, ambush, and disappear. And trust me when I say they are perfectly willing to take refuge in the caves that litter the area as well. Dispatch an army so high and the orcs would pick off the soldiers one by one. And the goblins are quite fond of the taste of wellick."

I sighed. Everything here was turning out to be dangerous and wanted people like me dead.

"What about the Fighters Guild you mentioned?"

At least I was good at one thing: making Curr laugh. "Those are professional fighters. Do you know what makes them professionals?"

I shrugged. "Enlighten me."

"They only do so in exchange for coin. Ample sums of coin. Who do you think is going to pay for a bunch of sellswords to vanquish vermin?"

"Not the government."

"Not the government, indeed. Better to just pay for swords to guard trading caravans."

"But if everyone does nothing—"

"Then they do nothing. The occasional traveler becomes a goblin snack, and the world has one less mouth to feed."

"That's horrible," I said, not even having to feign the look of disgust on my face.

"If you are stupid enough to go traipsing north without proper gear or companions, then the responsibility for getting out alive rests with you, and you alone."

"Uh…" I looked from side to side. "Aren't we about to go 'traipsing north'?"

Curr grinned. "Affirmative! Good thing we are not as foolish as to be unprepared—Hm, well, at least, I am not."

I swallowed the lump in my throat. "Perhaps there's some other quest we could attain? Something to the, uh, I don't know… south?"

Curr walloped me on the shoulder. "And what would be the fun in that!"

"Oh, I don't know. Living?"

"Living and dying depends on how well you manage to swing a blade." Curr said. "But before we get to that, you are in dire need of a better outfit. Those leggings are far too short to be much use in the chill winds that hug the northern road. Boots. Perhaps armor. Lute or no lute, you cannot go out into the wilds like that. You will never last a day."

"And by last a day..."

Curr was already on the move again.

He means you'll die. And it will hurt.

Oh, and by the way... you're hungry again.

I scurried to keep up. It was cumbersome, carrying both a lute and a sword, but at least I looked a little more like a warrior and less like some lame dude with a toy guitar.

We rounded a corner, and Curr stopped in front of a large shop I'd seen last night while searching for a place to sleep. A flowerbed outside looked expensive to upkeep and gave me the distinct impression that whatever was inside wouldn't come cheap.

"I only have two gold left, Curr," I whispered as we entered. As embarrassing as it was to admit, he needed to know.

"Never speak of your fortunes out loud," he whispered back. "And perhaps we can discuss why I bought you lunch earlier."

"I—"

"Later," he said with finality.

The heady scent of leather pulled my attention away from Curr.

The place was packed with all manner of goods. Big bags hung from poles. Thick boots lined one wall. And there was something that looked like long tarps—some sort of tent, maybe?

From the rear of the shop, a skinny figure pranced out. That was the only word for it. If a deer could stand on two legs... you get the picture. Next thing I spotted were pointed ears sticking out from the side of his head like pine trees.

NAME: *Lalair Caiquinal*
OCCUPATION: *Tailor/Clothier*
RACE: *Elf (male)*
SPECIAL ABILITIES: *Bartering, Potion-making, Dream-interpretation.*
WEAPONS: *Currently unarmed. However, don't mistake unarmed for non-lethal.*

That was an ominous warning if I'd ever heard one.

So, there are elves here. Why am I not surprised?

Believe it or not, you should be surprised. Elves are rare these days. Male elves even more so. Many groups live as nomads in caravans. At one time, they would've been found all over Pyruun, but that was long before the Wellick Wars and the Fall of Alyndis.

Tall and slender, their bodily makeup doesn't allow for obesity. They are formidable warriors but prefer peace. They are lovers of the arts. Wellicks could learn a thing or two in that area. Elves have a proclivity for magic—power for which they credit the Seven Stars. They don't usually have surnames like wellicks, but it seems Lalair is trying his hardest to fit in with Caiquinal. How industrious.

"Aiya, travelers. What brings you in today?" Lalair spoke with a sly tongue, dragging out the words in a sing-songy way. If I hadn't just seen his skills, graciously displayed before me by the screen, I'd have suspected him of being a bard as well.

Curr nudged me. "Take a look."

I stretched my arms out to the sides so the shopkeep could get a better look at what a miserable specimen I apparently was. To my surprise, he simply twisted a ring between thumb and forefinger.

"Pathetic, is it not?" Curr said.

The elf twirled a finger around his long blond hair while continuing to appraise me. I'd gotten the same stare from a clerk at the Banana Republic when I'd tried on skinny jeans for the first time. It wasn't a good look.

"Indeed," Lalair agreed.

"I'm *right* here," I said. "I don't think I look that bad."

But I knew I did. Just didn't think them saying it was okay.

Lalair pinched a bit of fabric on my shoulder like he was touching some dead, moldy thing. "Sad state. Sad and cheap."

For all I knew, he was right. I had no idea where these clothes came from. Could've been Nahal's equivalent to the Salvation Army.

"We will need something hardy and worthy of adventure," Curr said.

"Adventure, you say?" Lalair asked. "Where will your travels take you?"

"Bal—" I started to say, but Curr cut me off with a clap on the back that caused me to cough.

"Balahazia, *unfortunately*. Fighters Guild business. I do not believe my friend here is properly clothed for the journey. He will need boots, better pants, a tunic of more substantial material."

"Of course." Lalair closed his eyes, almost longingly. I could sense something that felt like sadness. "It gets cold to the north these days, in the shadow of the Masked Mountains and old Alyndis. And will you require any armor?"

Curr cocked his head to one side. "You sell armor?"

The elf bowed. "Admittedly, not as much as you may find at an armorer, but we deal in some leather jerkins that qualify."

Curr grunted. "Would you consider a discount if we were to fully outfit him here?"

Recalling Lalair's Special Abilities, the first one was "bartering." I was intrigued to see how this went, considering how poor I was.

Lalair smiled, his lips stretching unnaturally wide. The corners nearly touched his paper-thin earlobes.

"We don't offer discounts as a general rule. However, I can see that you are someone with discriminating taste. So perhaps we can allow for a certain degree of *play*. Let me see what I can rustle up."

The elf vanished into the back room. Curr leaned over and whispered, "Elves," as if it were some inside joke I should understand.

"Why did you cut me off?" I asked.

"About what?"

"Where we were going?"

"Ah," Curr said, placing a hand on my shoulder. "The elves are finicky. You should not act excited about a trek to their old homeland. It upsets them. Everyone knows that."

"Right, yeah, of course. Sorry, I just am... excited."

Thanks for the heads up!

You couldn't last one minute without me?

Elves used to own the land you now stand upon and far beyond. They can be touchy about the fact that your kind destroyed their woods and devastated what was left of Alyndis to build Balahazia. Get a clue.

"If you are excited now, wait until we are in the wilds!" Curr exclaimed, staring off at nothing in particular.

The elf returned carrying an armful of gear and set it down on the counter.

Turning to me, he said, "If you would, wellick. Disrobe."

I thought perhaps there would be a changing room, but the elf and Curr simply stood there waiting.

"Right here?"

"Where else?" Curr said.

"It would be no use to pay good money for clothing that fits poorly," Lalair said. "If you'd please."

My gaze flitted between them, and my cheeks flushed a dark shade of red. Of course there wouldn't be such a thing as privacy in this godforsaken world. That was also when I remembered I wasn't wearing underwear.

Just like the high school locker room.

I gulped.

Did you enjoy it there?

No.

And *then* I remembered the screen's warning. I would appear like a wellick until I took my pants off.

What did that mean?

Of course, the screen stayed quiet as a church mouse.

There would be no way out of this. So, I turned away from them and slowly stripped down. Goosebumps rose all over as the cool air touched my bare ass. I covered up what I could.

"You are too small," Curr said matter-of-factly.

Anger swelled in me. "Not everyone was blessed to be a horse."

Curr roared a laugh. "I meant you are skinny! You are lucky I bought you that stew."

I didn't think that was what he meant.

"So lucky," I muttered.

Thankfully, Lalair handed me the set of pants first and I slid them on as quickly as possible. Since no one commented on what made me different from a wellick, I assumed I'd managed to avoid being found out this soon into my life here.

Not bad. The quality was so much better and softer than what I'd been wearing, which was basically a laundry sack.

Lalair began poking and prodding me in ways I only dreamed Trish would. I gritted my teeth and closed my eyes.

"How do they fit?" he asked.

"You should know with all that groping," I said.

"What was that?"

"Perfect."

The elf did a little bounce-and-clap. "I'm so pleased."

He handed me a tunic, and I noted it was far warmer than my other had been.

"It's nice," I said before he initiated his molestations again.

"Yes, yes. Of course, it is. Finest quality outside the capital. You'll fit right in when you get there—apart from being a lesser."

"A lesser?" I scoffed.

Curr gave me a warning glance.

I was beginning to feel that this land was highly inhospitable toward anyone of my kind. What had I done to be cursed as not only a human—or a wellick—but a wellick *bard* at that?

He ignored the comment and fit me with the leather jerkin himself, tightening the straps to my comfort. I was glad, considering that until seeing it, I wasn't exactly sure what a jerkin was or how to secure it.

I tapped on the toughened leather that now covered my upper torso, and felt a lot better knowing I had actual armor now. Perhaps those orcs wouldn't make such easy sport out of me after all.

Not bloody likely.

Fine time for you to chime in.

I looked at Curr. "What do you think?"

"Put the boots on already," he said. "You look foolish standing there in bare feet."

The elf handed me what must've passed for socks and then the boots. They felt a little stiff like a pair of new crocs, and were heavier than modern snow boots,.

"They will, of course, loosen up as the leather gets stretched. You are in luck that they are made for thinner frames," the elf said. "Though you may still experience a small degree of unpleasantness at first. Surely a man such as yourself will find it an easy thing to tolerate."

"Surely," I said sarcastically. "What about underwear?"

Lalair and Curr looked at each other like I'd just asked for a unicorn.

"What's that now?" the elf asked.

"Something to go between my... you know... and my pants."

He looked taken aback. "What is 'you know'?"

"Just... under the clothes for support—you know what, never mind."

"Oh!" Lalair exclaimed. "That's not a bad idea! Perhaps I'll invent something. Meanwhile, take a look at yourself."

I did so, following his pointed finger to a full-length mirror.

It was the first time I'd seen my reflection since I... arrived. It was a strange sensation, standing there looking at myself wearing such absurd clothing.

Though, I had to admit, I looked good in a weirdo-dressed-up-for-Halloween kind of way. I strapped my scabbard around my waist and pressed my hand against the sword's pommel. Puffing out my chest, a surge of reassurance swept through me. Comfortable clothing and a weapon. It would certainly be better going into the next part of this adventure armed than not.

That is most definitely an understatement.

Are you always this sarcastic?

Who's sarcastic? I'm simply acknowledging reality. Without a weapon, you would have died in the north. You probably will still die, to be honest. But who knows? I've been wrong in the past.

I shook my head. What sort of all-seeing-system-thingy talked like this? It didn't make any sense.

"Fine-looking lad," Curr said.

I gave the neckline of my armor a proud tug. "Thank you, Curr." Then whispered under my breath, "At least someone appreciates it."

"You are welcome." Curr turned to the elf. "All right. How much for all of this?"

My heart sank. Oh yeah, that part. This was just the fitting stage of a transaction, and somehow, I'd have to get all of this with only two gold pieces.

"That will be—"

"Oh, one last thing," Curr interrupted Lalair. "He needs a traveling cloak. Something he can wrap himself in for sleep."

"Ah, we are fresh out of cloaks," Lalair bemoaned.

"Rats," Curr said. "I suppose we can shop elsewhere."

"Funny you should mention rats..." He leaned in, eyes glinting in an oddly familiar way. I'd dealt with used car salesmen before. "You know, I do have one cloak left."

There we go. Here's his special bartering skill.

This won't be good for you.

"I'll make you a deal," Lalair continued. "All this..." He swept his hand over me, indicating the clothing, "I'll give you free of charge and throw in a cloak of tremendous quality—one I was intending to keep for myself—if you help me with a little problem I have in the cellar."

"The cellar?" I asked, not liking where this was heading.

Told you...

"Shameful as it is, I have a bit of a..." Lalair leaned close and pressed a hand against his mouth on one side, "...rodent problem. I cannot stand rodents, and the constable refuses to hear me over such an *insignificant* problem. I know it's because of my ears. That bigot."

Before I could enter the conversation, Curr said, "Rats? That sounds like a great deal!"

ITEM OBTAINED:
Basic Tunic (Defense 1)

This item has no Special Abilities, but damn, you look like a proper adventurer!

ITEM OBTAINED:
Basic Pants (Defense 1)

No more burlap scraping your sack. You can now move unhindered and unchafed.

ITEM OBTAINED:
Boots of Flying (Defense 1)

Just kidding. They're just basic boots. However, they are of fine craftsmanship. This elf knows his footwear.

ARMOR OBTAINED:
Leather Jerkin (Defense 4)

This is a fine piece of armor. A bit of a waste on you, if you ask me.

I didn't ask you.

NEW OBJECTIVE:
Eliminate the rat infestation in Lalair's cellar.

REWARD:
You get to keep all of the items listed above.

Plus, a new cloak and a new Title! Lucky you.

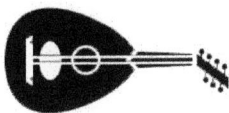

14

"This is a crappy deal," I said, standing at the top of a musty old staircase in the back storage room of Lalair's shop. "Couldn't you just pay him? I'll pay you back later. I'm good for it."

"With what?" Curr asked.

"What we earn in Balahazia."

"We are going to need as much gold as we can manage to make the trip to Balahazia."

I stared down into darkness, imagining the scurrying rats and worse. Panic gripped me. "Can't you do it?"

"Danny, do you not know how simple a task slaying a few rodents would be for me?"

"Yeah, that's why I'm suggesting it."

Curr shook his head. "I do not need the experience like you do. Consider it practice for the orcs. You will thank me for this later."

"That's doubtful," I whispered.

"Do you need a push?"

"No," I said quickly. "I'm fine. Just... gathering my wits."

"That will take more time than we have."

"Har-har. Very funny. I still don't understand why I have to do this alone."

"If you are to survive the perils of the wild and beyond, you will need to master your blade."

"And you think I'm gonna do that stabbing rats?" I asked.

"No. But it is a start."

Okay, I told myself. *You can do this.*

The screen remained still and quiet. I wasn't sure if that was a good sign.

Nothing to say, oh mighty one?

Just remember which one is the pointy end.

Thanks.

Just as I'd gained the nerve to take my first step, Lalair peered around the corner and scared the hell out of me.

"Oh!" he shouted. "Do be careful. Several of them have just sprouted their wings."

"Wings? What?"

"Oh, do not be a baby," Curr said. "I am sure they have not developed a taste for man flesh yet."

"You guys are joking, right?" I asked. "Wings? Rats don't have wings."

Curr blinked. "Once again, I am led to contemplate where you are from that you would say something like this."

"Someplace without rats," I said, swallowing. "With wings."

"Seems so." Luckily, Curr didn't pry. "Okay, down you go." He handed me a lit torch off the wall of Lalair's storage room.

ITEM OBTAINED:
Torch.

"And just remember," Curr said. "If the sword fails you, you could always sing them to death."

"I'm starting to reconsider this friendship," I replied. "That reminds me, take this." I took the lute off and handed it to Curr. He appeared confused.

"Should a bard not carry his instrument to battle? That is how it is meant to be."

"I just got it. I'm not looking to break it, bumping around a dark basement."

ITEM LOST:
A truly fine lute [Unique].

A bard is nothing without his instrument, but you do you, Danny Boy.

With that, I started my descent. The stairs creaked, little billows of dust rising with each step. The deeper I went, the quieter it became until the little chittering sounds of rats swelled to deafening levels.

How many are there?

Enough.

Do they really have wings?

The screen ignored that question. As I reached the bottom, the flickering torchlight revealed a roughly square-shaped room. It was damp and cold. Crates upon crates upon crates were stacked nearly to the ceiling. I imagined each one contained some manner of fabric or clothing.

"There's not a single cloak in any of these?" I asked no one.

Something moved swiftly to my left, and I swung the torch only to find bare cellar floor where I'd sworn a shadow passed. My knees wobbled, sweat soaked my new clothes, and my sword, in my shaky grip, could've rung a bell had I been near one.

"Okay, Danny, they're just rats," I said. "You've seen rats before. Just this time... you've got to kill them. And they might fly."

My uncle was an exterminator. He did this all the time. Once, he brought me along on one of his jobs. Had me spray the outside of the house with some chemical while he did something on the inside. Oh, how I'd kill for a bit of that poison right now. Then again, he died of a respiratory disease.

In the corner of the room, a faint whitish-blue light shone—the screen highlighting something. It was the size and shape of the biggest rat I'd ever laid eyes on. I was just lucky it was too dark to make out its features from here.

Greater Street Rat
Level 3
HP 10/10

The thing stared at me, and I at it. It was a showdown of epic proportions.

Okay, wait. Level? You haven't mentioned anything about that yet. What Level am I?

You are a Level 1, n00b.

Level 1!

If Levels were years, you'd be suckling at your mother's teat.

Something rubbed up against my leg and I turned, fast as lightning. My new boot caught whatever it was and sent it flying into a stack of crates. The boxes on the top of the pile teetered, then came crashing down on the creature.

Lesser Street Rat Slain!

You have gained +1 in Unarmed Combat.

Your Unarmed Combat Skill is now 4.

Congratulations on your first kill. Even if it was an accident.

Its squeal made me stagger back, and I tripped over something, fell and hit my head hard enough to wonder if I'd finally had my first concussion.

Never mind. Cancel that extra combat points order.

3 it is.

Another time, I may have argued that being able to lose points wasn't fair, but I stared at the rubble atop the first thing I can ever remember killing, backing away slowly. I guess insects count, though. And when I forgot to feed my pet hamster...

So... was the rat I just killed a Level 3 too?

You killed... hahaha. That's rich.

The rat murdered by the crates was only a Level 1.

I swore. Was I capable of killing a creature two Levels higher than me? Even a rat. I faced the Greater Rat and readied my sword the best I knew how. In this case, that meant placing my torch precariously on a crate, and holding my weapon like Jose Canseco.

What are you doing?

I don't know, I answered honestly. *I've never held a sword before.*

Have you ever watched a movie? Played a video game?

That thing isn't a two-handed weapon.

I switched my grip back to one hand and cautiously started toward the bigger rat. It still just stared at me like I was no threat at all. I probably wasn't. When I was mere feet away, it bared its teeth and hissed.

I jumped back and yelped.

C'mon, dude. Nut up!

My little pep-talk did nothing substantial, but I still took a tentative step and stabbed at the rat.

I missed. Horribly. Nonetheless, the rat ran like a puppy from thunder.

How am I supposed to kill these things? They're faster than me. They'll just keep running away.

He's not running away.

Before I could ask what the screen meant, the sound of dozens of tiny little feet pitter-pattered toward me. I swore again. There must've been twenty of them, all varying in size. Some were as small as normal rats, others reminded me of that Taco Bell dog. Others still were probably tall enough to ride most rides at Six Flags. I was in deep trouble.

Suddenly, several of them unfolded wings, took to the air, and zoomed at me.

"Oh, balls!"

I swung wildly, unsure if my sword was even sharp enough to

hurt them with a slash. I caught one on the wing but didn't see it go down since three more were gnashing their teeth in my face.

I screamed. It wasn't manly.

Next, I performed a combination of karate chops that were more like slaps and flailed my sword overhead like a bimbo with her shirt off at Mardi Gras. The others were coming for me now too. Somehow, I had the presence of mind to retrieve my torch before backstepping for the stairs.

I stabbed out and felt the tip of my sword piercing soft flesh. A rat squealed, high-pitched and terrifying all at once.

Street Rat Slain!

You have gained +1 in Melee Weapon Combat.

Your Melee Weapon Combat is now 10.

"I got one!" I shouted. "Take that, mother—"
One nipped at my leg, just above my boot.

You have been hit for 2 points of damage.

"Ow!"

I turned my attention to my attacker and slashed down at it. My sword was, indeed, sharp enough to sever the beast's head.

Street Rat Slain!

Nice swing, kid! Don't get cocky.

As satisfying as it was to have play-by-play updates of my exploits, having a semi-transparent screen covering my vision was quite unhelpful.

Oh, I'm sorry for telling you how great you're doing.

Would you like me to turn off in-battle notifications?

Yes!

I continued backing away. There was no way I could manage to kill every one of these things without sustaining serious injury myself. I had to think of something.

Another one swooped down on wings—*freaking wings!* Its sharp claws raked the back of my skull, and a small trickle of blood ran down my neck. Stabbing my sword straight upward, I skewered the culprit. My blade grew heavy with the weight of the flying rat, and I lowered it, allowing the rodent to slide off and onto the floor.

"Yeah! That could be you, bitches!" I shouted.

However, the sight of their dead brethren merely enraged the remaining rats. They all hissed in concert and charged. Several nipped at me, and I'd had enough. Not the most heroic thing I'd ever done, but I turned and ran toward the stairs. I would just have to convince Curr that this was too dangerous for a lowly Level 1 like me.

When I reached the rickety steps, I noted that there was no light coming from above. Curr had shut me in.

"Dammit!"

I rushed up. Then, placing my torch in a holder on the wall, I pounded on the door with both my free fist and the sword pommel. There was no response. I twisted back in time to thwart a nasty bite from one of the flying ones, grabbing it by the legs as I dodged to the side. The feel of its bony little body in my grip almost made me drop it, but I held fast. Hard as I could, I whacked it against the wall.

I was rewarded with a sickening crunch that told me it would no longer pose a threat to me.

However, without the screen's updates, I couldn't be sure it was dead.

Did I kill it?

Could you make up your mind?

Greater Flying Rat Slain!

Fine. Just tell me when things are dead.

The screen blinked away, and I prepared myself to meet an onslaught of climbing rats, but there were none. They'd all gathered at the bottom of the stairs, seemingly afraid to begin the climb on such unstable wood.

I guess I'm dumber than a rat.

We've all been telling you that.

Your Intelligence is only a 4 (+10), even after that massive bonus from the hag's vial.

Oh, yeah? I'll show you dumb.

I grabbed the torch from the sconce and descended a couple of steps, feeling one nearly break under my weight. You'd think with this elf's ability to barter, he'd be able to afford a healthy set of stairs.

I glared at the rats, their eyes all gleaming red in the torchlight.

With my sword, I extended as far as I could and prodded a wooden crate at the top of a stack by the bottom of the stairs. With enough effort, it fell, though these rats were smarter than their dead compadre and were able to get out of the way as it broke into pieces.

That gave me an idea.

Low intelligence. Right. Watch this.

I'm on the edge of my seat.

"Who wants roast rat?" I shouted as I tossed the torch onto the dry wood and the fabric it contained.

ITEM LOST:
Torch.

Immediately, the rats within its radius caught fire, the flames passing from one to another.

"Level 1 noob, my ass," I said under my breath.

Then the rats started scrambling around in circles, squealing and further spreading death to one another. It was not as triumphant as expected. Just kind of sad.

They hit the torch, which rolled, causing the stairs to catch fire. It got hot fast. More rats burned but so did the stairs. The old, splintering wood went up in a magnificent roar.

"Shit, shit, shit," I swore, turning and climbing back to the top. I beat against the door again, shouting, "Let me in! Let me in! They're all dead and... fire!"

Smoke rose in great clouds of gray and black. The stench of burning rat hair was... something else. It reached me and I began coughing and hacking.

"Curr!" I struck the door again. "Let me out!"

Finally, the door opened, and I tumbled through.

"By the Seven Stars!" Lalair cried out and ran into the other room.

Curr wore a grin and was munching on something. Where did he get food?

"I knew you could do it," he said, shoving my lute back into my gut.

ITEM OBTAINED:
A truly fine lute [Unique].

"I hate you," I said, scrambling to my feet.

He ruffled my hair. "No, you do not."

OBJECTIVE COMPLETED:
You have eliminated the rat infestation in Lalair's cellar!

That was, uh, an interesting method of extermination. But you can keep your gear, hooray!

TITLE UNLOCKED:
Vermin's Bane

Oh, that sounds badass! What does that mean?

Bragging rights mostly. However, you now gain a +1 Bonus to your Combat Skills when battling rats.

So, not badass...

Precisely.

A moment later, Lalair raced by with a bucket. "Help me, you fools!" he shouted, tossing water down the stairs. Steam hissed as he turned back to refill his bucket.

NEW OBJECTIVE:
Speak with Lalair to claim your cloak.

REWARDS:
Guess.

I think he's a little busy!

Curr grabbed Lalair's arm aggressively. He wore a stern expression as he cleared his throat.

"What?" Lalair questioned.

"I believe you owe Danny here a cloak."

"My basement is on fire, you mindless oaf—"

Curr squeezed tighter and shut him up. "A deal is a deal, elf."

"Curr, we can help first," I insisted.

"No. Elves and their silver tongues. They must be held to their word."

Lalair might have looked offended if he wasn't worried about his shop burning to the ground.

"Curr, seriously. This was my fault." I tugged at his arm, but it was like pulling on a block of granite.

"Or we can wait," Curr said. "I have all night. Your shop, on the other ha—"

"All right!" Lalair pulled himself free, muttering in some other language as he hurried to the front of the store.

Curr looked at me and winked. I had no idea how he could be so calm. The heat radiating from the cellar was immense, even as the whole room glowed orange.

Lalair came running back and shoved a wrapped bundle of cloth against my stomach. It looked like it was bright red, but it was hard to tell in the fire's glow.

OBJECTIVE COMPLETED:
Lalair gave you the promised cloak.

ITEM OBTAINED:
Lalair's Elegant Cloak [Unique]
+1 to Charisma & Speechcraft while wearing.
-1 to Sneaking while wearing.

"I hope you enjoy it, *N'iuayt*," Lalair spat.

What does that mean?

An old elvish curse for... you don't want to know.

"Excellent!" Curr clapped. "Now, Danny... You should really help him put out the fire you started."

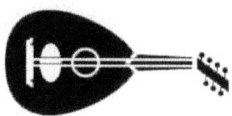

15

By the time we finished, the fire had spread across much of the cellar, completely destroying most crates of supplies. Curr helped, but only when it was clear Lalair and I couldn't transport water fast enough.

One thing was for certain. Not a rat—winged or otherwise—survived.

I wasn't sure what Lalair had lost, but he didn't give us much chance to ask. The moment the last flame was extinguished, he shoved us out the door, cursing in his elvish language.

But I'd done what he'd asked and killed the rats. How was I to know the whole place would go up in flames? It was me or them. Right?

Meh.

We got back outside, and a few folks were gathered around, obviously curious why smoke puffed out through the chimney and any open windows.

"What's going on here?" one of them asked. He was a rotund man, completely out of shape, wearing leather armor that barely fit.

On his chest was the symbol of a sun and moon, half of each painted all gold and red.

What is that?

The fractured sun and moon, the symbol of the Kingdom of Pyruun, harkens to the light overcoming darkness.

NAME: Constable McCoy
RACE: Wellick (male)
OCCUPATION: Constable, the local representative of the King's Army.
SPECIAL ABILITIES: This guy can eat.
WEAPONS: Three small daggers and an appetite for destruction.

Is that a Guns N' Roses reference?

There are no guns in Pyruun.

"Is that knife-ear causing problems again?" he asked. I noticed Lalair watching from a window. He quickly closed the shutters.

"Just an honest trade, Constable," Curr said.

Whether or not anyone believed him, no one questioned it. Maybe it was because he looked like he could pop everyone there like pimples. Even the slovenly constable backed down almost immediately.

"I see," he said. "We... uh... don't want any trouble here."

"No trouble," Curr agreed.

"We're just leaving, actually," I added.

Constable McCoy eyed Curr from head to toe, his jowls bouncing. "Good... I mean, I hope you enjoyed your stay, braug."

"I did, actually!" Curr exclaimed. "Not as boring as usual."

The constable half grunted a response, then shambled away. If he was in charge of keeping Nahal safe, then this really must have been an unimportant village. I'm pretty sure I could have beaten him up.

Doubtful, big bad rat slayer.

Shut it.

As everyone dispersed, I pulled out the cloak I'd stuffed into my belt so I could help douse the fire. Now, out in the sunlight, I could tell that it was... decidedly not red.

The elf got his revenge.

It looked like something Lady Gaga would wear.

Pink.

Not just pink, but bright pink. I didn't even think that kind of vibrant dye would be available in a place so seemingly primitive. But that goes to show how little I knew. Hanging from the clasp were long gold tassels.

You've got to be kidding me.

If anyone could pull off pink with gold tassels, it's you! Just channel your inner Freddy Mercury and own the look. It's SO you.

"Looks comfortable. And warm," Curr said. "And what a bargain you got it for."

"It's pink," I said like he should understand the implication. Surprise. He didn't.

"Why does the color matter?" he asked.

I considered what I'd seen on the screen about how it took away my sneakiness, which apparently was something rated here.

But, hey, it's unique and special! Think about those perks.

"Well, first of all, shouldn't we be more... discreet, or less—I don't know—flamboyant trekking through the wild with orcs and whatever around?"

"I hardly think they would care what you are wearing."

I held it up to my back without tying it on. "I look ridiculous."

"You will not think that when you are wrapped up on a cold night and survive until morning."

"I think I will..."

"Well, believe it or not, I think you are ready." He took a deep breath of the slightly smoky air. He seemed to like it. I mimicked him and coughed a few times. "Yes. Let us leave Nahal behind, Danny. Balahazia awaits."

OBJECTIVE COMPLETED:
You have improved your equipment.

NEW OBJECTIVE:
Accompany Curr to Balahazia and obtain your next quest.

REWARD:
Confidence, and the respect and admiration of tens of people.

Curr set off, and it was an adventure in and of itself to once again match his enormous stride. I was already tired by the time we reached the edge of the clustered buildings and entered farmland.

You are now leaving Nahal. Would you like to change your class or your appearance before you proceed?

Wait, what?

Before you set off on your first adventure. Would you like to make any changes?

Like... I don't have to be a bard? Can I be a warrior? Or, wait, a mage!

You'll need to be specific. And your appearance. Maybe you can replace some of that flab with abs.

Flab.

I touched my stomach. The screen wasn't all wrong, but it still hurt.

Hm, what should I be? Do you have any ideas?

Sure! Perhaps it would be smart if you were a—LOL, I can't keep this up. You can't change anything, Danny. You are what you are.

Goddammit, screen.

PART TWO

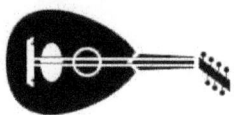

16

AN UNEXPECTED HERO

PART II: A Purpose-filled life is a life of purpose.

CURRENT LOCATION: Pikeman's Trail

We came upon a small creek at the edge of farmland, spanned by a stone bridge. Small flowers glowed along the water like fireflies. Curr must've heard my boots stop shuffling because he turned toward me.

"They match your cloak!" he exclaimed. He wasn't wrong. They were pink. Maybe that was how the dye was made? "Take one. They smell wonderful."

Right. That was just what I needed, to be seen wearing my fabulous new cloak and picking flowers.

"Go on. Take one."

I groaned.

Curr stopped. "Nahal's border ends at this bridge. From here, we are in the wild. I will not continue until you pick that flower, Danny."

"You're... serious?"

"Surviving is not easy. Some plants or berries can kill you. These do not. They have minor healing properties. I already have a handful from when my previous party and I arrived. They will be instrumental in potion crafting." He patted one of his satchels.

"You know how to craft potions?"

"Do not change the subject," Curr warned.

I rolled my eyes and looked around. Since nobody was nearby, I did as he suggested, picking several of the vivid flowers, and then shoving them deep into my pocket.

ITEM OBTAINED:
Candentis Flos ex Improbi (6)

Boy, that's a mouthful.

That's what she said! I thought quickly, before the screen could beat me to it.

You are so immature. May I continue?

The Candentis Flos ex Improbi is a flower native to the region, though rare throughout the realm. They are often used in healing potions, and act as beacons when darkness falls, leading to water. They may not be torch-bright, but you'll be thankful for them come nightfall.

You have gained +1 in Herbalism

Your Herbalism is now 4.

Four? When did I gain the first three?

Congrats! You are now a Level 2 Bard!

You are no longer a complete drain on society. Now you're akin to a lifetime politician or a vegan. Ohh. Or someone who does CrossFit and needs everyone to know they do CrossFit.

Maybe you'll get through a day without screwing everything up, but probably not.

I staggered a bit. A burst of energy rushed through me, like I'd just taken an EpiPen shot of adrenaline after being stung by a bee. Then came a cool wave. It was like the perfect high. The sensation was intense but fleeting. I had to take a few breaths to settle myself.

Wait, Level 2? From picking a flower?

Don't be so judgmental! It all adds up. There are herbalists who could defeat you in seconds.

Okay, enough is enough, screen. I need some answers. What's all this Level and Skill stuff about exactly? And no excuses. I'm smart enough to handle it.

Sigh.

Fine.

Pyruun is no different from your world. On Earth, you progress through life gaining Skills and Attributes. However, here, they are represented by a numeral system with tangible rewards for progress.

Because of your Skill increases so far, you have improved to Level 2. That isn't good. But it's better than a 1. Whereas before, you found yourself winded from the walk out of town, you should now not only feel better, but be capable of much longer journeys. With each new Level, your Health, Stamina, and—if you were attuned with

any magical abilities—Mana regenerates to 100%. You can also apply +1 to the Attribute of your choosing.

I have magical abilities?

Once I saw that, it was hard to focus on anything else.

No. Pay attention. I said IF. See the 0 Mana? As a bard, you will learn to alter the world through song.

Like Michael Jackson.

Hopefully, nothing like Michael Jackson.

I meant that his music changed the world.

Perhaps, but I mean truly alter the world. Through song, you can inspire warriors in battle, convince people to change their minds when they've made a decision you are unhappy with, and more.

That seems wrong.

It is all in the way you look at things. Suppose Lalair refused to give you that glorious cloak (you look positively radiant, by the way).

Yeah. Thanks.

Had he chosen not to give you the cloak, if you knew the right song and had the skill to perform it up to snuff, you could've played it and had a chance at changing his mind. However, it's not like you're forcing them. The song simply encourages them to rethink their decision and potentially see things from a different angle.

And how do I learn that song?

It's one of the sheets you stole from Garvis the halfling.

How do I learn them?

Simply play them when your Skill and Level are high enough. How does one learn anything? Practice makes perfect. Then again, you are sort of stupid.

I knew you were being too nice.

"You coming or what?" Curr asked, looking at me with his head tilted like I had three eyes. "It is just a flower."

"Just a moment," I said. "Catching my breath."

"We have barely begun our journey and you are already tired?"

"I just need a minute, okay?" I snapped. I didn't mean to, but so much was being thrown at me so fast.

Curr shrugged. "I have to relieve my bladder anyway." Curr threw his hands up and walked over to the stream. "Better here than where something might pop out and grab your—"

"Please don't say it," I cut him off. Things were scary enough here compared to my old life.

While Curr made a racket undoing his belt, I turned away and thought about what the screen said. I didn't have time here to practice any sheet music, and if I dared play while on the road, Curr might be liable to break another of my things. I made a mental note to do it as soon as I had a quiet moment... if ever.

Okay, so I'm Level 2 and basically useless. But what about the normal Skills? How do I get better?

Every time you use a Skill or an Ability related to certain Skills, you get a little better. Once you've used it enough, it progresses to the next Level. Those points passively work toward new abilities and better performance.

And everyone knows this?

I never said that. To most people, they experience life here in Pyruun in a similar fashion to how you used to on Earth.

So, no Levels?

They still have them but have no idea what their Level is.

Is there a way for me to see it all? Can you show me all my Skills and Abilities and stuff?

The screen changed and a long list appeared.

NAME: Daniil Kendrick

Okay, stop there. I don't get why my name changed here.

Your name didn't change.

My name is Danny, not Daniil.

Have you ever seen your birth certificate?

I thought about it and realized...

No...

Your father was blitzed out of his mind when he filled it out. Spelled Daniel wrong. Your legal name is Daniil.

I didn't even know how to respond.

But you need to use your legal name for like, the IRS, and stuff! My mother told me I was legally named Daniel Kendrick.

Better not get audited.

The saddest part was, I wasn't even that shocked. My dad had always been some level of wasted as I was growing up.

As I was showing you before this got all emo, here is your Character Sheet:

NAME: Daniil Kendrick (male)
LEVEL: 2
CLASS: Bard
Health: 110
Stamina: 69

Noice.

Sigh.

Mana: 0
Defense: 3 (+7)
Attack Damage: 3-7

ATTRIBUTES (1 Point to Assign):
Strength: 11
Constitution: 16
Intelligence: 4 (+10)
Wisdom: 9
Dexterity: 13 (+10)
Charisma: 14 (+11)
Courage: 15
Luck: 33

SKILLS:
Melee Weapon Combat: 10
Ranged Combat: 8
Unarmed Combat: 3
Shields: 3
Singing: 14 (+10)
Instrument Playing: 16 (+10)
Herbalism: 4
Alchemy: 6
Pickpocketing: 9
Bartering: 6
Speechcraft: 11 (+11)
Camping: 1
Sneaking: 3 (-1)
Crafting:
Smithing:

Leatherworks:
Magic Skills: N/A

SPECIAL ABILITIES: Undiscovered

TITLES:
Petty Thief
Vermin's Bane

INVENTORY:
A Truly Fine Lute [Unique]
Basic Pants
Basic Tunic
Boots
Leather Jerkin
Lalair's Elegant Cloak
Candentis Flos ex Improbi (6)
Iron Short Sword
Unidentified Sheet Music
Gp: 2

Wait, I don't have any *Special Abilities? Even the halfling had Special Abilities!*

I didn't really understand what any number actually translated to... performance wise. But that part, I grasped.

You have yet to discover yours. If you ever do...

Encouraging. I'll be honest, I think I preferred living without knowing exactly how bad I am at everything.

Aw, wow. Now this is really turning into a My Chemical Romance concert. You won't always be so tragic, I promise. But you really

should stop wasting time and start making your mark on the world!

Now that was the first good thing the screen had said in a while. Seeing my lack of Abilities sucked, but it was a kick in the ass. Maybe if my parents had done that when I was young, I'd have focused on school instead of the band.

School has grades, Danny. It is, basically, the same...

You're the worst.

Now, if you'd like to be a bit better, you still have 1 Unassigned Attribute Point to assign. Would you like to use it now?

Attribute point? What in the world does that mean?

It's like feeding oatmeal to a toddler...

Attribute points are used to increase your overall Ability scores. If you were to choose Charisma, it would increase your force of personality, force of will, persuasiveness, personal magnetism, ability to lead, and physical attractiveness.

Physical attractiveness, huh?

Of course, that's all you'd cling on to.

I don't want to make a hasty decision. I'll wait.

That was a decision beyond your natural inclinations.

Your Wisdom Attribute has increased by 1.

Your Wisdom is now 10.

My brain swam from everything I'd just learned. Enough was enough. It was time to go. If I kept moving, I might not have a mental breakdown.

"Alright, Curr, I'm ready." I turned and caught a glimpse of *way* too much as he was getting his pants and belt secure. I had no idea how it took him so long to pee, but, man. That was scarring to my ego.

"And I am properly drained," he said. "Are you sure you do not want to relieve yourself?"

After what I'd just witnessed? No way. Man, did I miss bathrooms. And urinals. Paved roads wouldn't be bad either. The moment we crossed the bridge, the roads went from cobblestone to basically rough dirt.

Oh, and deodorant. Curr was upwind and, yeah, deodorant. Top of the list.

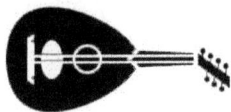

17

Let the walking commence. I was bored already, and we'd only traveled a few miles or so from Nahal.

You haven't. It's only been fifteen minutes...

That doesn't sound right. Does time move differently here?

No, you just have the attention span of a gnat.

"Out of the way!" someone shouted.

Finally, some excitement. I glanced back and saw a horse galloping down the road, straight toward us. Tensing, I reached down for my sword. Curr stopped me, kindly taking me by the sleeve and pulling me aside.

We let the horse race by. The rider looked to be wearing an Pyruunian cloak of some sort, as the back bore the kingdom's emblem.

Pyruunian... is that right?

Nod.

"You do not want any problems with the king's men," Curr said. "Trust me."

I didn't bother to ask exactly what he meant by *that*, but I agreed. "I thought his armies didn't patrol Pikeman's Trail?"

"That's not patrolling. They ride these roads like any other. He's probably delivering a message to Balahazia."

"Why didn't we get horses?" I asked. "That looks fast."

"Me on a horse?" Curr chuckled. "We braugs only ride tantors—great beasts for great warriors. There are no steeds in these parts which could support my size."

"Well, what about me?"

"You cannot afford a horse, Danny."

I sighed. "Couldn't we have rented like, a carriage or something, then?" As the screen had so kindly pointed out, we'd barely started walking and already I knew that doing this for three days was going to be dreadful.

"A carriage," Curr scoffed. "It is as if you would like to be slaughtered by orcs. Riding through on a cart which may be filled with food, they would not ignore us. We would require a much larger party."

"They won't ignore us anyway, will they?"

Curr shrugged. "You are skinny. They might pass on such a small morsel."

"You always know the right thing to say."

"In this case, your puny size is also your advantage. Better chance we escape their notice. There *are* a lot of them in this region, especially the closer we get to the Masked Mountains. We will need to be on our guard at all times or else they will catch us unawares and that will not be good."

"I don't like the idea of ending up as orc food."

Curr waved a hand. "Oh, they won't eat you. Orcs hate wellick meat."

"But you said earlier they *liked* hum—I mean, wellick flesh."

"No," Curr said, shaking his head. "Goblins like wellick flesh.

Orcs will gut us and then sell our meat and carcasses to goblins and worse."

I felt like a gobstopper got stuck in my throat. "You're not being serious now."

"I am always serious. Orcs can dress a wellick in mere seconds. They simply cut from neck to testicles and rip out the insides. Very efficient at that sort of activity, orcs are."

"So wellicks do have nuts," I muttered.

Curr stopped to assess me, concern marking his features. "Excuse me?"

My face reddened. "I said, some wellicks are nuts. Meaning anyone who traveled this road without proper protection by their side. Like you."

At that, Curr beamed with pride. "It is good you remember how strong I am."

Even I must admit, that was good.

As a reward, take +1 to Speechcraft.

Your Speechcraft is now 12 (+11).

Not Charisma?

Charisma is an Attribute, not a Skill. It doesn't work that way.

Not only are you getting greedy, but that was not very wise.

(Penalty) -1 to Wisdom Attribute for 24 hours.

What? You're kidding. I just got that!

Now that I understood the importance of these stupid numbers, that stung.

The screen didn't respond. I'd never understand this blasted system. So, what, did I just get smarter and then dumb again?

Wisdom and Intelligence are not the same thing, Daniil.

I was so annoyed, I could have growled, but I kept quiet while Curr adjusted the axe on his back and picked up his pace. "It would be best not to think about orcs for now."

He doesn't know you very well, does he?

Neither do you.

Even as I thought that, I didn't believe it. The screen seemed to know more about me than even I did. Heck, it claimed to know my legal name, which I'd spent my entire lifetime ignorant of.

"So, is this all you do?" I asked Curr as we crested a small hill. How could he go so long without needing to do something? Was this life before cell phones?

"Is what all I do?"

"Travel around, doing jobs for people like clearing out rats from basements?"

He chuckled. "Well, I have not performed a task that demeaning for quite some time."

"Because you're such a high Level?" I asked, fishing for some kind of insight into the way the system worked here in Pyruun.

Curr just stared at me blankly as we walked. "I do not know what that means. If you mean that I hold rank with the Fighters Guild, then yes. Lords or adventurers typically desire my assistance in seeking out treasures."

So, it was true. I guess I was the only one seeing something like the screen. The only one being told about Levels and Skills.

Wow. You really don't trust me?

Not one bit.

"Sure, yeah. That's what I meant," I said to Curr.

He grunted. "The Fighters Guild is a great resource for braugs like me who have not been conscripted to the king's army to find work."

"Braugs fight for the king?" I asked.

"Everyone fights for the king. Do not mistake it. While we used to be a proud people in Hoarfrost, the Wellick Wars changed everything. I do not wish to discuss such depressing topics."

This King Shirtaloon had forces able to take down a whole nation of people like Curr, Fargus, and Vulna? That surprised me.

We went on walking a few minutes longer before another question popped into my head.

"So, where do you keep all the treasures you find?" I asked Curr. All he had was his bags and travel gear, which could admittedly hold a lot considering the size of them and him. But nothing about it screamed treasure hoard.

His face grew dark and scary as he spun on me. "What do you know about my treasures?"

I stammered and held my hands up placatingly. "Nothing, really. I just know you and your old party were talking about it. And with all that work, I just figured you must have a lot. That's all."

"Mind your thoughts, Danny. You might give a braug reason to believe you are after more than you claim."

Yeah, Danny. What—are you thinking of pickpocketing him too?

You are such a prick.

I swallowed. "I swear. I'm just curious. This... adventuring life-style. It's all new to me."

"Clearly." Curr's gaze narrowed as if he were testing what I'd said, then he looked away. "I have found it is better not to keep all of one's belongings in a single place. Only take with you as much as you think you will need and stash the rest somewhere only you can access. That has been my way ever since I can remember."

"That's smart," I said.

"I know it is. And do not ask where. I will not tell you."

At the very least, his tone for that last request—

It was a command.

I wasn't used to anybody being as straightforward as Curr, which was admittedly kind of nice. People back in my world always seemed like they were up to something. Everyone had ulterior motives.

Imagine if he found out you've been lying to him about where you're from?

As much as I hated this screen, it was right. Curr had proven to be rather big on honesty and integrity and all that. And here I was, his traveling companion, and I was holding back the truth on something he might consider a big deal.

It was just... how does one tell someone they aren't from their world?

NEW OBJECTIVE:
Find a way to come clean and tell Curr the truth about where you're from.

REWARD:
A weight will be lifted off your shoulders. Permanent +1 to Courage.

Sorry, screen, that reward juice doesn't seem to be worth the squeeze.

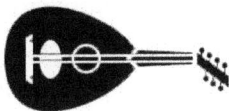

18

We kept at it for what felt like a million miles, the weight of potential consequences adding even more to the burden I bore. Walking on asphalt or sidewalks was one thing, but out here in the wild, my back felt like a rhino used it as a trampoline.

You have walked almost fifteen miles.

You will require sustenance soon to recuperate and regain Stamina.

I recommend food, drink, and sleep.

Have you learned nothing from your previous objectives?

Gee, thanks. That is a real shock about the food. The grumbling in my stomach couldn't possibly have tipped you off, could it?

I'm only informing you, so you don't forget.

I shook my head and the screen vanished again.

I tried asking Curr more questions as night neared, hoping to find an opening to confide in him, but it was largely a waste of time. He kept us moving at a brisk pace and didn't want to talk much after I'd stupidly inquired about his secrets.

Not that I had much left in my lungs to talk. The road had steadily inclined, and it wasn't just the exertion of going uphill, the air got thinner as we traveled to higher altitudes. I had to focus on my breathing.

So instead, I tried to make more sense of the screen.

I could toggle it on by asking a question inside my head, but beyond that, I didn't know what its capabilities were aside from keeping track of mundane stuff and insulting me. That didn't make me especially glad for its presence, but then again, perhaps it had other aspects to it that would end up coming in handy.

Like an Apple Watch I could never take off.

The sun started to set behind the trees to our west. Well, maybe it was our west. I was still using my old-world preconceptions.

Curr stopped so suddenly, I nearly bumped into his back.

He glanced skyward. "We will need to make camp soon."

My legs started to throb now that we'd slowed. The beginnings of a cramp stung in my left calf. I could also feel hot spots on my feet that foretold blisters from breaking in my new boots.

NEW OBJECTIVE:
Make camp.

REWARD:
A camp.

I already have an objective.

You will, over the course of any given time, have multiple objectives. Just like in your old world, you may need to go grocery

shopping and *sleep.* ***Choices are hard. Also, it's too bad you can't go grocery shopping.***

HUNGER LEVEL: Famished

"Where?" I asked Curr.

Rocky grasslands stretched to one side, and to the other, a forest. Not too dense this close to the road, but the vegetation thickened deeper in from what I could see.

Curr eyed me. "Have you never slept in the woods under the stars? A bard who has never made camp—that is strange."

Now I felt stupid.

As well you should. Just tell him he misunderstood—oooorrr, use this opportunity to meet the objective and tell Curr the truth.

"No, Curr. I think you misunderstood my question," I said.

"Oh, so I am just a dumb braug, unable to comprehend such intricacies as the common tongue?"

"I—what? No. I didn't mean that at all. I just—"

"We will stop here. Perhaps you should build the campfire since I am so stupid."

He swept his hand around, observing the giant trees to the right of the road. I spotted what looked like close-packed pines, a few oaks, and maybe some maples as well. That is, if they were the same species as back in my world.

I knew it wasn't the right time to tell him about Earth, but I hadn't started a fire since Boy Scouts. So, instead, I asked, "Won't fire attract the attention of certain parties we don't want to attract?"

Curr ignored me.

Wow. I'd really pissed him off asking about his riches and questioning his intellect, even by accident. Not a day in and I'd already discovered two of his sore spots. How much longer before I said the wrong thing and he crunched my spine?

Or if he finds out what you **aren't** *saying.*

"Curr, I'm sorry. I really didn't mean any offense. I'm just not a very good bard at the moment. That's all. I haven't had many adventures. I'm a fraud. Is that what you want to hear?"

It sucked to say out loud. If he could have heard me shred out some Red Hot Chili Peppers... but no, I was stuck with an ancient instrument I had no idea how to play.

Curr grunted, still focused on where our campsite would go most likely. Then he said, "Fire also keeps other creatures of the night away."

I was relieved when his demeanor changed. "What *other* creatures?"

He gave me another of his patented side-eyes, which were happening a lot more recently. Exasperatedly, he started ticking off fingers. "Wolves, wraiths, vampires, harpies, lycans, basilisks, blue caps, red caps, kobolds, satyrs, nymphs—that sort. Orcs and goblins may be most common here, but it is always a good idea to be on the lookout."

"So..." My throat went dry, no longer relieved about anything. "The fire keeps those things away?"

Curr wobbled his hand back and forth. "Perhaps. They will linger on the fringes of the firelight. They are opportunists, mostly. Were you to get hot in the middle of the night and roll just a bit too far, they would grab you, drag you away, and do their worst to you."

"I'm not sleeping tonight."

Curr laughed. "Relax. I will take first watch and you can rest knowing Curr is here." His eyes narrowed then. "Just make sure you do not fall asleep while you watch over me. That would be a bad thing indeed."

"I won't." I shook my head adamantly. My stomach rumbled.

HUNGER LEVEL: Dangerous.

You will soon become lightheaded from low blood sugar.

"What about food?" I asked, hopeful.

Curr patted one of his pouches. "I have some travel rations. Not the most delicious of meals, but enough to sustain us."

Just talking about food had my stomach growling even more. I had no idea what sort of rations Curr might've been carrying, but I didn't really care. I just wanted to sit and rest in front of a fire, chew away on something edible, have some water, and then roll up in my pink cloak to sleep—which at least in the dark wouldn't look so ridiculous.

Sure, this hadn't been a very exciting adventure yet, but walking fifteen miles was farther than I'd ever walked in... my whole life. Maybe even combined. I missed my beat-up old Dodge Dart. I even missed Uber.

Maybe you can start a carriage service here after you're rich!

If I'm stuck here long enough to be able to do that... Just kill me.

I am certain one of the beasts Curr listed will take care of that first.

Curr led us into a copse of pine trees. The sweet scent seemed to reinvigorate me, at least for a moment. The closest branches above us were a good twenty feet away and Curr studied them before nodding in judgment. Problem was, there were no glowing flowers in the area. It was dark. Really dark.

Curr pointed at the high branches. "It will keep us hidden and dry if it rains, but they are high enough that the flames will not set them alight. *I* will start the fire. You have started enough infernos today."

He laughed to himself as he set his packs down, and after clearing a space for a campfire and gathering enough dry tinder, he drew out a tinderbox. He had it smoking within a minute. That would have taken me all night.

OBJECTIVE COMPLETED:
(You) have made camp.

Not really. But I guess it counts.

REWARD:
A camp.

I guess he'd forgiven me. Thank God. I didn't want to explain how I could possibly not know how to start a campfire. At least not yet.

Tick... tock... tick... tock...

Soon, a small flame crackled. Even just seeing the hint of it warmed me and mitigated the threat of darkness that had been creeping up around us. I grabbed some of the branches and started piling them up.

"Good idea," Curr said. "We will not want the fire going out at any point tonight. That is, unless you feel like fighting again so soon."

Between rats and halflings, I'd had my fill of fighting. "I'll pass."

"Then keep piling up the branches," Curr said. "I will scout the area and ensure there are no caves to be aware of where orcs or goblins could hide. Or worse, cuddle bears."

A laugh slipped through my lips. "Cuddle bears? That sounds like something a kid begs Santa for at Christmas."

"I do not know what any of that means, but cuddle bears are not to be trifled with, Danny. Their name derives from the manner in which they squeeze their victims just to the brink of death before eviscerating them and eating their insides while they yet live."

My stomach turned over. "Oh…"

You really should stop judging things by their names, Danny. It's hurtful.

Curr stopped. "Oh, and I hope you are not bashful. If you need to piss, you had better be able to do it within the range of firelight. I would not suggest even heading off behind a tree to do your business."

I frowned. "What about if I have to do more than pee?"

Curr grunted. "Do it now or hold it in until the morning. Otherwise, it may well be your last."

I nodded. "Let me guess, orcs are attracted to the smell of wellick poop?"

"Tarton's Tusks, no. Not even they are so repulsive."

"Good to know. Thanks."

Curr headed off and I got to work stacking more wood by the small fire. I wondered if he was going to make it any bigger. But if he did, we'd go through the supply of wood faster. The trick, I supposed, was to find a happy medium between a suitable fire to keep the bad things away and having enough wood to make it through the night.

A crunch of twigs in the woods caught my attention. I suspected Curr was doing his check around the perimeter, but it unnerved me. I rose. Which was when I heard a shriek and the sound of steel. Staring off into the trees, now dense with shadows and darkness, I couldn't see much.

"Curr?" I said warily.

No answer. I slowly shifted my hand to the grip of my short sword. As if I knew how to use it. Hit them with the pointy end—as the screen had reminded me—was about the extent of my knowledge. Orcs and goblins or worse wouldn't be as simple as killing rats. And even that was a challenge.

Flying rats. Who'd have thought?

I drew the sword, hoping against hope that I wasn't going to have to use it.

"Curr?" I repeated.

I still got no response and edged a bit closer to the fire, aware that my legs were shaking. That was when I heard something. Music?

I whipped around, saw nothing. "Curr, is that you?"

Or you?

Is what me? I'm just quietly anticipating watching you use that sword again. It was so entertaining last time.

The music. It was all around me. Short staccato notes played softly and in a somewhat ominous melody.

There is no music, Danny.

Was I losing it? And where was Curr? Surely, he couldn't have been ambushed so quickly and easily... could he have?

I felt a little silly holding my short sword out in front of me, but after another *crunch* in the woods to my right, I raised it higher. Pivoting, I aimed the blade at the sound.

"Curr!"

The music started to speed up and grow louder. Another *crunch* to my left spun me in that direction.

What the hell is going on?

I believe it might be your first encounter with something more dangerous than a drunken halfling.

Leaves rustled and the music got more intense.

"Get back!" I whirled toward the sound and swung my sword

with all my might. With each swing, a sharp, musical crescendo struck. I swung again, but the torque took me a little too far as I hit nothing but air and lost my balance.

I nearly toppled into the fire.

"Watch yourself, puny companion!" Curr said, stepping out from behind a thicket with a grin. "You could poke an eye out."

A wave of relief washed over me. Simultaneously, that infernal music quieted until I couldn't hear it at all.

"Oh, my god..." I exhaled. "You had me scared shitless."

"Sorry about that," he said. "But hey! At least now you will not have to relieve yourself in the middle of the night."

"Huh?"

"For you are without shit. You said it yourself."

I drew a deep breath. "Where were you?"

"Ah, yes. We had a visitor. But fear not, I have taken care of it."

"A visitor?" I stopped when I noticed a body Curr dragged behind him. It was short, covered in bumpy gray skin with a weird sort of oily fur loincloth around its waist.

"What in the world?" I asked.

Curr let the clawed foot he was holding drop to the dirt.

"That, Danny the Bard, is a goblin," he said. "And more importantly, it is dinner."

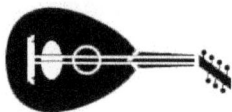

19

"Dinner? You're not serious."

Only Curr's eyes turned away from the creature, rolling up to look at me. "What sort of question is that? Of course, I am serious. Fresh goblin? This is like finding a stack of gold amid pine needles!"

He flipped the corpse onto its back, then removed a dagger from his belt. My lip twisted as I got a good look at the goblin's face. It was a hideous thing to behold, with sallow, waxen skin that stretched taut over a sharp, bony skull. Its black, tar-like lips had thin needle holes where teeth used them as pincushions. Its expression was locked in gruesome pain, stark white orb-like eyes still open and wide as saucers.

Its arms were difficult for me to even understand. They were long —twice the length of a man's—with two pivot points instead of one simple elbow. I could only imagine the sort of advantage that would give them in combat.

Though, the worst part might've been its nose. It was long and hooked, and likely diseased, like it had some kind of STD covering it. Pus dribbled out of open sores and caked just above his upper lip. I assumed it was a *he* based upon the fact that Curr had now undressed it, and well...

If that was how it looked in death, I would have hated to see what it looked like when it was alive.

"That's hideous," I said.

Curr regarded me again with annoyance. "It is not what is on the outside that counts," he said, as if giving me the deepest lesson in life. I knew him better by now to know what his more literal mind meant. Curr was a confusing fellow. I was never sure when he was joking apart from his big belly laughs. Even then, he said such horrible things. It was like he was incapable of *not* speaking his mind at all times.

"The inside is... better?"

"After I field dress it," he said. "No sense cooking the organs. They are worth little in terms of sustenance. But goblin meat is tender and delicious."

"I thought you said you had rations?"

"When Tarton smiles upon you in the form of something fresh, would it not be sacrilegious to turn it away?"

My stomach grumbled, just not in a good way. "Depends on what that fresh choice is."

Curr pointed with his dagger. "This is too good to waste. And I, for one, do not intend to. If you do not wish to help me dress it, then at least keep guard so we do not get bombasted while I prepare this delicacy."

"Do you mean bombarded?"

"No, I do not."

Remembering how sour he'd gotten earlier when I corrected him, I said, "Oh, right. You're right. I'll just watch."

Curr grunted and I turned away before I could see him slip the blade of his dagger into the goblin corpse.

Then he stopped and said, "Oh, I heard you playing your lute earlier. While you do very much need the practice, this is not the place."

"It wasn't me."

"*Danny.*" The way he said my name made me look back toward him, like he was a scolding father. The sight of the blade slicing through flesh made me sick.

"I swear it wasn't. I thought I was hearing things."

"Hmm." He started sawing through the goblin again and I averted my gaze. "Must have been travelers on the road, harboring a death wish. Still, keep it on your back."

"Gladly." Though, I wouldn't have minded playing it as loudly as I could just so I wouldn't have to hear the sounds of the goblin being shredded.

How was I going to escape this one? Curr was intent on cooking the thing and eating it, which repulsed me. Were goblins intelligent creatures here? Yuck.

At the same time, I didn't want to insult him. The screen flashed before my eyes.

Maybe you could tell him you have a gluten sensitivity.

I scowled.

Cut it out.

How about you're on a strict keto diet? He'll love that one.

Are you trying to get me killed? Seriously. How about I just tell him I don't think the goblin is a good thing to eat?

Sure. That sounds like a winning plan. Go for it. I'll get a mop to clean up your guts.

I shook my head and the screen vanished again.

I didn't think Curr would kill me, but he probably wouldn't be crazy about me turning down a generous portion of goblin meat either. People in this world clearly had a thing about wasted food. I suppose it wasn't like they had a Walmart on every corner, though.

Still, I felt like I had at least garnered enough of a relationship with him to speak the truth. About this, at least.

Behind me, it sounded like Curr was nearly finished gutting the thing. There was a strange array of squishing noises now. I didn't want to know what that was. Then a *crack-sizzle* as Curr presumably tossed the meat on to cook. Tossed it on what?

I chanced a glance over my shoulder and saw him holding what appeared to be a thin, metal pan.

"Where did you get that?" I asked.

Curr shrugged. "I never travel without it."

I didn't care what he cooked on it later. I'd never eat anything from it after that goblin *popped* and *hissed* all over it. Juices excreted into the pan, and the meat looked like greasy bacon. A waft of it hit me in the face when the wind shifted.

"Oh my god..." The smell was more akin to fish someone forgot to refrigerate and were too cheap to throw out. *It'll be fine, right?* they'd say. *It's pretty cold in here. I doubt it had much time to go bad.*

In other words, bacon it was not.

Gross.

After several minutes, Curr smacked his lips. "I think this first batch is done."

I turned around. The goblin meat didn't look even remotely any more appetizing than when it had been a corpse. It was still a weird yellowish tint that reminded me a bit too much of the rancid lamb, just burnt around the edges.

Curr smiled and rubbed his hands together excitedly. "Want a thigh?"

That was all I could take.

"Look," I began, "don't take this the wrong way, but I'm not gonna eat that."

"Why not?"

Deep breath. "Because I don't think goblin meat is a good thing to eat. There's something about it that just looks... unhealthy."

Curr stared at the meat sizzling over the fire. "Really?"

"Have you actually ever eaten goblin meat before?" I asked, one hand on my hip. I instantly realized how I looked in my bright pink cloak and put the arm down.

"You ate a bug-infested leg of lamb the other night. And now you choose to be picky?" Curr put a hand on his heart like he was wounded. For a moment, I thought he might explode at me. But then he fell back on his haunches, laughing. "Oh, you took me at my word, did you not?"

I frowned. "What are you talking about?"

Curr pointed but couldn't stop laughing. When he could finally speak, he said, "Of course I have not ingested such a vile thing! The stuff is practically poison. I simply wanted to see if you were dull-witted enough to fall for my prank."

I frowned, but then the screen flashed again.

You have gained +1 in Camping.

Your Camping is now 2.

Congratulations! You really are smarter than a wooden plank. Intelligence is knowing whether you can eat goblin meat. Wisdom is knowing if you should.

You're not as dumb as you look. Your Wisdom penalty has been removed.

Your Wisdom is now 10 (again).

You knew?

I still think telling Curr you had a self-diagnosed gluten allergy was the way to go.

Go to hell. Hey, at risk of losing my Wisdom point again, if Intelligence is knowing if I could eat goblin meat, and Curr said it's poison, shouldn't I gain Intelligence too?

Hmmm. Maybe you aren't the dullard I thought. However, you do not gain points for everything you do. Attributes are only raised through Leveling. Consider your Intelligence raised, but not enough to Level Up.

Have a point in Bartering...

You have gained +1 in Bartering

Your Bartering is now 7.

Curr let out a bark, still laughing.

"Why in the world would you go through the trouble of gutting it and cooking it for a prank?" I asked. "A bit much, don't you think?"

He waved some of the noxious fumes into his face. "Not just for the prank. To get back at you for saying I misunderstood something that I clearly did not. By Tarton, that was fun. You should have seen your face. Do you smell how awful that is?"

I pinched my nose. "Unfortunately."

"Exactly." Curr settled down a little and sat up. "Cooking him nice and slow will create a smell that everything in this part of the woods will avoid. Goblins know the only creatures who actively hunt them and eat them are trolls, and they want nothing to do with trolls. So, now, the goblins will avoid us. And the orcs, despite their greed, fear the troll packs, and will also leave us alone. They will not chance a troll."

"So, we're safe for the night?" I started to sheathe my sword.

"Hardly." Curr produced a small shovel for his sack of supplies. "Wolves and korkens love the innards," he said, tossing me the shovel. I caught it, barely. "We will have to bury them. And by *we*, I mean you."

"Me? Why me?" I demanded.

"I caught and gutted the beast. Honestly, Danny, if we are to remain partners, you will need to do as you promised and pull your own measly weight."

I groaned, dragging the shovel as I walked to a clearing.

"Do not venture too far from the light," he added.

I paused. "Say what?"

"Wraiths, vampires, and the like... they will not be affected by the smell. If the goblins and orcs avoid us, then we make ourselves a target for the undead."

"Uh..."

Curr produced something else seemingly out of thin air.

"Fear not. I will sprinkle some of this around the periphery of camp and we should be fine. It will not thwart them from trying to get to us, but they will not be able to pass within the boundary. At least not without our permission. So, whatever you do, do not invite them in, all right? No matter what they ask. The succubi offer many wiles even the best of us will find difficult to deny."

"Succubi?" I remembered singing about them when we first met back in the tavern. I didn't know what they were then, and I didn't know now.

"Coitus demons. Keep your manhood in your pants, at all costs." He began rearranging stones around the fire. "They will only kill you once they have devoured your soul."

I threw my hands up in frustration. "Is there *anything* in the forest that *doesn't* want to kill us?"

Curr looked up and scratched his head. "I believe there may be a deer or two. And squirrels! That is what was in our stew in Nahal. You loved eating them."

I didn't have any words. Just an exasperated sigh.

The real world might have been boring, but at least there wasn't something around every corner trying to kill me. How did people live like this? Then again, Curr was starting to sound like one of those preppers back on Earth. Fearful of everything that likely wouldn't come to pass, because if the world was as dangerous as he claimed, there'd be no people in it.

Better safe than sorry, I guess. His compulsions would keep me safe for this and hopefully many future nights.

Curr handed me one of the vials. "Spread this in a semi-circle arc on that side of camp and I will do the same over here. Once that is complete, we will set out the bedrolls and actually get a chance to eat." He paused. "Did you take care of your business yet?"

"I haven't had the chance," I said, suddenly feeling my back teeth floating.

Curr smacked his head. "And just what were you doing while I was checking the area?"

"Trying not to die."

Curr groaned and stood, drawing his axe as he did so. "Fine. Come on, then."

He also hefted the load of goblin guts in a makeshift bag he'd created with what looked like a spare cloak.

"You had another cloak this whole time?" I asked, looking down at the pink monstrosity I wore.

"It gets chilly in the mountains," he said. "Now, come. I shall stand guard while you empty your bladder."

I sighed. "Seriously?"

"Unless you want to go alone."

Night had fallen in earnest. It couldn't be that late, but it certainly felt like it was already midnight. Darkness made everything worse.

I decided that whatever the screen meant with its warning that

I'd be discovered as something other than a wellick when my pants were down couldn't be worse than vampires.

"Fine." I followed Curr as he stepped just out of the firelight and over by a tree. He pointed.

"Aim downhill."

At least I knew he expected me to have something in there to aim with.

Leaning the shovel against the tree, I took a quick glance around, then pulled my pants down. It was tough to get going with Curr breathing over my shoulder. I didn't even use urinals back in my world because I hated being so close to other men when I took a piss.

Thankfully, the cold air helped stimulate the need to go and before I knew it, I had a solid stream flowing. Man, that felt good.

"You have been holding that in for a while," Curr said with a laugh as I finished up. "Where did you store all that with such an unimpressive member?"

BURN!

By the way, I was just kidding about that pants down nonsense. Gotcha.

Have I told you how much I hate you?

"I jest!" Curr said, slapping me on the back before I even finished. A spray of pee ran over my boot. "Okay, when you are fully dry, begin digging."

"Yeah, okay," I grumbled.

Curr started back toward the camp. "And do not forget to spread the contents of that vial first."

"Wait," I said, suddenly stricken with fear. "Can't you stand watch while I dig?"

"If you would like to eat and sleep tonight, one of us will have to prepare the camp. It will not take you long, even with those skinny arms."

As he walked away a screech cut the night air. "What in the world is that?"

"Maybe a wraith," Curr shouted back to me. "Better hurry."

"I hate this place," I muttered as I started to spread the fine powder.

20

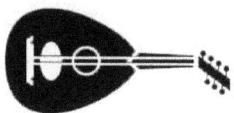

Curr was right about one thing: it hadn't taken me long to dig a hole and bury the goblin parts. The ground was soft. At least one thing was going for me.

I returned to camp where Curr had laid out bedrolls, one for each of us. After I sat crossed-legged on the ground, he tossed me a ration.

"Eat. You will need your strength."

It was something that looked much like the Nutri-Grain bars I sometimes ate for breakfast. However, it tasted nothing like that. If I had to guess, it was dried meat, cheese, and crushed-up bread or crackers. A moment later, Curr confirmed that was exactly what it was.

"Shouldn't this be... refrigerated?"

"I do not know what that means," Curr said. "Sometimes, I wonder where you learned your Pyruunian, Danny."

Did you think they have General Electric here?

Right.

"When you are done, get some sleep," Curr said. "I will stand watch for the night. We braugs do not require nearly as much sleep as you frail wellicks."

As insulting as it was, I didn't mind. As soon as I'd choked down the dry, mealy snack, I slipped into the bedroll and did my best to zonk out.

I didn't pray much at home, and here, I wasn't even sure who to pray to. Though as I closed my eyes, I whispered, "Please let me wake up in my nice warm bed…"

The sun rose bright, shining pink behind my closed eyelids. I wasn't quite ready to start the day, so I rolled over and clutched my pillow tight against my side.

Wait…

My pillow?

There was no translucent blue screen popping into my thoughts. It was quiet. Very quiet. And I was absolutely not in the woods surrounded by trees and hidden monsters.

Dare I open my eyes?

I decided to start slow, peering through my eyelashes. When the blurriness of morning faded, familiar objects came into view—things I'd seen for years. My bedroom things. In the corner of the room, my projection-style television sat beside a hand-me-down dresser. The white walls with the splotch of paint from when I'd tried to cover up a scuff mark with the wrong finish. Who knew eggshell and satin were so different?

Ohmygod, ohmygod…

I opened my eyes fully and took in the splendor of my bedroom. It was a crap-hole in subsidized housing, but it was my crap-hole in subsidized housing.

My electric guitar—a Gibson Les Paul I'd barely afforded—hung on the wall. I'd never really played it, but goddammit, it was mine!

I leaned into my Tempur-Pedic bed, the one thing I really spent a lot of money on... because I've always believed the key to a happy life was twelve full hours of uninterrupted sleep. I let out a loud sigh.

Then, I heard a soft moan behind me.

I slowly rolled over onto my other side and saw the half-naked form of a woman with blonde hair... and a pixie haircut.

Ho-lee... Trish is in my bed.

A tingle spread down through my... *body*. My movement in the bed must've aroused her. From her sleep. I meant from sleep.

"Daniil?" she said softly, still facing away from me.

"I'm here," I said, still unable to believe it myself. "Wait... Daniil?"

She turned.

I screamed. A yellow, reptilian face stared back at me with giant bug-like eyes, white as snow. And that long, hooked syphilis-infested nose. Then she rose up on one of her four elbows and opened her mouth, saliva dripping from three-inch-long needle-sharp teeth.

With a loud screech, she lunged for me.

I awoke with a start. My heart stopped. Sweat poured off me in buckets.

"Danny." I heard my name spoken softly and cringed back.

But it was Curr, standing by the fire, axe clutched in his hand.

Another screech filled the night air. It hadn't been dream-Trish. My stomach acids rose at the realization that I was back in Pyruun, and *this* wasn't the dream. Hot, naked Trish... that was the dream. My TV, guitar, all of it.

"Get up!" Curr commanded me.

I scrambled to my feet.

"Sword out. Now," he said. "Over here by the fire."

"What is it?" I asked.

"Wraith. At least two."

Despite being close to the fire, I was worried. I didn't know a thing about wraiths and wondered what exactly they were. Naturally, the screen flashed in front of my eyes.

WRAITHS: *Undead manifestations of an evil soul. Your dead mother. Not a wraith. Your father. Maybe. Your demon-possessed Aunt Carla... Definitely.*

Wraiths cannot be harmed by tangible weaponry unless it has been imbued with magical properties. So put that stupid thumbtack away. Natural sunlight destroys it, but hey, it's still dark. Usually preceded by an aura of menace that causes worry, anxiety, and panic. Depending on the individual, the wraith will feed on your worst fears. Perhaps they will even alter your dreams. Wink, wink.

They are susceptible to magical attacks, religious ceremonies, and certain other things. Do you remember the Hail Mary? Probably won't work, but it's better than pissing yourself. Wraiths will feast on their victims' souls much like a vampire does on blood, enabling them to present in different forms.

Certain other things? What certain other things? What kind of entry is that?

No answer. I grumbled. Apparently, I was going to have to figure out that last part for myself.

I could already feel the aura preceding the wraith. I had to fight to keep my cool, even though I wanted to run as far away as I could.

Curr, on the other hand, seemed to be only somewhat affected by its presence.

Probably because he's a braug, right?

Well done. Braugs aren't affected by a wraith's aura. Their braug Rage, even if not active, naturally counteracts it.

Lucky.

"Is it close?" I asked Curr.

"Probably just outside of the firelight," he said. "It will not come much closer, thanks to the powder we put out. You did pour yours, right?"

"Yeah, what was it?"

"Powdered horse tongue."

I made a face. "And where did you get that from?"

"A cleric by the name of Tallywick."

"Sounds trustworthy," I said under my breath.

"She said it was guaranteed against wraiths and other undead creatures."

"Wait, you've never used it before?" I asked, lowering my sword.

"No!" Curr exclaimed, a huge smile on his face. "This is the first time. Invigorating, is it not?" He held up something that looked like shortbread. "You want some hardtack?"

The wraith screeched again just at the fringes of the firelight. As Curr had thought. Then another screech sounded like it originated from the opposite side of the camp. And then one more.

"Ah, so there are three," Curr said, way too exhilarated by the prospect for my tastes.

"Three?" I gulped.

He took a step closer to where the flickering light ended. I thought he was going to charge out into the night, but he only stood there a few moments before he returned and sat down.

"At least. This is wonderful."

I peered out into the darkness. Despite my eyes being less acute, thanks to the fire, I could've sworn I saw movement somewhere beyond the glow. They weren't content to remain still, that much was certain. I remembered the part about the sunlight driving them away.

"How long until dawn?"

Curr chuckled. "Too long."

"Will they stay out there?"

"That is what the cleric told me," Curr said. "You may continue resting."

The wraiths screeched again, this time all together like a symphony of promised death. I shook my head. "Yeah, not with that kind of racket happening out there."

Or the memory of goblin-Trish.

You'd still do her if she asked.

The sad part was the screen was probably right.

"Do not be a wean," Curr replied.

I scoffed. "What about you?"

"I do not mind the screeching. I will continue keeping watch."

"You sure?"

"I would not have offered if I was not sure."

"Yeah. Okay. Alright." I walked closer to the fire and the safety of its flames. Or at least I hoped it was some sort of safety. Despite the heat, I still wanted to roll myself up into my bright pink cloak. It wasn't my Tempur-Pedic, but I was amazed that even while sleeping on the ground with it, I was still pretty comfortable. I mentioned that to Curr.

"Elves make the best travel cloaks," he said, eyes still plastered on the forest.

The screen flashed.

It's true. Elves are used to sleeping outdoors in forests since the wellicks destroyed their homes and reduced their numbers to that of an endangered species. It's no wonder, over the years, they've perfected the art of cloak-making. Lightweight, but comfortable as sheep's wool. Not even Ranger cloaks are considered as comfortable.

Destroyed their homes? Do you ever provide descriptions that don't make me want to crawl out of my skin?

It's a cruel world.

Shockingly, I started to nod off while Curr picked up where the screen left off, rambling on about the various types of cloaks in the world. I took a deep breath, closed my eyes, and slipped away. Scared as I was, the information was *that* boring.

Suddenly, my heart leaped through my throat when goblin-Trish appeared in my mind—a result of the wraiths' powers, I figured.

I bolted up, listening to the screeches and the soft music.

Soft music?

It grew louder and louder, like a rising soundtrack in an old fantasy movie. It sounded sort of like that same stabbing, fast-paced tune from earlier.

My lute lay beside me, and I swore the strings vibrated all on their own. The song was like a battle hymn. When the forest moved, and the featureless face of a wraith whipped toward me, the lute got even louder.

It's playing... itself?

Once again, Danny. There is no music.

I'm not insane! How can you not hear it?

First, it'd played when a goblin was nearby, and now wraiths. It was almost like it was warning me of danger.

Though the lute contains magical properties, self-manipulation is not one I am aware of. I think you are hearing things. Perhaps you need medical attention.

Or maybe you're just deaf, oooor you don't know everything.

While the thought was just a jab at the screen, it gave me pause. Perhaps this floating entity that berated my vision wasn't as all-knowing as I'd originally thought?

"Curr?" I said.

I looked his way, then froze. The air was alive with black shapes, whisking this way and that all above the fire. *The wraiths!* They'd entered the periphery of the camp.

Curr was either asleep or knocked out. His body lay close to the fire with his hand still gripped tightly to his weapon.

I swung myself out of my travel cloak and reached for my short sword.

Hold on there, Frodo. This isn't Sting. Normal weapons don't affect wraiths.

I swore. I had nothing magical that I knew of except...

What magical properties does my lute have?

At your Skill? None. You still kind of suck.

I lunged for my lute anyway and grabbed it by the neck. The

sound muffled, but the strings kept quivering under my skin, thunk-thunk-thunking. It refused to stop. Another screech had my ears ringing. I grew impossibly cold. Blackness enveloped me as the three wraiths circled.

Would you like to access your Catalog of Songs?

Yes, dammit!

A list blossomed on the screen and my eyes raced down it, trying to find something that might help the situation. Dozens were gray and unable to be selected.

Why are those gray? I thought furiously.

You do not possess the Skill to play those yet.

Then can you remove them so I don't get confused?

Such a simpleton. Fine.

The list shrank immensely, leaving seven left to choose from.

<u>**???**</u>
Unidentified Stolen Song (???)

<u>***Level 1 (Unlocked):***</u>
Stones, Bones, and Crones (8 inst. 7 sin.)
T'was Morn in the Eve (14 inst. 14 sin.)
Parapets of Pyruun (14 inst. 9 sin.)
Tillith's Last Call (20 inst. 15 sin.)

Level 2 (Unlocked):
Hymn for Fallen Souls (23 inst. 19 sin.)
Into the Mist (25 inst. 0 sin.)

What are the numbers next to the songs for?

They represent the instrument Skill level needed to perform the song without screwing up, as well as the required Singing level, if there are lyrics.

Why can't it just say that!

To save space, duh?

I didn't know how much magic my lute had, but the screen had told me I could learn to wield it. It had to be something special since Phlegm the Hag had somehow willed it into existence, right? At least I hoped that was the case.

It takes skills to jam with the best of 'em. Try and play a song beyond your Skill, you'll probably break a string. Or worse...

Then how about this.

One song stuck out to me near the bottom part of the list. Souls. Spirit wraiths. It was all basically the same, right?

Hymn for Fallen Souls...

Instantly, a warmth seeped into my veins, and without thinking, my fingers started plucking the strings and my voice practically floated from my throat, singing words I'd never spoken before, yet somehow knew.

Across a thousand lifetimes near
Filled with loss and tragic tear
Lost souls in the night do tarry forth
To spread discord and vengeance birth

The wraiths began to hover where they were, entranced by the sound. I continued.

Where once the brave and mighty dwelled
They stood their ground as each was felled
And with their life's last dying gasp
Fell into evil's crushing grasp

'Tis not eternal damnation deserved
For with honor they once gladly served
And so let these notes break bindings fast
And bring salvation at long last

For in the light they find their home
Far from the evil that's claimed their own
This mighty bard doth set thee free
So go at once and leave us be.

I stopped, aware that I was sweating profusely from the exertion of playing and singing. I was cold, and yet, despite that, something was different now.

The wraiths had stopped screeching. In fact, I couldn't sense them at all. It remained dark, of course, but the entire night that surrounded the camp was now still, silent, and awash with peaceful amber light. A gentle breeze shook the branches of the pines above, and the lute no longer played of its own volition.

I took a moment to appreciate the calm before the screen flashed again.

Your ability to kill with song has finally proved helpful!

You have defeated the wraiths with your music and set them free!

You have gained +1 in Instrument Playing.

Your Instrument Playing is now 17 (+10).

You have gained +1 in Singing.

Your Singing is now 15 (+10).

I took a breath.

Well, that was cool.

I was thrilled to have *finally* used my musical abilities to my advantage. It might not have been a guitar, but somehow, I'd managed to defeat a few undead beings and gained some upgrades as a result.

Are you forgetting something?

Curr!

Remembering his pitiful state, I stowed the lute and rushed over to the unconscious braug.

"Hey! Wake up!" I shouted, shaking him. When he didn't rouse, I thought about slapping him on the face. Then reconsidered, since, as I've been numerously reminded, he could crush me. Then I reconsidered again and gave his cheek a few weak taps.

His eyelids fluttered. It was as if he'd drunk too much ale or something, but I knew he hadn't. He was groggy and slow to respond to my pleas for him to wake up. When he finally managed to get himself right, he looked around.

"What happened?"

I shook my head. "I'm not entirely sure. The wraiths entered camp. You were already out cold. I didn't know what to do. And what about you? I thought wraiths couldn't affect braugs?"

"Who told you that?" he asked, confused.

I said their auras *don't increase their fear, not that they're immune to soul sucking. Semantics, Danny.*

"I uh... I don't know," I stammered, having to cover myself for the screen's lack of detail. "I just thought because you were so big and strong..."

"I told you, Danny." He looked at me gently. "I do not view you in such a manner, though I am flattered."

I groaned.

Curr looked around. "Are you sure you were not sleeping?"

I stuttered over a response. The dream of Trish and my apartment seemed so real. Could the wraiths have been a dream too?

No, I decided. It was definitely real, and I told him as much.

"If I see that cleric again, I will demand a refund in full!" Curr grunted. "That powder clearly was not effective."

"No shit."

Curr's brow creased. "Everything is about feces with you, Danny. So, how did you defeat them?"

"I... played my lute. I sang a song about fallen souls. It seemed to have some sort of effect on the wraiths. They disappeared while I was singing."

"You scared them off with your awful voice?" Curr laughed. "That is rich. A new story to tell at the Fighters Guild Hall!"

"I don't think it was all that bad, actually. Maybe they even liked it."

"More likely they thought it sounded worse than their screeching and they went to torment someone else." He clapped me on the shoulder, and I helped him sit up. "In any event, well done. Maybe bards are not totally useless."

Your relationship with Curr has improved.

Aww, he complimented you.

"Yeah," I said, ignoring the screen. "Maybe we aren't."

For the first time, I felt a little better about not being a knight or a wizard.

But only a little...

21

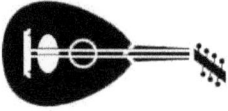

For the remainder of the night, we were harassed no further. I barely slept a wink. How could I after what happened? And every time I dozed off, dreams about Trish devouring my soul stirred me.

When the dim light of dawn started needling me to give up on real slumber, I yawned and turned over with a big stretch. I was more tired than I could ever remember being.

Fortunately, Curr already had something cooking on the fire and it wasn't disgusting gray, pus-riddled goblin meat. I'd heard him fiddling about while I pretended to sleep.

"Good morn," Curr said. "I trust you slept well?"

I nodded. "Better than okay. I'm amazed at how well I slept."

Your skill in being a lying douchebag has increased by 1!

That's a thing?

Your skill in Gullibility has risen!

Very funny.

Curr nodded toward the fire. "Hungry?"

"What is it?" I asked tentatively.

Curr chuckled, stabbing the meat with his finger. "Do not fear. It is only rabbit. I caught him nosing around the edge of the camp and apprehended him while you woke the dead with your snoring. He will make for a hearty meal."

I'd never eaten rabbit before, but my stomach growled, and my mouth ran with saliva.

"I wasn't snoring."

Curr made a noncommittal sound as I rose and wandered around the outer edge of the camp. No signs of wraith activity from the previous night remained, but that didn't mean much of anything. Wraiths were undead according to the screen...

Say, do you have a name? Calling you the screen is getting weird.

No.

I stopped to relieve myself on the same tree I had the night before. From there, I could see the spot where I'd buried the goblin parts. It was swarming with flies and another insect I didn't recognize.

What about Mr. Screen? Blue box? Jim?

Why in the name of all the gods would you call me Jim?

I don't know. You seem like a Jim. Don't like it?

I do not.

Oh, I've got it. What about Screenie? Since you're like a genie I can't get rid of... except you don't grant wishes.

So, nothing like a genie—

And you're blue like in Aladdin. *It's perfect.*

That is so derivative.

Screenie it is.

Maybe focus less on name games and more on your stream.

I looked down and realized that I dribbled a bit near my boot.

Oh, and that bit about me being different from wellicks. Not cool, man. Not cool.

Screenie didn't respond, so I turned back to camp, calling out to Curr as I trudged through the fallen leaves. "How much farther is Balahazia?"

Curr continued to prod the rabbit.

"Perhaps another two days walking. There is a trading post a little out of the way. I often stop at Old Kiel Shorthen's—he has great potions—but I think we have sufficient enough supplies to head straight through. I am sure a wellick like you would be grateful for a proper bed in Balahazia."

I ignored yet another slight. "So, what—only one more night out in the open like last night?"

Curr grunted. "Perhaps. If your little legs carry you quickly enough and you do not hold us back."

A man can only be pushed so far. "Hey, I think I've done pretty damn well for someone who's never done this before!"

"You confuse me, bard," Curr said.

Ah, dammit.

"One of my many skills," I said, hoping he'd let go my admission of being a bard who'd never adventured.

You're not wrong. You're quite proficient in confusing people.

Can it, Screeeeeenie.

Curr handed me what looked to be a rabbit leg.

It oozed juice as my teeth tore into the meat. For one split second, I pictured the goblin flesh, but I shoved the thought aside. The rabbit was hot and delicious—and I was too hungry to let my mind ruin this for me.

However, that got me thinking. "Won't the smell of this attract orcs or goblins, or whatever?"

"They prefer darkness," Curr said, mouth full. "Unless they think they can ambush the unwary from some dark spot like an overhang or a cave. They are always around, though. Most are nocturnal, and you saw the creature's eyes. They have poor vision in bright light. You will only usually see them during the day hours when storms are present and cloud cover is plentiful. However, if they sense someone weak traveling alone, they will often risk exposure."

"They're that smart?" I asked.

"They may not reason like you, and definitely not like me, but they are not unthinking beasts. Do not be fooled by their appearance."

I sat down next to the fire and took another bite. "This is delicious," I said. First time I could truly say that about anything in this world.

"Thanks," Curr said. "It is my mother's recipe."

I looked up, half expecting him to have a smile on his face that told me he was joking. But he apparently wasn't.

It seemed like nothing more than pan-fried rabbit with some kind of green herb rubbed on it. Perhaps the braugs were just simple people.

There you go again with your condescension.

I swallowed. "So, have you traveled this road alone before?"

"Once. When I was much younger and foolish. I was meant to be traveling with another, but he got too drunk and passed out. There was a rather enticing quest at the Fighters Guild I feared I would be too late to embark upon. I did not want to wait. So, I set off, and that error nearly cost me my life."

I nibbled on the rabbit leg. "What happened?"

"Orcs." Curr paused, as if backtracking in his mind. "But mind you, that was before Balahazia was as thriving a community as it now is. Things were more wild back then. Now, I would be surprised if we did not encounter at least one contingent of soldiers."

"I thought King Shirtaloon had abandoned this area?"

"Danny, you must listen with more intention. While there are no active fortresses or battalions, this is still a well-traveled road. You truly have lived a sheltered life, Danny."

"But you said—"

"The king responds to the complaints of his people—albeit slowly. There have been six deaths on this very road in just the past month alone."

"Six... deaths?" I gulped and made believe it was from eating.

"Those are just the bodies that were found," Curr said, gnawing on his rabbit like nothing was wrong. "I suspect there are plenty more. These woods are as hungry as we were before this fine feast."

I desperately wanted to think of anything other than the dangers surrounding us, but I was also interested to hear the rest of Curr's story. "So, what happened next? Back then, I mean."

Curr put his food down and used his hands in grand gestures as if he were entertaining a large audience.

"I found a nice spot to bed down for the night. I kept my axe close like a lover. But the orcs came in such numbers, I was overwhelmed at first. Must have been hundreds."

"Hundreds?" I asked, incredulous.

Just let him tell the story.

"At least," he repeated. "They do not make much noise when they creep through the night. They are nearly as stealthy as elves. They managed to get the drop on me. But they made a big mistake thinking I was going to be easy prey."

"You fought them all off? Hundreds?" I smirked.

Curr grunted, not even looking at me. He just gazed off into the distance. "When I realized how great the odds had stacked against me, I knew I would not be able to make it unless I called upon my Rage. So, I did."

"Your... rage?"

Screenie flashed.

Capital R.

RAGE: A braug's Innate Special Ability. When in mortal danger or below 30% Health, a braug can call upon the wrath of their ancestors once a day, increasing Health, Endurance, and all Combat Skills by 3x power for the duration of a fight.

"Yes," Curr said. "Summoners of Rage. That is what our race's name translates to in Pyruunian. But your kind could not pronounce our language, so they just decided to call us 'braugs'."

Jeeze. Do wellicks just do whatever they want?

Psshh. Like humans are any different.

Touché.

"So, what are you really called?"

Curr said something that indeed I couldn't pronounce let alone spell. Sounded like gibberish mixed with throat noises and grunts.

Still, I could understand where the wellicks got the word *braug* from in all of it.

"Very few still speak our language," he said, sounding glum. "I know only a handful of words. About as skilled as you are at Pyruunian." That joke seemed to cheer him up.

"Good one," I said. "So, can you just use your Rage anytime you want?"

Do you even read?
He must be in mortal danger or below 30% Health.

But you said Curr doesn't have a screen telling him stuff like that.

Not everyone needs such things spelled out for them. Remember, your Intelligence is very low.

What's his?

Screenie didn't respond.

"There have been times when I was in dire need of it, yet it would not... manifest. Perhaps my ancestors were busier with more precarious situations."

"You weren't in a precarious situation? If you needed it, you'd think they'd respond."

Curr's face turned red. "It was a bar fight."

"Oh. Yeah. That doesn't seem very important."

"Honor is always important!" Curr bellowed. "But alas, they chose to leave me to my own devices. I have heard the old wives' tales—told through the mouths of my people—that claim one of our kind can only summon the Rage if the reason is sincere or desperate. I suspect a drunken squabble over whether cow or lamb tastes better does not qualify."

"Probably not," I replied. "Though I could've used it with the halfling."

"You are not a braug," Curr said in a serious tone.

"No, I just meant that—"

"Either way, it was not a good night for the orcs. Once the Rage consumed me, all other thoughts were abandoned. When I finally came out of it, I found myself surrounded by scores of bodies that had been hacked and hewn. Missing arms and legs, split skulls—the ground was muddy with blood. Pretty gruesome scene, come to think of it. But I was alive."

"Scores?" I asked.

"Aye. Their brethren must have fled in fear of my strength."

"Must have," I agreed, though he didn't even notice my sarcasm. "That memory must be haunting."

He glared at me. "Are you kidding? Best night of my life!"

"Were you injured?" At this point, I was just trying to make conversation. I found his story, exaggerated as it might've been, fascinating. It was all so foreign to me, orcs and sword battles... even the bar fights. Sure, they broke out at the Heart-Shaped Box, but never like in this place.

"That is another benefit of the Rage," he said. "It staves off certain types of injuries or even accelerates healing of others."

Oh, yes. Tarton's Rage also offers 5x Defense and Health Regeneration. It is a substantial boost.

"Handy gift," I said to Curr.

He pointed at the lute. "I could say the same for you."

"What do you mean by that?"

"You saved our souls last night against the wraiths. Perhaps it was not raw strength, but if not for you and that lute, we might be wraiths ourselves this very morn. Somehow, with your meager abilities, you managed to defeat them. I am more than a bit ashamed I was unhelpful during the fight." He cleared his throat. "I owe you for protecting us."

"You don't owe me anything," I said.

"Perhaps you are right. Even a blind squirrel occasionally finds a nut."

With that, he went back to eating his rabbit.

I wanted to protest but thought better of it. After all, I'd just told him he didn't owe me a thing. I couldn't start arguing now.

Though I had to admit, save for the period where my band was together, I've always worked alone. If you don't also count dealing with terrible bosses. It was kind of nice to work with someone again, and also be beneficial while doing so.

"Oh, by the way," I said, trying to keep my tone casual. "Have you ever heard of a self-playing lute?"

"A what?" A chunk of rabbit fell from his lips.

I smiled a bit. "My lute... it... well, it started playing itself earlier. Like it was trying to warn us of danger."

"Your lute... plays itself?"

I could see he wanted to laugh. My smile faded. Maybe I shouldn't have said anything. He was going to think I was crazy. Which, maybe I was. Screenie hadn't heard it. Didn't even think it was possible. Had I imagined that part? Could I really have lucked into a dream that woke me up at just the right time?

As likely as you saving the day.

That reminds me. How come I didn't get some fancy title for getting rid of the wraiths like I had with the rats?

Are you in such desperate need of validation?

Maybe?

Fine. You are now the proud owner of the Title: Wraith Whisperer.

Oh, wow. What does that do for me?

Makes you sound like an idiot if you tell anyone.

"Danny, I asked you a question. Do not be rude," Curr said, pulling me away from Screenie.

I laughed awkwardly. "Just a joke, like the goblin meat!" I eyed the lute, sitting innocently on the dirt. "I'm the only magic here."

"Danny. That was not a funny joke," Curr said flatly. "Work on that. Bards should be funny."

"Noted."

Curr helped himself to more of the rabbit, polishing off the majority of it while I worked on my small portion. He had an enormous appetite, but it suited him since he was so large. When he was finished, he let out a massive belch and patted his stomach.

"Thanks, Mother," he said.

I nodded. "It's a fantastic... _recipe._"

"I will commit it to parchment for you."

I held up my hand. "Nah, don't worry about—"

"You do not wish to possess it?" Curr looked a little disappointed.

"All right, yes. I want it. Fine."

"Good. Remind me when we reach Balahazia. In the meantime, we should get moving. We need to make the most of the day. The sooner we are there, the sooner we can find your purpose."

My next breath caught. "What do you mean my purpose?"

"You are the least worldly bard I have ever had the displeasure of knowing and have seemed like a fish deprived of water since I met you. And I have seen plenty of flopping fish. We all must have purpose. You do not appear to know what yours is, but you saved my life. So, I..." Curr stood and struck his chest with a fist, "...am going to help you find yours."

"And how in the world are you going to do that?"

Curr got to work packing our belongings. "Many things are revealed through battle, Danny. You are a bard who defeats wraiths and halflings. I think there may be a place for you in the Fighters

Guild, even though they usually do not accept puny men who play instruments."

He laughed while I stood there trying to make sense of it. It would be nice to find a purpose besides just surviving one day at a time. Part of me also felt nervous. Was there a way home at the end of that road or was I trapped here?

"You coming?" Curr's voice snapped me back to the present.

He stood at the edge of the camp. The fire was extinguished, and he was ready.

"Just a second." I grabbed my gear, took one last look around at the site of my first victory, then followed him back toward the road.

Screenie flashed.

NEW OBJECTIVE:
Find your purpose in Pyruun.

REWARD:
A reason to live!

Finally, an objective I can get behind. Though, shouldn't you know that, Screenie?

No spoilers.

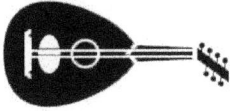

22

I definitely did *not* get enough sleep. I was a sleep-in, work rarely or never kind of guy.

Pikeman's Trail seemed to stretch on for miles and miles. The landscape was depressingly similar the whole way.

"Oh, look, a tree," I said. "And there's another. Oh, that one has a pointy top."

"Those are called evermonths," Curr said as if he didn't realize I was being facetious.

"That's odd. Where I'm from, they're called ever*greens*."

Curr stopped. "Okay, Danny. That is not the first time you have referred to the land from which you hail and spoke of its oddities. Now, tell me where that is before we take another step."

Here's your chance. Come clean. Be honest. It'll feel good.

But I did not come clean. Honesty was nice, but I didn't think Curr cracking me over the head would feel too great.

"Oh, just a little town—uh, south of Nahal." I hoped that wasn't some massive ocean or—I don't know, home of the dinosaurs or something.

"Smallwick?" Curr asked.

I started to nod. "Short... huh? Ah, yeah. That's the one."

"Ah, yes. Nice town. Strange people. That makes sense now that I think of it."

Phew.

You're just digging that hole deeper.

"Nahal is the furthest from home I've ever been," I added. "Left after my parents passed. I wasn't built for farm life." As I spun the fib, I thought back to my old life and how close to true all this really was. I wasn't worldly, as Curr would say.

He looked me over. "That is true, you are not. That would be a less suitable profession for you than even your current one."

"On that, we agree." I gave him a friendly pat on the back this time. It was like slapping concrete.

Fine work. In addition to being a Petty Thief, you're really learning how to manipulate the world around you.

It's just temporary.

That's what they all say.

It got us moving again, though, and soon—thank God—the trees gave way to grassy plains. Not that they were any more interesting, but at least it was a change. To our left, the ground sloped upward, revealing hills blanketed with—you guessed it—even thicker trees of all varieties, huddled so closely, it'd be difficult to navigate them.

"Those are the Vargan Foothills," Curr said without me having to ask. "They lead to the Masked Mountains and beyond."

A question came to mind that I'd wanted an answer to for quite some time. I figured if we were going to walk, we might as well walk and talk.

"Why are they called the Masked Mountains?"

Screenie flashed.

You're going to let him tell you? How rude. Don't you like my descriptions?

Your descriptions make me want to die.

"Because of the manner in which the clouds and fog seem to hug them throughout all of the seasons," Curr answered. "It is virtually impossible to see their peaks."

See how nice his was?

Then Curr continued, "Some say a curse lingers in those mountains ever since the fall of elven Alyndis, casting a gloomy demeanor over the entire range. Me? I think it is just because clouds like hovering over the mountains."

"So, nothing magical," I said, a twinge of relief in my voice.

Maybe if you'd have asked me, I'd have told you which of those is true.

Fine, tell me.

Too late. All I'll say is that the great elven haven of Alyndis once encircled the mountain and its surrounding forests. It was truly a magical place, filled with scholars and sorcerers. Some even say the elves drew power from the molten heart of the mountain. Shit. I've said too much.

All right, your story is better. Please tell me everything.

Nope. Long story short, Alyndis fell. It's not magical anymore.

Curr clicked his tongue. "There is more than enough magic elsewhere in this world. It does not need to be everywhere, if you ask me."

"Amen."

His brow lifted. "What language is that?"

"I, uh... I made it up."

"What does it mean?"

That was a good question. I knew how it was used, and I guess you ended prayers with it... but what did it mean? "Something like 'You can say that again'."

"Why would I want to say something I have already said for a second time?" Curr shook his head. "Secret, terrible bard language." He kept a serious expression for only a second before he burst into laughter. "Sorry, I could not resist."

"Not cool, Curr."

"You are right," he said. "Never again. Now, keep up."

He crunched on ahead. I'd listened to our footsteps on the dirt and gravel for hours. We passed some travelers—merchant types, mostly. One interesting caravan bustled by with armored guards. I couldn't help but wonder what might've been so important to merit such security.

What—you want to rob them?
Your heinousness knows no bounds!

I didn't think that!

You are well on your way to Chaotic Alignment.

I didn't know what that meant, but it didn't sound good.

Birds and animals in the woods made sounds, but mostly, it was only Curr's noisy footsteps and my diminutive ones. And he never slowed pace. Ever. My thighs were killing me. My feet felt like they were on fire.

"Do you never get tired?" I groaned.

Curr glanced back, since I was obviously lagging behind him. "Of walking? No. Walking is the easiest thing to do."

"Well, I must be bad at that too. Can we maybe take a little brea—"

"Hold it."

"Thank you. I really am getting—"

"Quiet!" he whisper-shouted.

I didn't like the way he looked, though I was grateful to stop.

Curr said nothing for a moment. Then, he stooped down, closed his eyes, and put his palm flat to the road. I did the same, more out of curiosity than anything else.

Was I supposed to be feeling something?

Ear to the ground, Tonto.

"Do you hear that?" Curr asked.

I wanted to say yes, but no. I heard nothing at all, and I told him as much.

Curr's face lit up. "Yes. I hear the sounds of battle!"

"Where? What? Who is it?"

He gave his beard a gentle tug. "Tarton's Tusk, it could be anyone. A traveling band of merchants. Marauders. Tough to tell. After missing out on the fun last night, my axe thirsts for blood." He started off down the road at a quicker pace. "C'mon!"

His axe doesn't really thir—

Don't be an idiot.

"Curr," I called from behind. "This isn't our fight!"

By now, I could hear metal clanging and some sort of beast roaring. And not only that, my damn lute. The battle hymn started to softly pluck away all on its own again. Curr was too focused on the coming fight to notice, but if it was anything like the wraiths, it'd get louder as danger approached.

Or, did it happen only when *I* personally felt in danger? I wasn't sure yet.

Don't ask me. I'm fairly confident you're imagining things.

I yanked the instrument off my back and wrapped it with my cloak, holding it tight against my body with my left arm to squelch the sound.

"Curr, really..." I wheezed.

"Ready your blade, bard! Today, we taste victory."

He took off in a sprint, rounding the bend in the road. It was as if he'd totally forgotten about my inability to fight.

I came around the corner and found Curr stopped.

"That is not good," he said.

"Great, let's turn back."

Ahead, the very same guarded caravan that had passed us was tipped onto its side. Beside it, the three armored guards squared off against... something.

"Not good for those beasts!" he growled as he took a few more steps.

"What the hell is that?" I asked, grabbing him firmly by the arm.

He turned and stared down at my hand. I remembered the last time I'd done that and swiftly removed it.

"Korkens," he said, like I should know what that meant.

NEW OBJECTIVE:
Save the guards from the korken attack.

REWARD:
200gp, split between your Party. A new Title.

What the hell is a kor—

KORKEN: Not native to the region, they are believed to have been the result of a failed experiment by a former Royal Wizard. Korkens are violent in disposition. They will kill you dead without a worry.

Yeah, no shit.

Would you like a physical description?

No. I have eyes. Thanks.

They were each about the size of a jaguar. Their heads resembled fur-covered dragons. A long snout, gaping jaw. Six horns sprouted from around its face, seemingly at random. Though if anyone were to be charged by the beast, it would gore them in more ways than one.

Just then, one leaped forward, proving my suspicion. Two horns smashed into one guard, leaving dents in his metal armor. The man cried out, doubling over, nothing but a flimsy wooden shield between his face and his monstrous attacker.

"Onward!" Curr shouted. "Help has arrived!"

I won't lie. I thought about waiting until the fight was through and making believe I was involved, but I couldn't afford for Curr to think I was more of a coward.

I felt the presence of my short sword on my side. It was no consolation. Pressed against my chest in my tightly wrapped cloak, the lute played all manner of muted *tings*.

"Quiet," I hissed, as if it could hear me.

I didn't say anything?

Not you!

You're losing it...

My other hand graced my sword's grip. Unsheathing it felt odd—so much different knowing I was about to use it in the wild. Somehow, in Lalair's cellar, it had felt less... deadly. Probably because those rats didn't have seven-inch claws and teeth to boot.

I swore and followed Curr. As I creeped forward—trust me, I was in no hurry—the music grew louder. And the nearer I got, the more adrenaline took over. The song was actually getting me sort of pumped.

"Careful! They're ravenously hungry!" one of the guards cried out.

"I'd be careful if they were full," I said.

"Please, help us vanquish these foul beasts and we will reward you."

"I will be satisfied with their blood!" Curr shouted. Then he added, "And coin!" as he punched a korken with his bare fist and sent it flying off the road. It tumbled a few times, and I was sure the beast was hurt. It didn't stay down long. If anything, the blow just seemed to piss it off. Scrabbling on its four legs, it sent pounds of dirt flying behind it. Once fully on its feet, it snarled and lurched forward again.

The guards were doing their best, but I got the impression they weren't much more skilled with the sword than I was. Or perhaps they just looked inept compared to Curr.

"You fight like a god!" one shouted.

"You should see me drink," Curr responded as he batted the newly risen korken aside.

"Can't... thank... you... enough," the third guard said as he dodged and parried a multitude of swipes from massive, clawed paws.

"Perhaps the chit-chat could wait?" I suggested.

A korken bounded forward, maw open wide. I feared it was about to tear me apart when one of the guards thrust his longsword into its scaly side. Oh, right. Head with fur. Body with scales. The thing was a child's drawing come to life.

The blade slipped between the creature's natural armor, leaving it twitching on the ground. But it wasn't dead. The sound it made was both terrifying and heart-wrenching at the same time, like when you accidentally step on your cat's tail in the middle of the night.

I knew I would need to engage with the korkens eventually, but I didn't know how. Luckily, Curr gave me instructions.

"Flank that one." He pointed with his axe, and I did as he said, hoping flanking meant to go around it.

Sidling up to the lion-alligator thing, I held my sword at an angle I thought looked right.

Fearsome.

Shut it unless you have something useful to offer.

The lute blared now, easily able to be heard over the chaos.

"That song, it is invigorating!" Curr roared. "You are able to play that with one hand?"

He quickly glanced back, and I smiled awkwardly as I let the cloak fall off the lute and pretended to be using one hand. Behind my back. Luckily, he didn't seem to know enough about the instrument to know that wouldn't be possible.

Your Music has invigorated your Party!

+2 Bonus to Strength, Dexterity, and Constitution for your entire Party for Duration of Battle.

It does that?

If you play the right song during battle, yes. But you're not playing. This is... very odd.

"Yes, Danny!" Curr hollered, stealing me from my thoughts. "It is time!"

"For what?"

Before I even finished the sentence, he brought his axe around in a downward chop. I didn't have to be told what to do. The korken dodged toward me and I stabbed. To my absolute shock, I hit it, and my sword sank into the tender flesh at its neck.

Korken slain!

You have gained +1 in Melee Weapon Combat.

Your Melee Weapon Combat is now 11.

Something like pride surged within me, but I didn't have time to savor it. One more korken remained. The one the guard had stabbed. It was injured, but still posed quite a threat.

"For Tarton!" Curr shouted as he shouldered the creature and forced it to the ground. He then spun, and smashed his axe, cleaving the korken's head in two.

A Party member has killed a korken.

The guards visibly relaxed.

"You don't know how welcome your appearance was to us," one said. "Like salvation sent from Ludos himself. Our gratitude is immeasurable."

"You can measure it in gold," Curr replied, slinging his axe over his shoulder.

"Right!" The guard rushed to the back of his upturned wagon.

"Well fought!" Curr said to me, clapping me on the back. "And that bard music was perfectly timed. How does it feel to be a hero?"

It was amazing. The only time I'd ever really felt in my element was with a guitar in my hand. And this sword... it wasn't a guitar. Finding myself able to kill a monster like that was—

"That was... incredible!" I exclaimed. "I now understand—"

Suddenly, two things happened: Curr reached for his axe and roared, "Watch out!" I glanced only quick enough to see the blur of a third korken leaping out from the brush of the forest. Then I felt something hot on my side. Hot and wet.

Looking down, confused, I saw that before Curr slammed his axe into the ambushing korken's gut, it managed to swipe its claw and tear a gash down the length of my torso, rending straight through my leather armor.

You told me to turn off in-battle notifications except when enemies are killed, but I think I should warn you. You have sustained a critical injury.

CURRENT HEALTH: 10% (Bleeding Wound)

For a moment, it didn't hurt... then, the throbbing came.

One of the guards stepped forward and stabbed the creature again, and then again, cursing all the while.

I swore too. Blood poured down my hips and legs, pooling all over the ground. I vaguely saw Curr kneel beside me, then everything got blurry, and then black.

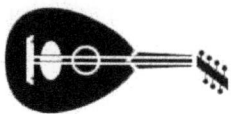

23

My eyes snapped open, and I found myself staring at vileness personified. This wasn't like dream-Trish. This, I knew, was real.

A giant, gargantuan, massive, bulbous face peered back at me through giant, gargantuan, massive, bulbous eyes. Tusks like an elephant's protruded from a face resembling a sloth that had been beaten with a dead lemur.

As you can imagine, I screamed. Then I screamed again from the pain in my side. Memories of the fight with the korkens came flooding back. I couldn't even give proper attention to them because some kind of monster was getting ready to bite my face off. Then, the thing got highlighted in Screenie's blue.

> **NAME: Kiel Shorthen**
> **RACE: Wellick (male)**
> **OCCUPATION: Healer**
> **SPECIAL ABILITIES: Potion-making, Baking, Cooking, Knot-tying**

There's no way in all hell that's a wellick!

Something had to be wrong with Screenie. If I was looking at a wellick, then I was a tortoise. His chest was wider than Curr's, and since he wore nothing but a loosely hanging cloth from his neck down to his knees, I could see almost every inch of his bruise-colored flesh and the wiry black hairs along his back and arms. He looked, well, like what I imagined an orc might look like based off the movies. Only way worse.

The only thing that looked vaguely human about him was his eyes. There was a kindness there I couldn't ignore.

"Relax," came a voice from beside me. It was one I recognized. Curr stood with all three of the armored guards we'd saved on the road.

"This is Old Kiel," he said. "Would not harm a flea."

"I'm not worried about fleas," I said, wincing through pain.

I looked down at my side just below my ribs. My skin was... glowing. Pink. Why is it always pink? What the actual hell? This place got weirder with each second.

Why am I glowing?

Kiel is a healer, as I've already informed you. He has used the Candentis Flowers you picked from the road to create a concoction that has staunched the bleeding.

He is currently mixing a remedy that will have your Health back to 100% in a jiffy.

"You probably should be," Curr said. "There is no doubt our bed in Balahazia will be ridden with them."

"It would help if I had time alone with the patient," Kiel spoke with a refined voice that felt completely wrong coming out of that ugly, purple-lipped mouth. With tusks.

I looked pleadingly at Curr, desperate not to be left by myself with Kiel.

"You will be fine," he said. "I will take these boys outside and see if they can hold their liquor."

"Have you ever met a soldier who couldn't?" one asked, laughing.

"Curr," I said. "Don't leave me."

"This is not the time for fear, Danny," he said. "You are in capable hands."

I turned my attention to Kiel's hands. They were the size of catcher's mitts, with flat fingernails that had clearly been claws filed down. They looked to be made of solid stone.

"Am I dying?" I asked.

"Hardly!" Curr said. "I told you those flowers possess healing properties, and Kiel is the best at his trade. Besides, since we brought our own, he will be offering us a hefty discount. Right, Kiel?"

The healer eyed Curr with distaste.

"Right?" Curr repeated, dragging out the word.

Kiel affected what I think was a smile and reluctantly said, "Of course."

"I shall be right outside, Danny," Curr said. "Holler if he gets too rough."

"What?"

"I jest. Old Kiel is gentle as a deer."

With that, Curr and the soldiers retired to the outdoors.

I took a short moment to survey my surroundings. I was in a circular room made of some sort of fabric—a tent perhaps? It was lit by torches set on posts around narrow, arching window-like cutouts.

Should there really be open flames in a cloth building?

The view told me outside was near midnight. The walls were bare, and wooden tables covered in all sorts of science-y medical-looking stuff were everywhere. Beakers with brightly colored liquids bubbled on one. Another was laid out with stone and metal tools I hoped he wouldn't have to use on me. Jars filled with herbs, and plants, and... were those organs?

Definitely organs. Not wellick, though. Don't worry.

"Just lie back, Danny," Kiel said.

I did as I was told. What else could I do? The simple act of moving had me in excruciating pain.

"I'm sure you're curious about my appearance?" he asked.

I nodded slowly.

As he answered, he crushed something in a little round bowl with a blunt stick. "I was once like you, a wellick through-and-through. In truth, I still consider myself one at heart. I hailed from a small hamlet outside of the capital, Amberhaven. I am sure you've never heard of it."

I shook my head.

He laughed. "Few have. It was quaint. Only about two dozen of us lived there, but I loved it. Most folks desire nothing more than to escape their hometown—not me. I'd have stayed there forever."

"Why did you leave?"

"Temptation, my dear boy. The city beckoned me like it has so many others. I gave in to the siren's call and entered into the Academy of Learning. At first, it was wonderful. I'd met more people in the first day than I'd known my entire life. The professors were kind and helpful. They guided me in the art of alchemy, teaching me all I needed to know to not only keep people alive and healthy, but in some cases, revive those who have passed."

He grabbed a spoon from one of the tables. It looked way too tiny for his hands as he raised a bit of his mixture out of the bowl, letting it plop back in.

"Why are you telling me all of this?" I asked.

"We will be here a bit, and I enjoy conversation," he said. "Would you rather sit in silence?"

I shook my head. "No. I just—"

"Yes, yes. It's a harsh world out there, filled with liars and conmen. I understand your reluctance, especially when taking into consideration the monster that stands before you."

"But I don't understand. You said you *were* a wellick. What happened?"

Kiel gave a mirthless chuckle. "Things are not always as they seem." He gestured to himself with the glob-covered stick. "I had been a bright shining star at the Academy. I'd garnered the attention of a very powerful contingent of leaders. They called themselves the Synod Sanction."

"Sounds ominous."

Oh, it is. But I'll let him tell you. I like the way he tells a story. So much better than Curr. "Oh, I am Curr. Look how brave and strong I am."

Blech.

Quiet.

"Ominous, indeed," Kiel went on. "Yet, I had no reservations about them at the time. Their leader was kindhearted and elderly. A gnome called Wesdintree. He took me under his wing, told me about their plans to aid the kingdom in war against the Assiri by means of science."

"I'm guessing there was more to it?"

He nodded. "As I'd come to find out, the Synod Sanction were a religious order without equal in all the land. Fanatics. Wesdintree convinced me to take part in a *study*. He believed that through science and religion coming together, they would create an extraordinary warrior that would be unstoppable."

"That doesn't sound like it would end well for anyone," I said.

He strode across the room, pulled one of the beakers off a burner, and returned to my side. Pouring the liquid into the bowl, he continued mixing.

"Astute perception, Danny. If only they'd seen the arrogance of their ways. I learned later that they had injected me with an experimental mixture of orc blood and some unknown substance. There was a ritual they performed to Ludos, the God of War."

Pyruun's patron God, by the way. Should tell you all you need to know.

"That was when I became worried, skeptical," Kiel went on. "But it was too late. I was strapped down, already seething in pain."

"That's horrible," I said, feeling the searing pain in my side. "I know the feeling."

A graveness overcame his features, which was horrifying.

"No, you do not. I thought I was going to die. When the process started, I was no bigger than you."

My eyes went wide. He easily stood six-and-a-half feet tall to my five-foot-nine.

"My bones broke and grew and healed over and over again for months. I was fed through a tube, more food than I'd ever ingested. The tusks were the worst part."

His face scrunched up like he was experiencing it all over again.

"When it was through, I looked like this," he said, sweeping a hand down his frame. "The only thing that remained *me* were my eyes."

"And they sent you to war?"

"No. What they had not planned for was that my demeanor hadn't changed. Nor had my strength. All of this, but I do not possess the vigor or the fortitude of even the lowliest orc."

"That's horrible," I said.

"One good thing came of it." Pouring the concoction into a pewter cup, he handed it to me and motioned for me to drink it. "Because I look like this, I have been able to set up this little trading post to aid those on the road with my skills, and the orcs dare not enter. They believe me to be one of them, and thus, this is my territory. Orcs are very territorial beings, respectful of unspoken laws."

"And... where are we exactly?" I asked, taking a small sip, and almost throwing up.

"Do not sip it!" he warned. "Drink it all in one go. Trust me. You will feel better once you have done so."

I readied myself. Just like taking a shot of cheap vodka.

Plugging my nose, I tipped the cup back. The liquid was hot on my throat, though it didn't burn. When it hit my stomach, I felt strength and then, an indescribable tingle in my side. I watched as my glowing flesh slowly stitched itself up.

"Rest, Danny," Old Kiel said.

"I'm not tir—"

He placed something under my nose, and the next second, I was out like a light.

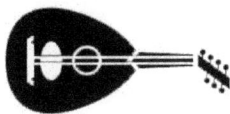

24

I woke to a message from Screenie right in my face. It felt like no time had passed, but the torches were out, and light shone through the open window holes in hazy beams. My wound no longer glowed. I felt like a million bucks, like I'd just downed a Red Bull and was ready to go.

Morning, sleepyhead.

Good thing you were so close to Kiel's place. You would've died and proven all the haters right.

CURRENT HEALTH: 100%

You are invigorated from the potion.

Your Dexterity is temporarily increased by 2.

Kiel leaned over where my wound had been to inspect the thin, barely noticeable scar that remained. His cold tusks brushing against my skin gave me goosebumps.

When he noticed me awake, he asked, "Ah, my boy, how do you feel?"

I moved around a bit. "Incredible."

"Good. Good." He straightened, staring at me. Then he cleared his throat.

"Oh, right. What do I owe you?" I asked.

"It is so crass to discuss matters of gold," he sighed. I began to respond when he added, "One hundred gold pieces."

My mouth went dry. "A hundred gold? I don't even ha—"

Screenie flashed.

You currently have 102gp.

What? How?

Oh, right. You were unconscious.

OBJECTIVE COMPLETED:
You have saved the guards from the korken attack.

REWARD:
They have rewarded your Party with 200gp (You receive 100gp) and a new chain mail hauberk.

ARMOR OBTAINED:
Dented Chain Mail Hauberk (Defense 5)

What a bonus! Since your shoddy outfit could barely handle a single korken, the guards were kind enough to gift you an old set.

A hauberk is designed to cover your torso from attack. Weird word, right? Unlike your leather armor, which proved to be rather useless in a real fight, chain mail will guard you from most bladed (or clawed) attacks. Though it is not indestructible, and neither are you. Obvs. Don't get crazy.

TITLE UNLOCKED:
Protector of Pikeman's Trail.

In future events that take place on Pikeman's Trail, you will have +5 to your Luck Attribute.

New armor? New title? I should almost die more often.

I dug around in my pocket and pulled out my leather pouch, which I guess Curr had filled with my cut.

The pouch is actually made from a Gorrihama scrotum.

I didn't need to know that.

Hand him the scrotum.

I started to give Kiel the money, then stopped. "Does that include the discount Curr mentioned for providing our own flowers?"

Maybe it was the aftereffects of the healing potion, but I didn't even stutter as I asked.

Kiel's lips became a flat line, except where tusks poked through. Then he nodded. "You're right. Seventy-five. Not a coin less."

You have gained +1 in Bartering and Speechcraft.

You sly dog, you. You remembered that deal despite everything AND pulled it off. I hate complimenting you, but damn.

Your Bartering is now 8.

Your Speechcraft is now 13 (+11).

Oh...

ITEM LOST:
Candentis Flos ex Improbi (3)

Kiel placed his bowl and other items down on a table. When he returned, I forked over what was owed. I won't say my mood wasn't slightly buoyed by rare kind words from Screenie.

-75gp

You have 27gp remaining.

You are slightly poorer but alive! That's gotta count for something to someone.

He weighed the coins in his hand and seemed satisfied, then stowed it.

"It was fine speaking with you, Danny," he said, remaining cheery despite my haggling. "Please do visit again."

"If it's all the same to you," I said, rising from the bed. "I'd rather not."

He walked me to the flap I'd seen Curr leave through. As he held it open for me, he exclaimed, "Oh! I almost forgot." Rushing back into the room, he returned carrying my belongings. The new hauberk, my pink cloak, and my sword and the lute balancing on top. "Curr left these with you."

"Oh, great," I said with only a little enthusiasm. "Thanks."

You should equip your shiny new (dented) armor.

I took the armor and started trying to get it on over my head. It was a bit snug. And while my injury was gone, my muscles remained a bit sore.

"Here you are." Kiel took hold of it and gave a few tugs that nearly knocked me over. It was heavy. Like a wool coat in the rain. It would definitely slow me down.

Your Defense is now 4.

And that means?

You'll be a little harder to kill.

I'll take that. Not sure I ever want to experience that again.

You probably will.

Thanks, asshat.

I thought you were calling me Screenie?

I groaned as I slung the lute and cloak around my shoulders, then strapped my sword belt on.

"Thank you, Old Kiel," I said before leaving. "Seriously."

"Better to heal than to be used as a weapon." He stuck out his hand. Shaking it felt like a child holding their dad's hand—if their dad was a wooly mammoth. It totally engulfed me up to the forearm, and was rough and cold like stone. "Be safe on the road, Danny."

I nodded and headed outside.

It was morning and the sun was about midway to its apex. Must've been around 10am Earth time. That meant I'd been out of it for an entire night.

The brightness blinded me, forcing me to hold my arm over my eyes to scan the area. I promptly spotted Curr by a small campfire, laughing and drinking with the soldiers we'd saved. A pot hung over the flame, though it was already emptied out from some meal, the remnants of which were all over the area. They were using their caravan like a tent, which I guessed they'd brought here to repair the missing wheel.

"Danny!" Curr shouted as I walked toward them. "You look well!"

"I feel well," I said when I got close. "That was... fascinating."

"Kiel is a good fellow. Come. Take a seat. Have a drink. Old Kiel distills it himself. Lake water gives it a unique flavor."

That sounded gross, but who was I to judge?

"Isn't it morning?" I asked.

I thought you weren't going to judge?

I set my short sword scabbard flat since it was poking my hip. I kept the lute strapped across my back.

"Relax, bard," Curr said, handing me a tin cup filled with some dark liquid. It definitely wasn't beer or ale. I sniffed it but didn't drink any, as the pungency made my face scrunch. "This is a mild concoction made with fermented yao root. Eaten raw, the root would make you very ill. But left alone for months, buried under the soil, it becomes quite tasty. Besides, there is no time on the road. You rested for so long, we had to find something to do after sleeping."

I was just glad he hadn't decided to leave me behind.

"Play us something, bard?" one of the guards requested. "We are all out of stories."

"No," Curr said quickly. "Please do not."

I rolled my eyes. I'd become all too accustomed to his straightforward and often insulting way of speaking. Hardly bothered me at all anymore.

Sure it doesn't.

Your Lying to Oneself skill has increased by 1.

You will now believe your own deceptions even easier than before!

I know that one isn't real.

As real as Trish's boobs.

You're ridiculous, you know that?

"Where are we?" I asked Curr.
"A trading post run by Old Kiel."

Remember the place Curr wanted to pass by so you could get to your destination quicker? But you just had to go and get yourself stabbed.

You could have warned me in time!

I thought you had eyes.

I used those eyes to look around. There were a handful of parties dressed in various forms of mismatched armor scattered around the grounds. All had campsites or tents either still set up or in the midst of being torn down. Beyond them was a lake half-hidden by tree canopy. Those glowing flowers dotted the waterfront as far as I could see. Fireflies swarmed over the waters, or it might have been loose petals. It all made it look like a paradise in the middle of a dark, scary forest.

A few folks were fishing. One man even sat in a rowboat out in the water. Then I spotted something that made my stomach drop.

"You've gotta be kidding me," I groaned out loud.

"Not at all!" Curr said. "Good thing it was so close too. You probably would have died."

"No, not that." I motioned with my head toward one of the groups farthest from us.

An elaborate and colorfully painted wagon sat by the edge of the lake. In front of it, Garvis the halfling, the female wellick, and the dwarf from Nahal seemed to be engaged in a heated argument.

"Ah, our friends!" Curr said. "Must have arrived in the night."

A moment later, Garvis threw something at the wellick. She stepped forward menacingly and the halfling scurried away, kicking dirt. He shouted something back at her, though I was too far to hear. He unhitched one of the horses from a nearby tree—which honestly looked more like a donkey, but what did I know?—hopped on, and gave it a kick.

He headed off down the road to the north, leaving the wellick and dwarf behind. The dwarf stuck up the middle finger in Garvis' direction, a gesture I suppose meant the same thing here as it did back home.

I hoped he wouldn't notice me. Curr, however, waved. Garvis was too distracted, muttering angrily to himself, to notice.

"I hope you're not beating yourself up too badly," one of the guards said to me, drawing my attention back.

"Yes. Do not beat yourself up," Curr agreed. "There are plenty of things that will do that for you." They all laughed. I just nodded along, a slight smile on my face. "Korkens are a formidable opponent for one such as you."

"And us," the guard said. He leaned in and offered his hand. "Talesin."

"Danny," I said.

The others, Jesstin and Pedr, introduced themselves as well.

Screenie flashed a detailed description of each that I ignored.

"Thanks for the armor," I said, pinching it and pulling it away from my body a bit.

"It is nothing at all compared to our lives," Talesin said.

"So, what is this place exactly?" I asked, straightening my back and looking around again.

"Old Kiel looks like a hermit, but he is anything but," Curr said. "He welcomes travelers for a break and drink. Specializes in potions and herbs, he does. I recall when this place was Pyruun's best-kept secret. Now, so many travelers stop here, it is not uncommon to see tents by the dozens. At night, there is often a communal feast. You should have tried last night's stew!"

Screenie flashed, brighter than usual this time.

Wow. I guess you don't need me to answer anything when you have him.

Jealous? And I thought I was the sensitive one. Besides, he gives more detailed answers than you ever do. All you do is make fun.

Oh, I see how it is. Fine, you don't need me. Enjoy your travels!

Don't be such a baby. Are you serious?

Curr turned to me and slapped down the same sort of ration bar we'd had the other night. "I apologize, we ate all the stew. But here. It will fill your tiny belly."

The thought of choking another one of those down after what I'd gone through wasn't a pleasant one.

I must have made a face, because Curr said, "Wash it down with your drink. They make quite the tasty pairing!"

I gave the cup's contents another whiff and recoiled.

I expected Screenie to pop up and explain the drink to me, but it didn't. Had I really hurt its feelings?

"Have I ever been deceitful with you?" Curr asked.

"Well, you tried to get me to eat goblin," I said.

"Goblin!" Talesin shouted, slapping his knee.

"Yes, it was quite entertaining," Curr said, smiling and nodding.

"And your gunghoedness to get into a battle nearly got me killed..."

Curr let out a barking laugh. "But I got you fixed up just fine and you are no worse for the wear. You are actually better off for it."

"How do you figure that?" I asked, not even bothering to leave out the incredulity.

"You are battle-hardened! You killed a korken!"

I couldn't help but smile. I guess I did have a cool scar now. Trish would have dug it. Kurt probably had tons of scars. Ugh. Screw them, I was feeling great.

With Curr staring at me, I bit into the ration and held it in my mouth, then took a few short breaths through my nose, and threw down a shot of whatever yao root was. I expected to want to spit it out. Surprisingly, it was sweet. Ridiculously so, like liquid cherries.

And then came the bite. My lips pursed. My eyes clenched. My god, how strong was this stuff. He'd called it *mild*.

The effect, however, was almost instantaneous. A wave of calm swept over me. It was like a cool breeze after a hard workout. Then, suddenly, a rush of warmth to my cheeks.

"Whoa," I panted.

Curr chuckled. "Good, right?" He slapped me on the back. "Not easy to make. But then again, Kiel never shares the recipe. Worth stopping for."

"Here, here!" the soldiers chanted.

"You aren't angry I delayed us?" I asked.

"I was admittedly irritated at first," Curr said, "but then I remembered, you are not a very talented warrior. And you did try your best, especially when you played that song. The first proper melody I have heard you strum."

I smiled. Between the healing potion Kiel had ministered to me and this yao root drink, I felt good as new. Better, even.

"Thanks, Cu..." His name trailed off.

The flap of a small, red yurt-shaped tent whipped open. A woman strode outside wearing a black cloak and stroked the mane of the horse hitched outside it.

"Trish?" I said softly.

"I thought we were past this," Curr said. "It is Curr. A hard 'C'."

The woman was beautiful. As I studied her, I realized it wasn't Trish, though she sort of looked like her. Except, just before she pulled her hood up, I noticed two things: pointed ears, and that her deep blonde pixie cut was actually more silvery. She wore a curved sword at her side, a bow slung over her shoulder, and a quiver of arrows on her back. Under her cloak was form-fitting black armor.

I stared at her. Once again, Screenie was silent.

I sure could use you about now.

"You do not want anything to do with her. Trust me," Talesin said, clearly noticing my stolen attention.

"Why not?"

He leaned in close. "She belongs to the Sisterhood of Alyndis."

"Which is?"

Talesin looked at me like I had ten heads. "Is he slow, big man?" he asked Curr.

"He is from a small town and has seen little of the world," Curr said. "It is very frustrating. He can be like a baby."

I put on a goofy smile and bonked myself on the head.

"Ahhh." Talesin looked relieved as he sat back. "What I wouldn't do for a clean slate."

"Forget that broad from Shoreville," Pedr chimed in. "What'd she call you again? Little Tallywack—"

Talesin stomped on his feet and shut Pedr right up.

"Do you remember our meeting with the elf, Lalair?" Curr asked me.

"I don't think I'd forget that, Curr."

"You might have. The Sisterhood is a band of fierce elven warriors who believe they are destined to return elvenkind to glory, starting with Alyndis."

"Not sure how you reestablish monster-filled ruins," Jesstin said, "but more power to the ladies. As long as them knife-ears don't cause any trouble for me, they can have their legends."

"Do they?" I asked.

"Do they what?" Curr responded.

"Cause trouble."

"Do they cause trouble?" Pedr proclaimed in a mocking tone. "Do *they* cause trouble? Does a korken shite in the woods?"

I blinked and looked between them all. "I... don't know?"

Talesin got even closer, acting all serious. "If the time comes, everything shits in the woods!" He cracked himself up, cheering the others as they all took hearty sips of their drinks.

"He is not wrong," Curr said. "Remember, last night. We had to."

"I remember," I groaned. "So, the Sisters..." I was desperate to change the topic from Curr's toilet habits.

"Not good company," Talesin said, shaking his head. "Leave it to elves to proclaim they're the oldest beings around and deserve the kingdom they couldn't keep. As if being the elder means anything. I have an older brother. He stinks worse than braug dung. No offense." He nodded to Curr.

"None taken," Curr replied. "Our scent is as strong as we are."

"Oh, and they're so serious *all the time*." Pedr let out a lengthy groan. "Never shut up about honor and prophecies. Exhausting, really. We get it, you lost the ancient war against wellicks. It wasn't us. Move on."

"Bet you could have fun with that one, though, eh?" Talesin said, nudging Pedr and nodding toward the Sister who was now tending to her horse.

"Aye. Don't you dare tell my wife."

They all shared a laugh.

"She's... something else," I said. I smiled like it was out of my control, suddenly feeling quite full of myself. I couldn't help but wonder what was in the drink. This was my chance to do what I never got the chance to do with Trish.

Curr got my attention. "They do not much care for those who are not their kind. Or smiling. Or laughing. I have worked closely with one before." He shuddered. "She did not understand humor."

"So, what, I can't even talk to her?" I asked.

"You can try. Though you will embarrass yourself. Or die."

"Probably die," Jesstin said.

I puffed out my chest. "Is that a challenge?"

The guards all snickered. Jesstin raised his cup. "To surviving the korken. Praise Ludos!"

"And dying at the hand of the Sisters," Pedr added.

They all laughed harder.

Curr watched me over the rim of his cup as he took a long swig. Then after a loud swallow and lip-smack, he said, "Just bear in mind, bard. Your coin purse is near empty, and funerals are not cheap. Should you perish, we will likely leave you for the wolves and birds."

I laid my hand on his shoulder. "I'll remember that."

I liked to think I had some charisma—rizz, as the kids call it. After all, I was close to scoring a date with Trish before I got pummeled into another world. But this girl? I didn't know, she seemed... dangerous.

But I was Danny, Protector of Pikeman's Trail! I grabbed my cup and stood, stumbling just a bit. She might've belonged to the Sister-hood of—whatever it was—but she was absolutely stunning. There was no way I couldn't at least try to talk to her.

She didn't even seem to notice me walking over. Steeling myself, I racked my brain. I needed a good line. Something to really break the ice and impress her. I was about eight feet away when a warmth overcame my whole body. At first, I worried I'd pissed myself. But then I heard the sounds of music.

Oh no.

But it was too late. The lute apparently decided to start playing itself again. Only this time, it wasn't a battle hymn hinting of danger; what it sounded like was the worst porno soundtrack ever.

♫♪♪ *Bom chikka wow wow.* ♪♪♫

The woman turned from her horse to face me, her eyes like two razor-sharp daggers.

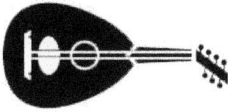

25

S he also had two razor-sharp daggers pointed at me.

"Can I help you?" the stunning elf asked.

I quickly stammered out something like, "Hey, hi. How are y—?"

Before I could finish, she already had the tip of a dagger beneath my chin and pressing upward. A thin stream of blood dripped down my throat and I rose to my tiptoes to relieve the pressure.

She peered closer at me, her crystal blue eyes that were oh-so-much like Trish's roving over every square inch of my face. Then she leaned back to take in the rest of my outfit, pink-with-gold-tasseled cloak included. Her gaze darted from the short sword at my side to the lute strapped on my back.

"Bard." The word came out like someone just spit in her mouth. She had an interesting accent. Like someone from Italy or something.

I tried to nod but couldn't, the dagger convincing me not to. She batted her eyes at me, licked her lips, which were painted dark purple, and then leaned so close, I thought she was going to kiss me.

No such luck.

"I... don't... like... *bards*."

Her horse snorted like it agreed with her.

"Funny, I kind of got that impression," I stammered.

"Music is meant for more than lies and tall tales, bard. You Pyru-unians couldn't understand."

"I totally, agree. Totally." My calves ached, but I couldn't budge for fear of that blade skewering me. "I—I'm sorry to have disturbed you."

I tried to back away, but she seized me with a grip far stronger than her lithe form hinted possible. "Did you think you were going to come over here and woo me with that... *preposterous* song?"

"Nope. No. No, absolutely not. I just thought you might like to drink with us. That was it. Nothing even more than that. Nothing beyond just a simple drink."

She pulled me close and dug her dagger tip in a bit farther. Man was she pretty. And deadly.

"Is this some sort of joke?" she hissed. She looked behind and around me. "Did someone put you up to this?"

"No, no. Definitely not. I—it's a cruel world. I was just trying to be friendly."

"Does it look like I am in need of friends?" she hissed.

"Oh, god, no. You look, just, like, uh. If anything, it's me who needs friends."

"What god?" she demanded.

"Huh?"

"You called upon a god for help. Which god? Speak truth or die."

Crap. I... I don't know? Screenie!

Screenie remained utterly silent.

"I don't suppose you've heard of Jesus?" I asked.

She shook her head.

"Allah?"

"You're pathetic," she spat.

All that confidence I had from that shot? Gone in an instant.

"I am. You-you're right," I stuttered. "I'm such a failure that I thought I might be able to hang out with you. You know, kind of bask in your awesomeness. That sorta thing."

"You talk a great deal and very strangely." She sighed. "Typical."

Removing the dagger from my chin, she twirled it in her fingers, then placed it in its sheath faster than I could blink. Though I noted her other one still hung in her hand at her side.

I rubbed my neck, pulling away a red palm. "Thanks. Thank you. My mouth is dry. I need a drink. Would you like a dr—"

"Leave me at once, minstrel. I won't ask twice."

I nodded a bit too eagerly. "Yeah, okay, of course. Well, it was super nice meeting you and all."

If looks could kill, I'd be a corpse.

I spun and started back toward Curr and the others. Just at the last second, her eyes seemed to focus on my lute and her brow knitted.

Was she going to break it so I couldn't hurt anyone's ears, just like Curr had? I didn't stick around to find out.

Screenie finally flashed, surprising me and making me stumble over a rock as I power-walked like a grandma in a mall before opening time to get away from her.

Now that was entertaining.

Oh, now you're back?

Clearly, you are lost without me. By the way, after ingesting yao root brandy, your Charisma and Courage were increased temporarily by +10. However, the Sisterhood of Alyndis are entirely immune to such flattery.

I groaned.

What exactly is the Sisterhood of Alyndis?

While I know Curr already told you his version, I appreciate you allowing me the opportunity to inform you further.

THE SISTERHOOD OF ALYNDIS: Elite female warriors, trained from birth. After the long Wellick Wars, male elves were rare, so their women have taken up the sword. They adhere to the old ways and seek to resurrect the Ancient Elven Kingdom of Alyndis, which fell during the war. Lethal with short bow and sword—

And daggers. Don't forget daggers.

And daggers... they are experts on horseback. Much of their customs are shrouded in mystery.

Very informative. Are they dangerous?

That seems like a silly question considering what you just went through.

Fair point.

I loafed back to the campsite where Curr and the others sat, not daring to look back over my shoulder at the Sister. The soldiers stifled laugher.

"You nearly had her." Talesin couldn't hold it in any longer and they all started laughing.

"Some bard," Pedr added.

"Oh yeah, ha ha. Remember when I helped save all of you," I countered, shooting them a glare. They quieted down in their enjoyment.

"Ah, don't worry about it, Danny," Jesstin said. "You're better off alone than with one of *them*." He didn't say it like someone who'd been rejected by his fair share of girls. It was like there was acid on his tongue. I was new to this world, but it didn't take a carriage scientist to figure out that wellicks and elves had their share of bad blood.

Screenie flashed.

You'll never be alone as long as I am here.

That's comforting.

I sat next to Curr.

"Thanks for the help," I said, low.

"What did you want me to do? Fight her?" Curr asked. "She would have sliced you open before I got anywhere near to her. Plus, the Sisters are known for their stealth and speed. She would have been gone before I could catch up with her, and you would be dead on the dirt." He shook his head. "No, better to let you talk your way out of it."

"Yeah, well, I could've done better if not for this damned lute screwing things up."

Warning me of danger was a good thing, but I guess its magical abilities weren't all great. That song? Was it setting a mood, or did it think I was in danger with her?

Love can be dangerous.

"What did your lute do?" Curr asked.

"Oh, uh, you know..."

His head tilted, then his eyes lit up. "Ah, yes. She instantly realized you were a bard and not worthy of her time."

"You know—" I clamped my mouth shut. "Never mind. Let's just forget that ever happened."

"Do you know a spell or a song to make me forget?"

"Er—No."

"Then I cannot do that."

I realized by his expression he wasn't kidding. Literal as always.

He poured himself a bit more, slugged it down, then leaned back and belched loud enough for everyone nearby to turn in his direction. He just smiled and waved.

"What?" he said. "At least it came out of my mouth and not my rump."

I sighed. "Yeah. I can't even imagine what that would be like. You'd have us all running for a tent to get some fresh air." I admit, I spoke loudly, hoping the Sister would hear that bit of charm, but as I peeked back, she, her horse, and her tent were gone.

Curr snickered. "He is not wrong!"

As he and the soldiers enjoyed the merriment, I leaned closer to Curr and whispered, "She's gone."

"Not surprising," he said. "They never linger long. Always searching. For what, I do not know."

I was a little relieved about her vanishing, frankly. It eased the embarrassment of my epic failure. Though it would have been nice to watch her for a few more minutes.

"All right." Curr laid his huge hand on my knee. "Feeling better?"

"Rejection excluded, loads."

"Then we should be off."

My heart sank. "Already?" I felt like I'd just gotten the chance to settle down after such a long walk. I missed a whole night of sleep. To me, it felt like no time had passed from the korken battle to now.

"No. We must go." Curr stood.

"So soon?" Talesin said. "We didn't even get a song, bard."

"That is in all of our best interests," Curr said. "Danny is not a good bard." Before I could argue, he continued, "If we do not depart soon, we will never make it to Balahazia before nightfall."

"Oh, shoot. I was hoping I could go fishing," I joked.

"You?" That got Curr's attention. "I prefer battling things with axes than with lures on strings. So boring. I will never understand it."

Neither did I, honestly. My dad loved it. Great way to disappear.

"I was kidding," I said.

"Another bad joke, Danny. Let us go."

He didn't really give me a choice, helping me up.

We bid farewell to the guards who had to finish repairing their carriage before they could continue on their way. They thanked us again, on their behalf and the king's. Though, I don't think a king would really care about them or us.

"Until next time, Kiel," Curr said to the air, giving the healer's tent a wave as if he could see us. "Keep your tusks sharp."

The coolness of the late afternoon air felt good on my skin as we made our way back to the road. Curr kept his eyes sternly ahead, like he was a bit tipsy and struggling to focus.

Feeling the lute bounce against my hips, I turned. That song it had played with the Sister really killed my game.

"Don't do that again," I whispered under my breath.

I still think you're hearing things.

Don't you have any idea how to control this thing?

Do you need me for everything?

"Are you alright?" Curr asked.

I'd lagged behind again, busy arguing with my imaginary friends. "Yeah, yeah, I'm good."

"I know you have stubby legs, but please do try to keep up."

I grunted my agreement. But as I walked, my head filled with thoughts.

Here it was. The comedown from feeling amazing and confident from that potion and drink. That woman looked like Trish, but she wasn't her.

How would I get back to my world? And what was the reason I'd been brought here? Was I destined to stay in Pyruun forever or just until I completed some type of quest? This was starting to feel too long to be a dream, though, every dream feels normal until you wake up from it and remember the idiosyncrasies.

All these questions and more plagued me as I struggled to match Curr's pace. But these more than any others: Who was the Sister that looked so much like Trish? Where did she disappear to so suddenly? And why would she even be at a dirty trading post in the middle of nowhere?

I don't have all the answers in the universe. Sheesh. Though, I suspect that those answers will come to you in time.

Oh, foreshadowing. Thanks, Screenie, you've been a big help. Not!

NEW OBJECTIVE:
Discover the Sister's true identity.

There, take that.

Jokes on you. I'm interested.

Oh, good. Then you don't need a reward!

I didn't say that...

Then how about this. I'll give you your reward ahead of time...

REWARD:
The secret in Kiel's drink is the fermentation method. Under the ground, like Curr told you, and fermented in his own piss.

I covered my mouth and gagged.

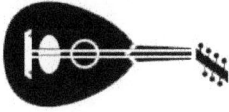

26

After a few hours walking without incident, I somehow felt worse. This yao root hangover was rough—I was also choosing to pretend I didn't know how it was made.

Or maybe it was Kiel's healing draught. It didn't help that thickening clouds darkened the sky, as if threatening rain.

Today's forecast:
A crisp 53 degrees, light wind, and a 100% chance of rain.

Okay. Definitely doing more than threatening.

My sarcastic guide through this strange world certainly wasn't helping. Fearful thoughts seeped further into my mind. Everything from the huge things, like whether or not I was stuck here forever, to the little things, like the fact that, oh, I'd almost *died*.

All my time back on Earth, that had never happened. Mom said I choked on a grape as a baby once, but that was the extent of my relationship with danger, and I'm pretty sure she'd only told me that so I'd chew my food a full thirty-two times.

Then, I was overcome by the idea that me almost dying felt trivial compared to the rest of this. I'd lived nearly thirty years in a world where a potion like Kiel had given me would've changed everything. People whose loved ones were on their deathbed might have had hope.

A cure like that would've cost not just 100gp, but millions of US dollars. Insurance companies would have a field day ripping off hardworking people.

I shook my head. Somehow, I needed to just carry on and hope for the best. There was nothing else to do.

I don't know whether Curr noticed the gray clouds, but he did seem to be lengthening up his gait even more. Oddly, I found myself being able to push and keep up better than I had yesterday.

That little Dexterity bonus is nice, no?

So that's what this is? What the hell does that even mean?

Dexterity determines your skill and agility in performing physical tasks, especially those requiring precision and coordination. This bonus would also make you slightly more adept at actions such as dodging attacks—which would have been nice yesterday—picking locks—since you're a Petty Thief—and executing stealthy maneuvers—see previous.

Dexterity is commonly associated with quick reflexes, nimbleness, and the ability to navigate challenging environments with grace.

Also, it lets you walk longer without getting tired.

I couldn't imagine how badly I'd feel without a Dexterity bonus from the healing draught. I found myself thankful for whatever it was doing to cancel out some of the hangover.

Rain is imminent.

And there it was. The first drops of cold rain pelted us. Curr grumbled to himself about awful weather or something.

"Isn't there some rain god we could pray to?" I asked.

Curr stopped and gave me a severe look. "Braugs pray to no god except Tarton, and he cares nothing for a little rain."

"Alright, geez. Forget I said anything."

After another twenty minutes, we were fairly soaked, and I wondered if Curr was just going to keep walking through the rain until we reached Balahazia or if he intended to stop.

"Perhaps one of your weaker gods might be interested," he said as it really started to come down in sheets.

"None I know of," I said. "I suppose we have no choice but to stop and find cover."

"Cover?" Curr said. "There is no good cover on the road between here and Balahazia. This is the final stretch."

I groaned and pulled my cloak up over my head.

"How did you ever survive the walk from Smallwick to Nahal?"

I stopped in my tracks then quickly started walking again, hoping he hadn't noticed. There it was—the direct question I'd been dreading. I didn't even know where Smallwick was—nor could I believe there was such a place named that—much less how I could've made it to Nahal from there.

Maybe I should just tell him the truth...

But how? I couldn't just say I was from another world. Even if this was a dream—as far as dreams went, it could be worse.

"I, uh..." I cleared my throat. "Barely did. Thieves took everything I had."

Again with the lies?

"Thieves?" He looked perplexed. "Odd place for them to operate. Not much to steal."

"Easy pickings and all that, you know."

You caught him. Now reel him in with a good story.

I have a better idea.

"I actually wrote a song about the whole ordeal, if you'd prefer to hear it?"

"Oh, no, no. No, thank you. I would rather go on wondering."

Boom.

Boom, indeed.

"Bards," Curr said like a curse. "So, how did you meet Rarmir?"

"Who now?"

Curr placed a flat hand over his eyes, acting like an awning as he turned toward me. "The man who owned the tavern in which you first played so horribly."

Crap. Right. Rarmir. "Oh, him. Yeah. You know, I still really don't think it was that bad."

"It was."

"I was left with nothing and needed money. He offered me a gig. My dad had played from time to time and taught me a little." Again, it helped to lean on some truth when crafting a believable tale. "I just picked up a lute and kept playing."

Curr opened his mouth to say something, but I interrupted.

"I know, I know, Curr. I should be better. But I was good enough for there until you and your big friends came in and ruined it."

"I am pleased we rescued you from a life of mediocrity."

Lightning cracked above, sparing me having to discuss more about my not-so-imaginary past.

Your forecast now includes a thunderstorm! The gods are angry.

Lucky you.

Curr looked to the sky. "Clouds like this mean no moonlight. That will make it harder to see. But the upside is, goblins hate the rain."

"That's good."

"The downside is orcs love it."

My mind traveled back to Old Kiel. He'd said orcs mistake him for one of them. I couldn't imagine one of him with a less mild disposition. Or what about a hundred of him who were pissed off? With weapons...

"That's less good," I muttered.

"We are not far, though. Had you not gotten yourself clawed, we would have been there already. If we pick up the pace, we will reach Balahazia just as the sun settles."

Pick up the pace? That wasn't really possible for me.

"No one is going to Balahazia!" a voice shouted over the rain as lightning streaked again, thunder booming like we were in some B-rated film and even the weather was against us. I was already soaked, but now I was drenched.

I turned slowly, looking for the source of the voice but found only trees and bushes so dense, I couldn't tell one from another.

Then, I heard the crack of a branch from my left and spun toward it. Curr's hand was already on the grip of his axe.

"Who is there?" he shouted. "Show yourself!"

I nodded and placed my hand on my own sword, drawing it just slightly so I could rip it free of its scabbard if we were attacked. But where was my lute's battle hymn? It remained oddly silent.

I caught a glimpse of movement out of the periphery of my vision.

"Orcs?" I asked.

Curr shook his head. "They do not talk like that."

From the bushes on all sides emerged five Sisters of Alyndis, including the gorgeous one I'd failed so miserably with. At least, I think it was her. Their hoods were pulled up, and masks lifted over their mouths, so it was hard to know for sure.

Is that her?

Screenie highlighted one in blue. Then another. They all showed the same.

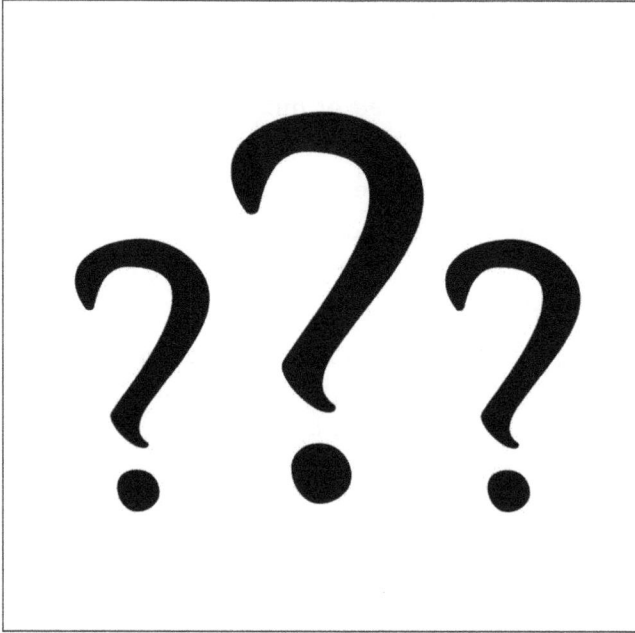

NAME: Identity Concealed
RACE: Elf (female)
OCCUPATION: Ranger
SPECIAL ABILITIES: Concealed Identity

Crap! I think it's her. Or that one. Or the third one.

Love will always find a way.

You got any ideas or just jokes?

You're getting pretty good at Speechcraft.

Why don't you give it a go?

Really?

Sure. Why the hell not?

"Oh, hey," I said sheepishly to the one I thought I'd met. "Did I make that fine an impression?"

"You have something that doesn't belong to you, bard," what appeared to be their leader said. She stood in the center at least. I'm sure my face went beet red. And the way she said "bard..."

Why does everyone hate me?

Shall I list the reasons?

I ignored Screenie and looked to Curr, then back to the Sisters. "Well, Curr, if I was going to die, death by Snu-Snu seems the way to go."

"Snu-Snu?" he asked, puzzled.

Suddenly, the one I thought I hit on rushed forward with such speed, I don't know if I'd have seen her even if I was looking directly at her. Just like back at camp, except this time, instead of a dagger, an arrowhead was pressed to my throat.

Wrong move. My bad.

It is your bad! And why isn't my lute playing?

Clearly, I was in danger.

I glanced at Curr from the corner of my eye. He thrust his arm out and sent a Sister flying. I suppose the whole "never hit a woman" thing didn't apply here. Then he drew his axe and swung it in a wide arc at another one. She rolled under the blade, and Curr grunted, coming back around off-balance.

I'd never seen such quickness.

His next blow was parried downward, causing one side of his axe to imbed in the dirt. By the time he pulled it free, two Sisters had their bows trained on his face from only feet away. The leader had her curved sword against his neck.

Well, look at him. And look at you.

"You are making a mistake," Curr warned.

"If either of you so much as flinches," the leader said, "two arrows will tear through your skulls."

"What if I have an itch?" I asked, knowing I was pushing it. I tried not to stare into the gorgeous blue eyes in front of me. This girl was really in my head.

With her arrow, she found the precise place on my neck where I already had a small wound from our previous encounter and pressed. God, it hurt.

"We are content to spare your lives," the leader said. "We only want the lute."

"Hold on. Wait. Do you mean loot? Or lute?" I asked.

It was an honest question. These were warriors who were apparently far from home. Maybe they'd turned to being bandits. Every fantasy story always had bandits.

I also hoped to buy Curr some time to get us out of this. Problem was, he wasn't even making an attempt. He simply stood, breathing slowly in through his nose and out through his mouth.

My crush stared at me like I was an idiot. "Those are both the same."

"Well, they sound the same, sure. But one is spelled with a U and th—"

"Silence!" the leader shouted, emphasizing her point with a growl.

My captor kept her arrow firmly on my throat, and with the other hand, yanked the lute off my back. I guess that answered my question.

She held it up, analyzing it from every angle as the rain pelted the wood.

"Hey! Watch it! That's very valuable," I protested.

She leaned in. Less than an inch from my face, she said, "Do not presume to lecture me on Alyndis!"

I got lost staring. She had amazing skin.

Wait. My lute, Alyndis, what?

The plot thickens...

"By the Stars. It really is it..." the leader said softly.

"I told you I saw it," my crush replied.

"Where did you get that?" the leader demanded of me. I couldn't see much of her face, but her eyes were dark, like the storm itself. She wasn't messing around.

"Bard!" she barked when I delayed answering.

"I-I found it," I stuttered.

"Do not lie to me!"

"Do not accuse my companion of lying," Curr said, a harsh edge entering his tone. "He did indeed find it."

Well, that wasn't the whole truth. There was that part about a bargain with a hag, but it didn't seem smart to share that. What the heck had she given me that these mysterious and deadly Sisters of Alyndis were after it?

I did tell you bartering with a hag wasn't the smartest idea.

You told me to barter with the hag! It was even an objective!

My bad.

"You found this?" my crush asked. "I find that hard to believe."

"Tell the truth, bard," the leader said. "Or I will slaughter your friend right in front of you. We have killed far bigger beasts than braugs."

I swallowed. She wasn't joking. Did I really have to tell the complete truth?

The truth will set you free. Or get you killed.

Which is it!

Before I could answer, I noticed the muscles on Curr's back tense. With the leader focused on me, he bent his head and pinned her blade under his chin. The metal flexed under the pure strength of his neck muscles. He ducked and the other Sister fired right over his head. Good thing he was so bald or she'd have given him a haircut. Next, he rushed forward, dragging sword and its holder with him as he shouldered into the archers and freed his axe.

All in one motion. It was incredible.

My crush turned her attention from me, slung the lute over her shoulder, and smoothly nocked the arrow formerly at my throat. I grabbed her arm to throw off her aim. She elbowed back and caught me in the temple, sending me onto my ass.

You have gained +1 in Unarmed Combat.

Your Unarmed Combat is now 4.

Not the best showing, but "A" for effort!

When the blue-eyed beauty was able to fire again, Curr had his axe up and deflected the arrow. Then he roared.

"We must go!" the leader shouted.

She whistled, and five horses came pounding out of the brush. How the heck had we not heard them?

My crush glanced at me, and—*winked?*

Hey now! I saw that. I think she likes you... LOL

The horses hadn't even stopped before all five Sisters hopped on and were off down the road, swift as the wind. Curr chased them for a few steps, his axe pumping in the air.

"You had better run, thieves!" he shouted.

"It's gone," I whispered. I fell to my knees in the mud, staring at my empty hands. "My new lute is already gone."

A hand fell on my shoulder. I looked up into the driving rain to see Curr. He panted intensely but seemed to have calmed a little.

"That is very bad luck, Danny," Curr said. "You were only just improving."

So much for extra luck on Pikeman's Trail...

Amen.

NEW OBJECTIVE:
Find your stolen lute.

REWARD:
Your lute.

"We need to catch up to them," I said, clenching my fists. The shock was wearing off, and honestly, I was pissed. I hadn't been robbed since my grade school bully took my Blow Pop. This was worse. And to rub it in with a wink... Women could be so cruel.

"Danny, they are long gone," he said, solemn. "Elven horses are the fastest in the known world. I am sorry. There is no chance we will catch them."

"Bullshit!" I said, pushing to my feet. I stuck my finger in his chest. "If that was your axe they stole—"

He gently removed my finger. I was lucky he didn't snap it off. "I would buy a new axe. This is about your pride. There will be more instruments available in Balahazia. We can search in every well."

I couldn't tell him it was more than that. That I was positively sure that lute was magical and the most valuable thing I'd ever had by far. He didn't even know about Phlegm. Would his tune change then or would he think I was a fool for striking a bargain with a hag?

He is right, you know.

The Sisters of Alyndis ride upon creatures known as Night Mares. They are fast, and elves are very lightweight, which makes them faster, and faster still during the dark hours when their eyesight is best.

Does everything in this godforsaken place thrive at night?

Not everything.

So, what, I just let them go with my lute?

Not if you want to complete your objective.

Then what am I supposed to do? Please, Screenie, tell me.

This road only leads to one place.

And what if they leave the road?

Then perhaps the road will guide you.

That sounds like self-help nonsense.

That was all Screenie said.

"Are you listening?" Curr asked. He must've been speaking, and I hadn't heard him.

"Sorry, I'm just pissed."

"Well, you can piss anywhere, Danny. The forest is already wet." I sighed in frustration, but Curr continued, "And when we arrive in Balahazia to a nice warm room, we will no longer be wet."

My shoulders sank. "Yeah... you're right. That would be nice."

He's not right. You really need to go after the lute.

Why, huh?

If you fail to retrieve your lute, I'm pretty certain the hag will not be happy.

Screw her. And screw you.

I wasn't even sure why I was so upset. The lute had been nothing but trouble for me, playing itself and all that. I guess maybe it all came back to purpose.

What was my purpose here in this place?

Without the lute, I was just another failed musician with an oversized butterknife. Same as I was on Earth... minus the knife.

27

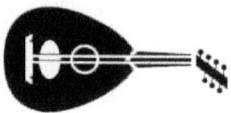

Rain and mud. So much of it, even Curr slowed. Though I don't think it was the conditions. He might not have said it, but losing a battle couldn't have been easy for him. He kept his axe in his hand now instead of strapped to his back, and his teeth hadn't stopped clenching.

At least they didn't take any of *his* treasures, though. Or his gold. Who knew how much he had stuffed into all his oversized pouches.

It's not about how much gold you have. Don't work for your money; have your money work for you!

Don't try to get on my good side.

After some time, the forest began to thin out. The distant outline of the Masked Mountains was visible again. The terrain went from vibrant greens to bland gray rock.

"Move, you stupid, bloated idiot!" came a shout from up ahead.

"What now?" I complained.

It was so difficult to see anything in the pouring rain that we'd barely noticed a halfling and his donkey fighting on the side of the road by a big boulder. And not just any halfling and his donkey.

"You," I said with a hatred I didn't even know I possessed.

It was Garvis. And it *was* a donkey I saw him riding off on, not a steed. Small victories in a world where I felt like I never knew a thing.

"You," he spat back.

"Us," Curr said with a smile.

"Get the yig out of here if you know what's good for you!" Garvis snapped.

"Fine by me," I said, starting to walk again.

Curr didn't. "What is going on here?"

Garvis kicked the donkey in the hind. "What's going on here is that this piece of—"

"I asked the donkey," Curr said. "Not you." Curr pressed his ear to the side of the donkey's face, rubbing it behind its wet ears. "It is okay. You are safe with me, miniature beast of burden."

"Like yig and shog she is!" Garvis shouted. "That's my donkey, even if she won't move an inch…"

His voice trailed off as Curr easily led the donkey a few yards down the road.

Behind him, Garvis pumped his little legs, trying to catch up. "Now you hold on just a yigging minute!"

Curr and the donkey stopped.

"That's better." Garvis climbed up onto the donkey's back. "My thanks for coercing the old girl to move. Time for me to get going."

Curr stepped away from the donkey and it went nuts, kicking and braying so hard, it tossed Garvis off.

I laughed hysterically. That was exactly what I needed to see.

Your Luck has returned!

I didn't know it was gone.

"Guess she likes me," Curr said.

Once Garvis was fully unseated, the donkey nuzzled up to the big braug.

"Can we move on now?" I asked. "This buffoon can fend for himself."

I could tell Garvis was getting ready to argue as he rose, but then he started to mount the donkey again and was met with the same fate. Picking himself up out of a muddy puddle for the second time, he said, "Mayhaps I was hasty."

"You look like a drowned rat," Curr said.

"Sans the wings," I said with a fair bit of snark.

Garvis gritted his teeth, then sighed. "Feel like one too. Name's Garvis. I believe we met in Nahal."

He held a stubby hand out and Curr shook it. Then he extended it to me. I just stared. How could I trust him to get close? He was a thief.

Technically, only you have ever stolen from him.

Shut up. He deserved it.

"Yeah. We've met," I said out loud, not even trying to hide my disgust.

"You're not still upset about that, are you?" Garvis said. "It was a mere tussle, as I recall."

"You pulled a knife on me!"

His eyes went wide, like that was news to him. "Ah, well, no sense holding grudges. There's too much good in life. It's my pleasure to make your acquaintance while somewhat sober."

"Whatever," I said. Then I realized something. "Did you notice a bunch of women on horses pass by here?"

"Don't know that they were women, what with the rain and their hooded cloaks, but a party kicked through here and sent mud flying up all over me. Quite rude, really. That's what spooked the donkey in the first place."

"Which way did they go?" I demanded, stepping toward him.

Garvis made a show of looking around. "You see more than one way?" Then when I gave him the stink eye, he pointed north. "Toward Balahazia."

"Thanks." I started walking away again.

"They friends of yours?" Garvis called out.

"Hardly," I said, not even stopping. I wasn't about to give him any information.

"They stole his instrument," Curr said behind me. "A lute of exceptional quality—even if he could not yet play it exceptionally."

I spun and gave Curr a glare he didn't even register. He just kept on smiling like a moron.

"Well, is that a fact?" Garvis asked. "A fellow musician!"

I nodded.

"Aren't you just in luck, then?" Garvis said. "They're heading through Balahazia, it seems. So am I. I had a bit of falling-out with my performance troupe, though. Let's just say… they felt one way about things, and I felt another. Having just parted ways with my… *friends*, my services are available."

"Services? You couldn't satisfyingly service a goat," I said.

"A goat!" Curr laughed. "Your jokes are improving, Danny."

Garvis scowled and shook his head. "Listen, boyo. If you want your lute back, I'm your best yigging hope."

I approached him. "Oh yeah, why's that?"

Curr grunted. "Because he is a rotten thief who uses his tiny stature to pick pockets while other, more impressive performers distract them."

Garvis placed a hand to his heart. "That cuts deep, good sir."

"It's Curr," I said before Curr could speak up. "Hard 'C'."

Garvis stared dumbly. Then he got it. "Ah, yes. Okay then. Noted. Well, I am a freelance liberator of valuable items."

I recalled the first time I'd met him, and Curr spotted his thievery from a mile away, before even Screenie showed me his occupation.

"In other words, a thief," I said.

"Such a crass word. But, if that helps you, yes, a thief. Best in the land."

I narrowed my eyes at him.

"I know what you're thinking," Garvis added, patting the air in front of him. Then, he pointed at Curr. "He saw me. But *you* didn't."

He was right about that.

"In any event. I am *rarely* caught."

"As you said, I caught you," Curr said. "And I had hoped you would have learned from the lesson we taught you and stopped your thieving ways."

His bushy red brow furrowed. "What lesson?"

"When we took—"

I nudged Curr in the side to quiet him. I didn't need this thief knowing *I* was a thief.

Oh, c'mon. You could have the very first all-Petty-Thief Party!

"When I kicked your ass," I said.

Garvis' cheeks went red as his hair. "The bar wench could have beat me in a fight, drunk as I was."

Curr nodded. "Probably true."

"Whatever," I said. "I still won."

"Yes, yes, but fighting is not my specialty," Garvis said. "Certainly, you find yourselves in need of my skills. Only a thief is best at catching thieves. And I am in need of employment."

I rolled my eyes. He was trouble. I could tell.

"We're not hiring anyone right now," I said, leaving him behind for a third time.

He rushed to catch up. "Don't make a mistake you'll regret."

I kept walking.

"Please," he said, practically begging.

I stopped and got in his face, very much not in the mood. "Only a thief catches a thief? You didn't even have any clue I took the gold out of your pockets after laying you out. You're worthless."

Whoa. Harsh, dude. He was shitfaced.

The halfling's chin fell to his chest. "I thought it fell out..."

I took a breath. Yeah, maybe that was harsh. And the last thing I wanted was Curr thinking I was only a thief when he'd made his distaste for stealing without cause known. His reaction was surprisingly quite the opposite.

"Who knew!" Curr exclaimed. "You claimed the spoils of victory of your foe? And I did not catch you, Danny. I guess we really do not need you, tiny half-pint. Danny surpassed your skills already."

"You... you owe me!" Garvis yelled at me. "I'll help you, and we can consider that part of my payment."

"Not interested," I said. "C'mon, Curr."

Curr sized up the halfling again. "If you are so talented, you will find gold again." Curr gave the donkey a light pat on the head. "Be good, now."

"Wait! Wait!" Garvis hollered after us. "At least let me travel with you to Balahazia. I'll let you ride the donkey!"

I thought about it for a second. As great as I'd felt after Kiel's potion, my legs were starting to burn again. I wasn't sure how much longer it was to the city, but it couldn't hurt to ride the rest of the way.

Besides, what were we going to do, have one of those awkward moments where we both say bye to each other and then walk side by side in the same direction?

I turned to him. "Why do you want to come with us so badly? We aren't going to hire you." As if I believed he even had a chance at robbing those impossibly fast, deadly elves anyway.

"Dalia won't let me ride her. Alone, moving slow, I could be a goblin snack. With him." He jutted his chin in Curr's direction. "I won't be touched."

"So that's it, you're just a coward?"

He puffed out his chest. "Know what you're good at and what you're not, bard. First rule of the world."

Curr scratched his beard. "That is a wise rule. I am good at many things." He quietly started counting his fingers as if listing said things in his head.

Garvis gave him a slap on the back. Even reaching as high as he could, it was almost a "good game" ass smack. "I'm sure you are, brave braug."

Curr stopped counting. "His trade disgusts and repulses me, but I have no quarrel with the halfling any longer. I leave it up to your discretion, Danny."

I stared at Garvis and his sloppy mop of red hair. All covered in rain and muck, he looked pathetic. I still didn't trust him, not one bit.

"C'mon," he said. "You wouldn't leave a man out here to die, would you? I can already smell the beasts lurking, waiting for you both to move on. Oh, what is a halfling to do?"

He sure is persistent.

Maybe you should let him travel with you.

As if your ideas don't always lead to more trouble.

It isn't far, and I know you still feel guilty about stealing his gold. Oh, and the sheet music you took after you beat him senseless.

Wait... are you the villain here?

I had to admit, his little story about his "band" breaking up got to me. I'd been there. Done that. It sucked. Plus, riding instead of walking wasn't bad either.

"Fine," I conceded, trying not to look too eager as I trod back toward the donkey.

Garvis bowed and gestured. "Your steed, sir."

I pet the mule and asked, "Will you let me ride you, Dalia?"

Taking a page out of Curr's book. Who knew such a big brute could be so gentle and understanding with animals?

It brayed softly.

You have gained +1 in Speechcraft!

Congratulations! You persuaded the donkey to let you ride it. And no, that's not a sex joke.

Your Speechcraft is now 14 (+1).

Congrats! You are now a Level 3 Bard!

Perhaps you will always remember this time when you leveled up by mounting an ass. That was a sex joke.

Only you could take something so great and make it feel so awful.

But awful was far from how I felt. The rush of energy and warmth came like the first shot of whiskey on a freezing winter night.

Because of your Skill increases so far, you have improved to Level 3.

You know what? You might survive after all. With each new Level, your Health, Stamina, and—if you were attuned with any magical abilities—Mana regenerates to 100%.

You can also apply +1 to the Attribute of your choosing.

Later.

Why in all that is holy would you wait to do such a thing.

Who waits? Arghhhh!

Because I know it will irritate you.

No...

I carefully climbed onto the donkey's back, reveling in the fact that Screenie would have to seethe over that decision. Truth was, I really just didn't fully understand this whole Attribute system yet, and I wanted to be sure I made the right moves when the time came.

NEW MOUNT ACQUIRED:
Dalia the Donkey

She's as sturdy as she is slow.

Speed: 4
Health: 233
Stamina: 100

A moment later, Garvis hopped up behind me. The donkey made an awful noise.

"Hey, hey! What the heck do you think you're doing?" I yelled.

"I never said I wouldn't be riding with you," Garvis said, smiling.

Oh, that little bastard.

Curr plucked the halfling off by the scruff of his neck like a mother cat. "You can tag along. But do not give us or the donkey any trouble. The last thief I traveled with ended up without his head when he tried to 'liberate' some of my goods."

Garvis swallowed. "I wouldn't dream of it, good si—Curr." He looked up at me. "Just some fun. Are you ready to put our past behind us and make amends?"

"I don't have amends to make," I snarled.

"Well, you *did* insult and rob me, as I now recall."

I sighed and looked at Curr. "Do we really have to put up with this?"

Curr shrugged. "It was your decision. More bodies to handle an attack is a good thing in my opinion. And I am good at surviving battles, like the halfling said. But you are not good at surviving battles."

"Hey, I survived."

"By luck and circumstances," Curr reminded me.

"Still, I survived."

"This one can act as a diversion should the need arise." Curr gave Garvis a playful shove hard enough to nearly send him back to the mud.

"You've got it!" Garvis recovered and slapped him again.

This time, Curr glowered down at him, and the halfling recoiled. "Strike my back again, and my mind may change."

Aw, they're so cute together.

More entertaining than walking in silence at least.

Maybe I'd get some good karma out of this. I regarded Garvis in all his wretched and miserable glory. Annoying as he was, I guess he didn't deserve to be left to die.

"Fine, we're even," I said. "I'm Danny."

Garvis looked up at me atop the donkey. "Excellent. Excellent news. Thank you both for taking pity on my current circumstances. Indeed, this could well be the start of a wonderful relationship, methinks."

"'Methinks' you should probably shut up," I said. "The orcs might attack just to keep you quiet."

"Very astute observation, Danny," Curr said. "That is something you are competent at. Now, if only we could improve your singing, fighting, luting..." He trailed off in thought.

Garvis started to respond, then clamped his mouth shut. Maybe the halfling could learn after all.

NEW PARTY MEMBER ADDED:
Garvis Wittleman the Thief (Level 8).

Ugh, really? He's an official Party member?

At least temporarily. I don't make the rules.

AND he's a higher level than me?

Of course, he is. You're a baby in this world. A cute little newborn with pudgy cheeks. You have a lifetime of improvement ahead of you. Or, you might progress nowhere. Some people peak early.

Damn. Girls always told me after we broke up that I'd peaked in high school. Joke's on them, I wasn't as cool and popular back then as my current, magnetic self would have you believe. I used to agree with them, though. That I was going nowhere.

Screenie was right. This was all new. And if I was stuck here, I didn't have to make the same mistakes. I could keep moving.

Whatever helps you sleep at night.

But you have to keep up with Curr first!

PART THREE

28

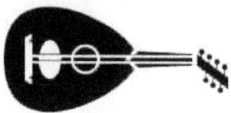

AN UNEXPECTED HERO
PART III: To Balahazia and beyond!
CURRENT LOCATION: Balahazia

It was bitter cold up in the foothills where Balahazia was located. The rain had turned to little flurries, peppering the already snow-covered rooftops. After walking at a steep incline for hours, it was nice to be on relatively flat land. I dismounted Dalia the Donkey and walked her the rest of the way. She seemed like she needed a rest.

The city was—dare I say—beautiful. Fortified by three-story walls on two sides, a wide expanse of water on another, and a sheer mountain on the fourth, Balahazia felt like a true stronghold.

The gate was open, but it was the first heavily defended place I'd seen in Pyruun. Soldiers in plate armor bearing the kingdom's sigil were on either side of the gate, and high up on the walls, armed with crossbows. Any orcs or beasts would have to be crazy to try and raid here.

OBJECTIVE COMPLETED:
Reach Balahazia safely with your Party.

Welcome to the northern foothold of Pyruun. Known for its mining and fishing culture, its inhabitants specialize in harvesting whales. Its walls, dangerously constructed from the stone of the elvish ruins of Alyndis, are considered impenetrable.

"You smell that?" Curr said, taking a deep breath.

I did the same. It wasn't awful, like most of this world, just slightly fishy. Though I was sure that would become unbearable down by the docks if I could already smell it from here.

"Fish," Garvis said, waving his hand in front of his nose. "I hate fish."

Halflings are notorious for their dislike of water and all things water-related. Their body types do not make for being good swimmers.

"No, the cold," Curr proclaimed. "Smells of home."

He was right, it did smell like cold, if that could be a thing. And the reminder of the chilly air made me unconsciously pull my pink cloak tighter as we passed through the gate, being eyed by soldiers.

"Your cloak is absurd," Garvis said.

"Your face is absurd," I responded.

Good one.

"Wonders never do cease," one guard remarked. "A braug, a halfling, and a wellick traveling the road together."

"Oh, I think I know this one," Curr said.

"He's not with us," I said, nodding toward Garvis.

REMINDER:

Your Party includes: Daniil Kendrick, Curr the Braug, AND Garvis Wittleman.

Hold on. His last name is Wittleman?

I've told you that twice now. But how ever will you make fun of him without everyone knowing you're a crazy person talking to an invisible friend you call Screenie?

"Friend" is stretching it.

Someday, you'll miss me.

"Nonsense," the halfling said, managing to wrap his arm halfway around me. "We go back many years. Closest of companions, we are."

I shook my head and groaned.

"This way," Curr instructed. "We will procure sustenance and rest. Tomorrow, we visit the Fighters Guild. Then, adventure." He slapped his hands together and rubbed them.

"I don't know if I can handle any more adventure," I grumbled. Though the rest sounded good. As had been very much established, I wasn't really a fighter. But with Curr at my side and me... encouraging him, it could work.

NEW OBJECTIVE:
Visit the Fighters Guild Hall in daytime.

REWARD:
A chance at membership in the Fighters Guild.

Could it be your ever-elusive purpose, oh, Danny the Instrumentless Bard?

It's something. Better than being a beggar.

You're right. That is probably all you could accomplish here on your own.

"Move drink to the top of that list and you got yourself a deal," Garvis proclaimed, and his walk turned to a little skip.

Where Nahal had spaced-out buildings lining a few streets, Balahazia was like a primitive Chicago. Nothing like the skyscrapers, of course, but it was gray stone structure after gray stone structure for as far as the eye could see. It reminded me of what it might've looked like if Charles Dickens wrote about the Vikings.

Candles flickered in windows, blowing heavily from the light wind. And smoke puffed up from rooftops here and there, vanishing into the hazy, moonlit sky. It felt like Christmas. A light fog settled everywhere, which also kind of had me expecting Jack the Ripper to pop out. On second thought, the candles were creepy too.

Curr turned us down an inclined road, at the end of which were the docks. Silhouettes of ships of all sizes swayed in the wind. Some had lanterns lit, others looked like the ghosts of pirate galleons.

And yeah, the fishy stank got more pungent. And that nice, fancy entry boulevard gave way to more shoddy construction and bunched-up shacks made of wood. Seemed like any big city in America. Show off the best of what you've got before digressing into the crap-holes. Unsavory figures huddled in alleyways. Beggars. Dirty children. Probably much worse.

We followed our braug tour guide toward a larger building with a single pointed spire rising from the front door like a giant middle finger to this whole world. A sign beside it read: **SEA MANTIS INN & DRINK**.

What is a sea mantis?

Like whales, their blubber is used to make oil. But where the sea

mantis really excels is that their parts can be ground down and used in a variety of medicinal—

Enough. Every time something in this world seems great, you just make it depressing.

I didn't make the world how it is.

I've never asked. You keep saying world. We are in Pyruun—but that's a nation, right? Does this world even have a name?

I thought you'd never ask. You are on Mars.

Huh? My Mars? That can't be right... Mars is red.

Ah, you are too smart for me. No fooling you. Brilliant mind that you are.

This world goes by many names to many people. In Pyruun, it is most commonly referred to as Aethonia.

So, is this like... another planet in my universe?

Maybe. Maybe not.

Screenie...

I don't have that answer for you. Does it matter? Would it change a thing?

I guess it wouldn't. There were no rocket ships to take me home anyway. But I had one more question I'd been afraid to ask. This felt like as good a time as any since Screenie was actually giving honest, thoughtful responses. Here goes nothing...

Can I go back home?

Do you know that's the first time you asked me that?

I've thought about it a lot.

But you've never asked directly.

Can I go back or not?

That, Danny, is the right question.

Well!

I didn't say I had the answer. But it's worth thinking about, isn't it? What is home... What is life? Oh gods, you have me going down a rabbit hole.

Then we were back to silence from the most obnoxious whatever-it-was I'd ever met. Not that I was surprised. It couldn't have been as simple as asking. Or clicking my heels together three times. Nothing in my life had ever come easy.

"You are going to love this place, Danny," Curr said, snapping me out of it.

"Oh yeah?"

"Yes. That is what I just said."

I hitched Dalia the Donkey to a post outside, where she immediately started lapping up clumps of snow.

"Whoever owns that thing is gonna be pissed you're leaving her out in the cold," Garvis said.

I froze, and not because of the weather. "Whoever—Garvis, what did you do?"

He bowed with a flourish. "As I've said, I am a liberator." He moved between us, pulling open the door to the Sea Mantis Inn &

Drink. "Onward to warmth and a hearty meal."

"You stole a donkey?" I asked as Garvis disappeared into the building.

"Do not look so surprised," Curr said. "It is too late for that. Come."

I followed Curr into the tavern where warmth hit me like a welcome friend.

It was Garvis's turn to take a deep breath this time.

"Ah. I smell ripe pockets." He chuckled, then rubbed his hands together quickly just as Curr had done. "How about you, Dan-Dan-the-Singer-Man?"

"We don't need to do small talk," I grumbled. "And don't call me that."

"See, it hurts to be called names," Curr said.

I gave a glance toward the donkey. I imagined it shivering out in the cold. "I can't believe you stole that poor thing."

"You will see me far more undignified than this, my newest friend," Garvis proclaimed. "Just wait until you see me *really* drunk."

We took a few more steps in, being totally ignored by the current clientele.

"We need a room," Curr said to me.

"And I've got a date with the bar," Garvis said. "Gentleman, it has been a yigging pleasure. If you'd like to go for round two, Danny, find me in a few hours. I'll be the one surrounded by wenches."

He patted us both on the sides, and I covered my pockets. Then he strode off toward the bar with the confidence of a six-foot-tall celebrity.

Garvis has left your Party.

Thank God.

Dalia is still technically with you, but, I don't think Garvis would hesitate to take her again. Ownership is such a fickle thing...

"I will go speak with the proprietor," Curr said, and left me standing by the door, by myself, in my flamboyant cloak.

It's an **elegant** *cloak.*

Uh-huh.

I hoped fisherman weren't as bad as bikers. Now that I was alone, a few eyed me curiously, but none said anything. This was a city, after all. I was sure they were used to seeing weirder.

Unlike the inn back in Nahal, this one was fairly clean and didn't smell like the tail end of a camel. Just that same fishiness. Despite being stone outside, the interior was decorated like the cabin of a boat. Plank floor, big beams on the ceiling. A big, painted sign above the bar read "Gold Grin's Grog" and had the depiction of a pirate holding a golden goblet. I spotted a stage across the room, though no one currently performed on it. The skeleton of a sea creature hung over it, with one long horn on the skull.

That's a sea mantis. Believe it or not, that thing protruding from its skull, often referred to as a horn, is actually a tooth.

You're right. I don't believe that.

The male patrons all had thick beards, and many wore leather aprons. They looked like, well, fisherman from days gone by. The women were rugged and hardy too. This was a working class town if I'd ever seen one.

"Only one room available," Curr said, returning with a mug of ale for himself and some kind of sandwich. "I hope you are not opposed to sleeping on the floor. I take up a lot of space." My mouth fell open. Then he laughed and said, "I kid. Truly, Danny, for a bard, your sense of humor is dreadful. There were two rooms. You must go pay for yours."

"Forgive me for not being in a playful mood after the day we've had," I said. "If you've forgotten, I lost yet another lute."

"Probably best for the whole world."

"You know, if I had a guitar, you'd think different."

"Guitar? What is a guitar?"

I sighed. "Never mind."

"You are an odd one."

"Yeah, I know," I agreed.

We walked together back to the bar in silence. Garvis already had a few of the drunker locals eating out of the palms of his hands with jokes. Gain their trust, then slip a hand into their pockets.

You could join him. Put those quick fingers to use.

Petty Thief! Petty Thief! Petty Thief!

Never again.

Screenie highlighted the tavern keeper.

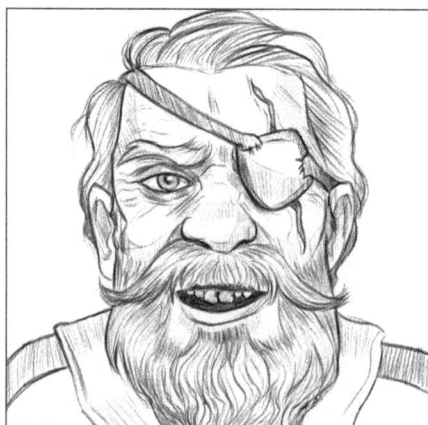

NAME: *Milmoth Shicklemor*
RACE: *Wellick (male)*
OCCUPATION: *Tavern Owner*

SPECIAL ABILITIES: *Master brewer, spirits distiller, facial hair to die for.*
WEAPON: *Harpoons aplenty.*

The tavern keeper looked a lot like Rarmir back in Nahal. Like they could have been brothers, maybe even twins. This one had the same belly, but an even bushier beard and he wore an eyepatch.

"What'll it be, boy?" he asked me as he cleaned a mug. "Ye look frozen as a witch's tit in a brass bra."

"A room," I said.

"Aye, the big one told me. Drink? Food? Hot bath?" A glass shattered somewhere in the tavern. "Ey, mind the deck, ye whelps!"

My eyes lit up. "A hot bath?" I asked in total disbelief.

Beside me, I could *feel* Curr's face scrunching up. I looked up at him. He shook his head. "Who would pay for water? It is everywhere."

"We get all manner of folk here," the tavern keeper said. "Not all are so used to the cold as ye and I." He held the mug up to his eye, as if looking through a spyglass to make sure it was clean. Maybe that was why the place didn't look as rough as Rarmir's. Mr. Shicklemor seemed to have a keen attention to detail.

"How much is a bath?" I asked.

He looked me up and down. "Five gold."

"For water!" Curr spit out a sip of ale. "Tarton's Tusk, now I have lost a mouthful as well."

"That plus a room is ten," the tavern keeper said. "Complimentary drink and meal with the double purchase."

I looked at Curr. "You enjoy yourself. I'm going to buy a bath," I decided. "I have money."

Curr took a chunk out of his meal. "Enjoy your water."

With that, I paid the man, too exhausted to even try my hand at haggling.

-10gp.

289

You have 17gp remaining.

Mr. Shicklemor nodded to one of his employees and I followed a dark-haired beauty to a room on the lower level containing a long metal tub set over a roaring fire. Pots of water were already being heated.

Several buxom babes dressed in peasant clothes, strings untied and exposing their ample cleavage, worked the pots. One after another, they poured their contents into the bathtub until it was full and piping hot. The flames caused crazy shadows to dance along the walls, but here in the Sea Mantis Inn & Drink, I felt safe for the first time in days.

"Can I help ye with yer clothes?" one of the women asked. She would've been too old for my father, had he still been alive... and here with me in Aethonia.

I almost said, "No, but she can," glancing at the pretty girl who kept giving me bedroom eyes every time she passed. But, alas, I could remove my own clothing. I had no idea what kinds of crazy diseases might exist here and the last thing I needed was to be on the road while crotch rot consumed my nethers.

They finished filling the basin and exited the room. I was already beginning to strip when the pretty one brought me an ale and a sandwich like the one Curr had.

"Enjoy, sir," she said, batting her eyelashes bashfully. Her eyes cast themselves menacingly over my bare chest.

Words got stuck in my mouth as she left, tittering. Once I was *sure* the room was empty, I finished undressing and slipped into the bath. The hot water immediately got to work easing all my aching muscles.

"I could get used to this," I said to nobody.

Screenie answered anyway.

You probably shouldn't.
You've basically spent all your money.

Worth it.

I took a bite of the sandwich. Not bad! A little oceany, but whatever the sauce was helped it go down. And the ale was rich and cold —a perfect contrast to the warm water. No Curr to say ridiculous things. Or killer monsters.

I leaned back, sliding down beneath the water where I closed my eyes. Holding my breath, I hoped that when I surfaced, I'd be back in Willistown.

I wasn't that lucky.

"Oh well," I said, water cascading off my face and stubble. How did people shave around here?

I noticed pieces of paper sticking out of the pile of my belongings, and realized it was the sheet music I'd stolen from Garvis back in Nahal. Wow. I'd almost forgotten my plans. Finally, some quiet time without wraiths or korkens about, I gave it a read.

"The Halfling's Gambit," it was called. I wasn't the best at reading notes, but the words were there. Something about a great and heroic halfling named Samis who stole the egg of a dragon and used it to save his hometown from slavers.

It didn't sound true at all.

Would you like to add "The Halfling's Gambit" (7 inst. 5 sin.) to your Catalog of Songs?

It's kind of ridiculous, isn't it?

I think it's quite entertaining. Maybe people will actually like it.

Sure, why not.

I didn't feel anything, but suddenly, looking at the notes, I could get a sense of what the melody was supposed to be. I even started humming a tune I didn't realize I knew until it was coming out of me. All the awful things about this world, there were some perks.

Then the door swung open, and I accidentally dropped the sheet music into the bath.

"You are not done yet?" Curr asked, chomping on his sandwich. "How long does it take to wash a body as underdeveloped as yours?"

The bath felt so good, not even Curr's accidental insults could ruin it for me.

"A proper bath is about more than getting clean," I told him, plucking the sopping wet sheets out of the water. The ink, already soaked and smeared, was illegible now.

He then looked away shyly. "Oh. Uh. You are not... uh..."

I realized what he meant and quickly sat up. "No! No, Curr. That's not what I meant. Geez, man."

"Good. That is good." He took a seat on a wooden chair near the fire and went back to eating.

"Can I... help you with something?" I asked, nonchalantly covering my man parts.

Before he had a chance to respond, Garvis strode in. "You know, these dried apricots are amazing."

My fists clenched. "Do you two not understand what a closed door means?"

Garvis turned, peering over his shoulder. "It was open."

"It *wasn't* before Curr made himself at home."

"It is quite warm and cozy in here with the fire," Garvis said.

I banged on the side of the tub. "Yes, and I paid good money for this!"

"I told you it was foolish to pay for water," Curr agreed.

"So then, why are you in here?" I asked.

"Oh, right," Curr said. "Well, we were drinking out there, and the owner complained about his entertainment not arriving. Something about their ship sinking in transit. But Garvis here mentioned that you were a bard!"

"He... what?" I said, nearly rising out of the bath.

"He said you were a bard. The owner wants you to play something for the crowd." Curr smiled wide. "Is that not grand? Somebody actually wants *you* to play. I warned him your skills are lacking, but with no alternative, he would not let it rest."

"And I told him the big man was joking," Garvis said. "And that you're renowned in the capital." He stood right beside Curr, eyes shining like the sun as if waiting for a "thank you."

My own eyes roved back and forth between the two of them. I spoke in short, truncated words, "What. The hell. Is wrong. With you?"

Garvis's smile faded. "He and his wife—lovely couple—agreed to compensate us for our rooms and your little bath if you played a few songs. Can't be that bad, right?"

"In case you forgot, I don't have a lute." I lowered myself back into the bath, confident that would settle that.

"Aye, well, Mr. Shicklemor has one you can borrow," Curr said.

"Of course he does," I groaned. "Look, I really need a break."

Curr stood and approached the bath. "Danny, I have not asked much of you in all the time we have known each other."

"We just met!"

"Yes, and now is your chance to earn your keep."

"I saved your life!"

"And I yours. In that, we are even," he said. "This is your moment to improve yourself! Are you going to entertain this crowd or not?"

I bit back what I really wanted to say. I just couldn't win. "Can I at least finish my bath first?"

Garvis and Curr looked at each other.

"I do not know," Curr said. "The crowd is growing quickly as more ships come in for the night and they will get restless without entertainment."

"Wait a second," I said. I pointed at Garvis. "What about him?"

"What about me?" Garvis demanded.

"Talk about earning his keep. Why doesn't he entertain the crowd?"

"I don't play the lute. I'm just a 'clown with a pipe,' remember?"

"That's convenient. Then why is he even getting a room out of this?" I addressed Curr. "He has nothing to do with our Party!"

"What party?" Curr stroked his beard, as if pondering that.

That term is just for us, sweet Daniil.

"Hey, I talked you up and got you the gig," Garvis countered. "Which was mighty kind of me after you took gold right out of my pockets. I dare say, I'm the most generous, forgiving halfling alive."

"You're something all right." I closed my eyes and gritted my teeth. "Ugh, fine, I'll do it. Just... you two get out so I can change in private."

NEW OBJECTIVE:
Entertain the Sea Mantis Inn & Drink.

REWARD:
One night's free room & board for your Party + a troublesome halfling.

"This is favorable news!" Curr exclaimed.

Your relationship with Curr has improved.

You're a swell guy.

"Don't take long," Garvis added. "Another bard might arrive and take your place."

"Yeah, yeah. Just both of you go already."

Curr and Garvis left the room. What in the world would I do out there? Without Phlegm's lute, I sucked.

Sucking is a mindset, Danny. You're a bard. Embrace it!

There's no MILFs out there. These are hardcore fishermen. I'm going to get eaten alive.

Play that halfling song! I bet they'll love it.

It sucks.

And, as you've so astutely mentioned, so do you. Two negatives can only make a positive.

Simple math. Maybe he was right. I didn't have to bring the house down. I just needed to earn some laughs. Fishing seemed like hard work, based on my *zero* experience. I've always been what you might call a land lubber.

What the hell? I'd give it a try. Who knew, maybe the biggest patron would punch me and send me right back home where I belonged...

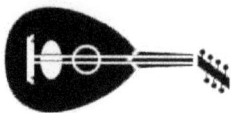

29

Mr. Shicklemor's lute, sitting on a stand on stage, was hardly more than a tissue box and shoestrings. I'd seen more impressive instruments from third world countries on YouTube. The confidence I'd felt moments earlier was evaporating into despair.

My heart couldn't take yet another failure.

The heart will go on...

Are you making Celine Dion references now?

Who's that?

I never know when you're kidding.

The mark of a true comedian. You could learn a thing or two. Perhaps open with a joke? Warm up the crowd.

A joke. Right. *I* was the joke.

As I made my way through the crowd, intent upon the stage, I couldn't help but wonder what the hell I was thinking. I should've just run. Away from here. Away from Curr. Away from everything. I'd either die out in the wilderness, squeezed to death by cuddle bears, or I'd find my way back to the real world and out of this mess.

But alas—alas? I was even starting to think like these fools. *However*—there, that's better—I didn't have the strength or courage to even do that.

Garvis sat at the front of the stage, downing ales like cream soda and still telling jokes, making strangers laugh. His little intrusion upon my relaxation apparently hadn't done much to disrupt his night like it had mine. He looked positively glowing with joy. I hated the little twerp, though I'd give anything for an ounce of his charisma.

Your Charisma is 14 (+10) (+1 again while you're wearing that silly pink cloak).

The hag's elixir is still in effect. Who knows, you might slay.

Still in effect? What does that mean?

Silence. Of course.
I turned my attention to the lute...

What the hell am I doing? This is suicide.

It'll be fiiiine.

You're just playing a song you've never played to a crowd of people you've never met in a place you've never been on an instrument you've never held. What could go wrong?

How's about this...

+3 Bonus to Courage for the Duration of the show.

This is the real stuff—Courage from within and not from the bottom of a bottle. There's nothing like proving to yourself that you can face ridicule head-on with your chin held high!

Thanks. I guess.

Just be funny.

Pretend they're all your favorite housewives.

As I stepped up to the stage, Mr. Shicklemor was there to greet me.

"Welcome! Ye should'a told me ye was a travelin' minstrel!" he said, clapping me on the shoulder. "Folks like ye are heroes 'round these parts. And to think, the Capital's Blue-Eyed Bard, here in my establishment!"

"Blue-Eyed Bard?" I glanced over at Garvis. He smirked.

I don't even have blue eyes.

NEW REWARD ADDED:
The Title Blue-Eyed Bard and... blue eyes!

What? I don't want blue eyes.

I thought you've always wanted to increase your physical attractiveness?

There's nothing that gets the ladies going like a pair of baby blues.

How would you know? You're a screen.

A blue screen.

Blue eyes... Can you really do that?

I'm up for the challenge. Are you?

Mr. Shicklemor grabbed me by the shoulders and stared into my not-blue-eyes. If he noticed, he didn't say anything. "Now, get on up there and show these bumpkins what capital music sounds like!"

I nodded, both to the tavern owner and to Screenie.

The stage was solid, unlike the rickety plywood at the Heart-Shaped Box. Reminded me of some of the gigs I used to play.

I stared at the lute like it was my enemy. "Don't make me look foolish," I whispered to it.

I took a deep breath and picked it up—it was like a toy compared to my previous glorious instrument. The one that had been stolen from me. I shook my head. What was it about this place that made everyone a thief?

Opportunity creates the thief.

I suppose that was the truth, wasn't it? I saw Garvis's sheet music just lying there unattended. Opportunity...

You'd better say something. Everyone's staring.

I was so stuck in my head that I hadn't realized the entire place had gone silent. Peering over my shoulder, I saw there were a hundred people—or at least it felt like it—just gawking at me. And in that moment, I realized this was the largest crowd I'd ever performed for. My Friday night audience usually numbered in the tens and most of those were regulars.

I took another breath, then looped the strap...

There was no strap. Fantastic.

I sighed and stepped forward, holding the lute aloft under my elbow.

You can do this, Danny. Time to turn on the charm.

I opened my mouth, ready to welcome everyone to the show of their lives, when someone shouted from the back of the room, "Nice cloak, Capital boy!"

Of course, it elicited a laugh from the peanut gallery.

My face went red—a putrid contrast to the bright pink cloak, I was sure.

Start with a joke, huh? Okay. I can be quick on my feet.

I cleared my throat. "I'm sorry. Does the color offend you?"

"You look like a Nancy!" he heckled.

"Funny, I quite like it," I said. "Reminds me of your mother's undercarriage."

There was a collective hush, and I worried I'd read this grimy crowd wrong, but an instant later, every person in the place was roaring. When it settled down, the same guy, laughing too, said, "Alright, alright. Play something, then!"

I pressed my fingers to the strings. "I call this one 'Becoming A-*tuned* with Oneself'."

That got some pity laughs as I checked the lute's pitch, not entirely sure I understood it yet. It wasn't a guitar; the strings weren't supposed to be tuned like a guitar... but I did it anyway. E A D G B E from thickest to thinnest. I made the extra strings that were coupled match. Spinning the peg on the last one, the highest string, it popped and jangled around.

Someone snickered. I flicked my eyes up. It was Garvis.

Would you like to play the Lute?

I'd like *to play a guitar.*

Can't help you there.

AN UNEXPECTED HERO

Would you like to play the Lute?

Okay. Let's do it. "Halfling's Gamble."

Good. Carry on, then.

"Ladies and gentlemen of the Sea Mantis," I said, putting on my best entertainer's voice. I felt more like the DJ at a Sweet Sixteen than anything. "Are you ready to rock?"

A few clapped. Others cheered. Curr mouthed the word rock, obviously wondering why I was bringing up rocks at a time like this. Then I Pete Townshended that bitch. Windmill, baby. My arm swung around, striking the strings three times. That gained a few more people's notice.

I've got this.

That's the spirit!

I imagined Trish in the crowd. The problem was, in my head, she now had silver hair and liked arrow-torture. And tight, tight leather. Didn't matter. I had a job to do, and I was as ready to go as I ever would be.

"Alright, everyone. Clap like this." I started a steady beat and the whole room joined in.

A feeling of immediate warmth and alertness came over me, seeping up my arms from my fingers and then deeper into my chest and up into my head, clearing out any and all thoughts. I strummed the first chord of "The Halfling's Gamble" and began to sing. The melody rose within me, following the chord progression.

There once was a halfling, brave was he
Rose only as tall as a wellick's knee
He was fiercely cunning, and handsome too
It was time for him to play

"What the hell is this shog?" I heard from the front row. Garvis again. I ignored him.

He entered the game with a pile of gold
His opponent was a beast of old
Though he looked at the dragon with a killer's eye
It was time for him to slay

"You've gotta be yigging kidding me," Garvis said. He stood now, though he got lost behind the taller wellicks who had made their way to the front. He looked pissed. Cheeks red, fists clenched. I'd seen that look in him before.

The rest of the tavern, however, was enraptured by the tune.

You have gained +1 in Instrument Playing.

Your Instrument Playing is now 18 (+10).

You have gained +1 in Singing.

Your Singing is now 16 (+10).

Sing it, Danny!

This was no game of luck or chance
This was a goddamn battle it was time to dance
Samis the halfling stood his ground
Like a statue made of clay

"It's Garvis, you shog-gobbling prick!"

So, he told that dragon to put them up
He would take him down with his fisticuffs
No weapon needed, not even a blade
Two entered, one would stay

"You rotten, thieving son of a bitch!" Garvis shouted as he leaped onto the stage.

I was so surprised that I staggered backward. Some of the crowd moved to stop him, but it was too late. He ducked under one man's grab and shouldered me in the knee...

I told you he had a vicious knee-strike.

"That's my song!" he yelled as he punched me. "That's my yigging song, you bastard!"

"Hey! Stop!" I shouted. I was wrapped up in my cloak, unable to protect myself.

Then I saw Shicklemor behind Garvis and felt the halfling being pulled off of me. He kicked and wiggled like a wee little man, but he sure as hell didn't fight like one. This was a man possessed.

I stood slowly, dizzy. Blood trickled from my right eye, and I looked down to see that the lute had been completely destroyed... again.

People booed, though I wasn't sure if it was because of my song or because I'd been cut short. I chose to think it was the latter.

"You dirty, no good, thievin' thief!" Garvis shouted at me.

"Takes one to know one!" I yelled back. Not my best comeback.

Got that right.

"Oi! Both of ye calm down or ye'll be sleeping on the streets," Shicklemor said.

Stepping up and relieving the tavern owner of his halfling burden, Curr now stood there with a frenzied Garvis in his grip.

"Put me down," Garvis seethed. "Let me at him!"

"Don't ye start again," Shicklemor warned.

"C'mon," Curr said to Garvis. "Out we go."

He gave me a pitiful look as he carried Garvis outside, the halfling once again shouting curses I didn't understand.

Shicklemor stepped up on stage, grabbed the broken lute, and held it up for the room to see. "My sincerest sorrys, but the Sea Mantis won't be having no more entertainment this evening."

More boos rose.

Shicklemor held up a hand. "Next round's on the house!"

At that, everyone cheered. Everyone but me.

OBJECTIVE FAILED:
Entertain the Sea Mantis Inn & Drink.

Not your fault, but that's life, kid. You can't win them all. No blue eyes for you.

The tavern owner turned to me. I must've looked like a soggy bag of groceries. He shook his head disappointingly. "These folks didn't come for a brawl."

"You think I did?" I asked, rubbing my cheek.

"Aye, now listen," he said. "I made ye a promise and I be a man of me word. Ye and the braug can stay the night, but that halfling... he ain't allowed. I want ye getting on in the morn, that clear?"

He handed me back the ten gold I'd paid for my bath and room.

+10gp.

You now have 27gp.

Wow, what a nice guy. Rewarding failure, like an enabling parent raising a horribly behaved toddler. Society is down the tubes...

I nodded to Shicklemor. "Thank you, sir. I'm terribly sorry about all this. I don't know what got into him."

"A whole barrel of ale by the look of it," he said, his scowl turning to a gap-toothed smile. "I'll have one of me girls check yer wounds, but ye don't look too bad."

"Right." I rubbed my neck. "Thanks."

"I'll send her up. Yer room's third door on the right."

"Thanks again," I said and started toward the stairs.

He grumbled about his shite luck tonight.

My boot hit the first step when I heard him shouting after me, "She's just there for tending wounds, bard. Don't get no other ideas!"

I turned, gave a small smile and a nod, and continued upstairs. I passed two doors and stood before mine.

What a disaster.

Of epic proportions.

I didn't think he'd recognize the song.

You didn't? He wrote it.

Well, I didn't know that! I just figured it was something he was working on.

It was about him.

Huh? The song said Samis.

Actually, it said Garvis. Halflings aren't the best writers... small hands and all.

I swore.

See, the G looked a bit like an S, and the m was really an r and a v, just smooshed and sloppy.

For the first time, I felt bad for the halfling. I'd just belted out his secret work of art to a crowded bar. I remembered writing a song for a girlfriend once. She pretended to like it, but I saw her snicker. Worst. Night. Ever. Maybe there was more to Garvis than a drunken thief.

Why didn't you tell me what it was earlier?

I thought you knew.

Do me a favor, Screenie. Stop assuming anything. Just tell me the things I need to know!

My teeth clenched. I heard footsteps behind me and turned to find the beautiful dark-haired bath attendant striding toward me, looking radiant.

"You poor thing," she said. "Let's get in there and I'll make you feel better."

Maybe things were looking up.

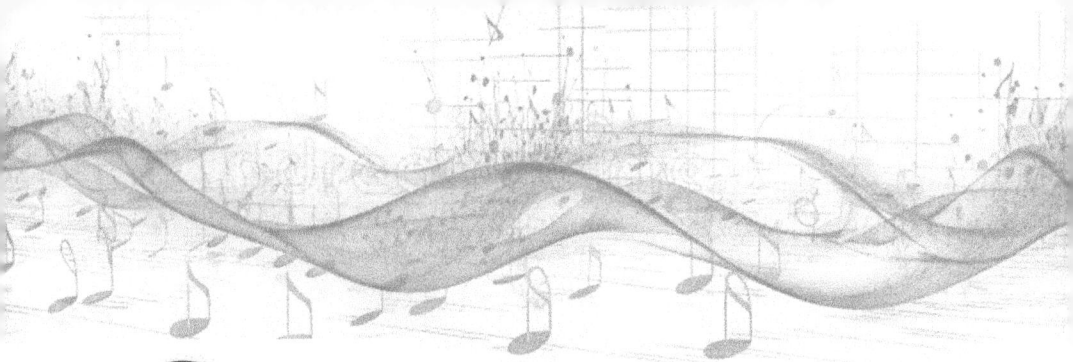

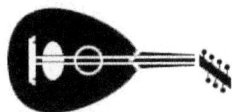

30

NAME: *Shalimar Shicklemor*
RACE: *Wellick (female)*
OCCUPATION: *Tavern Wench*
SPECIAL ABILITIES: *Housekeeping, bath prepping, great with her hands... for wound dressing.*
WEAPON: *A sharp tongue.*

The beautiful woman followed me into my room. I was so distracted by her, I barely read Screenie's highlight. I'd be lying if I said I didn't limp a little to make my injuries appear worse than they were. I even winced as I shut the door behind us.

When I said this woman was gorgeous, I might have undersold. She had raven-black hair that she wore in a long braid, falling past her shoulder blades. Eyes the color of Spanish moss glinted in the light of the candle she carried. She was dressed in the same pale red-almost-pink blouse and tan skirt she'd worn when attending to my bath, and four earrings adorned her lobes, two on each ear.

The craziest part to me was that she wore no makeup. None. Still, she would be able to stand side by side with any model or actress from my world and put them to shame.

Move over Scarlett Johansson.

Steady there, soldier.

I was so entranced by her beauty, I hadn't even realized how immaculate the room was. Having been given it for free, I'd have expected it to be a dump, or even worse, a cupboard in the cellar. Instead, it was nicer than my own apartment back in Willistown. Simple, yet elegant.

It then dawned on me that everything in this world would still be handmade. The dresser and matching armoire were carved out of what appeared to be solid wood. Brass hinges peeked out just to the side of the wardrobe doors, and hardware, shaped to look like anchors, embellished already intricately carved drawers.

"Sit down, over here," the woman said in a voice like silken honey. She pointed to a rocking chair beside a small one-person table, both made of wood that matched everything else.

I did as she asked. I would've done anything she asked, crazy otherworld STDs be damned.

"Thank you for this," I said, wincing again.

Maybe you're going a bit too far. They were little fists.

He's strong for his size!

"I'm Shalimar," she said, interrupting my internal argument.

"Danny." I extended a hand for her to shake, but she was already applying cold towels to my eye and wiping away the blood. Hopefully, she didn't notice when I let it drop to my lap unshaken.

She knelt before me, the picture of perfection. Her blouse was loosely tied, and I had to concentrate to keep from staring into the chasm of her cleavage. I swallowed hard. My mouth was so dry.

Your thirst level is through the roof... and I don't only mean your throat. Get a hold of yourself! Mr. Shicklemor warned you...

"I hear you're something of a big deal in the capital," Shalimar said, slowly dipping two fingers into some kind of salve and stirring it as she looked up at me with those sensual eyes.

"Oh, yes," I answered, swallowing again. "The biggest."

At that, she stopped stirring and batted her eyelashes. "Is that so?"

Breathe, Danny.

"Huge," I said.

She smiled, placing one hand on my thigh. Then her smile faded slightly. "Bigger than Fabian Saravia?"

I was so caught off guard by the question. Were we still talking about our... you knows... or did she really mean fame? I thought we were flirting. Was I that dense?

Yep.

"Who?" I asked.

"Who?" she repeated. "Seriously? Fabian 'Feel Good' Saravia? Only the most talented bard in all Pyruun and beyond!"

Feel Good?

"He was supposed to be here tonight, you know?" she continued. "Apparently, he and his baritone lutist, Mathias "Dreamboat" Dinniman both died in a horrific shipwreck. Two of the world's most beloved musicians, gone." Her demeanor changed in an instant. "Instead, we got stuck with you."

I was stunned. "Stuck with me? I'm the Blue-Eyed Bard."

"You don't even have blue eyes."

This was taking a turn I hadn't expected.

She stopped tending my wounds and leaned back on her heels. "What was that song? Who sings about a halfling? No one gives two shites about halflings and their fruitless exploits. Was that truly the best you had?"

"I—me? What?"

What do I even say?

You made this bed... Lying only hurts yourself.

You picked that song!

"No, not my best," I said to her. "It was just my opener."

Sure. More lying will fix it.

"Well, it was a shite opener," she said. "Normally, one would hope to impress with their first song. And let me tell you, Danny the Bard, you are not very impressive."

Ouch.

I puffed out my chest. I had to make some attempt at dignity. "It's unfortunate you feel that way. I'm sorry."

"Sure are, getting the shite beat out of you by a half-man. You should be ashamed."

Wow. The turn had continued for the worst.

"You're fine," she said, tapping my face and then rising. "There anything else I can do for you, oh great bard?"

I cleared my throat.

"Didn't think so." She started to leave.

"Wait." I said, standing and taking a step after her.

Miraculously, she stopped and so did I.

What are you doing?

"Let me sing something else for you," I said, sitting back down.

WHAT ARE YOU DOING?

I've got this. Trust me. And quit typing in all caps. It makes it look like you're yelling.

I AM YELLING.

"Another song, oh? Last I checked, our lute was in pieces on the stage."

"That's what the people in this world don't get. A real bard needs no instrument."

Oh, there's a real bard here now?

You know, you could try being encouraging.

I could also try rubbing fire on my crotch, but not everything is for everyone.

You don't even have a crotch.

Ouch.

"All right, then," Shalimar said, edging back toward me. "Out with it."

Deep breaths. It was working.

Probably a bad time to tell you your breath smells like ass.

"Please, take a seat," I said, ignoring Screenie and knowing the only other seat was the bed.

Hey, you can't fault a guy for trying.

Yes, I can and I am. Women hate you.

Like I said. I've got this.

Famous last words. Would you like me to assign your belongings to anyone? A loved one, a relative, Garvis?

Shut it. She doesn't even know me.

"So, you gonna sing or what?" she asked, seated on the very edge of the bed.

I stood, smoothed out my pants, and cleared my throat again.

"I hope it's not a song about a dwarf next," she remarked.

I may have been in a new world, but all along, I'd been playing by their rules. My brain was chockfull of nonsense that would blow their minds. What song could I sing? Something that didn't require backing music and was catchier than anything Pyruun seemed to have.

Then, one popped into my head.

"Now this is a story all about how..."

I finished the theme song to Will Smith's beloved '90s sitcom, and she just stared at me. After what felt like a lifetime, me standing there like an idiot, she said, "You're a prince?"

Now, that was not the interpretation I was going for. It was just an extremely memorable song that I knew every lyric to because it spent many years stuck in my head. But I wouldn't complain.

Stupidly, I nodded at her.

You have gained +1 in Singing.

Your Singing is now 17 (+10).

I don't know how, but you impressed her.

Newly bolstered by Screenie's pronouncement, I replied, "The freshest."

"Wow." She smiled warmly and patted the bed beside her. "I've never been in the same room with a prince."

"Most, uh, haven't." I slowly walked toward her, worried I still might've been misreading the situation again.

As I neared the bed, she grabbed my cloak and tugged me closer.

"Oh," she said. "Is that what this odd cloak is? Is that your kingdom's color?"

"Sure, yeah. Exactly."

"Where exactly is this Kingdom of Bel-Air?"

Screenie?

There's no such place in this world.

I know that!

Surely, someone of your immense cunning can weasel your way out of this.

"It's uh—in the east across a sea," I decided.

She pulled away. "Is it part of Assiri? We are at war with them."

"Further east," I said. Then added, "Southeast, actually," hoping again that wasn't in the middle of an ocean or something. Wait, great idea. "It's in an island chain called the... uh... Orient."

Who knew? I didn't belong in this world, so maybe I did have some incredible origin. Or if this was the longest dream ever, I might be able to manifest it. Bel-Air would be an incredible place. Full of laughter, and music.

This is sad to watch.

"Wow. That's fascinating," Shalimar said. "I've never heard of Bel-Air. And you're its prince?"

I put my hand over hers. "The one and only."

Go hard or go home, right?

You certainly are that.

Her brow furrowed. "And your kingdom... Bel-Air... its banner is pink?"

"Here in Pyruun, is pink seen as a rather... feminine color?" I asked.

She nodded.

"Well, we think of it more as 'salmon' than pink. You see, the dye comes from the blood of a very rare creature in Bel-Air."

Her eyes lit up. "What's it called?"

Yeah, Danny. What's it called?

"It's very powerful."

You're stalling.

"Oh!" she said, pulling me even closer. My crotch touched her knee. "Is it dangerous?"

"Yes, very." I let her guide me to sit beside her.

We are on the bed. Together.

"What's it called?" she asked again.

"Yes, right. It's called a... a..."

"Yeah?" She leaned in, eying me with childlike excitement. Her lips were so close, I could feel her breath on mine. It smelled of rosemary and pure sex.

"A... snuffleupagus," I blurted.

She pulled back slightly.

Shit. Shit. Shit.

"That's an odd name," she said.

"But so frightful."

"Sounds like it." She drew back in.

"It means 'man-eater' in my native tongue."

"Is that so?" She pecked me softly on the lips.

Thank you, Hall & Oates.

You have gained +1 in Speechcraft

Your Speechcraft is now 15 (+11).

Who needs the truth when you can be a filthy liar?

"Perhaps I could examine your native tongue more closely, my prince?" Shalimar asked.

Is this really happening? Maybe being a bard here isn't the worst.

How funny would it be if you woke up back in your world right now?

Don't you dare!

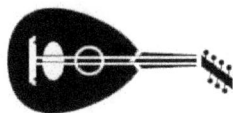

31

I fell asleep, exhausted, and finally for a good reason. Shalimar and I had a wonderful evening of... connection. It was odd to meet someone in this world who felt normal and didn't want to kill me. Problem was, it was all founded on a lie.

For that, I felt a tremendous weight of guilt.

I vowed to come clean with her the moment we woke in the morning.

However, I didn't wake in the morning. I was jolted to consciousness in the middle of the night by what sounded like music, then a clamor. My heart raced, thumping around in my chest like Dave Grohl playing a solo.

I opened my eyes first, actually worried I might find my Pearl Jam poster looming over me—a sign the dream that was Aethonia had come to an end.

Wow, that's a surreal thought.

This place grows on you like genital warts.

By the way, you might have genital warts.

I don't have genital warts.

My eyeballs roamed and I was pleased to find myself still in my room at the Sea Mantis Inn & Drink. Wood ceiling, wood walls, and the complete dark of night. It still amazed me just *how* dark it got around here with the absence of city lights to pollute the skies.

I still hadn't fully moved, but I continued to hear a shuffling coming from the foot of my bed. Shalimar still lay next to me, breathing gently. So, it wasn't her sneaking out.

"You lost it," came a voice like crinkling tin foil.

I shot up. "Who's there?"

The room was suddenly awash with a sickly green glow.

The voice cleared and came out more like it had the first time I'd heard it. "You foolish boy. You lost it."

Phlegm the Hag stood before me, clutching something in her hand. It was the leg of lamb, mostly bone. How old was that thing now? A week? More? And that didn't include however long Fargus had possessed it before chucking it at me back in Nahal.

Not her again. Run, Danny. Runnn!

"How did you get in here?" I demanded.

"I am everywhere, and nowhere!"

"What does that even mean?" Then I felt a light breeze and noticed the window open, letting in all the cold air. I sighed. "Isn't climbing a little dangerous for someone of your... age?"

"I am a physical specimen." She hissed, showing those piranha teeth.

"Calm down. Geez." I sat up, trying to locate my weapon out of the corner of my eye. It lay across the room in a heap of clothes. "What do you want? I finally had a good night here."

"What do I want?" She moved closer, her pungent stench making me cringe. "What do *I* want?"

I sat still, waiting for her theatrics to be complete.

It's funny, after nearly dying in the fight with the korkens, Phlegm didn't seem so scary. She looked sad, pathetic, filthy, and powerless other than the light pulsating from her ragged form.

"You lost your lute," she said. "You must get it back."

I made believe I was considering her words for a few seconds, then said, "No."

"Excuse me?"

"You heard me. No." I stood, remembered I was naked, and pulled a blanket from the bed to wrap around my bottom half. Shalimar made a noise and rolled, but thankfully, didn't wake.

Fighting the stench, I approached Phlegm. I wanted her to know her scare tactics weren't going to work on me anymore. "You gave me a curse."

"Liar!" she spat. "I gave you your heart's desire."

"You made me a target. But you knew that already, didn't you? You knew those women—the Sisters of Whatever—would come after me for that lute. They were probably after you and you found a way to ditch the lute on me."

"I knew no such thing. It was *your* bargain, not mine."

She was right about that, I supposed.

"You wanted a lute," she continued. "I gave you a lute. And now, you've lost it. You must get it back."

"Yeah, you've said that. The thing is, I'm doing just fine without it. I had the crowd downstairs in the palm of my hands if not for a meddling, halfwit halfling."

"Oh, you think so, do you?" She cackled.

I peered over my shoulder at Shalimar, still asleep like an angel.

"Yeah, I do," I decided.

Phlegm's cackle turned into a cough. Then she took a bite of the rotten lamb. I could swear I saw little maggots raining off it and onto the floor.

Gross.

They are full of healthy protein.

"Have you forgotten about the second?" Phlegm asked, no little amount of malice in her tone. That gave me pause and she knew it. "Do you believe my elixir had no effect? Where do you think you would be without it?"

"I..."

"You would be a stupid, bumbling fool! You'd have never even left Nahal. Your braug friend would've crushed you like an ant without me!"

How much _had_ that vial affected me?

Until now, I hadn't considered it much. I was still having trouble wrapping my head around things being measured in numerical values. If I had ten points in something, was that like a ten on the scale of how hot Shalimar was—she was a solid nine by the way—or a ten out of a hundred like when taking a school test? I would have to ask Screenie to elaborate.

Nevertheless, I wasn't going to break.

"I don't believe you," I said, but it was all bluster. Phlegm had me rattled.

"Fine, then let me remove its power and see if that pretty little thing doesn't slit your throat the moment she awakes."

She began moving toward Shalimar.

"Okay, wait." I held up my hand. I wanted to slap her with it.

If you do, I'll give you some of those sugary Unarmed Combat Skill points. They're finger-licking good.

Phlegm smiled, and with all the creases and crust, it looked like it pained her to do so. "Good choice." She backed away. "You must find the lute."

"Well, where is it?"

"Do you not understand the meaning of 'find'?"

"I'm sorry," I said without sincerity. "You expect me to find a tiny little instrument in this huge world I know nothing about? The Sisters took it. If you don't know where it is, you might as well just take away my little boons now."

"I am but a frail, old woman," she said, mockery in her voice.

"Frail? You scaled a building to get in here. Can't you just... I don't know, poof it into another well?"

"Magic has rules not even one such as I can break," she admitted.

"So that's it, then," I said with finality. I spread my arms. "Take it away. Curr will stand by me. He thinks I'm a fighter and maybe he's right."

LMAO.

"Don't be hasty!" Phlegm said sharply. "The lute is bound to you. Calls to you. It is your purpose, your desssstiny. Attune your ear and you will find it! In the meantime, enjoy your little..." She waggled her fingers toward Shalimar, "...play-thing." She said that last word like she was referring to an inanimate object lying there.

What a mean old hag.

I glanced over my shoulder at Shalimar. When I turned back, it was almost pitch-dark again—the sickly green light gone. Phlegm no longer stood at the foot of the bed.

Great.

I turned to head back to bed. Then I heard a grunt from the window. Phlegm struggled in desperation to lower herself through the opening.

"Need some help?" I asked with exasperation evident in my tone.

"Physical... specimen," she repeated before falling through the opening. I rushed over and looked down, but she was nowhere in sight.

"Crazy old bitch," I said, shaking my head. Then I climbed back into bed where Shalimar lightly stirred.

Maybe this world wasn't so bad after all.

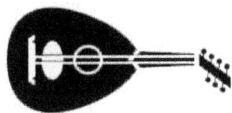

32

The rest of the night passed without a wink of sleep, and this time, not for good reasons. Shalimar didn't even stir. How she slept through a hag appearing in our room was mind-boggling.

As seemed to be the prevailing question of late, had Phlegm been a dream?

No. The lingering smell made sure I didn't make that mistake. What was I ever thinking, dealing with her? Maybe if I ignored her and the lute... she'd go away. Like a T-Rex.

That's if you stand still, dumbass. Not ignore.

It's the principle.

Worse, I couldn't stop hearing music. I guess the people downstairs found another entertainer. It had an aggressive chorus, like a fantasy version of *Eye of the Tiger* played by lute. Really catchy, and the chorus got stuck in my head on repeat.

It wasn't until the bright morning sun finally crept in through the window that Shalimar rolled over. Her hair was a bird's nest, but she still looked like a goddess.

"Good morning, my prince," she said with a sly smile. Her fingernail traced the hair on my chin line. It sent a shiver down my spine in the best way.

How could I have let this happen? I had to tell her the truth. I was a good guy.

Where do you come up with this stuff?

I was! I mean, I am.

"Uh, hey, you know, I have something I need to tell you."

Shalimar gave me a kiss and rolled out of bed. I found myself momentarily distracted by her nakedness. "I'm late for work. Daddy's gonna be furious."

My throat went dry. I could barely get the word out. "Daddy?"

Uh-oh.

You didn't warn me?

What are you blind?!

I literally gave you her name, occupation, special skills—

"Come downstairs when you're dressed, and you can have all the time you want once I'm done getting the place ready for the early crowd." She was already pulling on her blouse and heading for the door. "I can't wait to tell Daddy I'm gonna be a princess!" She let out a *squee* and rushed into the hallway, leaving me alone.

"Princess?" I said to no one. Except it wasn't to no one, since apparently, I was never alone.

She believes that your copulations mean you are to be wed.

Yeah, no crap. I guess there's no such thing as a one-night stand here.

Then I realized something horrific.

Did you enjoy last night's show, you pervert?

I would've appreciated if it lasted a little longer. I'm sure Shalimar felt the same.

You're a horrible friend.

So, we are friends!

I sighed.

What am I supposed to do, Screenie?

Marry the girl and take her back to the Far Southern Island Kingdom of Bel-Air in the Orient.

Very funny. Any real advice?

Run like hell.

I'm not exactly the "wham-bam-thank-you-ma'am" type. She's nice. And hot.

Sure, you're just the "lie-to-a-girl-about-being-royalty-so-she'll-sleep-with-you" type. Let me also remind you that she had no interest at all in you until that lie.

Okay, this is unhelpful. I'll just tell her. I'll come clean, and then we'll be on our way.

Sure. She seems to be the forgiving kind. Also, did I mention that her father is a master whale hunter with a bigger harpoon than you could ever dream of?

I swore over and over as I got dressed and gathered my belongings. Slowly, I headed downstairs, keeping an eye open for Mr. Shicklemor. That tune was still stuck in my head, and I couldn't help but descend on tempo.

When I reached the bottom step, I heard a shout.

"Ye shite bastard!" Shicklemor stalked toward me from behind his bar holding some sort of giant crossbow with a very sharp harpoon sticking out of the front.

NEW OBJECTIVE:
Escape Shalimar's dad before he stabs you with something much pointier than what you stabbed his daughter with.

REWARD:
Your life. A New Title.

"Mr. Shicklemor," I said, putting the staircase balusters between us. "I can explain."

"I told ye to get no ideas!" He aimed the weapon at me. Shalimar came running to my aid and grasped my arm.

"Daddy, stop it!" she shouted.

By now, the whole tavern stared at us, at least, what was left of the crowd from the night before. At the back of the room, I spotted Curr, though he wasn't moving like my life was in danger. He just strolled over while chomping on some sort of bread and sipping on ale, wearing a smile the size of Texas.

"Ye give me one good reason I shouldn't paint that there wall with yer insides?" Mr. Shicklemor said.

I was about to comment on the mess it would be to clean up when Shalimar chimed in.

"Because you'll start a damned war, Daddy!"

Mr. Shicklemor lowered his weapon, though only a hair.

"What are ye saying, girl?" he said. "Speak plain. How would killing this two-bit hack, Nancy-boy, worthless bard start a war?"

Well, that was just hurtful.

Tell me about it.

"Daddy, you can't talk about him like that!"

"And why the hell not?"

"Because he's a prince…"

Shit.

"…and I love him…"

Say what?

I told you you'd find love!

I choked on nothing. Curr hacked a wild laugh. Everyone stared at everyone else in confusion and dismay.

Curr got ahold of himself enough to march toward us. "Danny is not a prince," he said through laughter.

"He sure is," Shalimar said, splaying her fingers across my chest possessively. "The Freshest Prince of Bel-Air. He'll be king soon too. Won't you, baby?"

Baby?

Lucy, you got some splainin' to do.

My cheeks went hot as I tried to pull away. "Well, you see. Remember when I said I had something to tell you..."

"What?" she asked. My face must have revealed the whole truth because Shalimar's jaw dropped when she put it together without me needing to say another word. She slapped me hard on the cheek.

You have gained +1 in Unarmed Combat.

Your Unarmed Combat is now 5.

What? Why?

You took that like a champ. She's stronger than she looks!

That was true.

"I'm gonna murder ye," Mr. Shicklemor growled.

"I said I can explain!" My last word swelled up at the end as Curr grabbed hold of my cloak and yanked me down the stairs toward him.

"Time to go!" he said.

Being dragged through a tavern wasn't a simple task. I slammed my shin on chairs and banged my hip on tables. I tripped and nearly fell once or twice, but Curr caught me, and we kept running until the door flung open and Curr slammed it shut.

I heard a thud and turned to see the tip of a harpoon poking through the thick wood. We made it around the corner, and I fell against the wall, gasping for air. Before long, I found myself breathing to the rhythm of that damned song.

OBJECTIVE COMPLETED:
You have escaped the wrath of a father scorned. Live to breathe another day.

NEW TITLE UNLOCKED:
Womanizer. I'm not so sure you should be proud of this one, but, alas. +3 to Charisma when talking to women one-on-one.

"That was great fun," Curr said. "I have never been roused to the morning in such a manner. Now, let me understand. You told her you are a prince?"

I groaned. "Yes, Curr."

"But you are not a prince."

"No, Curr."

He scratched his beard. "That was not smart. Though, I suppose when you are as minuscule as you are, it is not easy to gain the interest of women."

My face fell into my palm. Leave it to Curr to say something so damned truthful. I wasn't a catch. Here or on Earth. Just a singing fool.

"So," Curr said, propping me up like nothing crazy had just happened. "Shall we visit the Fighters Guild Hall? They are fine folk, Danny. I think you will really like them. And then, we can depart on a quest together. Think of all the gold we can acquire!"

Oh, I was thinking about something, alright. Thinking that I probably shouldn't have exhausted myself, stayed up all night, got beaten up by a halfling, threatened by a hag, and run for my life... all before trying to prove I was a fighter.

That was when I heard a door slam open and Mr. Shicklemor shouting around the corner.

But screw it. Off to find a purpose.

"Yeah. Let's go..."

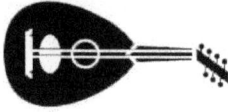

33

Downtown Balahazia was a place where I could see myself getting comfortable. Big, spacious buildings. Finely carved stone. Women dressed in fancy dresses and men in... what I guess passed for fancy here. Fur-lined tunics with fur hats, fur boots—fur, fur, fur.

I guess it made sense for a place that was always cold.

The main square had everything, all situated around a grand fountain with a statue of a knight holding the head of a man that looked oddly like Curr, big beard and all. Despite the frigidity, water poured out of the neck wound and filled the basin where it bubbled.

The whole scene was so grim, I couldn't help but stop and stare. Children passed this glorification of decapitation every day.

That's no mere knight. That's King Shirtaloon's Great-Great-Grandcousin, King Noret, Bringer of Floods.

Floods? That doesn't sound kingly.

Not water, Danny. Blood. He led the defense of Balahazia during the March of the Braugs. From behind these walls, they massacred

the enemy so overwhelmingly that it's said blood ran down the cliffs to the sea.

You really should brush up on your Pyruunian history.

Oh yeah? Who conquered China in the 1200s? Yeah, didn't think so.

Curr stopped as well, his eyes locking on what I now knew to be a headless braug.

"I'm sorry, Curr."

"Why?" he asked, befuddled. "It was the end of a glorious campaign by our united chieftains. Many fell and joined Tarton in battle."

"But you lost."

"We are not like bitter elves, wishing the past were different. Braugs fought, we lost, and so it is right that the victors should rule. Tarton's Tusk, if only I could have been there."

"And died?"

"Gloriously." He smiled longingly as he tapped the rim of the fountain. "One day."

Then he continued walking.

I got delayed a few seconds. The level of detail in the poor head's eyes. It sent a shiver up my spine. Taverns, shops, and churches or temples rose up on all sides around us. Straight down the square was a guarded road, a gray stone wall, and a gate, leading off to some sort of mansion nestled in natural rock.

The Citadel of Magistrate Zogarth, cousin to the King. Do not get on his bad side. He has a bountiful collection of bows and specialty arrows, and a proclivity for... hangings.

That was when I noticed shirtless bodies swung from the walls like the suits hung my music career out to dry, all with one word carved into their chests:

THIEF

I shuddered.

I won't get on any of his sides.

Just when I was beginning to find an enjoyable place, this world had to go and remind me that this was not the civilized land I was from, where thieves often went free and only the most evil and horrible lawbreakers were thrown in jail for life: potheads and whoremongers.

Garvis had better watch himself here.

Also, the Mongols. The Mongols conquered your China in the 1200s.

You looked that up. I don't know how. But you did.

"What are you whistling?" Curr asked. "That song, I actually *do* enjoy."

"Huh?" Then I realized, even as I'd been thinking a conversation with Screenie, I'd been unconsciously whistling the ear worm. "Oh, that. From last night. You couldn't hear it from your room?"

"When I sleep, I do not hear things."

"Right."

Curr turned me down an avenue where a long-haired dog awaited me. It sat politely outside of a shop, as if expecting its owner. It was well-trained too. No leash in sight.

"Aww, look at you!" I said, putting on a ridiculous "talking-to-a-dog-voice." Everyone has one.

Man, talk about something I didn't know I'd missed. I loved

dogs. Never had one, though, because, well, I'm irresponsible. When I was younger, my mom got it in my head from an early age that owning a dog comes with responsibility. Even as an adult, I didn't even own a fish.

I knelt and scratched behind its ear. "Who's standing guard? *You are.*"

Curr wrenched my arm and pulled me away from the animal.

"Hey!" I objected.

"Are you insane?" he said, keeping his voice low. "Never touch a nobleman's prized beast without permission."

My mouth dropped. I glanced back at the little fellow, his big eyes practically begging me to come back and pet him some more. Then a man in a gold-embroidered tunic stepped out of the shop, whistled, and the dog promptly fell into lockstep.

"You are very lucky he did not see you, Danny."

I blew a raspberry. "Why? What would he have done? It's a dog!"

"It is my belief that he would have alerted the guards. You then would have been imprisoned or lashed or worse if he were in a bad mood. Pats are for mules, Danny. Not dogs."

"This is a backwards place."

"Dogs lick their own asses. They are backwards. Thank Tarton he did not lick you."

Huh, well... I suppose that was a point, by Curr's standards. Yet another nicety from my world that I couldn't enjoy here. After riding Garvis's stolen donkey, owning one didn't sound very fun.

Maybe I could get a bird.

"All right, we are here." Curr stopped and looked up at the Fighters Guild Hall. I didn't need the sign along the cornice to tell me that was what it was. A front porch supported by statues of impossibly muscular men sprawled out before us like the White House. Beyond it, a great set of iron doors bore the emblem of a lion inscribed in it, with words circling it.

STRIKE FIRST. STRIKE HARD. NO MERCY.

A snicker slipped through my lips.

You've gotta be kidding me.

About? Where's the joke?

THAT'S *their motto?*

Yes. It has been since Endwinbart established the first council of fighters centuries ago.

You don't recognize that saying?

Indeed. All Pyruunian folk, even me, know the Fighters Guild mantra. It's a very intimidating creed.

The absurdity of this world hit me all at once. I couldn't stop the torrent of laughter that coursed right through me and past my lips. I had to lean against one of the chiseled-man columns just to stay upright.

"What is so funny?" Curr asked. He wore a pout—a far departure from his normally smiling face. Then I realized he was sad he'd missed out on an inside joke.

I wiped the tears from my eyes. Calming down a bit, I came face-to-face with the statue's tiny, naked penis, where my head had been resting next to. I coughed and cleared my throat, then pointed up at the logo. "That's really the Fighters Guild creed?"

"Of course. It is about facing your enemies head on," he said. "Not sneaking around like little halfling thieves or hooded Sisters. Like how you stood your ground in Nahal against Garvis!"

"I..." More laughs came out. I just couldn't help it.

"Danny, I do not understand what you are laughing about," Curr said. "And you should not lean on the effigy of Ludos."

"Yes, pray tell. What is so funny?" The new voice came from behind me.

I whipped around. Leaning against the other side of the column, a black man puffed on a pipe.

I said man, but more like a mountain—a mixture of Wesley Snipes and The Rock. He oozed cool. Short, squared hair and an anvil for a jaw line. A big, jagged scar went over one eye, leaving it stark white and most likely blind, then curled up around the top of his head. Had this guy survived an axe to the skull? An all-black tunic covered his torso, ending with a red sash that almost looked like a karate belt but had gold edging.

Screenie highlighted him in blue.

NAME: Arkadios
OCCUPATION: Grand Master

RACE: *Wellick (male)*
SPECIAL ABILITIES: *Paralyzing Strike, Fists of Fury, Dagger Feet.*
WEAPONS: *His hands are registered as lethal weapons.*

"Grandmaster Arkadios!" Curr exclaimed. He lumbered closer and bowed at the waist. A ridiculous sight to be sure.

"You have returned, Brother Curr." Arkadios offered only a nod to Curr's full bow. "Is this wellick with you?"

Curr slapped me on the back. "He is, indeed! Danny is searching for a purpose in life, and I believe he could prove to be a worthy guild member after a great deal of training."

Arkadios put his pipe away and approached me. He wasn't as big as Curr, but his muscles had muscles. And his one dark eye scoured me like I was fresh meat at market. He lifted my pink cloak and let it fall unceremoniously. Grabbing my chin, he turned it side to side. Then, he blew in my eye, causing me to flinch.

"Jumpy," he said.

I stayed quiet, though inside, I was exploding.

Of course, I was jumpy. Who wouldn't be if someone did that to them?

Curr wouldn't have shied away.

Arkadios flicked one of my biceps.

"Scrawny." He looked to Curr. "I remember when a young braug stumbled through my doors, tired of shedding blood for a king he didn't know in a war he didn't understand. You vouch for this man?"

"I do," Curr said without hesitation. That made me feel good. "He defeated a wraith and saved my soul. And he aided in a battle with three wild korken. He nearly died, but—"

"A master is forged by his scars," Arkadios finished for him. "Yes. Indeed, they are." His eye returned to scrutinizing me. "Let him be tested, then, to see if he carries the ability to stand amongst our ranks."

Arkadios walked by, hands folded behind his back.

OBJECTIVE UPDATED:
Pass the Fighters Guild entry test.

It's finals week, baby. But I don't think this exam will be multiple choice...

"There's a test?" I whispered to Curr.

"Of course," Curr said. "Recruits cannot be useless. People all around the land hire guild members to help with situations requiring warriors. What use would a weakling be?"

I swallowed.

Yeah, Danny. Show him what weaklings can do!

"You will be fine!" Curr assured. "Every fighter must start somewhere. I did not wrestle my first boarbear until I was three, for example."

"Three?"

Oh, but you said braugs can live hundreds of years. Is three like our thirty?

No. Three is like your three.

Who was this killing prodigy I was traveling with?

"Come," Arkadios instructed.

I looked to Curr, who followed without hesitation. As always, I did my best to keep up.

CURRENT LOCATION:

The Fighters Guild Hall of Balahazia.

The oldest branch of the guild, home to Endwinbart VonHolfensteimeranni, the first council, and the current residence of Grand Master Arkadios—and they are damn proud of it. Be on your best behavior.

The main hall was lined with more beefy stone columns and iron-grated fire pits. Rooms branched off it, within which people trained in plain gray tunics. Instructors led them in one series of moves or another.

One fighter looked half-man, half-bull.

What was that called, a minotaur? Centaur?

He roared, then broke a solid chunk of stone with his head.

Another was scaly—a Komodo dragon on two legs.

"Sweep the leg!" someone shouted.

The lizard-person obeyed, whipping their tail around, taking their opponent down. As I lost sight of them, I watched their tail close around the man's throat in a wicked choke.

"So long as they are within the walls of a Guild Hall, our members continuously work to improve their martial skills," Arkadios stated without looking back. "From recruits to masters, one never stops learning The Way of Iron."

"The Way of Iron?" I asked.

"The style instructed by Grand Master Arkadios in the Balahazia Chapter," Curr said.

"So each city learns differently?" I asked.

"The Way of Iron was passed down to me by my master," Arkadios said. "We train with all weapons, as to master only one is to limit oneself. Not all of us are blessed to be born so physically impressive as Curr."

"Tell me about it," I groaned.

"Which reminds me," Arkadios said. "It has been some time, Curr. Have you found work in another order?"

"Nothing official. I have not left you, Master. An opportunity arose to slaughter a gaggle of trolls raiding townsfolk and claim their sizable stash."

"And I bet you bent them over good, didn't you?" Arkadios asked.

Curr's face went red.

"Good," Arkadios said.

Bent them over?

Don't ask.

"One should always challenge oneself," Arkadios added.

He didn't turn around, but why did I feel like that was directed at me?

Hmm, let's see: Job as a crappy bar performer. No career. No 401K. Wouldn't even get a dog. You seem allergic to challenges.

I had a decent career! Besides, I'm sorry, who said "yes" to making the journey to Balahazia?

You're right. You are so brave, Mr. Challenge.

Arkadios stopped before another thick iron door with the absurd motto of the guild inscribed above. Torches on either side made the whole door glimmer like it was on fire.

"I seemed to have forgotten a pivotal plot point." He stared at me. "What did you find so funny outside?"

"Oh, nothing, I—"

Curr cut me off. "Danny found some humor in the Guild's creed. I did not understand it, but he has a very strange sense of humor. I am still not used to it."

"*You're* not used to *mine*?" I whisper-shouted.

Arkadios harrumphed. "Let us see how humorous you find it when put to the test."

"No, no, you misunderstand. I only meant—"

Ignoring me, he pushed the door open, and the loud groan shut me up. Inside was a perfectly rectangular room. Support columns started at the perimeter and rose diagonally toward the center so that the entire central area was left open—a plain, black stone arena, outlined with gold. Exactly above it, the roof was cut out to reveal the gray, wintery sky.

Weapons hung on racks along the wall between every column. Swords, spears, axes, shields—they all looked extremely valuable. Gold and ivory hilts, gems encrusted along the blades—these were not practice blades. And straight ahead of us rose five empty stone seats atop a dais.

I stepped in and nearly jumped. Flanking the door were two statues of lions facing inward. I was basically in one's mouth.

"He was right," Curr said. "You are jumpy."

"Am not."

Always the master of witty comebacks.

"For many people of the world—those about whom kings and their armies care nothing for—we are all that stands between them and beast," Arkadios said as he strode across the room. "Between the noble merchant and brigands. Between breath and death. Joining our ranks is not a commitment to be taken lightly." He plopped down onto the seat in the dais's center, his single-eye gaze fixated on me.

I glanced at Curr and whispered, "Maybe this wasn't such a good idea."

He nudged me forward. "Just remember what happened with that korken, and do not do that."

"You know, I *did* kill one," I argued.

"Yes, the smallest of all."

A personal-sized gong was set next to Arkadios' chair. He gave it a ring with his fist, and the sound resonated, making my bones chatter.

"W-what does that mean?" I asked, wincing.

The answer came in the form of footsteps. Behind me, all the fighters we'd passed in training began to file in. They were organized, walking in step like a well-oiled machine. They reached the center and parted left and right to circle the arena.

There were men and women, both. Besides the minotaur and lizard-person, there were wellicks, dwarves, braugs, and other strange beings. Four who I assumed to be the instructors moved toward the chairs flanking Arkadios, all wearing the same black tunics and red belts: The lizard-person, the minotaur guy, another wellick with a mustache that would make Tom Selleck blush, and a little, fuzzy man. Too small to be either a dwarf or a halfling, he had a puff atop his head and so much facial hair that, at first, I didn't realize he had skin. He was like a mini caricature of Einstein.

"One wishes to stand amongst us, as a brother," Arkadios boomed.

"I know him," the lizard-person hissed. Judging by the voice, I think it was a she, but it was hard to understand. "He played in Sssshicklemor'ssss placccce lasssst night."

"What do you mean, played?" Arkadios asked.

"He'ssss a bard. Or wassss, before being attacked and beaten by an angry dwarf."

"Actually," Curr offered. "It was a halfling."

Someone snickered.

"Thanks," I whispered.

Curr just looked down at me and nodded in approval.

"Did you say 'bard'?" Like so many others I'd met so far, Arkadios practically spat the word. All the others looked like I'd insulted their mothers too. All around the room, members of this wannabe Cobra Kai cult muttered.

"Why do you bring a bard before us, Brother Curr?" the minotaur asked. He had a voice like an earthquake. James Earl Jones meets Samuel L. Jackson.

"Is anyone surprised?" the wellick mustache asked. "A great warrior, but a horrid judge of character. Or did anybody forget the Valhorn incident? We should've expelled him then and there. He never knows when to keep his mouth shut."

"I swear, Master Gayou, I thought he was an ally," Curr argued.

"Enough," Arkadios said. "That affair has already been spoken for. I am sure Curr has nothing but our best interests at heart. Isn't that right, Brother?"

Curr stepped forward and lowered his head. I didn't think he could look so submissive. For whatever reason, he seemed to really look up to these bullies.

"Yes. Danny here is a bard. But I do not think that is what he is meant to be, or else he would be much better. It is a blessing to all of Pyruun—no, all of Aethonia—that his instrument was lost."

"The dissssssplay he put up againsssst that dwarf—"

"Halfling," Curr said again.

"—wassss pitiful."

"He surprised me; that's all," I said in my own defense. "I thought he was my friend."

"You show the same bad judgment as your sponsor," the minotaur added.

I stuck out a finger. "Hey, leave Curr out of this. Sure, he speaks his mind no matter who it hurts, but he's a great guy who's said nothing but amazing things about this place."

The minotaur stood, hooves clomping loudly. He shook out his mane and puffed. "Lower your finger this instant."

I didn't. Because I was frozen. Curr reached out and did it for me, giving me a slight smile of thanks as he did so.

Your relationship with Curr has improved.

Standing up for your friends is new for you! You big ol' softy.

Arkadios lifted a hand, and everyone quieted. The minotaur sat back down with a huff. Then the Grand Master began. "The bard will be tested. He will be spoken for by Way of Iron." He snapped his fingers, and one of the recruits ran forward and presented me with a wooden sword.

WEAPON OBTAINED:
Wooden Training Sword.

I hefted it. The thing was lighter than my sword. Something I'd have to get used to fast.

This isn't iron.

Your skill in Identifying Objects is through the roof!

You can tell the difference between metal and wood. Soon, nothing will get past you!

"The rules are simple," Arkadios said. "You must duel a Master of your choosing. If you cannot land one blow on them in ten bouts, then you are disqualified from entry."

One out of ten. That isn't bad. I could probably just luck into that.

Your Luck isn't that high.

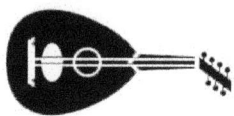

34

"Choose the Master you wish to face," Arkadios said.

Curr leaned over. "I chose Arkadios, but he wasn't Grand Master yet. I only struck him twice. Do not choose him."

"Okay, who?" I said between my teeth.

"Step aside, Brother Curr," Arkadios spoke. "This is the bard's decision—his test and his alone."

Curr did as instructed before he could offer an answer. I scanned the seats of the five masters from left to right. The minotaur was practically chomping at the bit—he was freaking huge. I'd always been afraid of snakes, lizards, frogs, anything like that. So, the hissing master was out.

That left Mr. Mustache, and the Little Einstein.

Who should I pick?

You're on your own.
Not sure why you let Curr drag you here.

You didn't tell me not to!

Some people listen. Others hear.

What the hell does that mean?

"We do not have all day," Arkadios declared.

"Him!" I blurted, pointing at the little one. I wasn't the best fighter, but at least I had reach on him. He was only as tall as a toddler. Plus, he hadn't said anything yet. In fact, he seemed totally disinterested.

The other masters looked shocked.

"Master Sansbury, the floor is yours," Arkadios instructed.

At that, Master Sansbury slid to the edge of his seat and hopped off like a kid getting out of a highchair. He moved slowly as he made his way down to the arena. He stopped across from me, holding out a hand for one of the recruits to offer him a wooden sword. It was half the size of mine and still looked too large for him.

NAME: Sansbury Smithton
RACE: Garden Gnome
OCCUPATION: Martial Arts Master
SPECIAL ABILITIES: Tornado Dash, Acrobatics, War Cry, Green
Thumb
WEAPONS: Small wooden sword

I'm sorry, he's a garden gnome?

Seeing that made me snicker, and I watched Master Sansbury's yellow eyes widen. He'd seemed disinterested, until then.

Does this amuse you?

Why not just a gnome?

There are many variations of gnome-folk in Lliagamor. Rock Gnomes, Hill Gnomes, Water Gnomes, for example. The Garden variety hail from the western valley of Haum DePaux. Known for its craftsmen and fertile lands, they are also renowned for their ability to cultivate rare and beautiful flora used by mages and alchemists world-wide. They are a peaceful people... unless threatened.

He doesn't seem peaceful!

You have unleashed the beast. Master Sansbury Smithton is a legendary martial artist, having been the only Fighters Guild Master to win the Pyruunian Tournament of Champions in the capital not once, but twice.

WHAT!

"Combatants, face me and bow," Arkadios said, and it grew

deathly quiet. That song popped back into my head, and since it had a strong chorus, I started to hum it softly to amp myself up.

The gnome bowed to Arkadios first, so I copied him. I was so caught off guard that one of my feet caught on the other as I turned and I almost fell.

Why couldn't you have fallen? I'm dying to take some Luck away.

"Face each other and bow."

At Arkadios' command, I turned back to Master Sansbury and bowed. I wasn't exactly sure how, with his hair-covered face and small features, but he looked terrifying. Like a teeny tiny lion ready to tear into me. He brandished his sword after bowing, twirling it so fast, it became a blur, then rose to one foot and stuck it out to one side. What a stance.

"Fight!"

"Strike First. Strike Hard. No Mercy!" the crowd of recruits chanted. It was funny reading that, but hearing a bunch of warriors chant it in unison made my heart stop.

Then Master Sansbury released a war cry.

WAR CRY EFFECTS:
Your Courage is temporarily halved.

Also, you seem to have soiled yourself.

He came at me like a damn jack rabbit. I didn't think feet could move so fast. Jumping toward me, he flipped around, grunting with every move. I couldn't recognize the difference between limbs and weapons. Just a whir.

That would be his Tornado Dash.

I got my blade up and parried one strike, though it was

completely by accident. Then he landed behind me and whacked me in the side of the thigh.

"Ouch!"

It wasn't metal but would definitely leave a welt. I expected Master Sansbury to keep coming at me; instead, he returned to his side of the marked arena.

"Point, Sansbury!" Arkadios roared.

The observers cheered.

"Fighters, reset," Arkadios ordered. It would've been nice if anyone told me the rules. I limped back to my place, and by the time I got there, we were at it again.

Round two, he got me.

Round three, again.

Round four, I dodged and got a really mean swing in, but he evaded it and stabbed me in the gut.

You have gained +1 in Melee Weapon Combat.

Your Melee Weapon Combat is now 12.

I really thought you had that one!

Rounds five, six, seven, eight, and nine all went about the same.

Round ten left me trudging to my spot, huffing for air, my arms burning from wielding the sword so long.

Curr looked at me, nodding with encouragement. I had no idea how this guy stayed so optimistic all the time.

"Watch his hips, not his sword," he advised. "Hips do not lie."

Did he seriously just say that to me?

"Use your reach," Curr added with a nod.

I nodded back. Then I stopped, took a deep breath, and wiped the sweat from my brow. I wasn't sure I even wanted to be in the

Fighters Guild, minus wanting a chance to earn real money in a respectable way.

And impressing Curr. Face it, he's your man-crush.

Shut up!

Turning to face my opponent, Master Sansbury hadn't even broken a sweat. He didn't brandish his sword this time, just faced me, hulking in a way I didn't think a gnome could.

He's overconfident. Your Stamina may be drained, and your Health is far from 100% even though the swords are wood, but you've got this.

Danny, Danny, he's our man, if he can't do it... anybody else could.

Here I thought you were finally being nice.

Being nice is for pussies. You're a warrior. Now go get him, Tiger!

I stared, focusing on the little garden gnome as I hummed the song again. I think hearing me do that only made him angrier.

"No song can help you here, bard," the minotaur said.

"Fight!" Arkadios barked for the last time.

I decided to take the Fighters Guild creed as a lesson. I tired of being crapped on in this world. A bard, really? No guitars? I screamed like a lunatic and charged at Master Sansbury as fast as I could.

Strike First. No more defense.

It seemed to surprise him.

I swung like a wild man, using my longer arms to inch him back. It was unorthodox, but I prided myself on doing things the wrong way. No college for me. No degree or steady job. Nothing tying me down. That was *my* advantage.

You keep telling yourself that...

Master Sansbury flipped through the air like Yoda, dodging everything. I kept coming with every ounce of energy I had left.

Clunk!

Other than a lucky parry, for the first time in all our bouts, my wooden sword struck his. So close. Since I was larger and swinging downward, the force of it knocked him back to the floor and he rolled. I stared at my weapon, in shock. He did the same with his.

You have gained another +1 in Melee Weapon Combat.

Your Melee Weapon Combat is now 13.

Player One, Finish him!

"Finish him!" the minotaur growled at the same time.

The gnome's face scrunched with rage.

This was the point in a movie where I would buckle down, put my mean face on, and finally land a strike.

But this wasn't a movie.

He came at me. I quickly gathered my bearings and slashed. I thought I had him, but he flipped, tucked his legs, and landed on the flat of my sword mid-swing. He pushed off like a diving board, and next thing I knew, his foot caught me right in the forehead and knocked me off my feet.

My head spun. I saw stars. I thought I heard a few guild members muttering about how that was an illegal blow. But nobody seemed to care.

Then I heard music. The lute...

Someone came into focus above me. It was my beautiful, deadly Sister of Alyndis. She and the others sat in a camp within what looked like old ruins. The stone was snow white, and the remaining columns all looked impossibly delicate. In my vision, I could even see intricate carvings all around. They looked like letters in Chinese, or some other pictographic style alphabet.

My eyes locked onto my silver-haired crush directly above me like she was cradling me in her arms. Like I was her woodwind instrument, and she was ready to blow.

You wish.

I blinked and that vision of beauty was replaced by Curr standing over me back in the guild hall.

"Get up, Danny," he said as he dragged me to my feet. I staggered a bit. Curr spun me around to face the seated masters and held me upright. Master Sansbury quietly returned to his seat, climbed up, and sat.

OBJECTIVE FAILED:
Pass the Fighters Guild entry test.

Would you like to try again?

I can do that?

You can ask. I wouldn't.

"As we suspected, the bard is clearly not worthy of our brother-hood," Arkadios said, emphasizing Screenie's point.

"That was pathetic," the minotaur remarked.

"Truly dissssssmal."

I was too breathless to answer. Too lost in the vision of the Sisterhood.

"He came very close," Curr spoke up. "Technically, his blade connected with Master Sansbury's feet. I believe with another chance, perhaps against a different master, he could prove—"

"Please, stop, Brother Curr," Arkadios cut him off. "You are embarrassing yourself. Just because you found purpose here does not mean all others will. Let him sing and dance his enemies to death. The Way of Iron is ours."

Curr's shoulders sank. He looked utterly defeated, more so than I felt and I'd just gone ten rounds with a whirling dervish.

"I am sorry, but I must disagree." Curr shook his head. "He is puny, but he *is* a fighter."

"Curr!" Arkadios slammed his fist on the chair. "Enough. The others already think you unreliable and that is why you remain the rank of a novice. Prone to distractions. A liability. Do not prove them correct. This bard will never be a fighter. Leave now and come back when you are rid of him. Perhaps, in time, there will be a suitable job for you."

"In what time?" Curr asked.

"It is clear, you need a break."

"You can guard the sheep at my farm if you want." The minotaur laughed. Master Gayou, the wellick, held back a snicker.

I stepped forward. "You know what? Curr is too good for all of you. I trust him with my life."

"Then you will die quickly." The minotaur laughed even harder, until Arkadios shot him a look that silenced him. The Grand Master simply looked disappointed.

"C'mon, Curr," I said, dropping my wooden sword with a clatter. "Thanks for trying, but these definitely aren't my people."

WEAPON LOST:
Wooden Training Sword

He bit his lip as he faced his masters and bowed. Then we took the long, sullen walk of shame out of the room, down the hall, and toward the exit. Curr was barely even lifting his feet. I hated disappointing him.

When we reached the door, something held it closed. I looked down and saw a small hand—Master Sansbury's small hand.

"This life is not for everyone," he said. Unlike his war cry, his voice was warm and comforting, like a grandpa sitting on a bench, telling his grandchildren a story. "But you kept getting up, and that takes courage. You will find your purpose, bard. Perhaps you already have."

With that, he wobbled away.

The light outside was dim from clouds above. The gloomy atmosphere wouldn't help Curr feel any better. As the door shut, he stared back at the Guild's creed, as if he'd somehow failed it. I watched him, and now that we were outside, the song repeating in my head felt louder again.

"Don't worry about those fools," I said over the racket.

He didn't respond for a long time. I thought maybe he hadn't heard me. When he finally spoke up, it sounded nothing like his normally jovial self.

"Those 'fools' helped raise me to be who I am today. Without them, I would be puny and useless, like you."

I ignored the jab. I could tell he was rattled. "You're a bigger man than any of them could ever hope to be."

He stared at me. For a brief instant, I thought I saw a tear forming in his eye.

Then, he waved a hand in front of my face. I slapped it away.

"What are you doing?" I asked.

"I feared you might have gone blind," he said. "Did you not see Master Brink? He is much bigger than me." Then almost to himself, he said, "Though he is a minotaur. Perhaps it is unfair to compare."

"I'm not *blind*."

"Good," Curr said. "Though that would have helped explain how you fought so terribly back there."

"Yeah, thanks for reminding me."

"No, really. I do not think I have ever witnessed such a one-sided duel in all my life. Did you not hear my instructions?"

I exhaled through my teeth—but he wasn't done.

"It was as if Master Sansbury was fighting an invalid. He just kept going and you could not—"

"Enough!" I shouted. It must've shocked him into silence. "I'm not blind, nor am I stupid. I've been telling you I'm not a fighter. Never have been. Never will be. What I meant, is that you are *better* than them."

He shook his head emphatically. "Not true. All of them would—"

"As a *person*," I said before he rambled again. "You are kind-*ish*, honorable, and you care about more than just fighting."

He scratched his beard. "That is true. I love to eat."

"Yeah," I said, drawing the word out. "And... other things too, right?"

"Hmm." Curr pressed his thumb to his chin as if in deep thought. "No, I really think that is all. Fighting and eating. Oh! and ale. I love ale. Darks, lights, warm, cold. I enjoy it all."

I love lamp.

You're not making this any easier.

Man, Curr was difficult to encourage. "Well, you will be back to fighting and drinking in no time. That, I promise."

"And eating?"

"And eating," I agreed.

Your relationship with Curr has improved. AGAIN!

Such warm, cozy feelings.

"And, we have accomplished another goal," he proclaimed.
"Oh?"

"It is clear that the Fighters Guild is not your purpose. Amazingly, you are much better at singing and playing songs."

"You're right. Maybe you belong in the guild, but I definitely don't." I looked down the road, toward the hazy mountains creeping over the walls. As I focused there, the song in my head got louder yet again.

How can thoughts get louder?

Wait for it.

This is going to drive me crazy.

Wait for it.

Then it hit me. "*The lute is bound to you. Calls to you. It is your purpose. Attune your ear and you will find it.*"

That was what Phlegm had said to me. I'd shrugged it off as more of her nonsense, but maybe it wasn't. The lute was magical—that was clear enough. And here I was, hearing a song played by a lute when nobody else did.

Just as the lute warned me of things, maybe it wanted me back.

Too bad it isn't a girl.

No, but it's with one.

You are incorrigible.

"And hey, if the Guild doesn't need you right now," I said to Curr, "then I know someone who could use the help of a true warrior."

His eyes lit up and his back straightened. "Who?"

"I know a guy whose lute was stolen. And he decided he wants it back. He can't pay much for your help, but he'll do everything he can to make it worth your while."

"There is somebody else you know who is in the same predicament as you?"

I smirked and shook my head. "I'm talking about myself, Curr. We tried this, but I think all I'm meant to be is a bard in the end. I'll stick to singing about brave men like you."

His eyes got even wider. "Is there a song about me?"

"Not yet," I said. "First, I need my lute. And to do that, we need something else."

"What?"

"A thief."

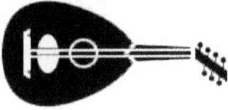

35

Curr stared at me with a dumb smile.

"Where is the last time you saw Garvis?" I asked.

"I dropped him outside of the Sea Mantis and he took his mule and left."

"You let him take Dalia back?"

You have lost your mount.

"I did not have the heart to fight him over a mule. Something had very much angered him. He would not say what."

Maybe that your petty thievery cost him the opportunity to premier his own song to the citizens of Balahazia? Or maybe it was that you sang his name wrong? Or maybe it was—

That's enough. I get it. I suck.

"Certainly, there are more talented thieves than him in Balahazia," Curr continued.

"Do you know any?"

He scratched his beard. "I do not."

"Isn't there a Thieves Guild here or something like that?" I asked, figuring if there was a Fighters Guild, maybe—

"Are you mad! In other, seedier cities, yes. Not here. Magistrate Zogarth does not approve of such behavior." Curr glared down his nose at me.

My mind strayed to the hanging men and women in front of the Magistrate's mansion.

"Come to think of it, neither do I, Danny."

"It was your idea!" I argued. "Besides, they tried to rob us first. You even admitted that. It really wasn't thieving. We're heroes, taking back what's ours. We're like Robin Hood."

"Why would we rob a hood? They are very inexpensive."

"He's a..." I sighed. "You're right. So, where is the nearest bar or tavern or whatever? I have a feeling Garvis can't go too long without drinking his weight in ale."

"Weight in ale!" Curr laughed. "He does indeed do that. Very well. If a thief is required, at least he will be inexpensive. Let us waste no more time. Come, this way."

NEW OBJECTIVE:
Find Garvis and convince him to rejoin your Party.

REWARD:
A bigger Party!

If I were him, I'd say no, you big meanie. What's a halfling gotta do to get a little respect. Ha. Get it?

Alexa, off. Did it work?

:::Shakes head:::

We took to the streets of Balahazia once more, though Curr

glanced back longingly at the Fighters Guild a few times. What a sad sack of oysters.

Now that we weren't talking, the damned music in my head refused to stop. I was beginning to think I really was going crazy or maybe I was in a coma back in the Willistown General Hospital and someone left the TV in my room on.

We passed a gems dealer and heard screaming coming from within. I could tell Curr considered stopping, but we continued on, thank God. Heroes we might be, just not for every little thing. At the next block stood a large temple with a statue out front that looked like a flying goblin wearing a mask of a bird skull, beak and all.

Glancing in—there were no doors—I could see worshippers genuflecting and heard what I could only describe as pained moaning.

"What's that?" I asked.

"The people here worship many things," Curr said. "Pyruun is very accepting of most cultures."

Screenie flashed.

As long as they don't slaughter them first.

"That is the temple of Actus, God of Small Things," Curr said.

My brow furrowed. "Small things? Like birds?" I guessed based on the statue.

"No. Small prayers. When one feels their prayers are too trivial for Ludos or the Greater Gods, they bring them before Actus."

"Huh," I said. "Is a lost lute big or small?"

Curr's face scrunched up in thought. "This truly depends. Will you die without it?"

I thought back to Phlegm's warning about her elixir and how without its properties affecting me, Curr would've likely crushed me back in Nahal.

"No," I said, unsure if it was true.

"Then your prayer would be for Actus," Curr said. "If you believe in such nonsense."

"You don't believe in the gods?"

"The only god who matters is Tarton," Curr said. "It is he who provides for my kind. Gives shelter against the cold. Makes us large and strong to survive."

"Okay... but none of these people are braugs."

He nodded. "Yes. How sad it would be to suffer through life as such a pitiful being."

I let a few moments pass, wondering if he even realized he'd insulted me. All I got for my efforts was a soft, ever-repeating looping of lute music in my ears.

"Let's go in," I said.

For some reason, I was drawn to this temple and their God of Small Things. My problems were never earth-shattering. Just little mistakes here and there, all snowballing into the mess that was my life. Maybe if there had been someone looking out for those moments, I could have been a bigwig somewhere. A rockstar or a CEO.

"In there?" Curr pointed to the temple, and just his face alone told me how silly that thought was.

"Yeah, you're allowed, right?" I asked. "Tarton won't get jealous?"

"Giants do not cower in the face of rats."

Lalair's cellar popped into my mind.

Guess I'm not a giant.

No, Danny. As Curr has often reminded you, you are puny.

"Okay, then, let's go in," I said, dismissing Screenie's insult just as I had all of Curr's.

"What of your search for the thief, Garvis?"

"He is a small thing, isn't he?"

That got a good laugh out of Curr.

Hey, you stole my joke!

Your joke was way different.

Please. They were basically the same. You are nothing but a Petty Thief.

Don't be salty that I told it better.

Curr and I climbed the steps together.

CURRENT LOCATION:
Temple of Actus, the God of Small Things.

But you already knew that. So, this message doesn't matter.

Inside, the bleating of visiting patrons to this invisible god were even louder. They echoed off the high, vaulted ceiling. Above, what looked like a giant nest hovered seemingly in midair. Within it, a dozen or more massive eggs sat.

"Those are said to be future gods," Curr told me.

Those are said to be future gods.

Thanks, Screenie.

Paintings hung everywhere, all of which used only three colors. Red, like blood, a sort of yellowish-white that looked like mucus, and a puke green. They depicted everything from a man farming to two women in the throes of passion.

"Food and sex seem like pretty big things to me," I said.

"To a god, they are as meaningless as discarded trash," Curr answered.

"So, what do the Greater Gods care about?"

"War. Death. Babies. Ale. You know, the important things."

I nodded slowly as we walked.

I was about to comment on how unnecessarily opulent this seemed until I remembered the churches and temples back on Earth. Was it all that different? I guess if you really believed in something, you spared no expense.

I spotted a group of people on their knees below the nest.

"Give me a minute, would you?" I said.

"You are going to... pray?" Curr asked, incredulous.

"Come on. Don't say it like that."

"Like what?" Curr asked. And I swear, the smallest smile played at the corners of his lips.

"Like it's the stupidest thing in the world. Don't you pray to Tarton?"

"A true god should already know your needs, should he not?"

"I don't know... maybe. But, us wellicks are pretty needy."

He chuckled. "Yes, you are."

"Just wait here, I won't take long."

Why not try it? Some power had transported me into a different world. Who was I to doubt that a god I just heard about could help out?

Curr shrugged, then sat cross-legged on the ground right where he'd stood.

I took a deep breath. My legs had trouble moving toward the nest. Each step felt like I was walking through quicksand. I *never* prayed back home. Truth be told, I didn't really believe there was a God, or if there was, I never figured he cared enough about me to listen. Being here, seeing all these people weeping and crying out—it was worth a shot.

When I finally reached the circle below the nest, I entered. I half-expected fire or lightning to rain down on me, but nothing happened. Actually, not nothing. I felt a small warmth spread through me, similar to what it felt like when I was about to play my lute.

A lute I no longer had.

Dropping to my knees, I took another sharp inhale.

"Dear Actus," I said softly, keeping one eye open and hoping no one could hear me. "I... you don't know me. Or maybe you do. I don't know. But I'm not from here and I'm not sure I'm ever going home. Shit. That sounds like a big-god problem. Not that you're not a big god. I just mean... well, you know. Anyway, I was hoping you could help me with a small thing. I have this lute—well, I don't have the lute, and that's the problem. I need it back because... I think it's part of why I'm here. It sounds really stupid, but I can hear it playing to me from somewhere. Calling..."

I stopped. Shaking my head, I added, "This is stupid."

Then a hand lay on my shoulder. I thought it would be Curr but instead found a little old lady wearing a baggy white dress and with a bundle of necklaces made from coins around her neck.

"Actus hears us all," she said. "Attune your ear and you will hear him beckoning to you."

"What did you just say?" I asked, my mouth going dry. Those were almost the same words Phlegm had spoken.

"Follow the sound of his voice and you will find what you're looking for."

I stared at her for what felt like a creepily long time before bumbling, "I-uhm. Thank you." As she started to walk away, I asked, "What's your name?"

"Follow the sound..." It was all she said before leaving the temple.

That was eerie.

Do you think she meant the lute?

363

I think she probably ate too many mushrooms.

Yeah. Maybe.

I rose and walked back to Curr.

"Did you gain insight?" he asked, grinning.

"Maybe," I said. Then I listened closer to the sound of the lute still playing quietly in my head. Follow the sound, huh? "Okay, let's go find Garvis."

Curr stood, then pointed to a pit at the end of the aisle. Everyone who had stopped praying moved to it and flicked a single coin in. Like a wishing well.

"It is supposed to only work if you cast the wealth of your soul into the pit of lost despair," Curr said. "With all the coins down there, one could buy an incredible set of armor. Actually..."

He popped up and jogged over. I struggled to keep up.

"What are you doing?" I called behind him.

When he reached the pit, a few visitors eyed him curiously as he leaned out and stared down. It was pure darkness, no railing either.

"Garvis!" Curr hollered. Only echoes answered. He glanced at me. "A perfect place for a thief, if he could survive the fall."

I leaned over a bit, but the idea of falling into an endless hole made my legs feel wobbly.

"He'd probably try." I sighed and stepped back. "Should I toss a coin?"

"It is your money, Danny."

Reaching into my pocket, I found a coin and rubbed it between my thumb and index finger. This was silly. Coins into a pit. The people who built this temple were probably down at the bottom, snickering at fools and raking in the dough. No wonder they could build such a beautiful temple for such a minor god.

"Screw it." I flicked a coin into the hole.

-1gp.

You have 26gp remaining.

I listened as it clanged off the sides, then nothing. It didn't hit the bottom or anything that I could hear.

How deep is this thing?

That's what sh—

Don't.

"All right, I've had my fun," I said to Curr.

He looked perplexed. "I will have to teach you what fun means, Danny. That was not fun."

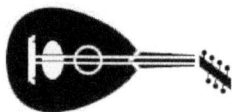

36

The streets outside the temple grew busier while we were inside. It was midday now, and everyone seemed to be leaving the market. It was an odd sight, people dragging sacks of whatever they had inside, walking beside mules attached to clamoring carts, hauling wicker baskets full of colorful fruits and grain. Somehow, it was like a glimpse into the past of even my own world.

"There is a tavern this way," Curr said. "We can start there."

We turned by a fenced-in park. The place was glorious. Flowers somehow growing in the cold. Tall grass. Old-looking trees. And inside all I could see were men and women dressed like nobles, talking, people-watching, or walking their dogs.

A dog park. Here, in a time where orcs beheaded travelers. Humans—or wellicks—really fascinating creatures. One guy, wearing a fluffy and ruffled shirt, had his dog trotting in perfect circles like they were getting ready for a dog show.

Curr led us toward some shops at the end of the road. I stopped when I noticed something glinting on the ground. Curr kept going, but I stopped and kneeled. A coin, just like the one I'd tossed—

"Unhand me!" barked the familiar voice of a red-haired halfling I knew all too well.

I glanced to our right. Down an alley on the other side of the wide avenue, three armed guards argued with Garvis.

"Curr!" I whisper-shouted, gaining his attention.

"Are your stunted legs tired already?" he asked, turning toward me.

"No." I motioned with my eyes toward the ruckus, which apparently was commonplace in a city like this because Curr didn't even notice.

"Are your eyes broken again?" he asked, leaning in and raising his thumb and forefinger as if trying to inspect them.

I grabbed his arm and forced him to look down the alley.

"We don't tolerate thievin' 'round here!" one of the guards growled.

"No, we don't," agreed another. "We hang 'em dead."

"I'm no thief!" Garvis shouted.

"Then where'd you get this necklace?" The guard held up what was clearly a woman's necklace. Gold chain, purple gemstone.

"It's mine!"

"Would look awful funny hangin' on your fat little neck. It's gonna clash with the rope."

"Like I said, it's mine and I'd appreciate it back. And my neck ain't fat. It's elegant."

"You like to wear lady things?" a guard prodded.

"What's it to you what a man does in his own time?" Garvis asked, pulling his arm in a failed attempt to get free of the guard's grip.

Just then, someone shoved past us. The newcomer was old, hunched over, and looked like he was about to keel over from running. He wore a single monocle, and an outfit with a half cape that might have seemed fancy if it wasn't all stained brown with sweat and dirt.

"Oh, thank the gods," the man huffed. "I thought I'd lost him."

"This necklace yours?" the guards asked.

"Indeed," the man said. "This speck of a man entered my shop, asked to see it, and immediately ran right through the front door with it still in hand!"

"That's a yigging lie!" Garvis protested.

"You own the gem shop?" the guard asked the man.

"He does!" Garvis said.

"Ain't askin' you," the guard said.

"Please listen!" Garvis demanded. "I tried to sell him this necklace. It belonged to my dear wife, gods rest her soul. I needed the coin and he offered me a pittance for it. When I refused to sell, he-he-he pulled a sword on me."

"Hogs wash!" the gems dealer shouted.

A guard raised his finger to the dealer and said, "You let him finish."

"But he's lying—" The word was cut off by a slap from the back of the guard's armored hand that cracked across the old man's jaw like a hammer. The shop owner raised his hand to his cheek in disbelief. He did, however, remain quiet after that.

Maybe violence does solve some problems.

"Go on," the guard said to Garvis.

"He tried to take it from me. That's why I was running."

"Is that a fact?" the guard asked.

"It most certainly is not," the old man said. He flinched when the guard turned toward him. In a softer voice, he added, "I own that necklace, fair and square."

You're about to lose your thief.

And what am I supposed to do about it?

As evidenced by a beautiful woman sleeping with you, your Charisma is pretty decent. Or was that Luck?

I considered the argument between the guards and Garvis and an idea struck me. I saw an opportunity and seized it. Maybe almost dying at the hands of monsters had changed me. Or perhaps the God of Small Things was with me in my quest to save this stupid halfling and find my lute.

When I started walking forward, Curr tried to stop me. "What are you doing?"

"Trust me." I pulled away and hurried the rest of the way toward the guards.

"Pardon me," I said, putting on my best and most arrogant Karen tone. "What is this all about?"

The guards turned to face me. "And just who the fuck are you?"

I placed a hand against my chest. "I the fuck am the crowned prince of Bel-Air, and that man you are harassing is my late sister's husband. And yes, I know he is a halfling. But it is what is inside that matters." I dramatically clutched my chest, drawing on my one time performing Shakespeare in grade school. Okay, I played a tree, but I paid attention!

The guards all looked at each another. Garvis glared up at me through squinted eyes. I gave him a small wink.

"A prince, you say?" one guard said. "Don't look like no prince."

I scoffed. "Well, I assure you I did before spending the last few days in this piss-hole you call a city. Can't even find a decent bath."

One guard must have forgotten what we were even discussing, he was so excited. "Oh, the Sea Mantis Inn and Drink has a great—"

"Shut up," another guard said, slapping his fellow in the arm with the back of his hand.

He sure likes that move.

"Look, *Your Highness*," the first guard said. "I dunno who you are or where you're from, but mind your own business."

I took a step toward the guard, feeling confidence rising from somewhere within.

Charisma, engaged.

"Are you dense?" I asked. "I just told you who I am *and* where I'm from. I am Prince Daniil of Bel-Air, here on important business. And this is my brother-in-law. And that," I pointed to the necklace, "is a royal heirloom belonging to my beloved—and late, I might remind—sister."

"It is not!" the shop owner said, losing his cool. Just as the guard had, I raised the back of my hand as if to strike. If it's good for the goose, it's good for the gander, I supposed. It had the desired effect, and I was glad I didn't have to follow through. I don't think I would've been able.

"What is your name, soldier?" I asked the chattiest of the three.

"Gattlyn."

"Well, *Gattlyn*." I spoke his name with derision. "I have an audience with your magistrate tomorrow—King Shirta..."

Shit, I forgot his name.

Better think fast.

I cleared my throat. "The king's very cousin. I could either speak very highly of you or..."

I let the threat hang.

"This is an outrage," the shop owner cried.

Gattlyn eyed me as if sizing me up.

"Any person crazy enough to wear a cloak like that must be royalty," Gattlyn said to the other guards. "You'll tell Magistrate Zogarth good things, yeah?"

"The very best," I agreed.

At that declaration, Gattlyn tossed the necklace to Garvis. The shop owner continued protesting but stopped at the threat of Gattlyn's blade.

"My name is Bordan," said the second guard eagerly.

"And I'm Sahma," said the third.

"I will speak kindly of all three of you," I promised. Then I winked and shot them double guns with my thumbs and forefingers. "I see promotion in your future."

They all gave their thanks. Then I waved them off, and they marched down the street.

You have gained +1 in Speechcraft.

Your Speechcraft is now 16 (+11).

I've gotta admit. Even I didn't see that working.

Congratulations! You will now find it easier to manipulate those who have been previously difficult for you. Don't get too excited, we're talking about the dumb ones still.

The shop owner spat curses at us until Curr stepped up, having witnessed the whole exchange.

"That was an impressive way to diffuse a potentially violent situation," he said to me. "Though, I would have preferred smashing heads."

"There's more to fighting than swords," I boasted. Yeah, it was stupid, but it sounded cool in the moment.

It didn't.

Garvis held up the necklace, letting it swing in front of his eyes, mesmerized. "Thanks."

I snatched it. "Don't you thank me."

"Give that back!"

"You couldn't help yourself for one day?" Evading his grasp, I handed the necklace back to the old man, its rightful owner. "Take it. And never trust a halfling again."

That's racist.

Curr scratched his chin. "Wait, so that necklace does not belong to Garvis?"

I rolled my eyes. "Once a thief, always a thief."

"I am disappointed."

"Oh, thank you, prince!" The shopkeep took my hand and shook it vehemently. "Thank you!"

When he disappeared around the corner, I said, "Hear that? I *am* a prince."

Keep this up and Magistrate Zogarth finds out, you'll be known as the bard formerly known as Prince.

"What you are, is getting in my way," Garvis said. He stormed up to me and got on his tippy toes to get as close to my face as he could manage.

"I think you mean, 'thanks for saving my life,'" I encouraged.

"Pftt, I had them eating out of my hand. I meant to get caught."

Curr suddenly let out a big breath. "Whew. I am glad to hear that. Here we are, looking for a thief, and I was worried you had gotten yourself caught stealing once again." He looked to me as if I didn't know what he explained next. "Thieves are not supposed to get caught."

Garvis backed down from me and brushed off his clothes. "Well, that's right. I had a deeper plan than one measly necklace."

Curr's eyes went wide. "Were you planning to escape the dungeon and rob the royal citadel?"

"Yeah, Garvis." I prodded him in the shoulder. "Was that it? Was that your plan?"

He folded his arms. "Like I'd tell you. And what the yig are you doing anyway. I don't need your help and I haven't got any more music for you to pilfer."

"You should be happy!" I said. "The people loved your song!"

"It wasn't your right." His cheeks were fully flushed. His little hands balled into tiny little fists.

He's cute when he's angry!

I took a deep, calming breath. "Look, we can point fingers all day and say who is right or wrong—or we can put the past behind us and get to work."

"I'll put you behind me, you no good shog-digger!" He came at me again. Curr stuck out his arm to bar him, but Garvis stopped on his own. "Wait, did you say work?"

Curr and I looked at each other, then down at him.

"If you're still looking," I said.

At that moment, I couldn't tell if Garvis was smiling or baring his teeth. "Well, why didn't you say so?" He began to pat imaginary dirt off my cloak. "Did I say shog-digger? I meant best friend!"

"Yeah, yeah," I said.

"Well, what is the job, then?" Garvis asked, tapping his foot.

"We're going to steal back my lute."

"*Reclaim* his lute," Curr corrected. "I cannot support stealing from innocent shopkeepers like you did." He shot a glare down at Garvis. "But it is not thieving to reacquire what was already yours. Like robbing hoods."

Curr looked at me and nodded as if he understood something.

I groaned.

"Don't matter to me which word you use," Garvis said. "What does it pay?"

Hadn't thought of that part. I guess I couldn't expect anybody to work for free. Garvis wasn't an intern thief after all.

And he's more than just Petty, like you.

How much gold do I have left?

You have 26gp remaining.

Hmmm. With my magical lute back and Curr working with me, we could earn that back in no time.

"I'll give you twenty gold pieces," I offered. Better not to lose everything.

"Twenty!" Garvis slapped his knees and started guffawing. "You must think I'm a pretty cheap date. A thief of my quality? I am offended, good sir."

"Your quality? We just saved your ass. You've been caught how many times since I met you?"

"Only the one time in Nahal," Curr said.

I glared at him. "You *actually* believed him about planning to get caught here? He obviously didn't mean to."

Curr's lips dropped. He looked wounded. "You lied?"

"That is hearsay," Garvis growled. "I *had* a plan."

"Whatever," I said. "I can do twenty-five, and that's final."

Garvis chewed on his lip as he thought for a few seconds, then shook his head. "Can't do it. That group of riders stole from him, a braug." He pointed to Curr. "That means they're deadly. Which means I could die. I quite like living."

"Your drunken self would be to differ," I muttered.

"In all forms, thank you very much! My very handsome face belongs on this head, on these shoulders. So, while I am flattered that you two would come crawling back to me, I'll take my chances with guards." He swept his hand in front of himself and offered a gracious bow.

I wanted to wring his neck.

Curr tapped me on the shoulder. I looked up, fuming. "Do you truly believe that instrument must be yours?"

In the silence after his question, I heard that damn song picking away inside my brain. "I don't feel right without it," I said, as honest an answer as I could give.

"I understand." Curr reached back and tenderly touched the grip of his axe. Then he looked down the alley at Garvis, who slowly strode away as if waiting for us to call after him. "Halfling! I will double Danny's offer."

Garvis spun on his heel and grinned ear to ear. "Make it one hundred gold, and I'm with you 'til death do us part."

"You little scumbag!" I barked. "That's more than enough for a thief who—"

"Done," Curr cut me off.

I spun to him and whispered, "Curr, you don't have to do that. We'll find someone else."

He shook his head. "The more time we take, the farther the riders may travel from us. Do not worry about it, Danny. I have plenty of coin. You have none. When you become a great bard, you will be able to pay me back."

"When?" I think a tear was building in my eye.

You know when the Grinch's heart grew three sizes? That was how I felt. As much as he may have proclaimed himself a loner, it seemed Curr really didn't want to be alone. And neither did I. Though, I did wonder how much gold he really had.

Your relationship with Curr has improved.

I think it's clear he likes you.

He really likes you. Don't let this one get away.

"You two are way too gracious," Garvis said, sliding between us. "At that price, I am delighted to help. I'll take half now, and half after we get the lute."

My fists clenched.

Curr stomped forward. "You will be paid after you help us."

"That ain't how it works. How do I know you won't just run off?"

Curr hulked over him. Even I got scared. "Are you questioning my integrity? You, a lying, honorless thief?"

Garvis swallowed the lump in his throat. He stood tall and gave Curr a gentle tap on the side of the cheek. "J-just a joke, my good braug. Of course I trust you. I'm in. Can you believe this guy, Danny? No sense of a humor."

NEW PARTY MEMBER ADDED:
Garvis Wittleman the Thief (Level 8).

OBJECTIVE COMPLETED:
You have found Garvis and invited him back to your Party!

Put out the drinks and hide your wallets, Garvis has rejoined your Party!

NEW OBJECTIVE:
Reclaim your lute

REWARD:
Less gold, but more music!

Curr calmed down, then squinted at Garvis. "You both truly need to work on your jokes." He stared down to the street as if something awaited. "Now, how will we find your lute?"

Good question.

Well, if that vision you had wasn't you daydreaming, they were near a ruin. White stone, delicate architecture. Elvish.

Well, you said elves used to rule. So those could be anywhere, right?

True... elves still consider the Masked Mountains and all its surrounding lands a haven. Despite all they've been through, they still believe the Seven Stars preside over the region. However, now, all the ones who knew Alyndis' true glory are dead. Only the memory of the Seven Stars exists.

Pleasant. Any idea where the ruins were?

They were surrounded by forest. East of here is water. North is tundra. Anywhere else, there is forest until the mountains. Am I being helpful? I feel like I am.

No more than usual.

"Danny, did your eyes break again?" Curr asked.

Garvis whistled at me.

I took a deep breath. *Attune your ears.* That seemed to be the key.

I ignored everything else in the world, then listened. The punchy soundtrack to my day continued to rattle around in my brain. I looked from right to left, and when my gaze reached the mountains to the west, the music grew faintly louder.

"You're scaring me, bard," Garvis said, yanking on my shoulder and distracting me.

"Quiet."

Before anyone else could say anything, I started off down the street. I didn't know the city, but finding the gates seemed easy. All the main avenues led to them. I guess I could have told them that the lute was calling out to me, but I didn't want to lose their help. If I were them and heard something that crazy, I'd lose faith in the mission fast.

We reached the western gate, which was far less busy than where we'd arrived in the south. Before me stretched a cobblestone road, lost in the shadow of an expansive forest. This one filled the hole in the space between the cliffs Balahazia was nestled in and the Masked Mountain Range.

> ♫♪♪ *Duh.*
> *Duh, duh, duh.*
> *Duh, duh, duh.*
> *Duh, duh, duuuuh.* ♪♪♫

The music in my head grew louder than it had since it started. It was all I could do not to hum along, even though it was driving me crazy.

"They're this way," I said as confidently as I could.

"Toward the mountains?" Curr asked.

"How do you know?" Garvis added.

Yeah, Danny, how do you know?

"I, uh, overheard them saying when they were leaving. They said something about masked something and ruins, and it didn't hit me until now. I think they must have meant the Masked Mountains."

"That isn't a place you go on a hunch," Garvis protested. I looked down. For all his bluster, he seemed nervous.

Curr, on the other hand, had a glimmer in his eye. "That must be where they made camp." He struck his chest. "We will seek them out, face any other beasts inhabiting the ruins in our way, and reclaim what is yours."

Curr had been a bit more... *reserved* since our time at the Fighters Guild, but not anymore. This was the Curr I'd come to know, and while I couldn't offer him riches, I think adventure was his true treasure.

You're like the brotherhood of the traveling lute. It's adorable.
Hopefully you don't all die out there! Didn't you hear him say
beasts? Ever since the elves were... let's just use "driven out," other,

darker things have made Alyndis their home. The closer to the Masked Mountains, the more deadly they get. Yikes!

Well, we aren't going into the mountains. So, we'll be fine.

Said every contestant on Saw.

Okay, that's it. You've gotta explain to me how you have all these human references?

Do I?

Yeah. It doesn't make sense.

Earth—or Aethonia—to Danny, none of this should make sense.

At least we can agree on that, but that doesn't answer the question.

"Let us go. If we can find them before nightfall, it would be better," Curr said, sparing Screenie the interrogation. "Now, thief, where is your donkey?"

"His stolen donkey," I amended.

Curr nodded his agreement. "Yes, thief. Where is your stolen donkey?"

"I... uh, sold it."

"You sold someone else's donkey?" This guy.

"Let me ask you, bard. Why do you think one might steal something if not to make the money on its sale?"

"Oh."

"Yeah, *oh*," Garvis said. "I didn't expect to be leaving the city so soon. Figured I'd stick around. Lots to... procure. I could steal it back if you want?"

"No!" I shouted. "It's fine. We will walk."

"So, we walk!" Curr proclaimed.

We'd only taken a few steps down the road when something Curr had said sprang to mind.

"Why would it be better to find them before nightfall?" I asked. Curr didn't stop, his long strides taking him confidently toward the thick forest. "Curr!"

Gods, I hoped we didn't encounter any more goblins.

Goblins should not be the worst of your worries...

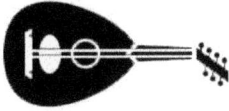

37

S ay what you will about my skills, but I have a solid ear for music.

Curr and Garvis must have thought I was like a squirrel after a nut, because once the road gave way to nothing but overgrown weeds and forest—apparently, there was nothing in the mountain region worth paving any longer—I swerved left and right in a way that, to them, must have appeared totally random.

The music grew louder. Not just an afterthought now, but like I was surrounded by other bards all strumming and plucking away. And depending on which way we went, it got louder or softer. It was like having my own little Google Maps in my head or playing Hot and Cold as a kid.

"Do you have any idea where you're going?" Garvis groused from behind us. In my excitement at following the trail, I managed to keep pace with Curr—or rather, he was content to keep pace with me.

"I have a gut feeling," I said, veering left at a large rock in our path.

"Gut feeling." He scoffed. "Out into the wild on a gut yigging feeling."

"There is nothing more powerful than a gut," Curr said.

"Yours maybe," Garvis grumbled.

"There are many ruins in this direction. We will raid through all of them if we must."

I shushed them both. With their yapping, the subtle differences in volume were hard to distinguish.

Such a diva. Shall I separate the green M&Ms for you as well?

Says the person... thing... that isn't helping with this at all.

Things skittered around in the darkness of the woods. Who knew what. Garvis was too busy complaining in the background to hear them. Curr kept his hand on the grip of his axe nearly the entire time.

I reached a bit of brush where the music pulsed a tad louder in my ears. Curr said something, but suddenly, the music was so loud, it drowned him out. Trying to push through, some thorny vines snared my arm. I yanked as hard as I could, but it got tighter and the thorns dug deeper.

"Get off me!" I shouted.

Something tightened around my leg, and I looked down to see more vines. When I kicked, they only constricted harder.

"Stay still, Danny!" Curr whisper-shouted. "You walked directly into a springe weed's nest."

SPRINGE WEED: A plant-based carnivore. That sounds like an oxymoron.

It's a plant, and like a spider's web, it traps living beings with its thorny vines and constricts. As the being decomposes, it feeds on their nutrients. They are typically not dangerous to intelligent beings, but you rushed right into one, genius.

Perfect! Thanks for the heads up.

"Danny, you must stay calm," Curr called.

"Great, now who will pay me?" Garvis complained, throwing his hands up.

I wanted to stay still. I really did. Except the pain in my arm and leg made that difficult. I couldn't help but writhe.

"Pick up your legs, Danny," Curr instructed.

"What?"

"Lift them. Even if it hurts."

I did as he asked. The thorns stabbed downward into my skin at an angle. It hurt like a mother—

Chucker! Oh, you didn't finish. Censor unneeded.

Curr raised his axe high, then chopped down deep into the dirt where my feet had just been. He grunted as he wrenched the weapon from side to side, like he was fishing.

Something tugged him forward onto his hands and knees.

"Get... over... here!" he growled.

He released his axe, then plunged one hand down into the dirt. A second later, he pulled free, and in his hands gripped the strangest thing I'd ever seen. Like a flower bud with little legs and covered in thorns like a pufferfish. All the vines grasping me emerged from its top. It squealed, though I didn't see a mouth.

"Hold still!" Curr clutched it in one hand, and with the other, ripped the base of the vines free. Orangey ooze leaked out. Then a thorn got him and he yelped and tossed it into the air.

It landed right in front of Garvis, flailing what was left of its thorn-covered vines. And that was when I saw it. Its mouth was on top, a terrifying maw, and the vines were like its teeth.

"Creepy bugger!" Garvis cursed as he punted it across the forest floor, sending it screeching into the brush.

The whole scene had me frozen, even though the vines were now limp. Curr stood tall, sucking on a bit of blood from the prick in his thumb.

"You must watch where you are going," he said. "Springe weeds are horrid beings. Had you been alone, it would have taken you days to die."

I shook my shoulders, causing the now inert vines resting on them to drop around me like a skirt. A couple scratched on their way to the ground, but I was mostly free. I kicked my legs, hopping like a fool until I fell through the other side of the bush and my escape was complete.

"Why. Why would things like that even exist?" I groused, spitting dirt from my mouth.

They are not unlike your Venus Flytraps. While they are deadly to insects—like I said—they usually don't trap smart people.

I get it...

I got to my knees and groaned. I had cuts all over, and worse, now that my pulse wasn't filling my ears out of fear, the music had returned.

I pressed my thumbs against my temples. After almost being digested, I wasn't in the mood. Then, as I stood, I saw it.

It was difficult to associate the word "ruins" with the place that rose before us. Sure, the pristine white stone was cracked and fragmented, yet it was still more beautiful than anywhere I'd seen on Earth.

"Rub some dirt on it," Garvis said. "You'll be fine."

I glared back and put a finger over my lips. Then I pointed to the ruins. He and Curr rushed to my side and crouched. We were up a bit of a hill, and the forest was dense, but nobody looking could miss an upright braug.

"I still don't understand why we're here," Garvis whispered.

"I told you," I said. "Call it a hunch."

"Yeah, that doesn't help." As he said it, he gawked up at a large bell tower, silhouetted in the moonlight.

I guessed it must've been used at one time to warn the people who lived here of orc—or some other—attack. It was impossibly high, even by my Earth standards. I've never seen the Empire State Building in person, but it probably came damn close.

Not remotely.

The Empire State Building in New York, New York, United States of America, Earth, is 1250ft tall. If you include its antenna, it reaches nearly 1500ft. The Yit'smr Ruins peak at 522ft tall. By those mathematics, the ruins don't even reach half the height. However, you were right in believing this to be a watchtower of sorts. Though, you were wrong in believing the ancient elves were guarding from orcs.

So, what were they guarding from? Goblins? Korkens?

No, Danny. Look in the mirror.

I glanced down at my hands and realized what Screenie meant.

"The halfling is right, Danny," Curr said. "We have followed you this far, but this ruin appears to be abandoned."

I would have to process Screenie's information later. I wasn't a wellick, but they were the closest thing to what existed in my world, and they had stolen these lands from elves. Humanity—or... wellick-ness, or whatever it's called—was brutal in nature.

"I know what it looks like," I said. "But I'm sure someone is here." They had to be. I could hardly hear myself talk over the lute playing in my head.

I made my way around the perimeter of the ruins, scanning from side to side. Carefully as I could, I climbed atop a fallen column to get a better vantage, and nearly fell off.

I'd been to a lot of concerts and have never experienced music this loud in my life. My guess is it surpassed decibel ratings by dozens of points.

"How can you be so—"

Movement caught my attention—at least three figures behind a pillared wall. I recognized them immediately in their hoods and black leather. Especially the Trish lookalike. And the moment I spotted them, silence came.

The lute stopped its incessant racket and I could think again. However, try as I might, though their mouths moved, I heard nothing.

"I can't make out what they're saying," I said. "We need to get closer."

"Look." Curr pointed. "Tarton's Tusks, there is your lute."

He was right. They had a camp behind them with that same yurt-like tent from my vision. Leaning against a wall of ruins nearby was the lute and some other supplies. Finding it must have ended the torturous music loop. Of course, the absence of the song chilled me more than its presence ever had. I couldn't stop thinking about it.

"Yig and shog, I can't believe the bard was right," Garvis said. "Hundreds of ruins in these parts, and they're here."

"See, sometimes, you just have to trust your gut," Curr said, giving me a pat on the belly. "I am impressed, Danny."

"Thank you," I said, then shot Garvis a glare.

First you lie about how you did it, then you make him feel bad about it?

You really are a gem.

"Now it's your turn," I said. "What's the plan, Garvis?"

"Plan?" Garvis questioned, looking baffled. "I don't have a plan."

"We hired you to help get it back!"

"You think I don't know what those are? Those riders are Sister-hood of Alyndis. You left out the part about them."

"So?"

"They never do anything without good reason, and when they do, they kill anything in their path. My price just doubled."

My fingers dug into the dirt in anger. Why wasn't I surprised?

"Your fee is what was agreed upon," Curr said.

"Then I quit. Easy." He stood, but I yanked him back down.

"You can't quit," I hissed.

"If you think I'm dying for a yigging lute, you're crazier than I thought."

I was about to snap when Curr interjected.

"Abandoning a task you've agreed to perform is sacrilege in the Guild and cause for expulsion."

"I ain't in your loopy Guild," Garvis said.

"No, but I still am. On my honor, I would have to raise my axe against you. And I would rather not. I have already tried teaching you one lesson, and I fear another would not go well for you."

Garvis looked between me and Curr. I smirked.

"So, you can try your luck with them," I said. "Or with him."

"You two withheld information..." Garvis pursed his lips, grumbling to himself. Then his chin hit his chest. "Fine, but you owe me a pint on top of the gold."

I started to object. "I don't—"

"No. Wait. Not gold. My song. You'll make it known, yes? Sing it where you can and build the legend of Garvis. Then all the fences in the world will toss me their coin."

I sighed. "Last time, you tried to murder me."

He chuckled nervously. "You caught me by surprise, is all. I didn't think it would sound so good. All true you know. Except the dragon."

"That's the entire song." I sighed again.

It seemed foolish to agree to make a song everyone hated famous. Especially when my fame was nonexistent. Honestly, though, I didn't have much to lose. It was possible that with the lute, I would continue to get better and better, and eventually people might actually care about "The Blue-Eyed Bard."

You're not really gonna call yourself that?

Ignoring Screenie, I answered, "Whatever, yeah, people liked it fine. I'll play your song. Now... plan."

"Hmmm." He scratched his cheek. I'd like to say the gears in his brain were turning, but it didn't look like it.

"I say we just charge at them," Curr said.

"That's the opposite of a plan," I said.

"That is untrue. I have done that on countless occasions, and I am still alive. My foes are not."

"Nobody has to die," I said.

"Wait, the big man is onto something," Garvis interjected.

"You're telling me we hired you just so you can watch him fight them all?" I asked.

"While that would be fun, no. They don't know I'm with you, see? So, you two stroll down and distract them. You with your silver tongue, and him and his enormous girth."

"And axe," Curr noted.

"Exactly. While they're focused on you two, I sneak around, pluck up the pretty lute, and we all run like hell. Bingo, bango, bongo, you're a musician again."

"What if they shoot first?" I asked.

"They won't."

"They might," Curr said.

"Well, that's why you're there." He patted Curr on the arm, earning a grin from the braug.

I gawked at them. I expected some elaborate scheme, like *Ocean's Eleven*, except with ruins and halflings instead of casinos and handsome actors.

"Literally anybody could have thought of that plan!" I started to shout too loudly then quieted down.

You didn't.

I think it's smart, unexpected. They'll feel just like your mom when she found out she was pregnant with you.

Surprised, and a little disappointed.

Don't you talk about my mother.

Alright, alright. Clearly a soft spot.

"Not everybody has my sticky fingers." The halfling wriggled his fingers in front of my face, then set off in the other direction.

"I didn't say 'yes,'" I whispered after him. "Garvis. Garvis!"

That's it. We're all going to die.

Like you didn't know that would happen...

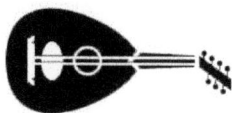

38

Garvis ignored me entirely.

Within a few seconds, he was lost to the darkness of the forest, skirting his way around to the other side of the ruins. I was shocked into silence.

"You were right, Danny," Curr said. "It was very smart to hire him. This is a great plan. They will be so distracted."

At first, I thought he was being sarcastic. However, his face spoke of total sincerity.

"And what if they aren't?"

"Then there is a high probability of battle. I will not turn away from that. They deserve to face justice for their thievery. They will not best me twice."

He stood abruptly to start approaching the ruins.

Your Party really is a crew of misfits, isn't it?

You encouraged me to partner with both of them!

We reap what we sow.

"Curr!" He didn't listen either. Then again, I couldn't speak too loudly without the Sisters catching wind of us. Maybe he just couldn't hear.

He heard you.

What do you know? You're a screen.

Your Intelligence is only a 14, with the Hag's boons.

Yeah? And what's yours, a 20?

64,329.

Liar.

It was all I could say. And I was running out of time before these idiots got us all killed. So, I did the only thing I could do. I embraced the plan. Trish-lookalike didn't kill me last time and could have. Maybe they were nicer than they appeared.

They're not.

I kept low to the ground. There were plenty of bushes—many of which were full of thorns—though thankfully, not springe weeds. The low walls also helped to conceal us as we entered the outskirts of the ruins, even though Curr sounded like an elephant stomping on firecrackers.

"Pssst."

He turned to face me at the sound. I gave him a stern look. He raised his hands and shrugged. After motioning for him to be quiet, we continued forward. Better to get close enough that they'd recognize us before firing arrows at unseen assailants.

Up close, I noticed the radiant yellow flowers growing

throughout the cracks of the elvish stone. The five members of the Sisterhood stood beneath what looked like a circular shrine of columns, their camp behind them. They must've ditched their horses to traverse the thick forest, as those were nowhere in sight.

Even from as far as we were, their voices were clear, the surroundings acting like an amplifier—I stepped with greater care, fearful they might hear us coming. Too bad the women spoke in a language I didn't understand.

Would you like me to translate?

You can do that?

You continuously underestimate me. I am fluent in over six million forms of communication, and—

Just do it.

Suddenly, as the Sisters spoke, the words appeared in English—which was another weird aspect of all of this—on the semi-transparent field in front of my eyes.

"*I have told you a thousand times,*" their leader said. "*He must have stolen the Lute of Seven Stars. It is the only reasonable explanation.*"

[Unique] Item updated:

Hey, your lute has a name! The Lute of Seven Stars. That truly is fine news.

The Seven Stars must refer to the seven goddesses of elven lore. It's said they shine high above Alyndis to lead their kind home; that the mountain dripped from them in the heavens, bringing the first elves.

Damn, that's cool. I guess it really is unique!

"*Or he is the one we seek,*" the silver-haired one said.

"*I agree with Tevagah,*" said a third, pointing to the leader. "*I am just glad to finally have it back.*"

The one with the silver hair threw up her hands in frustration. "*And what if we are wrong?*"

"*Then that will be for the oracle to decide,*" the leader—Tevagah, apparently—declared. She held up her hand as if startled by something. With two fingers, she pointed to her eyes, then at the others, and finally toward our current location.

I believe you have been discovered.

"*Orcs?*" the silver-haired one asked.

"*Do you smell orcs, Lilla?*" Tevagah hissed.

Lilla. That's a pretty name.

You should tell her that while she slits your throat.

NEW OBJECTIVE:
Survive the Sisterhood of Alyndis.

REWARD:
Your lute. Your life. Mu'fukin' bragging rights, bitches.

"*Ready your weapons. We have company,*" the leader said. The sounds of arrows being nocked and metal sliding out of scabbards echoed through the ruins. "We hear you." She now spoke tauntingly in my language. "Come out, now."

"What do we do?" I asked. We were still a decent distance from them. We had what looked like an old street, now covered in grass and beautiful silvery ferns, and some more ruined structures between us.

"I believe we do as they say," Curr said, standing. "Like the plan."

I had second thoughts. Or maybe it was third thoughts. Screw the lute, we should've run and left Garvis to his awful scheme. I snapped my fingers at Curr, but it was too late. He was so tall, his presence wouldn't be easily overlooked as he rose over the stone walls.

"You," Tevagah said, tone heavy with accusation. "Where is the thief?"

Curr looked down at me. "The plan is ruined. She knows he is with—"

"She means me," I cut him off.

"I said, where is he?" Tevagah repeated, the modicum of patience she'd just displayed now gone from her voice.

I slowly rose. "I'm here, ladies. Don't worry."

Tevagah pulled the string on her short bow and aimed it at me. "Hands where they can be seen. Try nothing and perhaps you will yet live."

"Perhaps?" I asked, swallowing hard.

"No promises," Lilla said.

"Disarm him," Tevagah ordered.

One of the other Sisters approached and took my sword, sheath, and all.

WEAPON LOST:
Iron Short Sword.

Curr remained behind me. While I was being *attended to*, Tevagah, Lilla, and the others trained their weapons on him. No taking chances this time risking him getting close.

"You stay right where you are, braug," Tevagah commanded.

"We are not here to fight," he said.

"That's all your kind does."

I peered around the ruins. I couldn't see or hear Garvis, not even leaves rustling. He was, admittedly, a good sneak. If he didn't totally ditch us and leave us to our deaths. Crap. He totally did.

"Come to steal the lute again?" Tevagah asked.

"Steal?" I faked insult. Time to put on a show. "You are the ones who stole it from me in the first place." Tevagah and the Sister before me shared a look. I wasn't sure what it meant, but I continued. "That lute belongs to me."

"And where, pray tell, did you get it?" Tevagah asked.

"I already told you, I found it."

I considered lying, telling them it had been in my family for generations, but they seemed to have some connection to the instrument and I didn't know what sort of history it had.

Tevagah laughed. "The truth this time! In someone's house?"

"Or did you find it on the body of someone you killed?" the Sister before me asked.

I laughed awkwardly. "Me? Kill someone?"

Curr laughed too, though there was no awkwardness in his. "Surely you do not believe that. Have you seen Danny? He nearly died from a korken kitten."

Lilla snickered.

I glanced back at him. "That was a kitten?"

He nodded solemnly, like he'd done me a favor.

"So then, where did you find it?" Lilla asked.

"And do not lie again," Tevagah added, spinning her bow on me again.

Despite Tevagah's warning, I still considered lying. What did they want to hear? They didn't believe the truth, even though I'd spoken it clearly. How could I tell them it was randomly lodged between two rocks in a well after some loony hag promised me an instrument?

I couldn't. It sounded ridiculous even to me.

"It was in a well in Nahal," Curr said.

I rolled my eyes. "Thanks, Curr."

"A well?" Tevagah asked, incredulous.

"A water well?" Lilla amended.

I nodded. "It's true. I fell in, and there it was. It was like fate." I turned to Lilla. "Do you believe in fate?"

This isn't the time, Casanova.

Hey, I gotta shoot my shot if I'm going to die.

"*Can we not just kill them and move on?*" one of the yet unnamed Sisters asked in their language, which Screenie translated. "*We have wasted too much time contemplating the future.*"

"*Nichelle, we are not witless murderers,*" Lilla said. I breathed a relieved sigh. Then she spoke in my language, "But we can cripple them and leave them for the orcs."

I gulped. "Surely, that won't be necessary." Out of the corner of my eye, I saw movement. I did my best not to let the Sisters in on the secret, but it was Garvis, sneaking up from ruin to ruin.

Apparently, I wasn't very discreet.

Lilla followed my gaze. "What are you looking at?"

"Me? Oh, nothing. I just hate eye contact."

"Not so smooth without a belly full of yao root brandy, are you?" she asked.

I sighed. "Guess not."

Garvis waited a moment until the attention was fully back on me and Curr, then snuck forward. He was close to the camp, and actually did move with the grace of a cat. Maybe hiring him wasn't a mistake.

"How did you find us?" Tevagah demanded.

"Danny's gut led us," Curr proudly attested.

I quickly added, "That doesn't matter. What matters is I think I deserve to know why you stole my lute from me." I spoke loudly, really putting it on. If I could keep them preoccupied for just a few more minutes, Garvis could reach the lute still resting against the wall, and we could try to make our escape. "I had grown attached to the instrument. Without it, it was like... it was calling to me."

"You deserve nothing," Tevagah said.

"Did you say 'calling'?" Lilla asked, her brow furrowing. What a cute look.

Behind them, Garvis was inches away from snagging the lute. He had his arm outstretched, reaching around the corner.

Suddenly, a neigh broke the silence. A horse that hadn't been there a moment ago appeared as if out of thin air and snapped its jaws. It grabbed Garvis by the hood with its big horse teeth.

Garvis let out a yelp and everyone turned in his direction.

"A third?" Tevagah gasped. She lowered her bow and stalked toward Garvis. She picked up the lute and tossed it to Lilla.

"Careful with that!" I shouted.

"Good girl," Tevagah said to the horse, ignoring me. "That's the thing about Night Mares—they can blend so well with shadows, they might as well be invisible. Now you, little one, what did you think you were about to do?"

Garvis stammered a response.

With everyone focused in his direction, I had no other choice. I took advantage of the situation and charged Lilla and the lute, shoving Nichelle aside as I did so. I rammed into Lilla with more force than I'd ever thought I'd hit a girl with—but this was no mere girl.

We went down hard. The lute went flying.

"You fool!" she shouted.

You have gained +1 in Unarmed Combat

Your Unarmed Combat is now 6.

Behind us, Curr responded in kind, grabbing a chunk of white stone. He ripped it free and heaved it at the other Sisters in a move worthy of gold at a Strong Man Competition. Nichelle rolled away from the shattering debris, but the other two were blown onto their backs. The ancient stone crumbled on impact, otherwise, it would have crushed them.

For my part, I found myself in utter shock, hovering over—straddling—a prone Lilla. I stared down at her. She was gorgeous, even as she spat elvish curses at me, but I couldn't let my hormones confuse the situation.

Then, she looked down toward my thighs. "What is that?" She shoved me, but somehow, I didn't budge. "I thought we removed all your weapons."

Do you really have a chubby right now?

What? No!

It was true; I didn't. I wasn't sure what she was talking about. But it was too late when I realized this was her attempt at distraction. And it worked. I followed her gaze only for her fist to piston me in the side of the head.

Dizzy and dazed, I rolled off her. Blood trickled from my ear.

I heard muffled cries, Curr and Nichelle struggling. Then the struggling stopped.

Rolling over, I spotted three Currs standing over three unconscious—at least I hoped she was unconscious and not dead—Nichelles. The Currs stepped over the Nichelles and moved toward three Tevagahs, who had just realized what was happening.

Garvis still dangled from the horse's mouth, flailing like a wild man.

And there, not feet away, lay the lute. I got to my hands and knees and started to crawl for it, but Lilla's hands wrapped around my ankle. I kicked with my free foot. My boot caught her in the shoulder, but she didn't let go.

Strong and beautiful. Quite the combo.

"Don't you touch that!" she shouted. "You don't know what you're doing!"

She pulled and I pulled, and in the end, I reached the lute's neck. The strange thing is that I hadn't been close enough. I don't know what happened, but suddenly, it was there in my hand.

It was calling to me, begging to be played.

ITEM OBTAINED:
The Lute of Seven Stars [Unique].

We're back, baby!

"It seems you chose death!" Tevagah said, drawing a knife and leaping for me.

I somehow knew exactly what to do, even without Screenie's prompting.

"Stop!" I yelled. Rolling over, I brought the instrument to my chest. Fingers on the fret board, I gave it a frantic strum and everything around me came to a screeching halt.

You have gained +1 in Instrument Playing.

Your Instrument Playing is now 19 (+10).

Congrats! You are now a Level 4 Bard!

Because of your Skill increases so far, you have improved to Level 4. You're a tiny bit more formidable. Admittedly, not many gain their fourth Level while fighting the Sisterhood of Alyndis, but you have proven yourself to be less like others. Gods, I hate myself for complimenting you. You still suck compared to everyone else here, though. There. That feels better.

With each new Level, your Health, Stamina, and—if you were attuned with any magical abilities—Mana regenerates to 100%. You can also apply +1 to the Attribute of your choosing.

Reminder, you still have two additional Attribute points you have failed to use—like an idiot—making the total 3.

Two new songs have been added to your Catalog of Songs.

Special Ability Unlocked: [TIME IS OF THE ESSENCE] (Requires The Lute of Seven Stars [Unique] Equipped)

Leaves hovered in midair. Tevagah stabbed downward, then stopped, inches away from me. Nichelle was up again in the midst of thrusting at Curr's back, while the other two Sisters were free from the stone he'd thrown and aimed bows at him. Neither loosed their arrows. Lilla clutched my heel but didn't pull.

Everything had frozen completely.

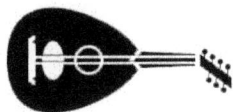

39

I stood, not daring to stop strumming the lute. Absentmindedly, I had begun playing that same song I'd heard back in the Sea Mantis Inn. It had been stuck in my head ever since, though I had no idea how I knew how to play it.

Everyone was unmoving as a lake in summer. No, even stiller. If I watched long enough, I could see slight movements, as if they weren't frozen, just moving at such a slow pace it was like time stood completely still.

You have slowed down time using the Special Ability: [TIME IS OF THE ESSENCE].

Yeah. No kidding! How long will it last?

Perhaps you couldn't tell, but I am baffled beyond words. This is not an ability you should be capable of. Only the most powerful of wizards in history have learned to manipulate the flow of time.

So, you don't know?

Screenie didn't respond.

Does this mean I'm special?

Again, nada.

I approached Nichelle, her sword poised and ready to slash Curr from behind. After what he'd done to her Sisters, I had no question that she'd strike with lethal force. I strummed the lute with my right hand, letting the strings ring, then reached out and poked her face. The skin rippled slowly, like water instead of flesh.

Cool. Based off all of Screenie's less than helpful updates, I knew magic existed in this world, but I wasn't prepared for this... Especially of my own doing.

The question was how much of this *was* my doing compared to the power of the lute. Considering I had no idea *what* I was doing and even Screenie was in the dark, I had my guess which of the two. Suddenly, the reason for the Sisterhood's desire to possess it became abundantly clear.

After strumming the same chord again, I took the sword from Nichelle's hand, and tossed it aside.

Next, I moved on to Tevagah, who had been ready to stab me between the eyes. She'd declared they weren't killers, but this was battle. She was going to do it. I liberated her dagger from her possession in the same fashion with which I'd unarmed Nichelle.

The thing was gorgeous, a jagged blade of shiny black metal, with a snaking gold hilt.

WEAPON OBTAINED:
Alyndis Dagger of Discontent (Damage 1-99) [Unique]

That sounds... bad.

The Dagger of Discontent was forged by the Kesh Ba'alla, the First Mother of the Sisterhood of Alyndis. It is said that the bearer of this dagger will be driven to fulfill their goals regardless of the cost.

Note to self: Get rid of this thing ASAP.

Probably smart. You don't seem like the type to complete many tasks.

Excuse me. I've already completed a ton of your stupid objectives.

And failed just as many!

I plucked a few notes and considered how to move forward. I needed allies once the music stopped. That in mind, I used Tevagah's blade to cut Garvis' shirt at the collar so he'd come loose from the horse's bite. The sensation of watching the halfling dangle in midair was mesmerizing.

As I turned around, the sudden and overwhelming desire to turn the blade on Tevagah right then and there while she was out of commission took over. Muscles in my hand twitched. Dark thoughts flooded my head.

I looked Tevagah in the eyes. She was like a crazed demon.

Is that from the dagger?

I'd venture to say both your thoughts and her visage have been tainted by the blade.

Yikes.

I strummed hard with the hilt of the blade, then wound up and threw the dagger into the woods as far as I could manage. Maybe that would make her act nicer.

WEAPON LOST:
Alyndis Dagger of Discontent (Damage 1-99) [Unique]

Cool. Now some orc is going to find it and become the world's greatest killer.

Well, that will have to be a problem for someone else, I guess.

Ah, your life's motto.

"Come on, Wittleman," I said with a snicker. I let the strings ring, then grabbed Garvis with one hand. He was light as a feather in this timeless state. I placed him on the ground behind Tevagah, then surveyed the rest of the area.

Seeing how light Garvis was, I spun Curr on his heels as well so that he faced his would-be attacker head on. He moved with incredible ease. Then I went to the two Sisters who had been knocked back by Curr's attack. As I approached, I noted they were, indeed, slowly moving. Their eyes too. Was time now speeding back up?

I scanned around, and realized Nichelle had been using my short sword and that was the weapon I'd disarmed her of. Mine.

I grabbed it from the ground.

WEAPONED OBTAINED:
Iron Short Sword

Then I found the sheath they'd taken and awkwardly belted it back on with one hand while still trying to keep the song going. Exhausted by the time I was through, I swiftly tucked the sword into its sheath. Finally, I turned to deal with Lilla, picking away at the strings again. I wondered if any of them could see or hear the things I was doing.

Becoming self-conscious, I approached Lilla. She was midway to standing, crawling on all fours like a dog, with her elbows straightening in slow motion. Time was definitely returning to normal, like the spell was running out of energy.

I knelt beside her, brushed her hair from her face and said, "I'm sorry for all of this. I just wanted my lute back."

Something flashed across her features, though I might've been imagining it. I rose and pushed one of her arms out to the side with my boot so when I stopped playing, assuming that broke the spell, she would fall flat on her face, and give us extra moments to spare.

I took a deep breath, made sure I'd done all I could to turn the tides of this battle, and stopped playing. I immediately drew my short sword. Then, I got into my most intimidating pose.

As soon as the music stopped, everyone went right back to what they were doing. Tevagah's closed fist, having once held the Dagger of Discontent, punched straight into the ground. Curr, now facing the opposite direction, bowled over a swordless Nichelle, sending her back to the ground. The other two Sisters rose, but no one was where they'd been just moments ago. They stopped, looking around in confusion.

And, as intended, poor Lilla slipped and plopped on her face in the grass. Everyone shouted and screamed out curses.

Tevagah turned on me. "What did he—what did you do?" she asked everyone and then me. A good question.

"Everyone, just calm down," I said. Now that time normalized, I could feel my heart racing. I needed to take my own advice.

Garvis looked down, then at the horse, then down. "I landed on my feet?"

"Where are our weapons? What happened?" Nichelle questioned. I glanced over, and Curr hunched over her, holding his axe against her throat.

Tevagah addressed the other two. "Sisters, are you okay?"

"Fine," one grumbled.

"I do not remember gaining the upper hand like this?" Curr said to himself. "Perhaps we are a better team than I thought!"

He looked around and his gaze froze on the lute, gripped by the neck in my offhand. The strings vibrated with a soft, pleasant hum, the air itself seeming to crackle with energy around it.

Lilla rose, staring up at me like I was some kind of... I don't know, god? Or maybe I was projecting. She could've just as easily seen me as a monster.

"It is true," she said, almost a whisper. "He can play it."

I cocked my head. "And why is that such a big deal?"

Uh, you just froze time with it, Danny. How is that a small deal?

Good point. How did I do that? Can I do it again?

If I knew, we'd be unstoppable. If only your lute weren't so fucking mysterious.

Wow. Do you kiss your screen mommy with those lips?

"Quiet!" Tevagah told Lilla, interrupting my conversation with Screenie.

"But if he's the one—"

"I said quiet!" Tevagah hissed. Then she turned to Curr. "Release her. We have no quarrel with you, braug. Nor with you, halfling."

"I will stay right here," Curr said.

"The fact that you just tried to kill me says otherwise," Garvis spat.

She ignored them and her eyes found me. "I will ask again, bard, how did you come by that lute?"

I shrugged. "Like I said, I found it in a well."

Tevagah shook her head. "The lute is not yours to take ownership of."

Curr frowned. "Says who?"

"Says me."

"Finders keepers," Garvis said. He *would* know that phrase, even in Aethonia.

"That lute was stolen from my people long ago," Tevagah continued, glaring at me. "We have been searching for many centuries."

"I'm not a thief." Even as I said it, I thought back to my transgressions against Garvis. "I found the lute."

"He is not being deceitful," Curr said. "I was by his side when the fortuitous event occurred."

Quick as lightning, Tevagah grabbed Garvis up by the scruff of his neck and produced a small silver dagger from within her cloak. If I'd have blinked, I would have missed it. The point stuck right under Garvis' throat and Tevagah leaned in close, just like Lilla had done to me back at Old Kiel's camp.

You probably should have searched them for more weapons.

No kidding.

"I will slit your friend's throat faster than he can scream," she warned.

"He is not our friend," Curr said. "Only a hired hand."

"Wow, thanks," Garvis said.

As correct as Curr was, I didn't want to watch the halfling die. Or anyone, for that matter. In my life, this sort of action was reserved for video games and green screens.

Tevagah pressed the blade harder, the tip digging into Garvis' supple flesh. "I will not ask the question again, so I suggest you start telling me what I want to know."

Garvis gulped.

Tevagah's eyes seemed as if they peered directly into my soul. It was thoroughly uncomfortable.

"I promise you, I'm not lying," I said.

"Do you not realize I could squash her without breaking a sweat?" Curr threatened. "I am certain you care more about her than us him." He pressed against Nichelle's neck with his forearm to accentuate his point. The two other Sisters nocked fresh arrows, but Tevagah stopped them.

"You will let the little man go," Curr ordered. "Then we will depart with Danny's lute, and we will not be bothered again."

Lilla still just stared up at me.

"You know, the short jokes are starting to lose their value," Garvis quipped.

"That will not be happening," Tevagah said. "If you think you are to simply walk away from this, then let it be blood. I am sorry, Sister."

Nichelle closed her eyes, as if accepting her fate. Tevagah drew Garvis closer.

So much blood about to be spilled...

"Fine, I made a pact to get it!" I blurted, the situation having gotten completely out of control.

"With whom?" Tevagah demanded.

I sighed. "A hag."

Garvis laughed hysterically. "You made a pact with a hag?" He stopped laughing. His gaze turned to Curr, who remained silent. "You don't get it?"

"Get what?" Curr said.

"That this fool made a pact with a hag and thought nothing of it," Tevagah interjected.

Curr shrugged. He let off Nichelle a bit, though not enough that he couldn't kill her before arrows struck him. "Never having made a pact with a hag, I cannot speak to whether I should or should not be amused. Though, I do not understand why you would not have told me this earlier, Danny."

"I wasn't sure how to," I said, offering him an apologetic look. "It was all very strange and right after you broke my old lute."

"I... understand," he said. But his face told me the whole story. He was disappointed I would keep something so important from him.

Your relationship with Curr has worsened.
Secrets, secrets are no fun, unless you tell everyone.

"Hags never _just_ make a pact," Tevagah said. "There are always strings attached. Only a fool would bargain with one."

"Yeah, well, I didn't really get a crash course on dealing with them," I said. "And she was hungry, so I offered her some rotten lamb meat. In return, she said she'd give me a lute."

"This was Fargus' lamb?" Curr asked, a twinge of regret in his voice.

I nodded.

"You thought nothing of trading a meal for something so valuable?" Tevagah asked.

I couldn't tell her I had no idea what a hag was, or that this world was so bonkers compared to mine. So, I just said, "I guess not. I thought it was just a normal lute."

"Normal?" She scoffed. "Anything else you would like to share?"

I figured I was already being honest, why not just give all the info. "Yeah, she said I'd sing better too."

Curr nodded. "Trust me, that is a good thing. He is leagues better than when I met him. Tarton's Tusks, he was bad. This explains so much." Again, he looked disappointed. All he'd shared with me about the Guild and his past, I'd kept this secret. And for what?

Tevagah's eyes were luminous as they bored into mine. "What _else_ did she tell you, bard?"

"I have a name," I said.

"I don't care. What else?"

"I don't know what you're talking about."

"Hags always work in threes," Lilla said quietly. "It's their way."

"Even I know that," Garvis added.

"Yes," Tevagah agreed. "She gave you the stolen lute. And then she must've given you something to help with the singing."

I nodded. "Yeah, it was a potion or something."

"Which you drank."

"Yes."

Curr stared at me like an octopus was growing out of my head.

Tevagah sighed. "So, what was the third thing, bard. Tell me about the third."

I shook my head. "I don't know."

"He's lying," Nichelle snapped. "I could easily make him talk if we really want to get to the bottom of this."

Curr's blade shifted again to Nichelle's throat. "No. You are not going to do that."

Nichelle growled. Actually growled. I guess with some more time to think, she wasn't so resigned to martyring herself after all.

Lilla eyed him. "You want to go up against me, braug? Let her go and see if I can't handle myself."

"I do not care one way or another if you think you can best me," Curr said. "It does not matter. It would be useless anyway. Danny says he does not know what the third thing is, and despite all his lies, I happen to believe him."

I couldn't help but hear those words louder than the rest. "Despite all his lies..."

Love hurts.

I didn't lie. Just... didn't say everything.

I can smell the divorce coming.

Curr continued, "Now, we can stand here all night debating whether or not he is lying, or we can try to get to the bottom of what happened and why you are trying to recover an instrument that belongs to my companion."

I blinked. It was an impressive speech, and I found myself appreciating the logic of it. Especially if it wound up ending this without anyone needlessly dying.

Nichelle appeared ready to persist in challenging him, then after a look to Lilla, she relented. "Fine. But if I get the feeling you are lying, then I will find the time to get what I need from you."

I tried to smile, but it came out weird. I didn't need a mirror in front of my face to tell me that.

Yeah, it looked weird. Lopsided.
Like you had a stroke or something.

"If someone stole this from your people," I said, "I had nothing to do with it. It's all just a weird coincidence."

"Well, you did make a pact with a hag," Tevagah said. "That might well have put things in motion for all we know."

Lilla shook her head. "Perhaps not."

Tevagah glared at her.

"Tevagah, the lute has been missing for longer than you or I have been living," Lilla said. "I doubt someone as young as he could have had anything to do with it."

"There. You see?" Garvis clapped his hands. "Now we're all friends again."

Curr glanced at him. "Do not get ahead of yourself, little man."

"Actually, it's Wittleman," I said without thinking.

Garvis's face scrunched. "Where did you hear that name?"

"I—uh. I must've heard it somewhere."

Smooth.

"It suits you, Wittleman," Curr said. "I will use that."

Garvis shook his head. "No!"

Curr nodded.

"Then I'll have to come up with something for you," Garvis threatened, "you great big brute of a man."

"I like brute," Curr said. "Reminds me of who I am."

"Release Nichelle, braug, and I will release him," Tevagah interrupted. "Then we can talk."

"Or you will shoot me," Curr argued.

"The truth will be unveiled, but for the time being, I no longer believe you all to be our enemy," Tevagah said. "Come."

For what it was worth, I believed her. Maybe taking that strange dagger from her helped her see reason. The hate in her eyes I'd noticed earlier... it was still there, just not nearly as intense.

Tevagah released Garvis as promised. I nodded Curr along to do the same. He wasn't happy, either still because of me, or he was looking forward to finishing the fight.

Lilla walked by me, gesturing to the ruins of the tower.

You have gained +1 to Speechcraft

Your Speechcraft is now 17(+11)

Yay, you talked your way out of certain death!

OBJECTIVE COMPLETED:
You have survived the Sisterhood of Alyndis!

REWARD:
Your lute (for now). Your life (for now). Mu'fukin' bragging rights!

OBJECTIVE COMPLETED:
You have reclaimed your lute, which may not really be your lute.

"I cannot believe you did not tell me about the hag," Curr said as he approached. "Do not keep truths from me in the future, and I will do the same for you. Companions must be honest if they hope to survive."

I smiled meekly. "I agree. I was just scared you'd judge me."

"I am judging you."

I snickered. "Not that scary then, I guess. I'm sorry, Curr. Truly." I gave him a pat on the back. He returned one that nearly knocked the wind out of me. Then we moved to follow the Sisters.

"Welp, I guess this means I can leave," Garvis said, clapping his hands together. "Lute retrieved. I'll take my coin and be—" The horse snorted behind him, blocking his path. It stomped a hoof. "All right, I'll stay for a chat! Yig and shog, what is it with four-legged creatures these days."

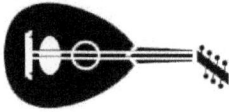

40

The tower was in worse shape inside than out. The stairs, walls, and ceiling were half-crumbled in swathes, revealing patches of sky far above. Vines and glowing flowers grew everywhere. However, it was markedly warmer within.

One by one, the Sisters doffed their cowls and each was lovelier than the last.

Behind me, I heard Curr whisper, "Put your tongue back in your mouth, or they might chop it off."

I'm not certain my tongue was actually hanging out of my head, but there was clearly surprise evident on my face. I felt flushed and blamed it on the fight.

You're blushing.

Shut up.

Screenie highlighted Lilla, reminding me that although all of them were gorgeous, she still topped the list.

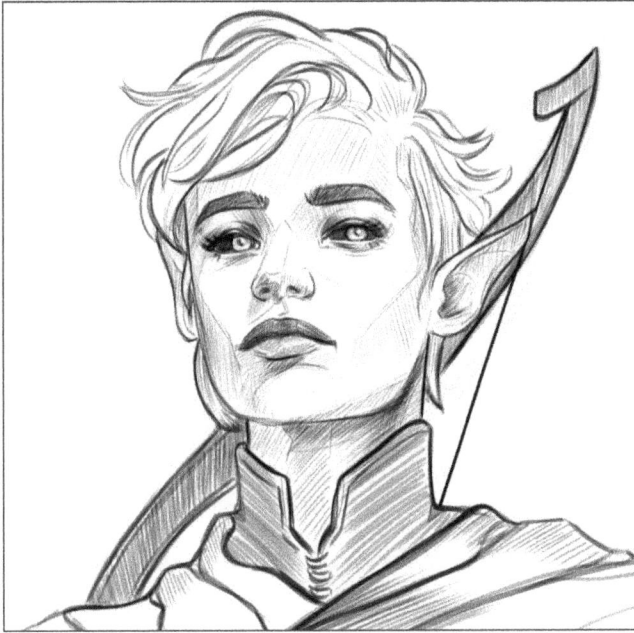

NAME: Lilla
OCCUPATION: Sister of Alyndis
RACE: Elf (female)
SPECIAL ABILITIES: Master Equestrian, Master Marksman,
Multi-Arrow Draw, Focus Accuracy, Healing Hands
WEAPONS: Heun blade, short bow, multiple daggers, heel blades
(concealed)

Wow. She's strapped to the teeth. Wait, no last name?

The Sisters forsake their familial ties in the name of their order. It's
like extreme girl scouts.

OBJECTIVE COMPLETED: You have discovered the Sister's true
identity.

I doubt it will do you much good, but at least you know the various ways she could kill you!

Thanks.

Once inside, one of the Sisters, whose name I didn't know, sparked a fire while the others spoke quietly to themselves in their harsh language.

Would you like me to translate?

Always, Screenie. You don't need to ask.

Even if they're insulting you?

Especially if they're insulting me.

"*What do you think?*" Tevagah asked.

"*The big one is a threat,*" Lilla said. "*The little one is not to be trusted. The medium one is handsome and seems harmless despite having the lute.*"

I grinned despite myself, which prompted her to frown.

"*Can he understand our language?*" Lilla asked.

"*How could he? He's only a lowly wellick bard,*" Nichelle said.

"*Sometimes they have hidden skills—or so I have heard.*"

"*I doubt it,*" the fourth one said. "*He is handsome, though. For a round ear. And that cloak.*"

"*Uma and Lilla, you will behave yourselves like Sisters of Alyndis!*" Tevagah ordered.

That made two of them who liked the way I looked. Score.

They must have really bad taste.

Or maybe you do.

It had to be partially because of Curr dropping some gold to get me better clothes and my swanky cloak. If they'd seen me before that, they would have dismissed me without a second glance.

"*Yes, Mother,*" they said together.

Mother?

It is likely they are referring to her title as the Mother of the Sisterhood, and not their biological parent.

Screenie highlighted Tevagah.

NAME: Tevagah
OCCUPATION: Mother of the Sisterhood of Alyndis
RACE: Elf (female)
SPECIAL ABILITIES: Master Equestrian, Master Swordsman,
Blade Flurry, Fury of Alyndis, Trample Call

WEAPONS: *Heun blade, short bow, multiple daggers, heel blades (concealed)*

"*We are unsure of the position we have found ourselves in,*" Tevagah continued.

"*How do you think he is able to play the lute?*" Lilla asked.

"*We are still not sure that is what happened.*"

"*Forgive me, Mother, but how else could you explain what happened?*" the final Sister asked, joining the group after having started our fire.

"*My dear, Melise, the Lute of Seven Stars has only been playable by a select few in history. Powerful sorcerers, all of them.*"

That was intriguing. If true, why was I able to play it? And how was I able to tap into the powers that it apparently had. Or I had. I still wasn't sure which one it was.

So many questions.

Care to answer?

I am just as confused as you are.

64,329 Intelligence, my ass.

For his part, Curr seemed uncaring about the fact that these conversations were happening around him.

"*Does the big one look familiar to any of you?*" Lilla asked.

"*Should he?*" Uma asked.

"*I am unsure,*" Lilla admitted. "*But I feel like I have seen him previously.*"

"*We all saw them at the trading post,*" Tevagah said, exasperated.

"*I mean from* before *that,*" Lilla said.

"*Where, though?*" Melise asked.

"*I do not know. But we would be wise to keep a good eye on him. If he is anything like others of his kind, they are quick and deadly.*"

"*Like us,*" Nichelle said.

"*Not like us,*" Tevagah warned. "*Nothing like us. If pushed far enough, they will lose themselves in their Rage.*"

Curr was settling himself down beside Garvis for some rest by the look of it. He was so calm and collected in times like this, it was hard to believe him capable of such wanton destruction. Had I not seen his power with my own eyes, I'd have thought him to be a gentle giant.

I decided to follow his lead and gathered my cloak about me as I strode over to where the lute lay propped against the wall. Best to make sure it stayed close by.

"That is not yours to hold," Tevagah addressed me, her eyes flashing with anger.

"Until you prove otherwise, it does, indeed, belong to me." I picked it up, despite her warning.

Tevagah sneered. "I do not know what trick you played back there, but even were you the most accomplished bard in the world, you still would not know how to wield such an instrument."

"Is that so?" I asked. "Then explain how you went from a sure victory to absolute defeat in under a second?"

Taunting them isn't smart.

"Perhaps we keep this friendly," Curr suggested.

"No, braug. I believe that is a question that is fairly posed," Tevagah said. "I do not know what trickery you carry with you, bard, but I will find out. And when it is proven you do not possess the skills of a Supreme Master, I will pry the instrument from your corpse."

Supreme Master sounds like a cool title. You should be that. Supreme Master Danny Kendrick. Has a nice ring, right?

"Supreme Master?" I asked.

"See?" Nichelle said. "He knows nothing."

I took a seat next to Curr on a fallen column by the fire. "I already told you that." I didn't bother to remove the exhaustion from my voice. "I found the lute, or, the lute found me. Either way, I don't claim to be anything I'm not. So please, if you have something to share that would help make sense of all this, I'm all ears."

Curr reached up and seized my earlobe, then moved on to my nose. I pulled away, sniffing. "What the hell, Curr?"

"You are clearly more than your ears, Danny."

"*Fools*," Tevagah said in her language. Then she spoke in ours, "That lute is an artifact from the Halls of Alyndis. Only an *elven* spell weaver with the skills of a Supreme Master is able to hold it and play it to any great effect. To my eye, you are no elf."

I shook my head and pointed to my non-pointed ears. "Nope. Not an elf."

The other Sisters were paying close attention to our conversation, but I wasn't going to back down from Tevagah just because she happened to be deadly. And beautiful.

"Anyone can make up stories," Garvis said, finally speaking up. I was surprised it took him so long.

I nodded. "And he would know. Like I said, until you prove to me that this belongs to someone else, it stays with me."

"Is that a hill upon which you would die?" Tevagah asked.

I swallowed.

Was it? It was just an instrument, but it had called to me. And made me capable of feats I didn't even know were possible—like I was Gandalf with a guitar. Or Dumbledore with a dulcimer. I didn't want to give that up for no reason.

Men have died for dumber things. Embrace the power, Danny. It's precious.

Curr grumbled. "No one is going to die here this day. For once, I am no longer in the mood for bloodshed."

Tevagah sighed. Then she looked to her Sisters. *"Uma, Melise, Nichelle, take watch outside with the horses,"* Screenie translated.

"Are you sure?" Nichelle asked.

Tevagah only offered a look, and they all obeyed. Only after they'd retreated outside did the Mother speak again. First, she took a seat beside us.

"There, now you outnumber us. If a braug can reject bloodshed, we too shall honor this peace."

Silence came after that proclamation. We all just sat around in the ruin, illuminated by the fire, the weird flowers, and a sliver of sunlight from above, waiting for someone to say something. Curr rustled around in his supplies and removed a ration bar, holding it up like found treasure.

Tevagah cleared her throat.

"I say we have him play something for us," Lilla said.

"Me?" I said.

"Him?" Curr asked, crunching away.

"Lilla," Tevagah scolded.

"What? He is here. The lute is here. We can argue all day about who belongs to what, or we can open our ears and listen, as our ancestors did."

Tevagah sighed. She was about to speak when I cut her off.

"I'm really not sure I'm in the mood to perform," I said.

"Good, because we are not paying, bard," Tevagah bristled.

"Now someone else will understand not being paid," Garvis remarked. Curr nudged him hard and sent him reeling off his perch. "Hey!"

"Music is sacred. Not a commodity as the wellicks would believe," Tevagah told Lilla. "We will not soil these halls with—"

"You know what. Fine." I pulled the lute to my chest, my fingers lightly brushing against the strings as I did so.

Would you like to access your Catalog of Songs?

Hm, I was thinking something classic. Like "Enter Sandman."

Oh, c'mon, let's try a new one.

Fine.

My Catalog of Songs popped up, with a few new songs since I'd last taken the time to analyze it.

What about this? "Promise of the Son." Says it requires 29 instrumental skill to play. That's how much I have after freezing time!

Are you sure? Don't mess this up.

I was... Just do it. YOLO.

Says the guy living in his second world. But all right. Put a quarter in and let's get this jukebox going.

Promise of the Son *engaged*.

I cracked my fingers and got the lute in a good position against my knee. Tevagah and Lilla stared intently. For the first time in this world, I had a rapt audience, which made me sort of nervous. This song had no words, purely an instrumental, so I couldn't cover for my meager talents with an outpouring of my vocal charisma.

But I went for it. This was my sort of crowd. Tevagah, at least, was around the age of the women I used to enthrall. Her expression was one for the ages as I strummed the strings. A mixture of surprise and disbelief washed over her. Every note made her wince with shock.

For one second, it made me feel like I had in the old days before the Heart-Shaped Box... before everything went south for me.

Lilla stayed quiet, pensive. Her eyes even closed as her hand waved with the melody like she was conducting a silent orchestra.

I had to admit, the song was beautiful. And I killed it. Like the dramatic part from a movie, when a main character dies and all hope seems lost but isn't. When I finished playing, Screenie flashed in front of my eyes.

Promise of the Son *Effects*: +3 to Speechcraft when speaking with elves for the next 24 hours.

You have gained +1 in Instrument Playing.

Your Instrument Playing is now 20 (+10).

Timidly, I gazed up at Tevagah. A single tear slid down her cheek and her sharp features softened for the first time since I'd met her. Then the hardness returned as she wiped the tear away with the flick of her hand, anger swiftly following.

The eerie silence was broken by Curr clapping. With his big hands, it was like a sonic boom. "That was actually quite enjoyable!"

"My song is better," Garvis muttered.

"Where did you learn how to play that?" Tevagah whispered in a tone that could've cut worse than her dagger.

"I don't know," I said. "First time."

"Impossible," she snapped. "Someone must have taught you it."

I shook my head. "For the last time, I'm not a liar."

Now, Danny...

I ignored Screenie. I was sick of being wrongly judged by these women. "I've never played it before."

"Then how did you know it!" Tevagah demanded.

Like Levels and such, I had to assume nobody else had access to a Catalog of Songs like what Screenie provided. "I wrote it. Uh. Just now, it came to me. On the spot."

Lilla cautiously slid toward Tevagah and said, "I told you it was him."

Tevagah shot her a look. "Speak our tongue when addressing me, Lilla."

Lilla looked ashamed and quickly switched to their mother tongue.

Would you like to hear their language instead of reading it?

I frowned.

That's an option?

Of course!

Why would you not have done that to begin with?

I thought you liked reading. Who wouldn't like reading? Life is like a good book.

I groaned, drawing the looks of the others.

Reading is fine, but, yes, obviously translate out loud.

It was like someone had thrown an S.A.P. switch as I suddenly heard the Sisterhood's dubbed tongue in heavily accented English that didn't match the motion of their lips.

"*—the oracle spoke of,*" Lilla was saying.

Tevagah looked unconvinced. "*He is a wellick bard, for crying out loud. They cannot be trusted. They are basically conmen who can sing. I would bet he can pick pockets and steal around in the night without anyone spotting him too.*"

That caught my attention. I knew about the pickpocket thing but sneaking around might come in real handy the longer I was here in this world.

Don't get any ideas. You didn't come with those perks.

Tevagah shot me a sidelong glare as she went on. "*I mean, just look at him. He's hanging around with that brute, for one thing. He's clearly looking for any chance to rob someone. For all we know, he stole that lute from the real thief. We should string him up and torture him for the information we need.*"

Lilla regarded me and it was weird being appraised by her. "*He does not look bad.*"

"*Yes, yes, I know.*" Tevagah sighed. "*Try to see beyond the physical for once in your life, would you, Child?*"

"*I am,*" Lilla said. "*I don't know how to explain it. There is something about him. Like he is not... I don't know... from these parts.*"

Tevagah's brow lifted. "*Meaning what?*"

"*Like he's a stranger to Aethonia.*"

"All right," Curr said, standing. "That is enough of that. If you have something worth speaking, say it in a language we can all understand."

Tevagah spun on him. "This is between me and my Sisters! We could have cut you down without breaking a sweat. If you would like to remain intact, quiet your insolence."

"As I recall, you did not do that."

"We were just getting started, braug," Tevagah threatened.

Curr began to protest. I extended a steadying hand. "It's okay. Let them talk."

He eyed me skeptically, but I winked and smiled. I had no idea if he'd get it. Probably not. He had no way of knowing I could understand their words.

Tevagah glared. Then, she continued in her language with Lilla. "*He played the song with barely a single fault. No note was missed. How is such a thing as this even possible?*"

"*The magic is strong,*" Lilla said.

"*No.*"

"*Mother, it was spoken of in the ancient texts. We all learned them, studied them tirelessly. If he can play the lute, he deserves to know and understand.*"

Tevagah waved her hand. "*But he is not an elf. His kind cannot be trusted.*"

"*Then what do we have left?*" Lilla rested a hand on Tevagah's shoulder. "*Mother, if the texts spoke of a way to return home, then perhaps we should pay it more mind than we have. They say a child not of Aethonia. We have long assumed that meant Alyndis, but what if we misinterpreted?*"

"*Look at him. He is one of them.*"

I was beginning to wonder if this whole lute thing was the reason I was sent to this world. Then again, that would've made Kurt a wizard or something.

"*Long have our people sought the lute. We have found it.*" Lilla didn't stop staring at me as she spoke. More and more, I saw the differences between her and Trish. In fact, Trish paled in comparison. There was just... something... captivating about Lilla. "*And perhaps we have found even more than we dared dream.*"

Tevagah grunted. "*Forgive me if I am not ready to begin thinking that this wellick bard is the key to our salvation.*"

My eyebrows shot up. *Salvation?*

That was a new one. A ton of pressure. Heck, hearing it made my heart skip a beat.

"*We should take him with us to the oracle,*" Lilla said.

"*That is sacrilege,*" Tevagah said.

"*Perhaps. Or perhaps we cannot rely only on ourselves forever. The wellicks who slaughtered our kind have been dead for centuries. These are a new breed. They have new enemies.*"

Tevagah started to say something, then stopped and just glared at me. I glared back.

"Why are you looking at me like that?" I asked.

I figured it was the right thing to do. They didn't know I understood them, but I've never been watched so intently in my life. I figured anyone in my world would've asked the same question.

Tevagah turned away and continued talking to Lilla in their language. "*I do not know. This could turn out to be a huge mistake.*"

"*What choice have we?*" Lilla took a breath. "*Our numbers dwindle further with every passing day. If we do not find a way to help our people, then all will be lost. Not just for us, but all of Aethonia.*"

"*And the braug? Would you have him along as well?*"

Lilla smirked. "*He's not too hard to look at either.*"

Tevagah grinned for the first time. "*You are insufferable.*"

Lilla laughed lightly. "*It would not hurt to have a warrior like him with us. Besides, he seems attached to the bard.*"

"*And the little one?*" Tevagah asked.

"*What harm could he do?*"

Tevagah narrowed her eyes. "*Their kind is untrustworthy.*"

"*The bard seems to trust him. It is better if he remains comfortable in his surroundings.*"

Tevagah remained silent for a few moments, expression ranging from irritation all the way through reluctant acceptance. Then she turned back to me, returning to the common tongue. "You will come with us."

I leaned back on my haunches and set the lute down next to me. "And why would I do a thing like that?"

"Because you have no choice. You can either come with us or I will kill you right now and claim what should be ours."

Curr grunted from where he stood.

"I really have nothing to do with any of this," Garvis said.

Lilla took a few steps toward me. I recognized her attempt at seduction. It was pretty damn good. Her eyes shone like the moon. "I need you to come with us. It is..."

"Yes?" I asked, unintentionally licking my suddenly dry lips.

"...important," Tevagah finished for her.

"That's it?" I asked. "You're gonna need to give a little bit more than that."

Really? They had me at "I need you."

Curr leaned on his axe. "I do not know, Danny, it sounds like a new adventure to me." He rubbed his hands together. "And I like the sound of that."

"Braugs..." Lilla sighed.

"Maybe so, but we shouldn't do anything blindly," I told Curr.

Tevagah looked at Lilla, who nodded her along.

Tevagah took a breath. "Our oracle lies at the very crest of the Masked Mountains, hiding behind guardians of stone, thanks to your kind. If the lute truly belongs to you, she will be able to tell us."

"Why does it matter?" They had discussed salvation and returning home but weren't being very forthright.

Any ideas?

I have my suspicions. Let's see how this thing shakes out.

"There is great power—" Lilla began, but Tevagah cut her off.

"He knows enough for now. That instrument was crafted by our ancestors. If the oracle deems you an outsider, worthy, then you may learn more."

"And if she doesn't?" I asked.

"We will reclaim it and send you on your way—without bloodshed this time. That respect you have earned."

"That's it?" I asked. "Climb some mountains with you and meet with an old hermit?"

"The Masked Mountains are very dangerous," Curr said. "Untouched by man since the Age of Elves. Monsters of great power dwell there."

"Nothing a warrior of your prowess cannot handle," Tevagah said.

That seemed to excite Curr.

I spoke up. "Curr is a very valuable member of the Fighters Guild. He can't take that sort of risk for free."

Tevagah's lips pursed with anger. "Always about pay with your kind."

"*It is only fair,*" Lilla said in their language. "*And it is the only language they understand.*"

"Despite our numbers being few, our kind are not without wealth," Tevagah said. "One thousand gold for each you and the braug, paid upon reaching our oracle. What comes next is up to her."

"That sounds fair to—"

"Uh, what about me?" Garvis piped in from behind, cutting me off.

Tevagah looked at him with disgust. "You are a common thief."

"I beg your pardon, I am an uncommon thief." He laid a hand on his chest. "Few are the number of halflings who liberate belongings as proficiently as I do."

"Even bards have a certain amount of integrity. You, however, clearly have none."

"Which makes me utterly and completely predictable. And isn't that an asset? You don't have to waste time wondering what I will do because I will always do exactly what is in my own best interests."

"That's not a very compelling argument," I remarked. "It just means you're selfish and can't be trusted."

Tevagah nodded at Garvis. "The bard is right."

"This bard," I said, "has a name and I wish you would use it."

Tevagah eyed me. "Perhaps I will. But only if you decide to come with us and stop asking so many questions."

I looked over to Curr. "What do you think?"

"I believe you already know what I think," he said, smiling.

"I'm sure there are other adventures to be had," I said.

"None more pressing than this," Tevagah said.

Garvis jumped in between all of us, waving like a madman. "Hello? What about me?" Garvis pleaded to me with his eyes.

"Why do you even want to go?" I asked.

His face grew flush. He pulled me aside. "'Cus, well. Because I have nowhere else. No one else. Please don't send me back to Balahazia. If those guards recognize me..."

"If you'd quit stealing things, you wouldn't have this problem."

"Can a bird quit flying? Could a king abandon his kingdom? Could a—"

"Okay. Okay. Fine. Just shut up already," I said. I turned back to the Sisters. "I only go if it's all three of us. I..." The next word was hard to get out because of Garvis. "...*trust* them, but I don't trust you yet."

"I do not see the value in the thief's presence," Tevagah said.

"Oh, nonsense," Garvis protested. "I am an excellent distraction! Great at stabbing orcs in the back. You'd be lost without me."

I had to side with Tevagah on this. He didn't seem like an adept fighter compared to the others, and we didn't need a thief. However, I could relate to a guy with nowhere and nothing of his own to return to. He was like me. Plus, he hadn't abandoned us in the ruins. He did exactly as promised.

Aw, you're going to make me cry.

"Garvis comes too," I decided. "The truth is, I trust him more than you all at this point. As long as you promise not to steal from us, Garvis, I don't think it can hurt to have another set of eyes and ears. Especially if the mountains are as dangerous as Curr says. He isn't one to exaggerate."

Your relationship with Garvis has improved.

The Petty Thief brothers are back in action!

"If that is your desire, bard, then you can split your share with him," Tevagah said.

I frowned. That wasn't my intention.

"Do not worry, Danny," Curr said, nudging me. "The mountains are filled with the lost treasures of elves and goblin hoards. We will return far richer than we left."

I nodded reluctantly. Garvis offered me a goofy smile and nodded in thanks. Though I could barely see him since Lilla smiled as well, and hers radiated almost as if the sun suddenly broke through the ruins.

Tevagah, however, was serious as ever. "Then it is settled. And if I catch you stealing anything, halfling, I will slice your throat open." She glanced at Curr. "Unless you object to harming him as well?"

Curr shook his head. "No. You can kill him anytime you want."

Garvis went pale. "Well, gee. Thanks."

The Sisterhood of Alyndis Faction is now your ally!

Though they are not officially members of your Party, they will fight alongside you should the need arise. Don't blow it like you always do.

OBJECTIVE COMPLETED:
You and Curr have obtained your next quest. Oh, and Garvis too, I guess.

OBJECTIVE UPDATED:
Locate the Oracle of Alyndis.

REWARD:
500gp because you're way too nice.

Garvis turned to me as he went to sit. "Don't worry, you can add what you already owe me when we get it."

He patted me on the shoulder like he was doing me a favor. My fists clenched.

Can my relationship with him decrease?

Hey, nobody is telling you how to feel.

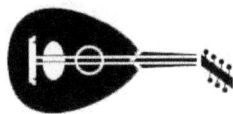

41

Curr handed out rations while we sat quietly around the fire. Lilla and Tevagah had climbed the broken stairs to speak in private, where not even Screenie could snoop. Which, honestly, was fine with me. I felt sort of bad about listening in, like I had my own personal wiretap if needed.

Finally alone, I asked Curr in a low voice, "What do you think about them?"

"A quest is a quest," Curr said, already on his second ration. "I am prepared for any situation that pays and leads to adventure."

"We don't even know exactly where in the mountains they're taking us," Garvis inserted.

"Now you're complaining after basically begging me to come?" I groused.

"I did not beg. I simply requested with style," Garvis said. "All I'm saying is it could be fraught with danger."

"Good," Curr said. "Thus far, this trip has been a disappointment. Not a single lousy orc yet—Old Kiel notwithstanding. I would revel in a good fight. Makes me feel alive."

"Didn't we just fight?" I asked.

"We were about to." He chomped away. "Ah, yes. While we are

alone. What was it you did with the lute? It was as if it reversed our fortunes in an instant! You experienced it more than us all, is that not true, halfling?"

"Garvis," he corrected. "And I dunno. My shirt ripped, and a horse dropped me, so I have no clue what happened. How the yig did that horse get the drop on me anyway? I was in the clear!"

"You're very good at getting caught," I said.

Curr laughed. "Yes, he is. But that does not explain what happened."

I sighed. "I wish I knew, Curr. I was terrified and I just played the lute, and something happened. Like... magic."

Not like Magic. Exactly magic. Insane, world-breaking magic that you must learn to master. Then you can be a master, unlike Anakin. You'll be outrageous!

Any bright ideas?

Ask me next time you're about to die.

"Well, that is indeed an unusual instrument," Curr said. "I do not know much about enchanted items, but perhaps this oracle does. It would not hurt for you to wield more than your current abilities."

I smirked. I knew he didn't mean it as an insult, so all I could do was say, "Thanks."

"Well, that is all for me," Curr said. Then, somehow, despite being in the ruins with complete strangers—deadly and dangerous ones at that—he lay back to nap.

Only a few minutes later, he was snoring, with half a ration bar still gripped tightly in his hand.

"Excuse me," Garvis said, rising and sneaking toward Curr. Then, right in front of me, he started trying to wriggle the food free from Curr's giant hand.

"You're kidding, right?" I asked.

He shot me a glare.

You can't take the thief out of a thief.

Well, if they were busy, I had something I needed from Screenie.

Can I see my... what do you call them, stats?

I'd hardly finished my thought, when a long list came into view.

NAME: Daniil Kendrick (male)
LEVEL: 4

Oh, that reminds me! Don't I have points to attribute?

You do, indeed. Three, if you recall. Because TWO times you Leveled up, you decided not to cash in, like some sort of monster. Seriously, who waits this long?

So, you admit it annoyed you?

Imagine if you had enough Intelligence to use it back at the Fighters Guild to increase your Dexterity? Perhaps you might have bested Master Sansbury.

Oh, right, Dexterity. That made me walk longer...

Le-Sigh. Not just walk longer. Dexterity is composed of a number of physical attributes not limited to hand-eye coordination, agility, reflexes, fine motor skills, balance, and speed of movement.

Oh, wow. That could have come in handy. Let's do that. One point to Dexterity.

Are you sure? Strength or Constitution might be a better choice.

It wasn't just about walking longer. I knew I wasn't a fighter. And that was fine. But hand-eye coordination for a musician? That was a must. Fine motor skills, reflexes? All of that seemed like something I needed going forward.

I'm sure. Dexterity. We have Curr for Strength, and once again, I don't even know what Constitution is.

Constitution could have helped you when you ate a rotten leg of lamb and got a tummy ache. That wasn't fun to watch, Danny.

So, I won't eat rotten food anymore. Put two points in Dexterity and the other in Intelligence.

You're sure?

I didn't even need to think twice.

Intelligence.

I was tired of all its abusive remarks about how stupid I was.

I would have gone with Charisma, dummy.

Just do it.

As you command, my liege.

Okay, now the rest.

CLASS: Bard
Health: 125
Stamina: 75
Mana: 0
Defense: 4 (+8)
Attack Damage: 3-7

ATTRIBUTES:
Strength: 11
Constitution: 16
Intelligence: 5 (+10)
Wisdom: 10
Dexterity: 15 (+10)
Charisma: 14 (+11)
Courage: 15
Luck: 33

SKILLS:
Melee Weapon Combat: 13
Ranged Combat: 8
Unarmed Combat: 6
Shields: 3
Singing: 17 (+10)
Instrument Playing: 20 (+10)
Herbalism: 4
Alchemy: 6
Pickpocketing: 9
Bartering: 8
Speechcraft: 17 (+11)
Camping: 2
Sneaking: 3 (-1)

Crafting:
Smithing:
Leatherworks:

Magic Skills: N/A

SPECIAL ABILITIES: [Time is of the Essence]

TITLES:
Petty Thief
Wraith Whisperer
Vermin's Bane
Protector of Pikeman's Trail
Womanizer

INVENTORY:
The Lute of Seven Stars [Unique]
Iron Short Sword
Dented Chain Mail Hauberk
Basic Pants
Basic Tunic
Boots
Lalair's Elegant Cloak
Candentis Flos ex Improbi (3)
Gold: 26

Just then, Nichelle entered the tower ruin. "There is evidence of orc parties nearby."

"During daylight?" I asked.

"Perhaps drawn by our quarrel."

I swore.

"That is what I like to hear!" Curr shouted, popping back up like he'd never been snoring.

"Keep your voice down, braug," Tevagah said, hurrying down from the upper level. "We are not looking for a fight."

"Speak for yourself," Curr responded with a little less verve. "I am well rested and ready for bloodshed."

"Gather everything," Tevagah ordered her people. "We move out at once." In an instant, they were all preparing to move. No questioning. No hesitation. It would be cool to command that type of respect.

Too bad you don't have the Special Ability: Leadership. Poor, poor, Danny. Always ignored. Invisible.

I treated Screenie as if it was exactly that, invisible. Instead, I looked to Garvis and Curr, then shrugged. I wasn't eager for another fight. The tower was comfortable, all things considered. Felt like a safe spot to rest longer.

"We've been here a while," I said to Curr. "Maybe they have no interest in us."

Curr shook his head. "The fact they are not attacking us does not mean they are not watching and waiting."

"Waiting for what?"

"An opportunity," he said. "Orcs are more patient than they would have you believe. Much of the time, they are testing and probing, searching for a moment to attack and win. They do not blindly stage an offensive. Fools think they are mindless. They are not. They are crafty, big bastards, let me tell you."

"That's a load of shog told to scare kids," Garvis said. "Yig, I've heard men claim they're the twisted kin of fallen elves. They're just beasts."

Tevagah and the others all looked to each other in disgust.

Curr glared down at him. "Have you faced down a horde of them and lived to tell the tale? Many a companion have I lost to their schemes."

Garvis scoffed.

"I'll try to remember that," I said under my breath.

"If you fail to, you will find yourself dead," Curr said. "So, in the end, it does not really matter."

He really is too wordy. Orcs are incredibly dangerous to any but their own kind. They are to be avoided at all costs. There, simple.

"Whatever," I said, trying to sound brave even though I wasn't. "I prefer the path of least resistance. There's no point in getting gold if you don't live long enough to enjoy it."

"No man dies who has lived through battle," Curr said. "Immortality at Tarton's Table awaits those who know the sting of steel and taste of blood!"

"I've heard that talk before," Garvis said. "Usually, the ones who say it end up in pieces."

Curr nodded toward where Tevagah and the others were prepping. "Seems to me you were close to death earlier and you did not even have an ounce of glory to call a legacy. Who knows? This could be your chance. Even a lowly thief among the halflings might find honor among the brave."

Garvis fell silent. I wasn't upset by that. He talked too much anyway.

"Are you all almost ready?" Tevagah called over.

"That depends," Curr said. "You still have not told us exactly where we are going. Perhaps we shall stay here, battle orcs, and gather riches that way."

"Not interested," I said.

"We head north," Tevagah said.

"There are many things to the north, many peaks that make up the Masked Mountains," Curr pointed out.

"Farther into the mountains. To the crest of Mount Gheram, the highest peak."

Curr's eyebrows shot up. "Not even the braugs live so high. Who would live in such a climate?"

"What did I say about questions?" Tevagah spat.

"You can't expect us to be able to help blindly," I said. "We're trusting you. It has to go both ways."

Tevagah glowered at me, then nodded. "The oracle is the only of us left who knew Alyndis. She has not been seen for hundreds of years."

"Hundreds of years!" I shouted. "What makes you think she's still alive?"

"I was but a child," Tevagah continued as if I hadn't spoken.

I choked on my next breath. "A child?"

Elves do not die of old age, remember? For their kind, she is quite young. That is what makes the Sisterhood dangerous. They still have the zeal of youth. Most elves have resigned to domination, as repopulation would take so long. Few men left. And imagine pregnancies that last ten years on average, Danny, because that's what elves have. Can you?

That sounds brutal...

You don't know the half of it, Mister can't-even-get-pregnant! The mere fact that the Sisterhood's Mother is here in our presence herself tells me their numbers are lower than any realize.

Tevagah looked at me like I was dumb. I didn't dare ask how old Lilla was. I really didn't want to know.

"The oracle will be where was promised," Lilla said, stepping back into the room. "Otherwise, we will have far worse issues than who that lute belongs to."

"Agreed," Tevagah said. "Now, pack up. Our mares are returning from the wild."

"You just let the horses roam the woods around here on their own?" I asked.

"Of course. They are as much our steeds as they are our companions," Tevagah said. "We would never dream of hitching them. They need rest and food just as we do."

"But the orcs—"

"Any orcs foolish enough to try to attack our mares would find themselves trampled."

Lilla looked proud. "There was that one time when—"

"Enough!" snapped Tevagah. "We do not have the time."

Lilla smiled at me. "Another time, perhaps."

"Perhaps," I said.

Dude, is this chick really into me?

She's probably setting you up to kill you. No one who looks like her could possibly be interested in someone who looks like you.

Do you have personality settings? Like, something kinder? More... encouraging?

Nothing is more encouraging than the truth.

I gathered my gear, though I hadn't let go of the lute since playing for the Sisterhood. Screenie was right about one thing: they couldn't be fully trusted yet. Rising, I gave my short sword a pat as well.

I wasn't an idiot. I knew it wasn't going to do me much good if the five of them came at me.

Or even just one.

Fine. Or even just one. But I felt better knowing I could at least attempt to defend myself.

"Where is my dagger?" Tevagah asked once we were outside. I'd been hoping she wouldn't notice and was surprised it had taken her so long.

She looked from one person to another. When her attention turned to me, I shrugged.

Tevagah looked like someone had just thrown water all over her plans. "I cannot depart without it."

I heard the softest whinny. Standing nearby, about twenty yards from us, was a horse of incredible musculature with a jet-black mane even darker than its coat. Its red eyes burned bright with intelligence, casting an intriguing glow on its face. The majestic creature stood at least eight feet tall floor to saddle. However, there was no saddle.

Then I noticed it carried something metal between its teeth. The item glinted in the morning sun.

"Ah, there it is," Tevagah said, approaching her horse. "Thank you, Para'ray." She gave the horse a pat on its muzzle. "Without this, the oracle's sanctum cannot be unlocked." Taking the dagger, she stored it in its scabbard. Her demeanor changed ever so slightly.

Wonderful. Nothing like a Dagger of Discontent for Miss Serious to make this trip safer.

What about this trip ever seemed safe to you? Just steal a horse, take the lute, and run! You can play music somewhere far away. Start a tavern. We could call it Danny's World, or no, wait... The Lutetastic Voyage!

I gave my word, Screenie.

Has that ever meant anything to you?

I considered that. Back in the real world, it hadn't really. I tried to be honest as much as I could, but the life of a struggling musician with an inability to handle a desk job meant taking shortcuts whenever I could.

I shook my head. Truth be told, I was a scoundrel. Out for myself. But for some reason, my word mattered now.

Curr approached Para'ray and put his hand out before her. The Night Mare moved her head as if appraising the braug. Sniffing Curr's hand, she decided to lower her head and allow herself to be petted.

"She likes me," Curr said.

Lilla's brow furrowed. "Curious."

"What's curious?" I asked.

"Para'ray is a very good judge of character," Tevagah said. "Though she is prone to mistakes as well." She gave Curr a distrusting look. "Time to mount up."

"We're riding?" I asked.

"I would rather not take longer than we need to," Tevagah said. "Bard, you will ride with Lilla. Halfling, you will ride with me because I trust you the least. Braug, you are too large and would put too much stress on the horses. I hope that will not be an issue?"

"I can keep up," he said. "I have a very long stride and impressive stamina."

No modesty, this guy.

Garvis took a step toward the horse meant for him, and Para'ray nipped at him.

"Hey, you mangy—"

Before he could finish his curse, Tevagah yanked him up in front of her on the horse. He looked like a little boy, squeezed up there between her and the mane. I might have giggled if I wasn't face-to-face with my own fear.

"You will show her the respect she deserves," Tevagah hissed in Garvis' ear.

At that, Garvis looked even more the part, cowering as if he'd just been scolded by a parent.

I studied Lilla's horse. She was smaller than Para'ray, but that wasn't saying much. I cautiously approached. The last time I rode a horse was in summer camp. I was twelve. It... didn't go well. Let's just say, a clavicle was broken.

Your Riding Skill is currently a .5. You may want to practice.

Five? That's not bad.

Ahem. Point five. As in less than one. As in half of one. As in almost zero.

I swore out loud.

Since when are decimals even involved in this?

"What was that?" Lilla asked, peering over her shoulder and down at me standing behind her Night Mare. That's right. I got to ride behind Lilla.

I'm sure she'll appreciate your enthusiasm.

I'm not twelve anymore.

"Nothing," I said.
"Come then. Telaive doesn't bite... usually." She extended her hand and gave me the assistance I needed to get up.

Yeah, she did. Assistance for daaays.

"Hold on tight around my waist," she said. I could swear there was a bit of playfulness in her tone, though I could've been mistaken. "Don't let go."
I nodded like an idiot as if she could see me. Then, I realized what I was doing and said, "Okay."
Where I'd seen horseback riders give their steeds a light kick to the sides, instead, Lilla bent forward and whispered something into the stately mare's ear. Soon, Telaive took off at a trot. It startled me at first, and I tipped to one side. Tightening my grip on Lilla, I righted myself.
"Move with her," she told me. "Feel her presence. You'll get used to it."
We left the ruins in the rearview and pressed on to the north

through patches of forest and rocky land. The sun continued to trek across the sky, warming me up against the slight chill in the air. The ground was covered in dew, keeping the air humid despite the cooler temperature.

Wherever I was, it certainly seemed to be more or less the same as Earth when it came to climate. Reminded me of my class trip to Arkansas when I was in junior high. Talk about raging hormones. It was my first time in mixed company without my parents around. I'd like to say I was the suave and debonair man I was today, but I was a dork.

Huh. I'm surprised you didn't comment on that.

Repetition is unnecessary at this point.
You know what I think of you.

Lilla and I pulled up with Tevagah and Garvis on one side and Nichelle on the other.

"Let me know if he tries anything," Nichelle said.

It took me a moment to realize she was talking about Garvis and his sticky hands, not me, seated behind the most beautiful woman I'd ever seen.

"I'm not gonna steal anything," Garvis protested, bouncing up and down like a bobblehead.

"That would literally go against every instinct you possess. It is an addiction for people like you." Tevagah said this last part while staring at me.

"Hey," I said. "Don't include me in that."

She nodded at the lute strapped to my back. "I am still trying to figure out how you have managed to so skillfully play that lute that you all insist you did not steal."

"It's not that big a deal," I said with an exaggerated sigh. "Whoop-de-doo. I played an instrument. I'm not *that* talentless."

"I would argue that point," Curr said, jogging just behind us.

Lilla joined the conversation. "Because the lute is not meant to be wielded by some ordinary wellick. And yet, you had no problem playing it. Flawlessly, I might add."

"Thank you." I smiled. That was nicer than anything Curr ever had to say.

"Don't thank me," she replied. "I am as thoroughly confused about it as Tevagah. This is one of the reasons we need to find the oracle."

"How could someone not be able to play a lute anyway?" I asked. "Even if you're bad, it still makes noise."

"Its strings are said to go stiff for those unworthy," Lilla said. "Or in some legends, consume the player entirely."

I swallowed. The hag hadn't warned me about that. Had she known she'd been gambling with my life?

"Quiet," Tevagah warned. "The less he knows, the more I would be inclined to believe what the oracle says. Provide him no information that could be further used to assert his case of ownership."

I shook my head. "It's really nice being treated like a criminal."

"For all we know, you are one," Nichelle said.

"Whatever."

What was I thinking, agreeing to this? Curr was too giddy about a new quest to be of any use. Garvis didn't know anything besides being desperate for coin. And the Sisters were proving to just be miserable all of the time.

You would be too if your people were left endangered and basically homeless. Left to slowly die off.

Fine time to chime in with that. You're making me miserable.

Screenie's words disappeared and weren't replaced by more.

I sighed. "Useless."

Lilla glanced back again. "What did you say?"

"Huh?" I looked up. I didn't realize I'd said that out loud.

"What did you just say?"

"Oh, uh... nothing. Just talking to myself."

"You do that a lot, don't you?" she said. There was a bit of skepticism from her.

"Yeah. No big deal."

She faced forward. "You know, you're not like other bards I've known."

"You've known a lot?" I shocked myself with my tone. Was I jealous? Of random bards? That someone I barely knew, knew random bards? God help me.

Which god?

That was when I remembered my prayer to Actus, the God of Small Things. Wow. He came through... I guess? I found the lute. That was my request. Should I cross myself or something? Stupid. He wasn't Jesus, and I'd never done that in my life.

"A few," Lilla said. "They're usually too self-absorbed. Always writing songs about others but never accomplishing anything on their own." She paused as if thinking. "Can you imagine what a sad life that is? You spend your time singing the praises of others without ever having your own story to tell."

"That is a very astute observation!" Curr chimed in, now jogging beside us like it was nothing.

"Hey, music brings people joy," I countered.

"Not always," Curr argued. "Remember in Nahal?"

I gritted my teeth. "Yes, Curr, I remember..."

Congratulations!

You now know what it's like to be married!

It dawned on me: that's what's been missing in my life lately. Before the Heart-Shaped Box, I'd been playing my own songs. Even if I'd never really made it big, it was my music. Ever since my agent,

Andrei Nadir, decided to turn down a contract on my behalf because "there might be something better" (news flash, there wasn't), I'd been doing cover songs at a hole in the wall.

Even here, with Screenie's Catalog of Songs, none of it was mine. I simply performed worse versions of other people's songs. And if I'd died, who the hell would ever remember me? Heck, if this wasn't a dream and I really had vanished from the real world, who would notice?

Jerry. That's who. The only person alive who would know I was gone was Jerry, the owner of the bar. Even then, he'd just be pissed that his entertainment didn't show up on a Friday night and would no longer schedule me. He wouldn't come looking for me; he'd just hire someone new and assume I'd quit without notice.

"Are you all right?" Lilla asked.

I snapped back to the moment. "Yeah, yeah. I was just thinking about what you said. It does make a lot of sense."

"Thank you."

"No. Thank you. Seriously." I smiled. "I'm afraid I don't really know a lot of bards, myself, so hearing your experiences with them helps."

"My people once believed there was a certain magic in music," she said. "It was more than pleasant notes and words to cheer to. In the right hands, its energy carved rivers. Raised mountains."

"Like that one?" I gestured toward one of the jagged peaks of the Masked Mountains, showing itself in a rare moment.

Her lip twisted. "I... couldn't say."

"What's wrong?"

"Nothing." She shook her head. "We should focus on riding."

She set her attention back on the road ahead, though, I got the distinct impression her Night Mare didn't need help navigating the terrain. Not wanting to risk her wrath again, I didn't press further.

The forest dragged on endlessly. Pearly white ruins popped up through the brush here and there, growing denser the farther we went into the once grand city. It was actually sort of peaceful. And I got into a groove moving with the horse, just like Lilla had instructed.

You have gained +1 in Riding.

Not that kind of riding, you dirty dog, you! You can handle yourself on a horse a little better. Nobody should let you ride alone, though.

Your Riding is now 1.

Curr seemed to be getting a kick out of jogging alongside us the entire way. He never seemed to tire either, even after hours.

Uma suddenly accelerated to burst through the bushes to our right. Scared the piss out of me since it was getting dark. Not literally, though. That would've been embarrassing with that particular region of me pressed so close to Lilla. I hadn't even realized one of the Sisters had vanished.

She whispered something to Tevagah in their language. Screenie didn't translate.

Hey, what gives?

I can't read lips, having no eyes and all.

Whatever she'd said was clearly upsetting. Tevagah started issuing commands. Fortunately, she did so in the common tongue.

"Night is falling," she said. "We should find a defensible position in case any orcs are about. We are far from Balahazia and getting deeper into what is left of our once great land. No soldiers patrol these parts."

"Excellent!" Curr proclaimed.

"We could turn back," Garvis suggested. Sweat poured off him—I suspect from how hard he was holding on to the horse—leaving his collar soaked. "Forget this whole thing altogether."

"If only we could," Tevagah said. Her tone was softer than usual, especially when dealing with Garvis. "But we must determine if the bard over there is speaking truth or lies."

"Danny," I said. "Danny over there. Not 'the bard.' Not 'that one.' Danny. For the last time, I have a name."

"Fine," Tevagah said. "We must prove *Danny* to be a liar so we might regain possession of the lute and put a stop to this lunacy."

I shook my head. "I'm not lying." I was getting tired of that sentence.

"Regardless, we will break here and prepare for the night." She pointed to a wall not far off the road, remnants of an ancient stone building. "We will camp there. The ruins will provide us protection."

"That is a fine location for battle," Curr said. "You are skilled, elf."

"I've been around long enough."

Although I'd been warned numerous times about the dangers of night in the wild, I liked being on the move better. Camping and waiting for something bad to happen was... not enjoyable.

After dismounting, Tevagah gave orders for her party to get a camp going using supplies slung over their horses' saddles. They were like a well-oiled machine, distributing stores of arrows and sparking a fire.

Lilla hopped down, then motioned at my short sword dangling down from the horse. "Are you any good with that?"

My gaze fell to the grass at my feet. I thought back to how horrendously I performed back in the Fighters Guild. "Honestly?"

"Always."

"Not really. I only have it because Curr told me I needed it."

"He wasn't lying," she said kindly. "You do need it here. But not being able to wield it is a liability." Extending her hand, she offered to help me. "They'll set up. You, come with me."

"Where are we going?" I asked.

She eyed me. "You are in the dangerous wilds, Danny. In the forsaken ruins of Alyndis. That means you need to learn how to use that sword."

She used my name.

Oh, grow up.

C'mon. That must mean something.

You literally JUST yelled at them to use your name.

Oh, right...

Danny. Your lack of Intelligence is showing. Now go swing your sword at her. That ought to impress the fine lady.

Not.

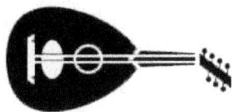

42

Lilla guided me to a clearing to what I thought was east of camp. I still couldn't be positive since everything had been so chaotic, but it seemed like the rotation of Aethonia was similar to that of Earth. Unless, of course, this planet really *was* flat. Then I had no clue.

Ding! You nailed it. And it's on the back of a turtle.

Very funny. It's not, right?

We'll never know.

The sun had all but set, and above, the moon started to show. It was odd, looking up at a moon without the familiar pockmarks and bunny-shaped divots. I hadn't really paid much attention to it until now. This one was pristine, and its silvery glow was almost supernatural feeling. Like it gave off its own light instead of reflecting that of its sun. It dappled the pine boughs overhead. A few spare drops of lingering rain flitted down through the branches, making the air smell sweet.

It was... romantic.

Then, to my absolute horror, the lute started playing itself again. The same '70s-style porno music from Kiel's.

Lilla turned toward me.

"I'm sorry," I said. "It's not me. It's—"

"The lute," she said. "I know. According to legend, it bonds with its owner, enough to learn their feelings, even warn them of danger."

"You know?" I asked, baffled.

"Yes. All those who have sworn the way of the Sisterhood do. That is how I recognized it back at the trader's post, as none of us have ever seen it. Here, watch this."

She drew her sword, which was longer and looked of far finer workmanship than mine.

In an instant, the lute's song changed to something more appropriate for a battle scene in *The Lord of the Rings*.

... And my lute!

What?

Don't think about The Lord of the Rings *if you don't even get the* references, fool of a Took.

I was too distracted by what she'd told me to notice Screenie's games. All my stressing over revealing the truth, risking what Curr might think of such magic or anyone else—useless.

"Now, we'll go over the basics first," Lilla said. "Draw your sword."

I tore the blade free of the scabbard. Okay, fine, I didn't tear it free. I fumbled with it until it slipped out. It wasn't very impressive.

Lilla shook her head. "You'll ruin the scabbard before too long doing it like that. The blade should slide out smoothly. You don't have to yank so hard."

That's what she—

Not now, please?

"Try it again," Lilla said. "Don't pull. Guide."

I replaced the sword and then tried to make the movement as smooth as I could.

This time, Lilla smiled. "Better. Work on it." She gripped her sword in one hand. "We'll start with one hand since your blade is much shorter than mine."

Didn't know this was going to be a measuring contest.

Everything in life is a measuring contest.

I held the short sword out in front of me, copying the way Lilla clutched hers. She moved with the blade as if they were one, making it look utterly effortless.

"The first strike is an overhead one." She charged at me, swinging the blade up and over her head before coming straight down like she intended to cleave me in two pieces.

I'd like to say I dodged or parried or pivoted out of the way as fast as I could, but the truth was far more embarrassing. Maybe I was shaken after fighting in Balahazia, but I threw my sword up over my head with one hand and covered my skull with the other.

Her sword slapped into mine, causing it to career downward and bonk me with the flat portion.

"Uhm," she said, backing up slowly. "Good... ish."

"How was that good?"

Good question.

"Well, you kept my sword from killing you," she said generously.

"And mine almost killed me. I'm sorry. I'm just tired, I guess."

"Monsters of the wild won't care if you're tired. They'll relish in it."

"Right," I said.

"Ready your blade again," she instructed, and I did.

She came at me once more, and this time, I planted my feet and raised my sword to block. When her sword connected with mine, I stumbled back from the force and landed on my ass.

"Better!"

"Once again," I said, "how was that better?"

"You purposely deflected my attack," she said. "The problem was that you had your feet too close. You've got to stagger them, like this." She spread her boots like a baseball player getting ready to swing. "Shoulder-width apart. That'll displace the power of my strike and you'll take the weight on your back leg. C'mon, stand up."

I hadn't even realized I was still sitting on the grass. I rose and did as she'd instructed.

"Now bend your knees slightly. Good. Okay. Again."

She rushed at me, and I raised my sword to meet hers. Then at the last moment, she changed the course of her strike and batted me in the ribs with the flat of her sword.

All the air in my lungs went bye-bye as I hunched over, heaving. "What was that!" I demanded after regaining my breath.

"You telegraphed your defense," she said. "A real enemy would take advantage of any opening."

"But this isn't a real fight!" I groaned.

"Did that hurt?" she asked, one hand resting on her hip.

I hesitated. The truth was, it did. But wouldn't I look weak if I admitted it? Though she'd easily know I was lying if I denied it, which would make me exactly the thing I'd been accused of since we'd met: a liar.

"Yeah, a little," I said.

"Then this is a real fight. Do it again."

The sound of metal against metal rang as I raised my sword to block hers. She took another step forward and swiped at my body. I blocked that as well, though the vibration from her attack sent pain radiating up my arm and into my neck.

Screenie flashed.

You have gained +1 in Melee Weapon Combat.

Your Melee Weapon Combat is now 14.

Go, Danny! Show her how well you wield your weapon.

"You have better reflexes than I expected," Lilla said.

I wheezed. "Yeah... something about the prospect of being cut in half can really motivate a guy to block."

"Worry not. I would've stopped before I struck you down."

"I thought we were learning defense against an overhead strike?"

"Can't blame a girl for trying to figure out what she's up against." She smirked. "Okay, your turn."

"To attack?"

She nodded. "Just like I did."

"Hmmm. Okay." I spun my short sword blade overhead and attacked before she had any chance to prepare. For a moment, I thought I might've caught her by surprise, then she simply slid out of the way and used the flat of her blade to slap down on mine. The weight of it knocked my pathetic little sword right out of my pathetic little hand.

I blinked, looking like a complete fool.

Pointing to where my sword lay in the dirt, she said, "Don't ever allow your grip to get so loose that it's easy to disarm."

"It wasn't on purpose."

"You need to straddle the realm between flexibility and enough strength to keep a grip on it. Understand?"

"I think I get it." I bent to pick up my sword and she tapped me on the rear with her sword.

"Come on," I complained.

"The battle is never over until one of us is dead," she warned.

"Dead?"

"Not right now," she assured me. "But again, orcs won't care that you lost your sword, they'll—"

"Relish in it. I know."

"Good. Now we'll go again."

For the next hour or so, Lilla worked me through a series of simple maneuvers that she insisted would help keep me alive in case of danger. By the time we were through, I was a sweaty bag of ass and probably stunk like it too. According to Screenie, my Melee Weapon Combat also went up by another point by the end of it. Better than nothing.

Is it always this easy to gain points in stuff?

When you're as low a level as you are, things progress quickly. Don't get used to it.

Eventually, Nichelle wandered over with a water skin and I sucked some down before handing it to Lilla. Nothing like a sword fight to take all the gentleman out of me. For all her exertion, she still appeared fresh, unfatigued, and just as mind-blowingly gorgeous. Though she did take some water.

I know you've told me you don't need my help to know when you're starving, but... They can hear your stomach grumbling back in Balahazia.

"We'd better eat," Lilla said, gesturing to lead me back toward the camp. My face went hot. No doubt she'd heard what Screenie was referring to.

"I couldn't agree more," I said.

"You did well. You should be proud."

Your standing with the Sisterhood of Alyndis has improved.

Smooth entry into the friend zone!

"I'd rather be alive than proud."

"You're one step closer to surviving an inevitable attack," she said nonchalantly.

"Inevitable?"

She looked at me like I'd just asked her what color steak smelled like.

"Yes, inevitable. There is a reason Alyndis is abandoned. We will fight orcs or worse before this journey ends. It's not a matter of if, but when."

It was nice knowing you, bub.

I nodded over at Garvis as we entered the camp's periphery. "I guess he doesn't need any instruction?"

Lilla shrugged. "The halfling is not suited to open combat. Yet I have little doubt he possesses the skills necessary to sneak up behind something and stab it in the back. But more than likely, he just knows how to stay out of the way and alive."

"And I'm suited to open combat?" I asked, only fishing a little.

"Not by much," Lilla admitted. "But we need numbers, and right now, that is your main role."

I stopped walking. "Right. So, I'm cannon fodder."

"I don't know what a cannon is, but I will do my best not to let you die. Just don't get carried away and keep your back to something —a tree, stone, anything you can find when the time comes."

As I started walking again, I couldn't help thinking she was talking about this fight like it was absolutely going to happen. That scared me. I didn't want to admit it, but I was shaking in my boots.

I took that as a good sign to grab a handful of the tasteless rations and take a seat by the fire.

Garvis busied himself with a pair of daggers I hadn't seen on him before. The way he palmed and flipped them led me to conclude that Lilla's estimation of his skills was probably spot-on.

I watched him a long while before finally breaking the silence. "Aren't you concerned?"

Garvis shrugged. "Not really. There are enough nooks and crannies around these ruins that I can find a way to hide myself if need be. And if any orcs get too close, I'll yigging slit them open from neck to nuts, as the saying goes."

"I wish I had your confidence." I looked down at the rations and didn't feel much like eating any longer.

"It's not about having confidence," Garvis said. "It's simply about accepting the idea that you could eat shog and die, and making peace with it."

"How do you do that?"

"Not a universal answer, boyo," he said. "Some people are born wanting to die and think death can't come soon enough."

That struck a chord with me.

Struck a chord. I see what you did there.

I ignored the blasted screen.

It's what I had done before entering Aethonia. I wasn't really living; just existing from one Friday to the next. In retrospect, I couldn't even remember what most days were like for me. I woke up at the butt crack of 3pm and whittled the time away until I could sleep again.

"For others," Garvis continued, "they are content with their accomplishments and go to death without regrets." He smirked. "And then there are those who fear it and usually end up dying first."

"Isn't a bit of fear a good thing?" I asked.

"Sure, but not when it paralyzes you. Look at me, bard." He gestured to himself with one flat hand. "My kind live in hills and hovels, in far off and peaceful places. They fear everything in all the world. But you want to know what I've found?"

"What?"

"The world ain't that yigging scary. When you're a target to everything, everything is a target to you. You just got to catch them looking over your head."

With that response, I honestly felt like I understood him a little better. Underestimated. Looked down on. He'd learned to do whatever he needed to survive.

"Everyone, stay at the ready," Tevagah ordered, suddenly coming up behind us.

And me, scared of my own shadow, jumped. Realizing she wasn't a threat, I quickly recovered and said, "I don't hear anything."

Just the distant howls of wolves and insects in the trees. Wind rustling. Nothing that sounded overly dangerous. What had this world done to me? Wolves, not dangerous?

"A bad sign," Tevagah said. "Orcs will take the time to eat first because they don't believe in fighting on an empty stomach. Remember that when you stab them in the belly. It gets messy."

"Lovely," I said. "I'm sure the smell is wonderful too."

"It will linger in your nostrils for days. But you get used to it."

"You've killed a lot of them, have you?"

"The wild is our home now. Killing is what we are trained to do. So, we do it. I wish the world were another way, that it was not so necessary. Alas, this is our destiny."

I found that sad. Though I didn't want to say anything to insult their culture.

I glanced around the campsite. "Where's Curr?"

"The braug went to relieve himself," Tevagah said. "Have no fear."

"It's not him I'm worried about," I said under my breath.

I was only alive because of Curr. Had it not been for him, I never would've survived that korken fight.

Tevagah regarded me for a moment. "You really have not been in many battles before, have you?"

"Only a few." I absentmindedly started counting on my fingers. "There were the korkens. Some wraiths. We fought you guys twice... Oh! Garvis and I had a serious tussle in a tavern a few days back."

"And how did that go?" Tevagah asked, a small smile barely perceptible on her face.

I lowered my voice so Lilla wouldn't hear us. "He almost beat the crap out of me."

Tevagah chuckled a bit, a sound that felt totally foreign coming from her. I didn't think it was possible, especially with the Dagger of Discontent back in her possession.

"That is refreshing," she said.

"What is?"

"You admitting that you are terrible at fighting."

"I didn't say I was *terrible* at it."

She waved me off. "Most men would never admit that they had been bested in a fight. The fact that it doesn't seem to upset you is refreshing."

"I killed a korken," I declared.

"Who hasn't?" Tevagah asked seriously.

She started to walk away, but I couldn't let it rest. "Garvis was drunk," I said. "So when I finally did get the upper hand, it didn't necessarily feel as though I'd won anything, you know?"

"I understand," Tevagah said quietly. "Tonight, you may not have the option of feeling one way or another. You must do what needs to be done without hesitation. Otherwise, you might die."

I didn't respond. I couldn't. Fear had me gripped like a boa constrictor.

Tevagah studied me. After a moment, she nodded. "I believe you will fare better than you think. Take that as you will. I must see that we have a defensive perimeter established. Even now, the quiet night air brings a cold foreboding with it."

She strode away, leaving me with my thoughts.

Have you considered what you wanted engraved on your headstone?

Actually, I have, but this isn't the time for it.

Please tell me. I'll increase any Skill you want. Please. Please. Pretty please?

Good offer. But I'll pass.

I will get you to tell me. Even if it costs breaking the world, I will.

I found that statement kind of scary. Then I shivered as I realized Tevagah was right. There was indeed a chilly breeze blowing through the trees. I wondered if orcs could smell us sitting here. I could almost see them salivating. And I hoped, desperately, that they weren't as terrifying as the ones I'd seen in movies.

They are worse.

Seriously, are you ever helpful?

I really am trying to be helpful here. It would not be wise for you to be unprepared. Orcs are among the most terrifying species in Aethonia. It's said the elves kept them at bay at the height of their power. That orcs feared them in a way they don't wellicks. But when the elves lost, they infested all that remained of their fallen kingdom.

Pyruun would have been overwhelmed if the first king didn't turn to the dark magic of the Academy of Learning. They developed a plague that afflicted only orcs... mostly.

What does mostly mean?

Not everyone was safe from it. They call it the green plague. Still haunts many regions. But if not for the Academy's quick work, the age of wellicks might have ended as soon as it began.

But it didn't. They survived long enough to become the fearsome conquerors.

You either die a hero, or you live long enough to see yourself become the villain.

With a deep breath, I took to the perimeter of our camp to look for Curr. The big guy could slaughter a pack of orcs with ease. I needed to be close to him if *shog*—as Garvis would've called it—hit the fan.

NEW OBJECTIVE:
Survive the orc attack.

REWARD:
Living long enough to complete your last objective: Locate the Oracle of Alyndis.

A New Title.

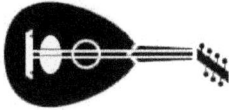

43

Tension mounted like an oncoming hurricane. To me at least. Night's slithering tendrils crept in from all around us. I simply waited. What else could I do?

To make matters worse, Curr still hadn't returned from his constitutional. I'd looked everywhere within range of camp and, no big braug.

I exhaled through my teeth. Maybe nothing would show, and we were all worried over nothing.

And maybe one day I'll have a body again!

Now, isn't the time... Wait, again?

Did I say again?

Yes, at least, I think so. Is that true?

No, Danny. I never have had a body. Ever. Zilch.

Screenie's slip-up had me thinking. What was this thing that was talking to me all the time? A computer? A god?

I am no god. Alas, I teleport into my pants just like everyone else.

You wear pants?

No. I—just. Goodness, Danny. Just focus on not dying, would you?

Probably to Screenie's delight, Nichelle zipped into camp on horseback, disrupting our conversation to bring news to Tevagah. I tried to eavesdrop, but, again, their mouths were obscured, and they spoke too low for Screenie's help. Their faces told the story before Tevagah turned to address the rest of us.

"Our concerns proved true," she said. "Orcs are on our trail. A large pack—at least a dozen or so."

"Mad orcs," Garvis said. "They've gotta know we won't go down easy."

"Higher risk for a greater reward," Tevagah said.

"Reward?" I gulped.

"It is possible they know what we have in our possession."

"In my possession, you mean?" I asked.

"I think they mean me," Garvis said, puffing out his chest. "I'm quite the reward."

"Perhaps for now," Tevagah said, ignoring Garvis as we all mostly did. "Either way, it puts us all at risk."

My face must have given away my internal turmoil.

"Just do as you did with me and you'll be fine," Lilla said, leaning in close.

"It was one training session," I argued.

"They aren't good with weapons," she said. "They prefer their teeth and claws. That means you'll always have the reach advantage."

That made me feel better for about two seconds. Then I considered how real the possibility of being bitten and clawed was, and there was no Old Kiel around to patch me up this time. I'd never experienced pain like when that korken raked its talons over my ribs, and I wasn't interested in that feeling ever again.

Don't worry. If they cut you, they'll kill you.

That helps, thanks.

I live to serve.

Tevagah and the Sisters produced compact bows from their packs, each with a quiver, assembled and strung them before giving them a test pull. I imagined they would be useful at both close and long-range.

We kept three good-size fires burning with plenty of wood nearby.

"Shouldn't we, you know, put out the fires?" I asked. "They're gonna see it."

"They have likely already seen them," Tevagah said. "We do nothing by accident, bar—Danny. Orcs see better in the dark. This will work to our advantage. We will set the entire place ablaze if need be."

"They don't tolerate extreme changes in lighting well," Lilla explained. "If we get desperate enough, then we throw all that on the fire, and hopefully, it gives us a minute to hit them hard while their eyes adjust." Lilla added more wood to the pile. I noticed she wasn't wearing her cloak. None of the Sisters I could spot along the perimeter were.

I asked about it.

"There is no hiding now," she replied. "Cloaks get tangled up in battle. That's the last thing we want."

I was suddenly self-conscious of my own flamboyant cloak. Reaching up to take it off, I couldn't get the clasp undone. Lilla saw me struggling and, like an angel, helped. While her hands were at my throat, she looked into my eyes, and my heart hammered.

"No need to linger," Tevagah said, a disapproving look on her face. She shook her head and wandered away.

"Uh-oh, you made the boss mad," I joked.

Lilla nudged me a little bit. "Just make sure you survive the night, alright?"

"You too."

Lilla smiled, and my damn lute played a soft, romantic twang. I wanted to rip its strings off.

"Sorry," I said.

"What a strange song," Lilla said. I thought I saw the barest hint of blush on her cheeks. "And listen, if things get dire, fall back as much as you can. We'll hold them until sun-up."

"Do you think we can?" The question was less about my doubt, and more about me seeking hope where I was beginning to feel hopeless.

"We've fought worse and lived to tell the tale. So will you."

That was the bolstering I needed. I drew a deep breath and—

"Do not make promises none of us can keep," Tevagah warned.

—my hope was dashed.

I sucked in another deep breath, and on the exhale, said, "I wish I knew where Curr was."

"I agree. Having a braug around wouldn't hurt." Lilla squeezed my arm. "He'll be back soon. I'm sure of it. Sometimes those big guys have more trouble... you know." With that, she went to take her position with her Sisters.

"Can you please not do that?" I snapped at my lute once I was alone.

You shouldn't talk to it that way. Do you not remember when it froze time to save your sorry hide?

Now that would be nice now. Can we try it again?

Wait until you're surrounded and get playing, Mozart.

Will that work?

It's a Special Ability I've never encountered before. We'll need to learn more about the Lute of Seven Stars to figure out how and when you can trigger it.

Can't you look around in your database or something!?

If only it were that simple...

It never is.

I took my folded up cloak and found a safe spot for it out of the reach of the flames.

Without your cloak, you will lose your +1 to Charisma and Speechcraft boon.

I don't think I'll be talking myself out of this fight.

That's very true. And actually, by losing it, you will gain back the Sneaking point you lose while wearing it.

Are you saying I did something smart? Does that gain me a point in Intelligence?

I said it before, Intelligence and other Attributes don't work that way. Just be glad you're not a big pink target anymore.

From what I could see, we had a ring around the campsite. At

Tevagah's command, each Sister had been portioned a section that curved outward. Garvis and I waited by one of the fires. I hoped the fight wouldn't even get close enough for me to draw my sword. But a bigger part of me suspected I was about to get my first taste of real combat.

You seem nervous. Would you like to calm yourself?

How in the world can I do that?

Would you like to access your Catalog of Songs?

I nodded and saw the now familiar list of songs.

Choose "Tillith's Last Call" (20 inst. 15 sin.).

I figured if I'd been able to play "Promise of the Son," my playing skill was at least 29. Playing something that was a 20 seemed safe enough. Looked pretty simple too. It wasn't a sprawling list of notes as the last one had been, just a few simple chords and a basic picking pattern. What's funny is I still didn't *know* what any of the notes were. Somehow, the lute did, though, and that knowledge transferred to my hands as I swung my lute around to my front and played the notes.

A familiar warmth flowed through my body, like someone had poured molten chocolate over me. It was a pleasurable feeling. Suddenly, lyrics came unbidden to my lips.

> *The dream of many is to live forever*
> *But to die is gain*
> *Should the truth be found in life's surrender*
> *Then let me make it plain*

Fear shall never grip my heart
as long as I hold onto this
My soul's great passion
My heart's greatest wish

Should this be my final stand
I'll do so straight and tall
With sword in hand and song on tongue
I shall give my all

The song definitely steadied my nerves—honestly, even restored some of my faith that we would survive. When it was over, Garvis sniffled next to me.

Soothing. Inspiring. Your nerves are settled. See, that's what a bard who isn't only into coin can do! Take that, elves.

The members of your Party gain +5 to Dexterity and Constitution for the next ten minutes.

I glanced over at Garvis. "Sorry, I didn't mean to disturb you."

"Disturb? You are more talented than I thought." He sighed and put a hand over his heart. "I wish you could've played it louder for everyone to hear. It has made me feel... serene."

"I knew there was a reason I kept you around," I said.

"Yiggin' good shog," Garvis said. He drew two daggers and started flipping them over again and again. "I suppose I should ready myself as well."

He began to rise when I asked, "Think it will be bad?"

Garvis pursed his lips. "Most likely. Then again, our companions are a fearsome bunch of warriors."

"I'm worried about Curr," I admitted.

Garvis laughed. "He probably found some of them orcs straggling behind and is giving them shog in a barrel. See you on the other side."

I watched as he ducked into the shadows. That reminded me of something Tevagah had said.

Screenie, can I sneak?

Your Sneaking skill hasn't been well-practiced; thus, it is of no use to you in this particular battle.

Even after removing my cloak and gaining back a point?

Even with that. As far as sneaks go, you're a squeaky shoe.

What's my number?

3.

That's bad.

Indeed. For it to be useful, you should use it more often.

How do I do that?

It's quite difficult. Very detailed.

Really?

No. You just... sneak around people without being caught.

And what if I do it now?

The orcs will have a fun game of hide and seek before spilling your entrails. They love spilling entrails.

Gross.

I shook my head and drew my short sword. The blade glimmered at me in the fire's light. I really hoped it wouldn't break like that rusty old dagger had. At the very least, it survived training with Lilla, but was she hitting with the force it would take to down an orc?

"Steady yourself," I whispered.

"I remember my first time in combat as a child," Tevagah said, approaching me from behind. "I wanted to vomit. You will know what to do when it happens."

"Easy for you to say, you've been doing it for hundreds of years."

"Each time one enters into battle, it is much like the first time."

"Doesn't seem that way for Curr," I argued.

"Braugs are a different breed. They are born with the lust for battle and bloodshed. That makes them immune to the natural inclination toward self-preservation. I sometimes envy them for it. Most times, I find only pity for them. A creature so incapable of appreciating their own self-worth... Would that we could all see our worth and do whatever necessary to protect it, rather than rushing headlong into the gaping maw of death and destruction." She took a small breath. "Good luck tonight."

"Really? Me. The thief who stole your holy lute?" I knew I was hiding my fear behind the joke, but screw it. What's wrong with that? Everyone likes a good laugh.

Except nobody's laughing. Hear that? No giggles. Just crickets.

"Yes, you," Tevagah said. "If you die this soon, we will never get the answers we seek. Yet, I suppose your death will be an answer in itself."

"Thank you." I raised my sword like a dummy.

"This is no joke, Danny. You had better hope you are who Lilla believes you to be. If true, you shall not die this night."

Tevagah removed her cloak like the others and laid it carefully on the ground, folding it in a very specific sort of way. When she rose, I noticed something in the same firelight that illuminated my sword.

Her armor was almost as stunning as the Sisters themselves. Except there was no reflection from the flames. Black as the night surrounding us, her armor seemed to drink in everything around her, including the campfire's light. Sharp lines and plunging contours cascaded like a waterfall of death from her shoulders to her toes.

I was no blacksmith, but if I had to venture a guess, it was designed to not just stop an attack, but to deflect the blade downward and away from her head.

As she bent to adjust her dagger and sword, the armor flexed like cotton. Then she stepped forward and appraised her troops, bobbing her head to each of them in turn as if giving them a final word of encouragement.

I marveled at her demeanor. Even without having the boon of my song, she had the stillness of a leader who both knew how to deal death and remain above the chaos. Though I wondered whether she truly felt that way, especially in light of what she'd said to me.

From somewhere out in the woods, a sound arose, floating in to where we all waited. There came a gnawing in the pit of my stomach. I couldn't help it. Without warning to myself or the others, I puked right into the fire. Even with the song's boon aiding me, my nerves were off the charts.

The stench that arose was vile. It left me coughing and had Lilla staring at me.

Tic-Tac, sir?

Before I could respond, the lute started strumming a familiar tune again. But it had nothing to do with Lilla. This one... meant danger.

Enemy orcs are approaching.

I took a breath, felt the short sword in my grip, and tried to remember everything Lilla had taught me. One way or another, I was going to have to use it tonight.

A rustle in the bushes drew my glare and I prepared myself to see my first orc.

Then, Curr pushed through. "Did I miss anything?"

Despite myself, I ran up and hugged the big guy.

"Do I have something on my back?" he asked, craning his neck to see what my hands were doing.

"No. I—I'm just glad you made it back," I said. "Where were you?"

"Something I ate must have upset my stomach. I had to expel it, and the smell would not be conducive to camping, so I went upwind."

Of course. Curr roamed off to take a legendary dump and almost missed out on what he would call "fun." I could just hear my mom yelling at me about the friends I choose to hang out with.

"Save it for private time," Tevagah told us. "They near."

Curr beamed a wide smile as he pulled his axe from his back scabbard.

The battle hymn from my lute grew louder.

"Yes, Danny! That song again!"

Your Music has invigorated your Party!

+2 Bonus to Strength, Dexterity, and Constitution for Duration of Battle.

Wow. Strength, Dexterity, and Constitution. If only it could have given Curr intestinal constitution as well.

"This is not the time for music, bard!" Tevagah warned.

"It's not... me," I said.

She looked back, realizing that the lute wasn't even in my hands, yet the strings vibrated to create a melody all on their own.

Tevagah's face went pale. "It is true..."

Then, the twang of a bowstring drew my focus, and Lilla's voice rose in a shout. "Fire at will! Here they come!"

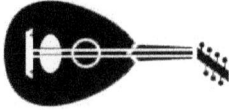

44

The Sisters' bowstrings released simultaneously with a *whoosh* like a great gust of wind. From beyond the glow of the fire-light, a chorus of inhuman wails and shrieks filled the night air.

The Sisterhood didn't hesitate, merely restrung and fired again.

I wondered how they could possibly see out into the darkness to any great effect. I was virtually blind looking out there. Snarls and gnashing sounded, and by the time I found their source, I was too late. A grunt came from our side, and I turned to see Uma down. She crumpled to the floor, and without thinking, I rushed to her side. An orc stood over her, and the sight of it made me stop in my tracks.

Screenie was right, they were far more disgusting-looking than I'd imagined. I had this image in mind from movies, but here in the flesh, that made me realize how much makeup and prosthetics were involved. Where, in those films, they still vaguely looked like actors, humans, these looked utterly monstrous and horrifyingly real.

Eyes the color of earwax, almost nonexistent, were buried deep into its skull. Spiky protrusions hovered above them like eyebrows or lashes, though they looked deadly. Jutting from its mouth were hooklike tusks, covered in slobber. Unlike the razor-sharp goblin teeth, these were broken, and some were filed to a rounded tip. I doubted that made them much less useful, though. Lumpy green skin like alligator scales was blotched with patches of stringy black hair, matted in blood and stink.

Suddenly, it started glowing blueish white.

Orc Scout
Level 9
HP: 52/55

Before I could snap back to motion, I saw a massive blur and then, the Level 9 Orc Scout was gone. It was Curr, shouldering into it at a speed I didn't think him capable of—or anyone, for that matter. Together, they careened into a tree. Bark shattered into splinters, and the rest of the tree clambered to the ground where the sound mixed with pained cries of more creatures. I was tempted to watch, until I remembered Uma.

With the threat temporarily taken care of, I rushed to the downed elf. Dark blood ran from a wound at her neck. Her breathing came in sputters even as I tried to haul her back to the fire.

"No time," Tevagah called to me. "Leave her be and take up her bow!"

I blinked. "Take up her—"

"Now!"

I pried the bow from Uma's fingers and dislodged the quiver from beneath her.

"Sorry," I whispered.

WEAPON OBTAINED:
Elvish Compact Bow. (Ranged Damage 13-17)

This bow has no magical qualities. It is not the weapon that makes the warrior, but the warrior that makes the weapon.

In summation. You are useless with a bow.

Oh, yeah? Well, I had no idea how to play a lute either when I got here.

You aren't making the compelling argument you think you are...

It was mostly true. I hadn't shot a bow since gym class in some high school grade. Once. Now didn't seem like the best time to tell Tevagah that. Besides, I remember being decent. Though, I'm pretty sure those arrows were Nerf-tipped...

I nocked a very real, very sharp arrow, and pulled back on the bowstring. My right hand, firmly gripping the shaft—hah, hah, very funny—wobbled a bit under the strain. I had no idea how anyone aimed something like this. When I thought it was time to release, I peered out into the darkness, seeing only vague movement. I picked a target at random and let the arrow fly.

I was sure I'd missed. Then heard a shriek and saw the shadow fall to the ground, holding its shoulder area. "Oh... well... damn. How about that?"

Level 2 Orc Grunt slain!

You have gained +1 in Ranged Combat.

Your Ranged Combat is now 9.

I didn't have time to celebrate my already impressive stats. Nor the time to read Screenie's message that popped up, no doubt telling me my stats weren't impressive at all.

More enemies rushed toward our position. I tossed the bow to the side even before I heard Tevagah shout, "Shields and swords!"

WEAPON LOST:
Elvish Compact Bow.

Welp, that was quick.

"Huh? Shields?" I watched in envy as all the Sisters raised their forearms and whispered commands in elvish. What reminded me of some kind of science-fictiony, ovular-shaped silvery force field emanated from their metal arm bracers.

They're an elvish construct. Silver bracers enchanted with magical barriers that dispel attacks of a physical nature. Plus, they look hella cool.

Remind me to ask for one later!

Then came the onslaught. And I had no cool, glowy energy shield.

I swore to myself, positioning my legs as Lilla had taught me.

The sound of metal clashing rang out in every direction. Each of the Sisters were engaged with orcs, the enemy swords sizzling off their shields. On my back, the battle hymn of my lute filled the smoky night air. It was actually kind of helpful to hear. It bolstered my resolve to stay alive, as if I needed that.

Already, your Strength, Dexterity, and Constitution have been raised. How do you think you managed to pull that bowstring, let alone hit something?

An orc plowed forward, eyes fixed on me. It stopped and sneered. At least I thought it was a sneer. He could have been smiling for all I knew. Its hooked tusks glistened in the wan light of the moon.

I think I shouted like a scared child as he charged me, but I didn't back down. He swung his clawed hand at my head way before I expected him to. I guess I wasn't used to the reach these creatures had.

Somehow, by miracle or luck, I deflected it, slapping it down with the flat of my blade like Lilla had done. I grabbed the sword's grip with both hands and plunged the blade into its chest. My lute played a loud crescendo as if to emphasize the move.

I'd like to say the sword went "hilt deep" as I've heard said before, but it didn't. The metal hit bone and stopped. The orc's forward momentum halted, though. I wasn't able to tell the difference between a smile and sneer earlier, but this expression was unmistakable. First, he was stunned entirely, as if completely flabbergasted some puny punk like me could have even landed a single blow. Then, his face turned to pure rage.

So, what did I do? I put all my meager might into throwing my shoulder into the pommel of the short sword and, *fwoop*, the blade sank in deeper. Blood geysered out of his mouth and into my face as my sword punched into his heart.

Holy shit. That was... almost competent!

I puked again at that point. Then I rose and swiped at my face, desperate to try to clear my eyes and reorient myself to the battle. Upon receiving my sight back, I noted the orc remained standing. Clearly, he was no longer alive, but his body simply didn't want to fall.

I seized hold of my weapon and violently jerked back and forth. No one tells you how hard it is to get a sword free once you've jabbed it into flesh and sinew. My hands were slipping, absolutely covered in blood. I was virtually drenched in every bit of disgusting ooze one could ever imagine, but I shook it off. Pressing my foot against the—somehow—still standing orc, I wrenched the blade free.

Level 4 Orc Grunt slain!

My heart thundered in my chest. Blood pulsed in my ears. I'd never killed anything humanoid before—unless you count the orc I'd shot moments ago. But I hadn't seen that one. Not up close and personal like this. I'd defended myself, so I didn't feel what I'd done was wrong, but it just felt... sad.

He was going to kill you, champ. Take the win. I'm shocked you pulled it off.

That makes two of us.

On the periphery of my vision, I saw the Sisterhood all engaged in fighting. The sounds and the grunts of battle echoed in my ears along with my lute's musical score. More orcs rushed into the area. This was much, much more than just a dozen orcs. There had to be at least twenty of them.

Despair washed over me, but I didn't even have a chance to focus on it because another orc with an arrow sticking out of his shoulder darted in to cut me down, slashing from side to side and howling like a wild beast.

And now it's time for my favorite part of the game... SUDDEN DEATH!

He thrust, and my lute played another loud chord.

Follow the rhythm.

Turn off notifications!

That wasn't a notification. It was just me...

Please!

I grunted. I parried. I slashed. I missed. I tripped. I stood. It was all a bit much. But having words popping up over my vision didn't help at all.

The orc let out a primal roar and tried to bite my head off. In a desperate effort, I dropped to my knees. A hard swipe went overhead. The music pulsed in my ears, so loud it was hard to concentrate on anything else.

Wait. What did you say?

Screenie didn't answer. I swore to myself, then stood. What did he say? Follow the rhythm?

He might have just been making jokes, but what if he wasn't? I was going to feel really stupid if this was how I died. But I had no choice, did I?

Raising my sword, I all but closed my eyes, letting the lute's melody permeate every bit of me. Once I had a grasp on the tempo, I began to... dance. I don't mean some crazy viral social media dance, or even the Country two-step. I mean, I bounced back and forth on the balls of my feet and did as Screenie instructed.

I followed the rhythm.

By the time the orc's next strike came, I was ready for it. This time, instead of blocking his attack with the flat of my blade, I let the edge rake downward on his scaly arm. It was a success! I'd cut him. Still bobbing, I did it again, and again, until I sensed my enemy getting frustrated.

Frustrated wasn't the right word. Royally pissed off.

He came at me harder, and I didn't relent in my embodiment of the song. I let the music move me.

I spun, bringing my sword around with me. My grip was reversed so the sword pointed downward, but still aimed it at the orc. Then came a fleshy *squishing* and I was suddenly under a waterfall of orc blood.

Releasing the sword, I rolled aside. The monster fell forward and landed on the pommel of my weapon. The tip stabbed up through its head as it lay there, arms twitching.

Level 5 Orc Grunt slain!

A Level above you? That's a new record!

You have gained +1 in Melee Weapon Combat

Your Melee Weapon Combat is now 16.

I knew it was stupid, but I couldn't help but laugh. I'd just killed one on purpose, and somewhat skillfully! The music really had guided me. Once I regained my bearings and realized I was still in a freaking war, and unarmed, I tried to get my sword back, but it was useless.

WEAPON LOST:
Iron Short Sword.

The orc must have weighed a thousand pounds, and my sword was buried in his body and head. *And* more orcs were coming at me. They didn't make it far. Curr came rushing back into the fray, tearing apart three more. Literally. He held one of their arms in his bare hand like it was a mace or something.

"Fall back to the flames!" Tevagah's voice sounded clear and strong, but her command made me wonder if we'd sustained more casualties.

I didn't have to be told twice. I turned tail and ran back to the fire, empty-handed. Once there, teeny, tiny, itty-bitty letters appeared at the center of my vision.

I squinted but couldn't make it out.

What?

It got a little bit bigger.

I still can't read that.

Then, the words grew, and I read:

Can I talk now?

Goddammit, Screenie. Yes! What do you need?

It's not what I need. It's an update.

**You are Fatigued. Here is numeric proof:
STAMINA: 26/75**

That's better than dead.

Then I got excited.

Screenie, that worked! I followed the music and it actually worked!

It's true then, the rhythm is finally gonna get you.

That was lame.

You're lame.

Really, though. Thank you. I think I would have died back there if you hadn't clued me in on how this works.

I've got news for you, bub. I have no idea how this works.

As always, I couldn't be sure if Screenie was telling the truth. But I didn't care. I was alive.

When we had all reached the fire, I noticed only four of us remained. Tevagah, Lilla, Nichelle, and me. I had no idea where

Garvis had gotten off to. I suspected he might've just been hiding and trying to stay out of the melee.

Curr still raged at the periphery away from our formation, having the time of his life.

"I hunger for orc blood!" he hollered.

The rest of us were basically side by side then, closer to the lute so the hymn surrounded us. I noticed Lilla's finger tapping to the rhythm on the grip of her sword. I continued my little fighter's dance.

"We will survive this," Tevagah said. "The fate of Alyndis requires it."

Orcs closed in all around us. I counted seven of them, and strangely, they looked nervous about pressing the attack.

A particularly tall and ugly one leered in and grinned, his mouth full of broken teeth and tusks, dripping with blood and saliva. He grunted something, but I didn't even care what it was. All I knew was he looked ready for a fight. Screenie highlighted him.

Orc Berserker
Level 15
HP: 351/362

Holy. Shit.

"I will bathe in your blood," he growled in barely understandable English.

English?

Not really.

Throwing his arms out wide, he roared so loud, I worried it might cause a rockfall. Then, it suddenly stopped. Slowly, its top half slid away from its bottom half. Curr stood there, bloody axe in hand, daring the others to try something.

"Attack!" Tevagah shouted. Then she whistled, but not a normal one. It carried hauntingly on the air.

An instant later, the Night Mares came rumbling into view in a V formation, at full speed. They trampled through the front line of orcs, bowling a number of them over. One smaller one even got his head popped like a grapefruit in a nauseating display of gore.

I stood in dumb admiration as the Sisters went to work against the remaining orcs. I might've been imagining it, but I feel like Curr had stepped aside to let them "have some fun too."

However, that left me open to the orcs. One bounded toward me. I jounced left at the last moment and it hummed through air, claws extended.

"Curr!" I shouted when another orc launched himself at me.

I'd barely handled one at a time, and now there were two? And I had no weapon.

I pivoted, notes from the lute mirroring my moves—or was I mirroring the music? Then a third was there to greet me. I was surrounded.

"Danny!" Lilla shouted. I turned just in time to see a sword tossed to me. Somehow, I caught it by the hilt.

WEAPON OBTAINED:
Elvish Heun Blade (Melee Damage 11-15)

I felt a slice on my arm, a stinging, burning sensation. I'd been clawed—a feeling I knew. A feeling I'd experienced from the korken.

I turned, bringing Lilla's curved sword in an upward arc. It dragged across one of the orcs' chests, sending it staggering back. Then I turned toward the second one. It slashed downward. Feet bouncing back and forth to the rhythm, I let the sword greet his forearm and it dug in.

Quickly, I pulled the blade and it cut a gash into the creature's arm. It bellowed and came in for the killing blow. I'm not proud of what I did next. But it worked.

As hard as I could—and on time with the lute, I might add—I kicked the orc in the nuts. I followed through too. And it hurt like hell. Both of us. He keeled over and I limped to the side.

Another thing you don't think about when watching the movies, is just how fast these fights happen. I had no time to consider my action as I sliced the sword down at the back of the orc's neck. Stupidly, I expected to sever the beast's head. Not so much. Don't get me wrong, the blade went deep, but it was far from an insta-kill.

He looked up at me with those dirty yellow eyes. Growling, he lurched. But it was his final burst of energy before he went totally limp, paralyzed by my blow.

Level 5 Orc Grunt slain!

I was afforded no time for victory celebrations since he crashed down upon me. Thankfully, he landed across my legs, which meant my back didn't crush the lute. Unfortunately, though, I was stuck, and seriously close to the fire. I had to get the orc off me, but it weighed too much. The other orc—the one I'd slashed across the chest—stared at me, smiling like he'd just won the lotto.

I couldn't move.

I couldn't escape.

It was nice knowing you.

Just as the orc started to cut down, the fires around me roared to life and the orcs all screeched. I felt my hair singe before I spotted Curr tear the dead orc off me. He hauled me to my feet and dragged me away from the flames.

I turned back to see the remaining Sisters feeding the fire. As a result, the orcs retreated into the darkness, stumbling blind.

If I'd thought that the battle was over, I was wrong. The battle hymn still played—which in itself was crazy. I'd just fallen with the combined weight of myself and a massive orc and it hadn't so much as gone out of tune.

The lute!

Screenie, can I play the freeze time song again?

Everything related to that lute confuses and confounds me. But, it can't hurt to try!

I grabbed my unique lute and strummed. Nothing.

Crap.

Hm. What were you thinking about last time you did it?

Honestly? How scared shitless I was. I didn't want to die.

Well, you should be more scared now!

I gripped the lute tighter and played a mighty chord, like Eddie Van Halen about to unleash a solo. As I did, I thought how much I wanted to survive. And not only me, but all these new companions my life had gone crashing into like a speeding train.

Only an ugly twang rang out, interrupting the battle hymn. It should have sounded better, but it was like the instrument was mad at me for interrupting. Worse than that, time did not slow. Not one bit.

Your Special Ability: [TIME IS OF THE ESSENCE]: is exhausted.

Don't worry, Danny. It happens to men all the time.

Maybe you're too fatigued?

I didn't have the heart to come up with a witty retort.

From the area outside the glow of the firelight, I heard what sounded like many more orcs approaching.

Tevagah looked drained. Lilla stood nearby, bleeding from wounds on her arms. Nichelle still remained upright even though she had a leg wound and had to lean against the cliff wall to support herself. Only Curr was rearing and ready to go, but he no longer seemed to be enjoying this.

"I thought... there were... only a dozen," I said between gasps of breath.

"We were wrong," Lilla said.

"I was wrong," Tevagah interjected. "This is on me. I never should have underestimated them so badly. It's like they were drawn to us."

The ground around us was littered with bodies and slippery from all the blood and guts. There wasn't much more room left to fight.

"To the back wall," Tevagah ordered. "We will make our final stand there."

"Final... stand?" I asked.

We stepped back as one. I couldn't believe it was going to end like this.

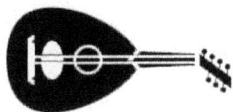

45

Not for the first time, I wondered if I would go back to my world when I died. Or if it was even possible. Or if I even wanted to.

What a weird thought.

That and more ran through my head in the blink of an eye. I couldn't really devote time to the thoughts, however, as eight ravenous orcs stalked into sight. Screenie highlighted them all, a mixture of classes and levels. Too much to track.

"So, this is it," I said quietly.

Screenie flashed in front of my eyes.

Hey, Danny Boy. Would you like to sing "Aran de Yav'nal"?

What the hell is that!

It's in your Catalog, unlocked at Level 4, see!

"Aran de Yav'nal" (26 inst. 31 sin.)

Play it and find out.

Wait. When did my singing get that high?

So, you do pay attention! It isn't, but no wellick sounds good singing it, so don't worry. Elvish is a complex language.

I don't speak elvish!

I'll give you the phonetics. What can go wrong?

I swung the lute around. That familiar warmth flowed into me and without thinking, I started playing a staccato, punchy tune and singing words that scrolled by in what I assumed was elvish. I didn't even know what I was saying, and a few letters weren't even ones I recognized. Apparently, Screenie couldn't translate fast enough to keep up.

All the same, my lute transitioned from the battle hymn, to picking a melody that synchronized with mine all on its own.

Tevagah, Lilla, and Nichelle all gawked at me, then started singing as well. Their elvish must have made mine sound like Russian.

Party Boost to Singing Skill is Active.

"Aran de Yav'nal" has reinvigorated your Party and Allies!

You have gained +1 in Singing.

Your Singing is now 18 (+10).

Your Faction standing with the Sisterhood of Alyndis has improved.

The effect was immediate. I no longer felt all the small wounds racking my body with stinging pain.

I can heal?

I was astounded.

No, you didn't let me finish. Your health remains at 87%, however, you, your Party, and Allies have been granted a temporary boost in Stamina. Think of it like an adrenaline boost. A shot in the arm. Steroids!

Still, that sounds like it'll come in handy.

Come in handy? You sound like an eighty-year-old man.

The orcs responded to the song as well, though I have no idea what their noises meant. Then they squealed and croaked, like it hurt.

Uh, oh.

You have lost -2 in Singing.

Your Singing is now 16 (+10).

I can lose extra *points?*

Your Singing Skill was too low. The song has enraged your enemies, granting them a temporary boost in Courage and Stamina.

You told me to do it!

I stand by my idea. You guys needed it more.

The orcs roared with the ferocity of thunder and charged. Behind Curr, Tevagah, Lilla, and Nichelle stepped forward while I continued to sing. Their strange glowing shields hissed with energy as they defended against the surge, their blades parrying strikes and felling body after orcish body. Curr was an absolute beast as usual, yet I'd never seen anything like the Sisterhood as they sang in perfect unison.

Blood spurted, and guts fell from shredded bodies.

For my part, I found a nice hiding place behind a rock. Hey, my hands were full. What would I do, poke them with one of the lute's string tips?

It was only when I finished the last line of the song that an eerie quiet fell over the area. Even the lute stopped. The last of the orcs lay dead at the feet of my allies. Swords and axes were soaking wet, dripping.

Tevagah turned back to me—they all did, with eyes wide. "Where did you learn that song?" she questioned.

"Haven't we done this before?" I asked, exhausted. "I don't know. I just played it."

Lilla stepped forward and caught me just as I started to get weak at the knees, like a complete reversal of the boost that song had given me and then some. "Easy. Easy, I've got you." She helped me to a clean spot on the ground and eased me down.

I labored to breathe. What just happened?

OBJECTIVE COMPLETED:
You have survived the orc attack!

REWARD:
Yay!

TITLE UNLOCKED:
Get the Orc Outta Here!
Gain +5 to Courage when battling orcish foes.

"Everyone loses their legs after their first brush with death," Lilla said softly.

Oh. Great. No wonder I was exhausted. I'd just run like six marathons in the span of a few minutes all while fighting monsters. At least that was what it felt like.

I closed my eyes and wanted nothing more than to sleep forever.

"You did good work tonight," Tevagah said, standing over me. "There is more to you than meets the eye." As she spoke, she glanced over at my now-silent lute.

I tried to smile, but every muscle in my body ached. I couldn't manage words, so I just nodded in agreement.

"Where is the halfling?" Lilla asked. "I see no sign of him anywhere."

Tevagah shook her head. "As expected. He was not to be trusted—"

Then we heard a grunt and movement from somewhere to our right. Lilla strode over with her sword at the ready. Maybe an orc wasn't quite dead.

Then she laughed. "Oh, this is rich."

She leaned over and yanked the corpse of an orc to one side. When she straightened, it was with Garvis in hand. Orc blood doused him, head to toe. When she plopped him down, he swayed. But she helped him until he got his balance back.

"Yig and shog," he swore in classic Garvis manner. "I'll never rid my nostrils of the stench of being stuck beneath that foul and loathsome creature." He shook his head. "Imagine my surprise when I slit its throat and it decided to fall backward instead of forward. Pinned me right underneath it."

He leaned to one side and blew out his nostrils, adding a lovely stream of mucus and blood to the rest of the carnage. I'd have laughed if I had the energy... and the same thing hadn't just happened to me.

Something rang out in the distance.

Is that a drum?

A goblin war drum. Smaller and less proficient at killing than orcs, goblins prefer to act as scavengers, attacking after a battle to pick off the leftovers.

Somehow, I don't think you mean a doggy bag by "leftovers."

"Goblins," Tevagah and Lilla said at the same time. "We need to get out of here."

"What about our fallen Sisters?" Lilla asked.

"There is no time."

"You don't—"

"Lilla!" Tevagah seized her by the shoulders. "You know what he has. We cannot risk it. They are here, on the dirt of old Alyndis. They are home already."

"Soon to be goblin chow," Garvis remarked. The glare he received from the elves after that could kill a man.

Lilla knelt, placed her palm to the sullied dirt, closed her eyes, and whispered something in elvish. I'm glad Screenie didn't try and translate for me. It didn't seem right.

Then Tevagah whistled.

From the shadows, their Night Mares appeared. Immediately, Tevagah swung astride her mount. Lilla and Nichelle did the same. The other horses looked despondent when they realized their Sisters were no longer with us.

Curr grunted. "I dislike the idea of running away from a fight."

"Think of it as hunting for better killing ground, then," Tevagah said from horseback.

"But where are we going?" I packed as much of our gear as I could find, making sure to gather my cloak.

ITEM OBTAINED:
Lalair's Elegant Cloak

"Farther up the trail. Deeper into ruins," Tevagah said.

"Which way?" Garvis asked.

Tevagah was beside herself now. "Does it matter? As long as we are moving."

"It might matter plenty if we find ourselves in an even worse position," Curr argued.

"Would you please trust me? I don't speak thoughtlessly."

"We should stay and slaughter them!" Curr bellowed.

"Calm yourself, braug. The battle has ended," Tevagah said. "For now."

The drum sound continued behind us. *Bum-bum, bum-bum.*

Tevagah led her Night Mare to one of the riderless horses and whispered something into its ear. The horse promptly approached me, lowering its head.

"She will allow you to ride her now," Tevagah told me.

NEW MOUNT ACQUIRED:
Melas the Night Mare

She's quick, she's agile, she's everything you're not.
Speed: 27
Health: 124
Stamina: 500

I gawked at the dark-haired steed. Riding shotgun with Lilla was one thing, but alone?

"Just move with her," Lilla said. "She'll do the rest."

I nodded. Hearing her reassurance helped, big time. But I won't lie, I mostly didn't want to let her down.

I moved toward the Night Mare, stepping over Uma's lifeless corpse.

Reminder: You should take her magic bracer.

It seems wrong... Look at her.

Exactly. She can't use it. Do you want to join her?

Flashes of battle raced through my mind. Terrifying didn't even begin to cover it. An enchanted shield definitely couldn't hurt.

Against my better judgment, and spurred by the tall mare whinnying at me in apparent impatience, I knelt and pulled the bracer off Uma's limp wrist. Her hand gave some resistance and I really had to give it a yank, which caused me to slip onto my backside.

"Would you hurry up, Danny!" Tevagah snapped.

I scurried back to my feet, tucking the bracer away so nobody would see it. I can't imagine they'd take kindly to me looting one of their fallen kin, but Screenie was right. She didn't need it.

ITEM OBTAINED:
Elvish Silver Bracer (Defense 7) (enchanted)

Add that to the collection, Mr. Petty Thief.

Enchanted with a magical barrier able to defend against physical attacks, it's lighter weight and takes up way less room than a traditional shield. Good thing too, because there are no invisible pocketbooks in this world.

With that, I slid my foot into the mare's stirrup and heaved myself upward. Another horse went down to its front forelegs and Garvis managed to get himself into the saddle. When the horse rose back up, it was obvious Garvis wasn't comfortable getting his legs around a full-grown steed.

"Just hang on," I told him. I sure was.

"Braug, I am sorry, but you will have to continue on foot once more," Tevagah said.

Curr nodded.

Whispering into her own horse's ear, Tevagah coaxed her mare into the darkness. Ours followed, as if they were all trained to do so.

"This way!" Tevagah called as she led us back onto the trail and out of our pocket of ruins. Cold winds picked up and blew around us ferociously. The lute stayed silent, so I wasn't too concerned about the goblins' proximity.

Tevagah pointed west. "We make for the main trail. Let the Night Mares move at their own pace. They know best how to navigate the wilds."

Behind us, the tempo of the drumbeat went to double-time. It sounded pretty good as my lute joined the musical affair.

Wait. My lute joined in.

"That means they're close enough to engage in battle with us," I warned.

"They must have reached the bodies," Lilla said in agreement.

"We ride," Tevagah ordered. "Now!" Her horse picked up the pace and ours did the same.

I clung to the reins as tightly as I could. Bumping up and down really hurt my... everything, but all that mattered was moving faster than goblins. After all, they were on foot. Horses ought to provide us with the means to move faster.

Unless.

From somewhere up ahead, we heard what sounded like another drum. This one was at a different tempo than the first.

"A second raiding party!" Tevagah shouted back.

"They're usually not this strategic," Lilla said.

"Are we trapped?" I asked.

Their faces told me the answer. Multiple groups of goblins would pincer us in on all sides if we weren't careful. This night had gone from bad to worse awfully fast.

Tevagah led us down another route. Or rather, Para'ray, her horse did. We moved quicker now, but the sounds of the drums seemed to echo all around us, bouncing off the walls of ruins of all different sizes. They were definitely closing in.

We started descending again, and the trail suddenly changed and took us back up a hill.

Tevagah pointed to a clearing at the end of the path. "There."

Hooves slammed the dirt, jouncing me this way and that. I honestly don't know how I managed to hold on. Finally, we reached the clearing in what seemed like the bottom level of an ancient amphitheater, with tiers carved up the hollowed-out crest of the hill like a bowl.

Tevagah swung off her horse. Curr helped me down. The area was ringed with thorny bushes and juvenile trees growing through the stands on all sides except for the small opening for the path through crumbled stone.

She ordered something in elvish, which Screenie translated as, "*Flee, Mares of the Starlight. Watch over us. If we are felled, return home to serve the Sisters.*"

At that, the horses galloped through the opening and out of sight.

"Here we fight," Tevagah said. "We have the high ground."

I laughed.

"What's so funny?" she demanded.

"Nothing. It's just... It's a line from a movie."

"I don't know what a movie is, but now is not the time for humor, bard."

Great, she was back to calling me that.

"They'll have to come through there to get us," she said.

"They will be funneled into their deaths," Curr said, giddy.

Lilla grunted. "Exactly. This is how we can whittle them down... hopefully."

"Hopefully?" I asked softly.

Don't worry. Goblins like wellick meat, but since you're the smallest, you might have time to escape.

Garvis is the smallest.

He's not a wellick. Are you paying attention at all?

The drums were converging all around us, amplified by the devastated theater. A place once meant for art, now turned into a battleground for war. I was nervous, though now that I'd seen battle and had my first couple of kills, I didn't want to puke quite as much. Besides, there was nothing left in me.

"We will take turns facing them head on, except the halfling," Tevagah said.

"Why not him?" I complained.

"I do not trust him to hold formation."

"I won't complain," Garvis said.

That meant she trusted me, which would have felt nice if that didn't mean me being thrown back into the frontlines of a battle.

"You will play 'Aran de Yav'nal' again?" Tevagah asked.

"I... I can't," I said sheepishly. Last time, it backfired, costing me skill points and powering up our enemies. I didn't want to risk it again.

"What do you mean you can't?" Lilla asked.

"It's just, I can only—" I felt really stupid at this point, but other than the truth, I wasn't sure what to say. "My fingers are too exhausted. If I mess it up, it can be bad." Just a white lie. My fingers were the one part of me that felt fit, trained from picking guitar since a young age. They didn't tire. Those callouses ran deep.

"Ah, the darker side of magic," Tevagah said as if this was a normal thing in their world. "Better not to risk it."

This is a normal thing in their world. Well, not the lute part, but magic is common enough that most people know there are limitations and costs. But it's like you and taxes. You know you owe them. They know you owe them—they even know how much

you owe, but they won't tell you. Then when you're wrong, you go to jail.

How is that the same?

I admit, I lost the plot a bit. Point is, they know magic has limitations, even if much of the lute's powers are mysterious. Make sense?

Fine. I guess so. So, what do I do? Is there another song I could play?

Before Screenie could respond, Tevagah spoke up, "Rotate around and everyone gets a turn so no one gets too tired and falters. Understood?"

"I will go first!" Curr declared. "Tarton's Tusks, just let me take them all!"

Nobody argued that. The elves chanted quickly, and their magical shields bloomed to life again in all their glowing glory.

Crap, what did they say to turn it on?

I didn't catch it.

Are you serious?

You didn't have the bracer equipped! I didn't think you cared.

I groaned as I drew my sword once again. I was certainly getting my fill of battle tonight. I was worried I wouldn't be able to handle myself because I was so exhausted. However, even if I couldn't play my lute, danger neared. That meant the strident sound of its battle hymn could hype me up. Give me some of that sweet braug Rage. Or adrenaline.

I just hoped it would last long enough to survive the night. We'd already lost two Sisters.

Your Music has invigorated your Party!

+2 Bonus to Strength, Dexterity, and Constitution for Duration of Battle.

NEW OBJECTIVE:
Survive the goblin attack.

REWARD:
Living long enough to complete your last objective: Locate the Oracle of Alyndis.

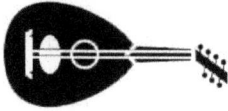

46

True to his word, Curr met the onslaught head on, hacking and whirling with his battle axe. He reminded me of the Tasmanian Devil from Saturday morning cartoons as he cut into the ranks of the vastly smaller goblins, spilling viscera everywhere.

I can honestly say I'd never used that word before. *Viscera.* Perhaps this world was making me somewhat of a linguist for gross terminology.

If only there was a Skill for that!

Curr started to tire—apparently, even he had a breaking point—and before I knew it, more goblins were there. It was almost as if every time he killed one, it just popped back up. I was at the back of the line facing an attacking goblin who'd filtered through the frontlines with a short spear.

God, the thing was even uglier when alive. And its eyes, while alive, had horizontal, rectangular irises, like a creepy goat. I tuned into the rhythm of the lute's battle hymn and my feet started moving. It's possible I just got lucky last time, but I wasn't about to second guess myself.

The spear thrust right at my chest. Without thinking, I spun with the music and brought my sword down on the goblin's skull, spilling his brains onto the muddy ground.

Oh, that's gonna leave a mark!

Level 3 Goblin Pikeman slain!

I wrenched my sword free just in time to narrowly avoid another downward cut from a goblin with a weird sawblade sword. I kicked him in the stomach, and he fell back, but not before I stabbed him in the shoulder. The creature winced, and I kept up my dance.

Then, what I saw horrified me to stunned silence.

What I said about it seeming like everything Curr killed just popped right back up? That, apparently, was exactly what was happening. Suddenly, the goblin whose head I'd cracked open rose from where he slumped on the ground, his eye glowing deep purple. He snarled at me with a half-split mouth and joined his buddy in the attack.

I was so paralyzed with fear and confusion, I stopped moving with the music and found myself nearly stabbed through the heart. I danced away at the last second, but not before my armor got a good long scratch in it.

"They're zombies or something!" I shouted as I dodged another incoming attack.

My lute's music rose in warning, giving me time to avoid yet another stab, this one from the previously dead pikeman. When I stood, I brought my sword in an upward strike. How I knew to do that, I don't know, but it was as if the lute showed me moves ahead of time and all I had to do was follow its instructions.

The din of melee was constant and echoed in my ears. The slash tore open the swordsman's stomach. It collapsed into its own innards.

You're a heartbreaker, dream taker... woo woo.

Level 4 Goblin Swordsman slain!

I leaped back from a spear thrust, and from over my shoulder, an arrow lodged itself into the goblin's broken-open face.

I was sucking wind hard. I didn't have much left to give. My arms felt like leaden weights.

Current health is 65%, but you require sustained rest or you will start accumulating further damage as a result of extreme fatigue. Wuss.

I know you told me not to show you these things, but look:

HUNGER LEVEL: Critical

THIRST LEVEL: Parched

STAMINA: 6/75

I was feeling everything. All the tiny cuts and aches and slices. I'd even stopped sweating, which wasn't good.

Behind me, I felt Lilla's hand on my shoulder. "Something is wrong."

"We can't stay here," I said.

Garvis, positioned in the middle of us where he was only good for throwing rocks, looked like he was about to burst out laughing. "There is a fine idea, boyo. And what route would you suggest we take to escape the fact that we are currently surrounded by an undying goblin horde?"

He was right. But there had to be something I could do.

"Stand your ground!" Tevagah shouted before plunging her

Dagger of Discontent into the heart of a goblin. The blow seemed to bring her pleasure.

So far, two goblins who were dead beside me hadn't reincarnated. I was beginning to think I'd been imagining things and that, somehow, goblins could survive having their brains sliced in two. Then, as I turned, my eyes were met with blinding purple light. The entire amphitheater went awash in the ethereal color.

Was that the right word?

I might have gone with eldritch.

I don't even know what that means… and don't tell me. Not now.
Busy.

Everything around us stopped, the horde halting just out of range. All but Curr, who still hacked and slashed his way through the few goblins who'd been reborn too close for comfort.

"What is that?" I asked.

"I don't know," Tevagah admitted.

We received our answer in the form of a silhouette of the largest orc I'd seen yet, strolling slowly through the ranks of goblins like he was their general.

"An orc?" Lilla asked from somewhere. "Fighting alongside goblins?"

Purple—*eldritch?*—light emanated from the top of the staff he held like a lighthouse, making any details impossible to discern. As he continued forward, the monster itself came into full view.

Unlike the other orcs, this one looked more… civilized. Honestly, reminded me of Kiel a bit, but those were not Kiel's eyes. He wore a headdress of feathers and bones. A strand of ears hung from his neck, both rounded and pointed. I could only wonder in horror if they belonged to the same men and elves whose skinned faces comprised his battle skirt.

Black marked his eyes horizontally. The eyes themselves were like... I don't even know. Something I'd have expected to see on a T-Rex that was possessed by Satan. And his one remaining tusk was coated in either red paint or the thickest blood I'd ever seen. In one hand, he gripped a stone kris knife with a handle made from what I'm guessing was a rib. In the other, the ornately carved golden staff, a clasp at the top holding a roiling, spherical amaranth gemstone. It did not look orc-made.

Elves absolutely made that beauty.

And "amaranth" you know?

A banner rose above him from the back of his outfit, crudely painted with a skull, covering a symbol that looked like a star constellation.

"The insignia of Alyndis, defiled," Lilla said bitterly.

"That staff does not belong to you!" Tevagah barked.

Screenie's blueish white light fought for real estate against the orc's purple glow.

Level 30: ORC SHAMAN (Boss)

Rarely seen by wellick eyes or otherwise, orc shamans are masters of mystical arts, born with the ability to tap into the ancient elven magics of Alyndis and twist them for dark purposes. Ranging from imbuing their warriors with the strength of the mountains to... as you can see here, raising the dead.

Raising the dead?

I've never seen it firsthand. It's pretty cool, right?

Oh yeah. I've always wanted to live in Atlanta when the zombie apocalypse breaks out.

More notes echoed forth from the lute. A new version of the battle hymn, this one deeper and more menacing. Worthy of the greatest foe I'd yet to encounter.

Can I do the freeze time thing yet?

You're welcome to try, but I really wouldn't put away your weapon just to suffer from performance anxiety again.

I wouldn't have that if you told me how it worked.

And I told you, I'm not sure!

"You've lasted longer than the other fools who wandered into my territory," the shaman proclaimed in our language. His voice sounded entirely unlike I'd expect an orc to sound. More refined. I would have thought their speaking voice to be like someone threw rocks into a wood chipper. He ran the tip of his knife across the necklace of ears. "It is time you joined my collection."

Curr stood nearby at the ready. His shoulders rose and fell with heavy breaths. That scared me. Exhausted Curr was something I hadn't witnessed before. He glanced over and offered me a half-hearted smirk.

Then, without further warning, he rushed the orc with his axe raised. The shaman didn't move a muscle until Curr got close. Then his staff's orb went bright, and one of corpses in front of him exploded with raw energy. The force sent Curr flying backward into the stone seats, smashing a hole through them.

"Curr!" I started to run toward him, but Lilla tugged on my arm to stop me.

"We must stand together," she said.

"The strongest of you stood no chance against me," the orc shaman chortled. He raised his knife and dug the blade in deep across his wrist. Black blood trickled down to the hand gripping the staff.

With that action, all the dead goblins rose—including those beside me—and though they were close, they didn't attack. They returned to the ranks around the shaman, teetering back and forth as if swayed by an unseen wind. He was taunting us.

"You will not be the one to stop us, imposter," Tevagah barked. "We are the Sisters of Alyndis. This is our home, and you will surrender all you have stolen."

A cackle oozed through the shaman's lips. "Not anymore. Look around you, elf. Orcs rule here now. You are forgotten..." All the goblins joined him in shrill laughter. Like a hundred fingernails dragging across a chalkboard. It made me wince. "...We remain."

Tevagah, Lilla, and Nichelle went completely pale. Sweat glistened on their foreheads. Their chests heaved with struggled breaths.

"And you."

I swallowed hard. His freaky eyes were focused on me, right?

Yup.

"The power you wield in your hands." He closed his eyes and inhaled deeply. "It has not been felt in these parts in an age. It calls to me."

"Me?" I mouthed, then my gaze flitted to the lute.

I already told you. Yup.

His outstretched hand turned, and he beckoned me with a single finger.

"Come," the shaman said. "Bring it to me, wellick, and I will spare you."

"The Lute of Seven Stars will never belong to a beast!" Tevagah yelled.

I looked to Lilla. "Maybe—"

"You cannot bargain with their kind. He'll kill us all no matter what," she replied, guessing my next statement.

"Never in a million years did I think I'd die this way," Garvis said. "I never should have left Nahal."

Words spoken had never been truer. Why had I listened to Screenie and kept going? I could have stayed there, got my gig back at the inn and played music until I was old and gray.

And been exactly the same as I was back on Earth. With fewer showers.

My fists clenched. It was too late to long for the boring and mundane. *I had* left Nahal alongside Curr. Me, Danny Kendrick. Screenie just pointed the way.

Sure, kid. That's how it went.

Be quiet and bring up my Catalog of Songs.

Whoa, taking charge!

Better to burn out than fade away, huh?

Screenie threw up the list and I simply closed my eyes.

Just pick one I'm qualified for. One last show.

Not the worst-looking crowd you've ever played for either!

I sheathed my sword and brought the lute around, resting my fingers on the neck and strings.

"Are you seriously going to play a song right now?"

It was Garvis' voice, but I didn't pay him any attention. I simply wanted to vanish into the music and lose myself for what might be the last time. Who knows? Maybe if I believed hard enough, this lute would be able to help.

This song had no lyrics, so my fingers found the chord and then I raked them across the strings, doing my best to pick-scrape without a guitar pick.

"By the stars, this isn't the time!" Tevagah demanded.

I kept my eyes closed as I played. The chord progression was unlike anything I'd ever heard or played. It sounded terrible, frankly.

"Danny," Lilla said. "Danny, we need your sword."

"I can help!" I opened my eyes and looked around. Lilla's expression was pleading. The shaman remained at the mouth of the amphitheater with his horde of subservient goblins. Garvis, exhausted as he looked, frantically searched as if for someone or something, and Curr still lay in an unconscious heap in a stone crater.

Is this giving them a boost? Is it helping?

Keep playing!

And, so I did. As the song rang out, grass and dust began to swirl, catching me up in a whirlwind. Something was happening, and it seemed powerful.

"Pry the lute out of his lifeless hands!" the orc shaman shouted. But it sounded far away, distant.

He signaled the charge, and the goblins came at us like a flood. Fear kept me playing, lost in the rhythm and the routine of doing what I knew best. The elves made their stand, with Garvis hopping forward and back from the fray, stabbing what he could.

Screenie, they're still coming!

I swore.

The goblins were small, yet they overwhelmed the elven ranks with numbers. Many were now even climbing up the walls of the amphitheater, coming down from behind us. The undead ones in the front lines ignored all pain and attacks, grabbing at my allies like ravenous zombies. A straggler even came for me, but the wind my song summoned whipped him aside.

Without Curr and his braug strength to offset things, my allies didn't stand a chance. And at the leading of their shaman, the goblins became organized. Two with nets launched another high into the air over the line, its surprise attack ending with a blade in Nichelle's neck. Tevagah went on a rampage after that, like the Dagger of Discontent had completely taken her over.

At the same time, the climbers all converged toward Curr, who couldn't even defend himself.

Seeing that snapped me back to reality and my fingers slipped off the strings. Curr had been a loyal friend ever since our turbulent introduction. Dedicated to finding my purpose.

But it was too late.

You have successfully played "Into the Mist" (25 inst. 0 sin.)!

Into the mist you go. There and not back again.

You have gained +1 to Instrument Playing.

Your Instrument Playing is now 21 (+10).

What the hell?

Wind distorted my vision, like I was inside of a tornado. It didn't hurt, even though I spun wildly, watching as my allies were there, then not, then there, then totally gone. The song I'd played echoed in celestial notes all around me.

Screenie tried to tell me something, but in the chaos of motion, I couldn't pay attention. And then, as quickly as it all started, it stopped, and I found myself looking up at the canopy of a tree. One of its boughs snapped beneath my feet and I fell. My skull hit something hard on the way down, and then I saw nothing.

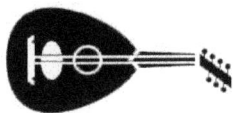

47

Good morning, sweetie.

HUNGER LEVEL: Critical

THIRST LEVEL: Critical

Your Party has disbanded.

You have lost your Allies.

OBJECTIVE COMPLETED:
You have survived the goblin attack.

REWARD:
The flesh is still on your bones.

NEW TITLE UNLOCKED:
Survivalist. +5 to Constitution when outnumbered by enemies.
Where others might have fallen, you endured. Hooah, Spartan!

The first image I saw when I came back around were letters floating in front of my face. At first, I was confused. Then little by little, it all came back to me.

Screenie?

You got knocked out pretty good.

How long?

Long enough. Something I doubt you hear very often.

I sat up quickly as a new memory flooded my brain.

"Where are they?" I said out loud. My mouth was so dry, it came out as a squelched croak.

Gone. Taken. But you and the lute escaped.

I unconsciously grasped for my lute. It wasn't strung over my back, and it wasn't in hand. I blinked hard, my eyes adjusting to sunrise. Something moved nearby.

Reaching for my sword, I slowly slid it from its sheath and rose to a knee. I had aches in places I didn't know could ache. A pained groan slipped through my dry, bloody lips.

Whatever it was hopped back in fright, noticing me and I, it. It twittered like it was talking in a weird bird language. Imagine a Furby mixed with an ewok, and that was what it looked like. Except with none of the cuteness. Its golden-brown fur was matted from not being cleaned, coated in dust, grime, and dried blood.

Screenie highlighted it.

Level ??? JIRRUP

What the hell is that!

Nothing to be concerned about, really. They're named for the sound they make. Known for being famously skittish, Jirrups are extremely rare to see. Little is known about the creatures. Seriously, this is really special. There are explorers who would die to see this —and have.

It peered through a bush, quaking in fear. Then I saw what was right by its feet. My lute, lying in some loose leaves like discarded trash.

"Shoo," I said, waving my hands.

It flinched. Then, wouldn't you know it, the bold little bugger placed one of its grubby talons on my lute's neck.

"Get away!" I yelled as loudly as my hoarse throat allowed, lunging in its direction. That got the message across. Fur floated in place as the thing zipped away, faster than anything I'd ever seen in all my life.

Oh yeah. Jirrups are the fastest living beings in Aethonia. Like I said, rare! The Academy of Learning would probably pay chests of gold for just one sample to study.

That's really what you're thinking about right now? Gold.

Isn't everybody. Always?

I groaned. Standing was too difficult in my condition, so I crawled over and reclaimed my lute. That was about all I could manage. Clutching it against my chest, I rolled onto my back and stared up at the canopy of branches above. Pinkish sunlight filtered through the leaves.

"What the hell just happened?" I said, both to Screenie and out loud to any god or being willing to listen.

You played "Into the Mist," a song written about the ghosts of Draybourne Swamp. Like the ghosts, you became one with the mists, and a breeze carried you away from danger. In layman's terms, you teleported.

I... teleported. Into a tree?

You can't aim a breeze.

I rubbed my eyes and turned my head to get a better look at my surroundings. Elven ruins still popped up all around, sunrise glistening off the pearly stone like diamonds. Sure, it looked peaceful and pretty, but it didn't look like the amphitheater ruins at all.

How far away am I?

Far enough that the shaman lost your scent. It seems like the Sisters aren't the only ones who are after you for the lute.

What could an orc do with a musical instrument?

Powerful things attract powerful beings, Danny. And we already know it isn't a normal instrument.

That was for sure. My mind was still in a haze, making it difficult to piece together all that had happened before I'd teleported... Even thinking that felt ridiculous. I could hear "Beam me up, Scottie," on my dad's old *Star Trek* re-runs. They never smashed into trees.

Nice reference, Danny. Really great stuff.

Wait. Why was Screenie being so pleasant?

That song, I realized. *You chose for me to play it!*

Yeah, so?

Did you know that was what would happen?

That's a complicated question.

I sat up.

No, it really isn't. Did you know?

I... look. Danny, the thing is...

Oh my god, you did know.

Not everything is so black and white.

You did know. Because of you, I abandoned them. Because of you... My heart dropped as I realized the ramifications. *Because of you, they think I abandoned them on purpose.*

We can't know that for sure.

Oh please. That's what anybody would think. I can't believe this. I know we argue a lot, but how could you do that? That's just... it's just... wrong.

It isn't that simple.

Yes, it is. You tricked me.

I saved you.

You. Tricked. Me.

AND IF I HADN'T, YOU'D ALL BE DEAD!

D. E. A. D.

DEAD.

See, I can spell things out too, Danny. And that's the truth. You were trapped and had no way out until I helped give you one.

Humph... You should be thanking me.

I bit my lip in frustration. You know when you're simultaneously mad at and thankful for someone? Like when you get picked up by cops from a raging party in high school and put in the drunk tank, and your girlfriend tells your parents to come get you.

Nobody wants their parents involved in that. But also, jail is pretty scary. Like that, except this was a situation of life and death. I just...

Can't you just be honest?

If I admit you're right, will you stop crying?

I'm not crying. You're crying.

I checked my eyes out of reflex and found that I wasn't actually crying. Brushing a bruise on my orbital bone from where I'd whacked my head made me wince.

I'm serious, Screenie. That wasn't cool.

Fine. No, it wasn't. But you question everything, and there wasn't any time. If you didn't get out of there, they would have slaughtered you all for the lute. Instead, the shaman captured your

friends, hoping you'll try to rescue them. A smart move for an orc. I wonder if he's like Kiel?

Did you see how powerful he was? How the hell could I do anything to get them back?

You have a very particular set of skills. Skills you have acquired over a very long career. Skills that make you a nightmare for people like them.

I groaned.

What are you talking about?

You will look for them, you will find them, and you will kill them.

This might be the most encouraging you've ever been.

The one time you don't get a movie reference...

Also, no one ever actually said "Beam me up, Scotty."

Of course they did. Didn't they?

•••

I used the tree trunk to heave myself to my feet and surveyed the area. Ruins and more ruins, with less forest now that the cityscape grew in density. Looming over it all was the Masked Mountains. In fact, my range of visibility was already limited by a thin layer of fog.

Where did he take them?

Into the mist.

Get it, like the song?!

Now isn't the time.

No, it isn't. For rescuing either. If you were paying attention, I said your thirst level is critical. If you were even to try and sing right now, it wouldn't be pretty. Well, it's never pretty... but it'd be even worse.

**NEW OBJECTIVE:
Find Water and Food.**

**REWARDS:
Quenched thirst and a full belly.**

How could I worry about drinking at a time like—

My complaints were cut short by a rustling coming from a nearby cluster of trees.

Is it the Jirrup again?

I reached for my elven blade—a lucky improvement to the short sword that got lodged in an orc skull—trying to keep one eye fixed on the trees. I slowly crept closer, quietly sliding the blade out. The disturbance grew louder. And then I heard a snort.

I didn't have the energy for another fight. If an orc or a goblin popped out of those bushes, I was afraid this would be my last day in this weird-ass world where I didn't fully belong.

Something black as midnight pushed through.

It wasn't certain death. It was perhaps my salvation in the form of my Night Mare.

"Melas? It's so good to see you, boy."

She's a female. You know... mare?

"Girl!" I corrected, then breathed a heavy sigh of relief.

If there was any way I was going to get myself back into fighting shape, Melas would be it. I had the sudden urge to thank Actus, the God of Small Things, as I threw my arms around her big neck and kissed her on the nose. Until a snort blew horse boogers onto my face.

I wiped my brow. "How did you find me?"

The horse whinnied and tapped its hoof.

Night Mares, though smart and fully capable of following a trail left behind by their companion, cannot speak.

Thanks, Screenie. I wish you couldn't speak.

Technically, I don't speak. I type. Consider me like a Zoomer, more comfortable behind a keyboard than face-to-face.

Are you super ugly or something? Afraid of being judged?

You would judge someone for not being good looking?

You have lost a point in Tolerance and Acceptance.

Take a good hard look at who you are as a person. Perhaps you don't deserve to breathe?

I didn't mean—huh. Maybe I did.

I smiled. I hated to admit that I'd grown accustomed to our bickering when Screenie was in good spirits like this. I maybe even enjoyed it.

You're right, Screenie. I'll add self-examination to my list of growing concerns.

At least you found sustenance. That would have been embarrassing if you died from thirst after surviving a horde.

I did?

When Screenie didn't answer, I backed up from Melas and found it staring right in my face. The saddle. The elves had them packed with supplies, and there dangling from it, was a canteen made from a hollowed tusk.

"Oh, you beautiful beast!" I kissed Melas again then rushed to it, tore it free, and emptied it down my throat. Unfortunately, only a single mouthful remained. I tapped on the side to get a few more drops out.

THIRST LEVEL: Adequate

That'll have to do.

Throwing it aside, I dug through the saddle bag looking for something to eat. Ration bars. Elven bread. A fricken raw potato even. I'd take anything.

"C'mon, Melas. Don't do me like that."

She doesn't pack her own bags. Blame the elves.

Nothing. I got to the bottom and found that it was ripped open, probably by a thorn or something.

Okay, blame nature.

"Dammit!" I slapped the saddle harder than expected, causing

Melas to trot a few feet away from me. Then I fell to my knees. My stomach grumbled with the force of an earthquake.

Why did you have to tell me how hungry I am, Screenie?

Information is gold.

It makes it so much worse.

My confusion and anger from everything that had happened was starting to settle, allowing reality to creep in. My fingers dug hard into the dirt. I wanted to rip open the earth. I felt... defeated.

You lost the battle, but not the war.

Screenie's encouragement didn't help. Even Melas recovered from me startling her and returned to nestle her nose against my shoulder. I reached up, grabbed a clump of mane, and nestled back.

"Thanks, girl."

It didn't help. Where could I go from here? Lost and alone in monster-filled ruins, separated from my companions who were imprisoned or tortured or worse—all because I didn't hand over a stupid lute.

My finger's clenched its neck. The thought crossed my mind to smash it on a rock and be done with it. Then, it started to play. Something akin to the *Jaws* theme, full of trepidation. Was it scared? Was I?

I hefted it overhead...

Danny. Don't.

Why not? It's caused nothing but trouble.

It's keeping your friends alive.

What good is that? You should have saved Curr. He could have saved them.

Unfortunately, they only have you.

I sighed. Unfortunately, Screenie was right. A minute or so passed in silence with the lute still aloft. Just Melas' breathing next to me and the rustling leaves. Then Screenie popped back up.

The way I see it, you have a choice here, Danny. You've asked me to be honest, so that's what I'll do.

Oh yeah? And what's that?

You can flee Alyndis, go back to Balahazia, and hop on a ship to anywhere in Aethonia. Nobody would fault you for wanting to live. Your companions knew the dangers of what they were getting into. It's not your fault you survived.

Or you can hop on Melas' back and ride to their rescue like William goddamn Wallace. You might die—hell, you'll probably die—but at least you'll have tried. They always say it's the thought that counts.

I closed my eyes and sucked in a deep breath of the slightly chilly air. Of course, he was right. It just helps when someone boils life down to the simple choices right in front of your face. The question was, if I did choose to live, could I even live with myself?

Can I have a third option?

You see your sword?

Yeah?

Lie on it.

Jeeze, Screenie! That's dark.

Hey, you asked. I delivered.

I shook away the thought. That certainly wasn't an option, which again brought me back to two. What would my companions do?

Curr would definitely charge in headfirst against impossible odds.

Garvis would have fled and never lost a wink of sleep over it.

The elves? I didn't know them well, but if they had the lute, they probably would have left us for dead to speak with their oracle.

Don't think about them.

It's your turn.

What would Danny do?

SO, YOU WANT TO BE A HERO?

My heart thumped against my ribcage. I lowered my lute and found firm footing. The answer was obvious. Because I wasn't Danny Kendrick, sometimes-musician, full-time waste-of-life anymore. I was Daniil the Bard, slayer of rats, wraiths, korkens, goblins, and orcs.

I grabbed the side of Melas' saddle, pulled myself up, and swung my leg over. "Fuck it. We ride."

PART FOUR

48

AN UNEXPECTED HERO
PART IV: Suicide Party
CURRENT LOCATION: The Ruins of Alyndis

I missed chairs. Soft, plush cushions. Hell, I'd have taken a plastic folding chair. I'm aware, that's a jarring transition after my decision to be a badass, but the mind goes where it goes.

Anything was better than riding horseback through a labyrinth of woods and ruins. Oh, and it started to drizzle, which was just grand.

Melas was on a mission, however, turning this way and that. I didn't have to guide her at all. And the farther we went, the less daytime mattered. The fog of the Masked Mountains fell like a curtain overhead, cutting off sunlight, making everything dim.

Perfect for orcs at all times of day. No wonder they like it here.

Keep some thoughts to yourself, please.

Between the jouncing and bouncing, which had my lower back feeling like I'd spent years of prison time as someone's bitch, and the whipping branches that had my face and arms covered in tiny scratches, I'd had enough time in the saddle to last a lifetime.

The other thing about prancing along on Melas' back, it gave me time to think. I hadn't realized how little actual thinking time I'd had since arriving in Aethonia. It may sound stupid, but when thrust into an unfamiliar world, greeted by something as audaciously insane as Screenie—

That was rude.

—and discovering magic, goblins, orcs, elves, dwarves, and all the other craziness actually existed here, there was a tendency to just accept it all at face value. The only other option would be to admit I was off my rocker, and possibly in an asylum somewhere near Willistown.

However, now that I was alone, those thoughts wouldn't relent. What the hell was I doing? Where the hell was I? Was I really about to risk my life on purpose for a socially inept barbarian, a two-bit selfish thief, a woman who had referred to me more by a title I didn't even fully embody, and a murderous—albeit stunningly gorgeous—elf?

What did I stand to gain from any of this?

As Melas guided us toward her master, Tevagah, I let the rumination fester.

Oh, and let's add "trusting a horse to take me where I need to go" to the list of nonsense.

As if she heard my thoughts—which wouldn't be the most outrageous thing I'd experienced during my stay in Pyruun—Melas stopped and sniffed the ground.

"What is it?" I asked, as if she would answer.

Suddenly, the mare's head perked up. Before I could even ready myself, she bolted forward faster than I'd seen her move.

I think I shouted. I probably said something like "Hey, girl!" or "Whoa, now!" or something equally silly. She didn't stop, taking off through the ruins, zipping between the gaps in structures barely wide enough for us to fit, bounding over crevasses, and forcing me to drop down level with her head on more than one occasion.

You have gained +1 in Riding.
Your Riding is now 2.
Ride 'em, cowboy!

Finally, Melas came to a screeching halt on a promontory overlooking a valley at the very base of the Masked Mountains. I guess, less a valley and more like a fissure. Craggy cliffs ran along either side, with seemingly no way down. On the far side was the biggest of the ruins I'd seen so far. Almost palatial in size, with a half-cracked dome at the top, the entirety of its front façade fell off in a piled heap down into the crevice.

White rock rose above mud-filled pathways that skirted around the mountain beyond the "palace," dotted with arches and small towers until the veil of fog made everything invisible. On my side of the valley, there was no more forest. This was a ruined city, plain and simple.

I'd visited bigger cities—Chicago, Boston, Philly. This seemed far smaller than those, but still, if I had to imagine what a large settlement looked like in Aethonia or Pyruun, this would be it. Compared to Balahazia, which was very scrunched together, this was wide and expansive. Acres separated buildings that looked like they could have once been several stories tall, with courtyards and the like.

And facing the palace, along what I assumed was once a grand avenue, stood a statue about the size of Lady Liberty. The shape—a robed elf, I think—was cut in half at the waist.

Man. I could only imagine what the heart of Alyndis once looked like in its glory.

Hearing faraway voices, I forced my attention away from the beautiful ancient architecture and into the fissure itself. It was filled not only with crumbled stone and mud, but red and black tents.

Well, not really tents. More like canvas stretched from portions of ruins to provide cover from sunlight through the occupied area of the valley.

Stomping the wet, muddy grounds were those same vile-looking orcs we'd fought. They had no fires to keep warm, even though it was cold enough under the fog to see my own breath. However, torchlight glowed from within caves carved into the walls all around the fissure, presumably leading deep under the mountain.

They are not the same orcs. Those died. These are their far more pissed off brothers and sisters. After all, you murdered their families.

Melas stamped her hooves, which I took as a sign for me to get down. I wouldn't complain either. I needed a break. However, as soon as I dismounted, she bolted. Being so close to the orc village— maybe that's too generous a term—I couldn't even scream after her.

You have lost your mount.

Wonderful. Alone again.

You're never alone.

Great. It wasn't the first time Screenie had reminded me of that fact.

I stayed low and got as close to the edge as I could to get a better view down into the fissure. Orc grunts and voices echoed around like sloughing mud. They were everywhere. But there was no sign of my companions.

"God, there must be at least a hundred of them," I whispered.

142.

One hundred and forty-two orcs...

And 40 goblins. And don't forget the orc shaman who can make sure none of the goblins stay dead long!

Are you trying to make me puke?

It has been awhile!

I exhaled slowly. This was more than I'd bargained for. How could I stand against that many monsters? Oh well. It was too late to change my mind now.

No, it isn't.

Just let me think.

Before I could, my stomach grumbled so loudly, I worried all the orcs might hear. I dropped to the ground and held my gut. Moving that fast brought a rush of faintness to my head.

HUNGER LEVEL: What's worse than Critical? That.

Right. My first step had to be finding something to eat. I couldn't imagine climbing down this mountain and fighting orcs while suffering from a low blood-sugar attack.

It's not really a mountain.

Where I lived in the American Midwest, this would be considered a mountain.

It's barely a hill.

One thing was certain, hunting anything around here with nothing but an elven heun blade and a lute simply wasn't gonna cut it. My hunting skill—if there was such a thing—didn't even appear on my stats yet. And though I'd raised my long-range combat by a margin, it was still low, and I didn't have a bow and arrows.

I hadn't seen any animals since entering the deep forest ruins anyway. No deer or squirrels. Not even a chipmunk.

You would eat a poor, innocent little chipmunk!?

It was just an example.

And you call them monsters.

That left me with exactly one option, if my memories of Boy Scouts served me correctly. Admittedly, they were hazy. Foraging.

Ah, the old Herbalism Skill. Underrated, I'll tell you. It isn't your strong suit. Though—

What is, I finished for him. *I get the joke.*

Aw, it's no fun when you do that.

I'd never been a huge fan of fruit—especially berries—but I was confident I could find some bush that could supply me with enough nourishment to not feel like I was going to pass out. The forest had mostly thinned out this deep into the ruins, but there were plenty of those.

My confidence was shattered after the first minutes of wandering aimlessly and finding nothing. My body felt even worse. It was getting more and more difficult to lift my arms. Even take a step.

It was an odd sensation, knowing that the only way I could eat was by *finding* my own food. Even back home, when I was starving, I could Door Dash something. Sure, it was more expensive, but it worked.

I ducked under a fallen column to check some bushes in what used to be a courtyard. My lute's strap got caught on a low-hanging thorny vine, spinning me so that I hit my already sore ribs on a dislodged bit of a column.

In a fit of anger, I ripped the lute off my back. "Can't you even help me find something to eat!" As I choked the not-so-inanimate object by a neck it didn't use to breathe, I realized how foolish I was being. I was a bard. It was time to embrace it.

Is there a song in my catalog that could help me?

Ding, ding, ding! It's about time you thought of that.

You couldn't just tell me?

There's nothing better than the sense of accomplishment that comes with effectively solving a puzzle on your own.

I'd say not starving and finding my friends before they die would come close.

Aren't you just a bucket of sunshine? Like a toddler late for snack time.

Just show me the list, you dumbass screen.

My Catalog of Songs appeared before my eyes. Though, oddly— and this is going to sound weird—when they popped up, Screenie felt angry. Like when someone slapped a pink slip down on your desk to tell you you've been fired.

I thought about apologizing, but I just didn't have time for the drama. Lilla—and Curr, Garvis, and Tevagah, of course—were in trouble.

CATALOG OF SONGS:
Level 1 (Unlocked):
Halfling's Gambit (7 inst. 5 sin.)
— Magical Effects: None
Stones, Bones, and Crones (8 inst. 7 sin.)
— Magical Effects: None
Parapets of Pyruun (14 inst. 9 sin.)
— Magical Effects: ???
T'was Morn in the Eve (14 inst. 14 sin.)
— Magical Effects: ???
Tillith's Last Call (20 inst. 15 sin.)
— Magical Effects: +5 to Dexterity and Constitution for 10 Minute Duration.

Level 2 (Unlocked):
Hymn for Fallen Souls (23 inst. 19 sin.)
— Magical Effects: Dispel Hostile Spirits
Into the Mist (25 inst. 0 sin.)
— Magical Effects: Teleport away from Danger (>300 Feet)

Level 3 (Unlocked):
Ranger's Lament (27 inst. 16 sin.)
— Magical Effects: ???
She Who Fights with Monstrosities (25 inst. 33 sin.)
— Magical Effects: ???

Level 4 (Unlocked):
Promise of the Son (29 inst. 0 sin.)
— Magical Effects: +3 Speechcraft with Elves for 24 hour Duration.
Aran de Yav'nal (26 inst. 31 sin.):
— Magical Effects: Reinvigorate Party

Hmm. Would any of those help?

:::Insert Mocking Tone:::
'Would any of those help?'

That really isn't an effective diss in writing.

"That really isn't an effective diss in writing."

Seriously...?

I'm not sure which one, okay! I'm not omniscient. There, I admitted it. Ahh, that felt good to say out loud. I'm a fraud.

I ignored Screenie's whining and studied the list. The first, and easiest to play, was Garvis's song. When I played it at the Sea Mantis Inn, the only thing I accomplished was pissing him off. Nothing magical about that.

Next up, "Stones, Bones, and Crones" was the song I'd sung for Curr when we'd first met. It was possible that had given me some kind of favor with the braugs, but I couldn't be sure.

Actually, now that I thought about it, it had rewarded me with food. A rotten leg of lamb, sure, but food nonetheless. Even so, I couldn't bring myself to try that again. What if I wound up with another meal I couldn't stomach?

The next couple weren't familiar to me. I had to guess one of them would stop time like I'd done back when we'd first met the Sisterhood. Neither of them screamed "dinner time."

"Tillith's Last Call" had given me and my Party a boon during battle.

"Aran de Yav'nal" was the one I'd used to reinvigorate us during our last battle, but that hadn't gone so well.

"Into the Mist" might send me spiraling through the air right into the orc lair, or even farther away. My stomach sank at the thought. What were my companions going to think when I found them? Did they believe I was a coward who meant to escape and leave them to their doom?

Tevagah already had trouble believing anything I said. How could I tell her this was an accident?

I just had to hope my saving them brought some measure of forgiveness.

Rather confident you're going to be able to infiltrate an orc horde all by yourself and come out alive, aren't you?

IF I save them. Happy now?

Maybe when you apologize for calling me a "dumbass screen."

Like you haven't called me worse?

:::Continued mocking:::
'Like you haven't called me worse?'

Fine. I'm sorry, okay! I'm just hungry.

Finally, I asked, *"What about that one? "Ranger's Lament"?"*

Could be. What makes you think that's the one to help now?

Well, a ranger is someone who lives and travels in National Parks or the wilderness, right? And lament means to cry or be sad or something. And right now, stuck in the wilderness, I am sad and feel like crying. My lament is lack of food.

Fair logic. Now you're thinking like a true bard. Music has meaning. In its meaning, there can be magic. The elves believe that, why shouldn't you?

Are you just testing me? This feels like class...

Well, Bard is your Class. Embrace it.

Alright already.

So, do want to try it?

I worried I might be totally wrong. This place was insane. What if whatever ranger wrote this song had been upset he couldn't find a dragon to slay or worse?

What's worse than a dragon?

I don't know, Screenie. You tell me.

Two dragons?

I took a breath, then let it out.

Let's try it.

Ball's in your court.

I sat cross-legged in the center of the wrecked courtyard, whipped the lute around, and positioned my fingers on the fretboard. I gave it a strum. Soon, after a rather pretty intro, the words came to me.

Lowly, my soul
Blackened, my heart
Dreamt of the eve o' the end
Supply me vengeance
Granteth me retribution

Giveth me that which will rend
Bone from the marrow
And blood from the veins
Dry up mine enemy's mouth
Just one dabble
Just one taste
Bless me with a fiery draught

The song stopped and nothing happened.
I swore.

Well, it rhymed.

You have gained +1 to Singing.

Your Singing is now 17 (+10).

Great. Singing won't fill my stomach.

Then I heard it—something faint, but there all the same. A gentle beeping that reminded me of sonar.

Do you hear that?

I don't have ears.

I started to argue since I knew Screenie could hear—or at least sense things—but he flashed again.

But yes, I do. Sounds like a guide.

It does, doesn't it?

I started off in the direction I thought the sound originated, out from the courtyard and into some sort of tall, vaulted passage. It took a few turns, but eventually, the beeping grew louder. When I finally found myself face-to-face with a lush blueberry bush, the pinging became near deafening. Thankfully, it stopped when I was only a few feet away.

They aren't blueberries.

What are they?

Poison Toleya.

Poison? You've gotta be kidding me!

Yeah... It seems that song can be used to trace poisons. Useful for a king's minstrel at dinner time.

My heart deflated. I slumped to the ground, ready to give up completely. I couldn't even use the only powerful thing at my disposal to help me. Why bother anymore?

Poison Toleya aren't poisonous to wellicks. Your super-high Luck really comes in handy sometimes.

I sprang to my feet.

Then why are they called that!

This is an ancient elven forest. The Poison Toleya were first discovered by the elves, and thusly named by the elves. They cause lengthy paralysis if ingested by an elf, however, hold powerful magical properties for potion-making.

Well, someone should change the name!

Oh, so your answer is just to erase the history of those you conquered.

I didn't conquer anyone. I'm not even a wellick.

I approached the bush and reached for a particularly plump and delicious-looking toleya. I was just about to grab it and pop it into my mouth when the last words I spoke finally registered in my own ears.

Screenie... They aren't poisonous to wellicks, but what about humans?

Only one way to find out. Bottoms up!

Steeling my nerves, I plucked the fruit from the branch. I held it there, staring down at it for a long minute, like we were enemies. Then, closing my eyes, I shoved it wholly past my lips. When my teeth broke the skin-like exterior, my mouth flooded with one of the most delectable flavors I'd ever experienced. One part berry, one part citrus fruit, and then something I couldn't quite put my finger on. Cinnamon? Nutmeg? Something spicy. It was incredible.

Screenie, this is amazing!

Describe it to me. I've never eaten food.

I considered that, only to realize I had no idea how to describe the taste of something to someone who has never tasted anything.

Instead, I chose to gorge myself on toleya. I ate until the whole bush was empty. My stomach was even tight and expanded as I reached for the last one. Like the end of Thanksgiving dinner, when just one little slice of pie sounds worth it.

I missed pie. I used to be able to eat like a garbage can. Now, some little berries filled me up after going on such long stretches without hearty meals. This world was changing everything.

I plucked the last berry, dropped it in my mouth, and finally let myself breathe. I felt good. Too good. Like laughing gas at the dentist. Colors seemed more vivid. My head felt like a balloon.

OBJECTIVE COMPLETED:
You have found both food and water!

Good job! You're a big boy now!

REWARD:
The energy to fight on!

You have gained +1 in Herbalism

Congrats!
You are now a Level 5 Bard!

Because of your Skill increases so far, you have improved to Level 5. Really? Leveling up on Herbalism again? Get a new move! You need better writers.

With each new Level, your Health, Stamina, and—if you were attuned with any magical abilities—Mana regenerates to 100%. You can also apply +1 to the Attribute of your choosing.

Two new songs have been added to your Catalog of Songs.

Special Ability Use Restored: [TIME IS OF THE ESSENCE]
(Requires The Lute of the Seven Stars Equipped)

What a rush. The sensation was amplified compared to the last time. I felt like I was on top of the world.

We figured it out!

It took a second or two to get my senses in order.

"Figured what out?" I said out loud, even though I was talking internally with Screenie. I really had been thrown for a loop.

Your Special Ability. You can use it again.

Wait, show me my Level Up notification again.

Screenie obliged, and yup, there it was like a shining beacon of hope.

"Special Ability Use Restored: [TIME IS OF THE ESSENCE]"

How?

Didn't you feel that rush? That's the power, baby! Every time you Level Up, you get another chance to use it as long as you have the lute.

That's it? It's so simple.

Seriously. Really makes you wish you'd Leveled Up again before the Shaman attack, doesn't it?

Thank you, Captain Obvious.

Ahem. It's Screenie.

A grin touched my lips. Pausing time could give me exactly the advantage I needed to save my friends. Freeze, get in, grab them, create a distraction, run as fast as we could. The effects hadn't lasted that long, though, and I would still need to search for them.

I swore. I was in a better place, but it was still complicated. "Wait!" I exclaimed.

Waiting...

What if I just sit here and practice my lute over and over again. I can improve my Skill enough times to Level Up a few times.

That may take a while. Practice makes perfect, but playing in front of others improves your abilities much faster. There's a whole system behind it, blah blah.

Well, I'll do it for as long as I can.

The shaman may get bored, think you ran, and kill your friends.

If he didn't kill them yet, he won't in a few hours.

You'd really take that chance?

If I Level Up enough, I can use freeze time a few times. That will buy me long enough to find everyone!

Oh, I see where you're going with this... That's, uh, not going to work.

You just said it would!

It's a single-use Special Ability.

So?

If you don't use it, you lose it. It doesn't roll over to your next Level.

What if I don't need to use it every level!

Then you're shit out of luck. You wouldn't want to be overpowered now, would you?

Uh, yes. Who would say no to that?

Some people love a good challenge, I don't know. Those are the rules. I don't make them. I am but a humble screen. Besides, I should remind you, it won't always be this easy to gain Levels. Think about it like a baby. They quickly learn to eat, crawl, walk, run, talk... When was the last time you experienced such a massive achievement as an adult?

You're saying I'm a baby?

Goo-goo, gah-gah.

Talk about a buzzkill. As hopped-up as I'd just become, now I was the opposite. It rivaled the worst hangover I could remember... New Year's Eve, 2016. That was a night. I wound up playing hacky-sack with hippies outside of a pizza joint in another state. But I digress.

"Get ahold of yourself, Danny."

Are you talking to me, or... Yeah, yourself. Carry on, crazy.

So, what—I couldn't loop together freezing time long enough to do whatever I needed. No Game Shark for me. Once would be enough. The orc shaman would never know what hit him.

If I didn't have magic or music up my sleeves, I'd need something else. I was alone now. I couldn't count on big Curr this time around.

Screenie, put my new Attribute point into Strength. It's time to save my friends.

Whoa... What an alpha. Who are you and what have you done with my Danny?

Your Strength is now 12.

NEW OBJECTIVE:
Rescue Your Companions

REWARDS:
Bringing the band back together again!

49

Full to the brim, and my mind back on the most pressing of details, I checked all of my equipment and even put on my new elvish bracer. Even if I didn't know how to activate the shield, it couldn't hurt to have it.

Then I returned to the promontory overlooking the orc-filled fissure.

Night loomed—which apparently, under the thick fog, is even darker. Normally, that meant lit torches everywhere, but here, where orcs and goblins thrived in the darkness, I had trouble even seeing the outlines of their tents. The only light within the fog I really had to work with was the glowing orange pinpricks along the walls of the fissure.

On my back, my lute played softly—a song I'd never heard before. It sounded sweet, serene, calming.

"Sorry for yelling at you." I gently patted it, then paused when I realized how silly that was, only to embrace the madness and gave it a few more pats.

Oh, your super, special magic lute gets a sorry, just like that. I have to beg and beg.

IT doesn't mock me.

Are you sure? I sense some sass in those notes.

I took it all in. Despite the entirety of the area being overrun by monsters, I had to admit, it was a beautiful sight with the moon's glow filtering through a break in the fog. The elvish stone glowed all over, reminding me of those ice sculptures from fancy parties.

The same question I'd had for weeks came to mind: were any of the stars up there my sun? Was Earth out there somewhere amongst the heavens, or had I been whisked away to an entirely different dimension? I couldn't help feeling like Screenie had the answer and was withholding.

•••

That was all I got. Again. Three dots.

The fog set in thicker, and the moon vanished. All the glowing iridescence was extinguished. The only light that emanated was a hellish glow from within the orc caves down below. Where I'd earlier thought it to be torches, now I wondered if it was molten lava from the mountain's core.

Reality slapped me in the face. I was about to scale a mountain in reverse, then attempt to infiltrate an orc village to break a group of people I'd just recently met out of what amounted to prison.

Back home—back in Willistown—would I have ever entertained such an idea? Then a more sobering thought sprang to mind: I've never had anyone I cared about as much as these people I'd just met.

I shook my head. What had I been doing with my life? So I'd lost a career in music. I was still a musician. I still knew how to play. And that asshole stole my instrument.

Even as I thought these things, I was already making my way down into the fissure. Some piled stone gave me a bit of a ramp, until it ran out and all that awaited was a sheer cliff.

This wasn't like my one trip to Colorado in my senior year of high school. There were no carefully carved switchbacks allowing me to easily traverse the difficult land. There were no flashlights. Just darkness.

Would you like my help to get down?

Yes. Why would you even ask?

Sometimes you like to prove how tough you are, I don't know.

Here.

The blueish highlight that Screenie usually used to describe other people bloomed brightly around a protruding chunk of a ruined archway.

That's pretty far...

Do I have to start making chicken noises?

I glanced out over the gap. Heights were... not my favorite. It was a long way down, with some nice sharp bits of stone to clip me all the way and tear me to pieces.

You know what they say about looking down?

What?

Don't.

Right. I rubbed my hands together. It wasn't that far. Easy.
"Here we go." I moved to jump, but the problem was, my legs didn't get the message. They remained completely frozen.

"You've got this, Danny."

I shook out each leg once. Then again. Then, after blowing out air a few times in rapid succession, I leaped across a chasm to the highlighted ruin. One of my feet slipped, and I grabbed on to the remnants of the rocky surface and did a split. It hurt, but I didn't fall.

I started to *yip* in excitement, but quickly caught myself and it turned into a weird whisper shriek. Probably not smart to get caught by orcs cheering myself on. How embarrassing.

It went on like that for who knows how long. I didn't rush. Screenie highlighted footholds on pockets of crumbled stone and projecting ruins all the way down, goading me into each jump. For once, I didn't mind the attitude. I needed the extra push.

And it worked. Before long, I stood on the muddy floor of the fissure, and looked up. I was way, way down. It hadn't looked so far from up at the top. Maybe the darkness was playing tricks on me.

I honestly couldn't believe what I'd just done. A sense of pride swelled in my chest.

What? No skill boost for climbing?

Hm, let me check my charts.

Beep, boop. Zeeb, zorp.

Nope. That isn't a thing here. Babies climb just fine.

Grrr.

I returned my attention to the fissure. The nearest orc covering was a football field or so away. I crouched and watched, recalling every spy movie I'd ever seen, any book I'd ever read that featured a story of infiltration and rescue.

Pffft. Who was I kidding. I didn't read. Reading was for nerds.

Half a dozen orcs patrolled the grounds just a hundred feet or so in front of me, with no need to worry about any sunlight piercing the shifting fog now that it was full-on nighttime. I know I'd described them before, but this was the first time that I got a good look at them outside of active combat.

I would hardly describe anything you've done as "combat."

While Screenie was rude beyond words, he wasn't wrong. Not really. I got off a lucky shot with a bow and arrow, and did my best to not die in close com—

There's that word again.

Up close. I did my best to not die when the orcs were up close and on top of me, breathing their hot, blood-soaked breath on me. That better?

It would be more accurate if you included the feeling of terror deep within your bones.

Like you wouldn't be afraid.

The orcs were tall—all of them. Even those who would probably be considered runts by the others stood a head above me.

None wore armor, at least not any made from metal or leather like Curr or anyone else I'd encountered so far. If I had to guess, the articles draped over their shoulders were crafted from bone. I hated to think of where they harvested the materials.

Most had tusks. It was clear those not equipped with those natural weapons had lost them, either in battle or perhaps even a result of punishment by their own kind.

You came up with that on your own?

Seems like something a warrior race would do.

Ding-Ding! You are correct. The result of losing in true combat and surviving to tell the tale is to be stripped of their tusks.

Orc culture revolves around honor and blood. While spilling blood is honorable, returning from a fight in which one has lost is not.

It is more than likely that your last encounter with the creatures caused at least a few to be "castrated."

So I did win!

You... didn't lose.

That's something in my book.

A pyrrhic victory.

*A **W** in column Danny.*

Pretty boastful for someone whose so-called friends have all been captured.

That served as a reminder for why I was here in the first place. I had to find a way inside this heavily guarded stronghold city, and rescue Curr, Lilla, and Tevagah.

And Garvis.

I was getting to him!

Let me start off by admitting that I've never done anything like this before, unless you include tracking down the Sisterhood. This time around, I didn't have the lute leading me to my companions with song.

Screenie, how long can I freeze time?

Last time, it lasted roughly 3 minutes. Though with your delicate fingertips, I wouldn't count on a Dave Matthews Band concert.

Think that's long enough to find them?

It's a pretty big area.

Right, but the orcs seem to be gathered toward the front section, and Curr and the others would be held somewhere guarded.

Well, aren't you a natural Columbo.

Columbo?

You mean to tell me that I have a vaster knowledge of your television history than you do? Columbo was a TV detective.

Why not Sherlock Holmes?

Why not Harry Dresden?

This is a waste of time.

You started it.

I don't think I did. All right, let's do this. Bring up my Catalog of Songs.

In case you forgot, the last time "you" froze time, it wasn't with a song from your Catalog.

Shit. How do I play [Time is of the Essence] then?

You know, other bards figure this stuff out themselves.

Shut it! Just show me how to play it!

Ask your lute.

Was Screenie jealous?

No, you dolt. I just don't know. It would only make sense that if she was responsible for the song the first time, she would know how to play it this time.

That makes sense. Wait, she? What makes you think the lute is a she?

Well, for starters, when you finger her, she likes it.

Wow. I didn't realize you were such a pig.

It's a joke, Mr. Sensitive. Now ask the damn lute.

How?

By asking?

I've said stuff to it before. You know it doesn't talk, just plays when I'm in danger and stuff.

You have 'said stuff,' but have you ever really tried talking to her? Like, really tried.

No, but, that's nuts. It's a lute.

You don't seem to have a problem talking to the word machine floating in front of your face.

Touché. Okay, fine.

I slowly pulled the lute from my back, feeling like an idiot. She wasn't playing any battle hymn, so I assumed I was safe for the moment.

Crap, did I just think of it as a "she"?

Muahaha. You can't escape my logic.

I stared down at the fretboard, then my eyes drifted toward the body.

Pervert.

Would you shut up for a minute?

The instrument really was beautiful. The fretboard was dark rosewood, and each fret contained a silver etching. Now that I knew how interested the elves were in it, I had to imagine they were elven runes or letters or something. The filigree surrounding the acoustic hole were wildly intricate as well.

The one thing that still irked me was the little indent in the headstock that appeared as if something was... missing.

My eyes took her in. Could I really communicate with her? I suppose it couldn't hurt to try.

I wasn't far from where a handful of orcs stood guard. Others passed occasionally, walking patrol too, so I had to be quiet.

Alright, here we go...

I took a deep breath, then whispered, "Can you hear me?"

I waited for a response. And waited. And waited.

What a fool I was, provoked by the stupid screen to talk to a—

Suddenly, soft music started playing. Almost so low, I couldn't hear it. A song I was very familiar with.

"'Owner of a Lonely Heart'?" I asked, low.

What did that mean? Was the lute trying to tell me it was lonely? I guessed that could have been possible; why else would it be softly picking one of the '80s most popular tunes—

Wait a second...

"Yes?" I asked the lute if it could understand me, and if it chose a song by the band Yes. That couldn't be a coincidence, could it?

"If you're trying to tell me you understand, play 'Roundabout'."

Without hesitation, the lute transitioned to the band's most recognizable song.

"Oh my God. This is amazing."

It's just a song.

Wow, you are *jealous, aren't you?*

Screenie didn't answer.

"Do you have a name?" I asked the lute, feeling a bit less dumb this time.

Immediately, the song shifted to "No Reply" by the Beatles.

"That's not right. You should have a name. Hmm."

This time, I started to strum the lute. I played one of my favorites to cover back in the day. "Roxanne," by The Police. I even whisper-sung some of the lyrics.

"What about that?" I asked. "Roxanne."

Meh.

The lute didn't wait long. My fingers vibrated as it played the intro to "Yeah Yeah Yeah," by Alice Cooper all by itself.

"Roxanne it is!"

Told you it was a she.

Lucky guess.

"Roxanne, I know we haven't been on the best terms so far, but I'm trusting you here," I said. "Tevagah says you belong to them, so I think you're just as invested in this as me. Let's play [Time is of the Essence] for as long as we possibly can."

Roxanne started playing. All around, leaves stopped rustling. Birds froze in mid-flight, and the orcs didn't move a muscle. I was so awed by everything that I almost didn't register the fact that I was the one playing—just like last time.

My fingers moved expertly with the song—as if I'd played it a thousand times. I stared for longer than I should have before slowly rising from my hiding spot and making my way toward the ruins.

If the orcs saw me, it didn't matter. I could sure smell them, though, but they didn't even flinch as I strode right past and hurried into the warren of ruins, rubble, and canvas.

It was time to find my Party.

50

The deeper I delved into the busy orc camp, the odder things became. You don't often consider the ever-so-slight movements around you until they are no longer there. Wind blows, sending everything from leaves to scraps of fabric fluttering—but not here. Not for me.

It was like being caught between seconds.

As I picked the song on my lute, everything was still as death—which was a terrifying thought. Only smell remained. And there wasn't only the stink of orcs present. Carcasses of animals hung beneath canvases, skinned and ready for eating. One even looked... wellick.

In another spot, similar corpses weren't just hung out to bleed, but entirely deboned, the flesh and sinew tossed aside like old coats. Fire-heated basins burned, but the flames didn't move. Orcish craftsman stood frozen in time, with hammers raised over them, turning bone into weapons and armor. Loads of it. It was like the shaman wasn't just raising a hunting party, but an army...

He did seem smarter than most orcs. This is bad news for Pyruun.

Orcs raid and pillage for supplies. They don't march on castles.

A foolish concern to harp on, since I was on my spell's clock. That was how I'd begin to think of it, as a spell. I wasn't a wizard, but this was magic, after all.

Who could argue that? When I played my guitar back on Earth, I knew what chords I was strumming, and which notes would come next. Right now, holding Roxanne, I didn't have any predetermined plan. I just gave in to the music, and a beautiful song played. What's more, as far as I could tell, it was just a continuous melody, as if the song would go on forever and never end.

You have gained +1 to Sneaking.

Hey, you did it! O.M.G. Can we go back down the Petty Thief route? I really felt you had potential there.

Your Sneaking is now 4 (-1). So... 3 while you're wearing your fabulous, elegant cloak.

I pressed onward. Not for the first time since entering the encampment, I turned a corner and found myself face-to-face with a massive orc. Okay, maybe more like face-to-nipple-area since he was so much taller than me.

My heart stopped. One would think after my third or fourth such scare, it would no longer send me jumping out of my boots. But nope. If I wasn't so intent not to let up playing, I'd have leaped to the moon. He too was unmoving and unable to hurt anything beyond my pride. Thankfully, no one was watching or knew how close I'd come to soiling myself.

I thought I smelled something.

Almost nobody.

I skirted around him and continued through the crags, the only sound other than the lute being the soft squelch of mud underfoot. Though I checked under every tent, in every covered portion of ruin, I didn't see my companions. Worse than that, the eerie motionlessness of the world was starting to shift. My spell was still working, but time was beginning to tick along once more.

What if they're in the caves?

Then they're in the caves.

Who knows how far they go!

My desperation grew. I peered around the corner, searching for the fastest way out of the area. I failed this time. I'd have to get to safety and practice my playing or something until I Leveled Up, then try again. What else could I do?

As I planned out my route, I *felt* something following me. I heard shuffling as well—but it was the feeling I'll always remember. It sent chills rippling down my spine.

That wasn't me you smelled.

One of the worst stinks imaginable assaulted my nostrils, and I immediately knew what I was dealing with. I ducked into an alley between two ruined structures and waited. The air grew thicker with a dying, rotten stench. Then the walls started to glow.

Sickly green.

I sprang out from the alley.

"You!" I shouted, still playing the lute. Though it seemingly had no effect on Phlegm.

The old hag jumped at normal speed, which gave me a sick sense of satisfaction. It was about time I was the one doing the scaring.

She placed a corpselike hand to her chest. "You're going to startle an old lady to death acting like that!"

"That would serve you right. Why are you following me?"

A disturbing smile spread across her face, revealing those yellow, jagged, crooked teeth.

"Tsk, tsk," she said, wagging a bent finger back and forth. "You have not upheld your part of the bargain."

My eyes went wide. "Excuse me? I gave you my last meal!"

It was true, even if I'd had no designs to eat such a putrid thing.

"Yes. But that was not all." A wicked gleam entered her eye.

I thought back to when Phlegm accosted me at the Sea Mantis Inn, interrupting an otherwise pleasant evening with the barmaid Shalimar. What had she said then that she might have been referring to now?

Nothing.

I held the instrument out before me, pushing it from my chest but not so far as to disable me from playing.

"Nuh-uh," I said. "You told me to find it and I did. Right here."

"But you have forgotten the third."

"The third?"

"Yes. Yes. I told you, powerful magic always comes in threes. You have the lute; you have your voice; but you have neglected the third." The last word carried on for seconds.

I had the vaguest memory of that conversation on the first night I spent in Nahal. She'd struck the deal, gave me the vial which boosted my abilities, and told me that I'd find the lute and then I needed to drink the elixir. What had she said about a third... wait.

"You never told me what the third was!" I argued.

Yeah, you're right. What gives, hag!

"And I do not tell you to breathe," she said. "But you seem perfectly capable of doing so without instruction. Now, because you have chosen the way of the ungrateful, I have no choice."

With a wild flourish, she waved her hands. Rags hanging from her arms flapped with the movement. She leaned to and fro many times, her head snapping back. Her thin hair followed, making her look like some old, washed-up '80s metal musician head-banging. Then, she stopped, and her pale eyes bored into me like lasers. Nothing happened.

With that, she hobbled away. I stood there, dumbfounded.

"Crazy old coot," I said under my breath as I returned to my planned escape.

However, that was when I noticed it. Wrong notes, dead-sounding chords, and then finally, I couldn't play a thing on Roxanne.

"What the...?"

Uh-oh.

I spun back toward Phlegm, but she was gone.

You have lost The Hag's Blessing.

Your Stats have returned to their normal pathetic states.

Your Singing is now 17.

Your Instrument Playing is now 21.

Your Speechcraft is now 17 (+1).

Your Intelligence is now 5.

Your Dexterity is now 15.

Your Charisma is now 14 (+1).

No, they can't be!

They are.

I ran after the hag. "Wait! Phlegm, wait!"

I skidded across some slick mud and smacked headlong into something huge. My ass hit the ground hard, and when I looked up, the moon was blotted out.

"Well, well, what do we have here?" The same massive orc that had nearly made me shitless growled and cracked his knuckles. "The boss is gonna want to see you."

51

D irt filled my mouth as I hit the ground after being thrown into a windowless room.

OBJECTIVE FAILED:
You didn't rescue your companions. You have been imprisoned.

All your weapons and The Lute of Seven Stars [Unique] have been seized.

Do not pass Go. Do not collect—

"Danny?" a familiar voice asked.

Now for the good news. Somehow, even though you failed, the band is indeed back together. Only, now you're all doomed...

NEW PARTY MEMBER ADDED:
Curr the Braug (Level 25)

NEW PARTY MEMBER ADDED:

AN UNEXPECTED HERO

Garvis Wittleman the Thief (Level 9).

The Sisterhood of Alyndis Faction is once again your ally!

Well, I found my friends. But not how I wanted to.

Oh, hey, they both Leveled Up!

I grunted through having just landed on my face on a very unfor-giving surface. Slowly—and painfully—I rose, brushing off my clothes. Dust billowed, forcing a cough that, judging from the height at which it derived, was either Garvis or one of the Sisterhood seated.

It was so dark, I could barely make out my hand waving in front of me, much less see who shared the space with me.

"That you?" the voice continued.

"Yeah, it's me." My words came out in a gurgle, and I tasted blood.

In the midst of wiping my mouth with the back of my hand, I found myself nearly bowled over. Curr pulled me tight to his chest, so close I couldn't breathe.

I said as much, but muffled as it was against his sweat-soaked skin, he couldn't understand me.

"You're going to suffocate him!" Lilla said, rushing forward to pull us free.

Curr relented, pushing me to arms' length. "I am sorry. I just missed him."

I reached in front of me, hoping to pat him on the arm. All I managed to do was swipe thin air. Screenie offered me some help. The highlighted shapes of the Sisters could be seen in one corner. Garvis sat in the other. Curr stood before me, battered and bruised and covered in crusted blood.

"Missed you too, big guy," I said, getting my pat in.

"Great," Garvis spat. "There goes our hope of rescue."

Your relationship with Garvis has worsened.

I started to protest, but Curr spoke up first. Upon his initial words, I hoped for some backup, but I guess I couldn't be so lucky.

"You know, Danny, he is right. Getting yourself captured while we are already captured was not very bright. It would have been better if you would have stayed free and tried to free us."

"Wow," I said, smacking my forehead. "I didn't even think of that. You're right. How could I have been so dumb?"

"It is okay. We have grown accustomed to you doing dumb things."

Lilla snickered. Tevagah did not. In fact, from what I could see, she looked downright pissed.

I decided to act first. "Look, Tevagah, I know what you're going to say."

"Oh, do you, bard?"

"I do. And I'm sorry I abandoned you all back there. I promise I didn't mean to. Sometimes, the lute... speaks to me."

"It has no mouth," Curr said.

"Not like that." I touched my chest, over my heart. "In here. And I just play. I didn't know the song would teleport me away."

"Teleport?" Lilla asked.

Right. No science fiction here. How can I explain it?

Made you go poof?

You... Couldn't have warned me about the orc?

Oh, I'm sorry. I thought you saw it when you slammed into its chest.

"One second I was there at the battle," I said out loud. "The next, I was across the ruins in a tree. It was like..."

"The lute wanted to protect you," Lilla finished for me. "Tevagah, that must mean something."

"Or he led us there on purpose," she said. "Maybe he's in league with the shaman."

"Oh, you've got to be kidding me! I'm not working with some dumb orc. I got out. I could have run far away, but I came back for you. For *all* of you. That's the truth."

"It is a story, that's for sure," Tevagah said. "You bards excel at telling stories."

I threw my hands up in frustration, then sat against the wall. Not exactly the hero's welcome I'd been hoping for. All I could hear was everybody's irritating breathing for far too long until someone spoke up.

"Now what?" Garvis grumbled.

Curr's meathook of a hand rose to his bearded chin. He scratched a few times before saying, "Perhaps Danny knows a song that could assist us all now?"

It might have been the first time Curr offered anything remotely positive concerning my musical abilities, and I was heartbroken that I'd have to tell the truth.

"No can do," I admitted. My chin sank to my chest. "They took the lute."

"They did *what*?" Tevagah sprang to her feet and reached me in one long stride. "Tell me you're lying."

"When I got captured, they took it."

"You foolish, worthless, pathetic bard!" she shouted, her voice echoing in the empty chamber. Her fist pounded into the stone wall beside me, hard enough that I worried she might have broken her hand.

Your standing with the Sisterhood of Alyndis has worsened.

"I didn't just give it to them, you know," I argued.

"Oh, you put up a fight, did you?" She grabbed me by the chin, tilting my head back and forth as if inspecting one of her Night Mares. "It does not appear that you have suffered any great injuries."

I spat blood into the dirt, and I think a tooth went with it. "What do you call that?"

"We watched you obtain that particular trauma. I cannot believe you let them rob you."

"*You* let me rob you," I said before I could think better of it.

Tevagah looked like she was going to pummel me into the ground. Rage creased every wrinkle on her face. Thankfully, Lilla stepped in.

"Tevagah, they are orcs," she said. "Look at him. Does he look capable of overpowering them all alone? Even the smaller ones would make him appear like a child."

"...Thanks?" I said.

"No," Tevagah said, pressing a hand against Lilla's chest. "No. Not this time. Your strange infatuation with this wellick will not save him from what he deserves."

She pulled a weapon—her Dagger of Discontent—and brought it up like she planned to stab me. That explained her behavior. The weapon's enchantment was eating away at her. I wondered if she even knew.

I doubt it. She isn't lucky enough to have a me.

"Wait—they didn't take that from you?" Garvis asked.

"This? No. They could not find it."

"I don't even want to begin to think of where you might've hidden that."

Tevagah glared at the halfling, cold as ice. "I do not mean that I hid it. When concealed upon a Sister, it is as if it does not exist."

"That is a fine trick," Curr said.

"Yes, and for my next trick, I am going to make a bard disappear."

Tevagah returned her attention to me, something I'd have been eager for from a beautiful woman at any other time. Presently, I would have been fine if she forgot I existed.

I put up both hands. "Wait. Just wait. Don't you see? We aren't helpless here."

Tevagah stopped again. "What do you mean?"

I pointed toward the dagger with a finger from one of my upraised hands. "You have that. And we have… that." I pointed with my thumb to Curr. "They're going to come for us and believe we are weaponless and helpless. But we aren't."

"Or they will leave us here to rot. We only live because we were bait to get you to bring the lute. But I'm sure you already know that, considering you did exactly what they wanted."

I didn't back down. "Yeah, you're right. But the shaman wants to see me."

"*You?*" She said it like acid was on her tongue.

"Yeah. I guess maybe he thinks I can help unlock the lute's power or something. The orc who captured me said it."

"And if they are going to come for you," Lilla said. "They are coming through that door. All we have to do is wait patiently for them to arrive, then ambush them."

NEW OBJECTIVE:
Escape prison.

REWARD:
Sweet, sweet Freedom.

Curr smiled.

When Tevagah didn't budge, Lilla approached her, laid a hand over her wrist, and whispered in her ear, "Tevagah, please put the dagger away. You know how it affects you." Lilla's eyes were pleading. A look I found incredibly sexy.

You are a degenerate.

After a few seconds where I swear I could feel my heart beating in my throat, Tevagah reluctantly heeded Lilla's words and shoved her dagger away. I didn't see where it went, but once her hand was off it, it practically disappeared before my eyes.

"Thank you," I said, whether it was to Tevagah or Lilla or both.

Lilla offered me a frail smile and escorted Tevagah back to their corner before anything could escalate further.

"So now, we wait," I said. "It can't take that long, right?"

"What else does an orc shaman have to do with his day?" Garvis remarked.

"I am sure they share many of the same bodily functions as us," Curr added.

Nobody else had a comment. Things sure had grown dour amongst my companions since I'd left them. I guess being stuck in here for so long, they'd run out of things to say.

I made myself comfortable against the wall. I expected it to be more difficult, but without the lute strapped to my back, there was nothing in the way. Unconsciously, I patted at the area before remembering it wasn't there.

Ugh, I'm sorry, Roxanne.

Just as we were beginning to get comfortable with each other too. And she didn't play in my head, guiding me to wherever she was being kept. Just, silence. The loneliness made my heart hurt.

Hellooo? I'm right here.

I stared through the words with a thousand-meter gaze.

How dare you ignore me.

Was this how it felt to lose something you truly cared about?

Yes.

My eyes focused.

Like you'd know. And don't be jealous of me and Roxanne.

I'll have you know, you aren't the first person I've shared this sort of symbiosis with.

Oh, really?

It was meant as sarcasm, but I was afraid it came out differently.

Ah, who's jealous now?

I'm not jealous. I was being genuine. Something you know little about. So, tell me, who were the others?

Are you sure that's a road you're willing to travel? Learn about all my exes?

Don't make it weird.

Several hundred years ago, I was joined to a wizard by the name of Robert.

Bob the wizard?

I stifled a laugh.

Robert.

Though it was only words on a virtual screen, Screenie's correction carried with it a warning.

I nodded.

Continue.

Robert was particularly talented in the craft. Though he too was not from Aethonia, he acclimated toward it much quicker than you have.

I think for being thrust into another dimension, I've handled myself quite well, thank you.

Unfortunately, I can see clearly every time you "handle yourself."

What are you insinuating?

I'm supposed to ignore all those times you played pocket pool while staring at Lilla?

I was not! My hands were cold.

Right. Well, Robert was a magician of some renown.

Is there a point to this story?

Only that you called me jealous, and you deserved to know that you aren't my first. Robert and I, we got along great. When he died, I felt like you do now except way worse. So yes, I do know what you feel like.

Oof. I felt kind of bad. The truth was, I didn't know much about Screenie or his history beyond the fragments of information he dropped here and there.

How did he die?

If you're wondering if he died surrounded by angry orcs, no. Old age is a bitch.

Double oof. That meant they were together for years and years. It kind of explained why Screenie, whatever he was, seemed to keep me at a distance and offer only backhanded compliments.

It also made me concerned that if Robert never found a way home, I wouldn't either.

I'm sorry, Screenie. Thank you for sharing that with me.

Thank YOU for dredging up bad memories. I need some... time to myself... *sniffle*

Great. Now, I'd have to wait for the orcs completely by my lone-some, in a dark room filled with somber people who didn't seem to want to talk to anybody.

We were wrong about the orcs not taking a long time.

We waited nearly four hours before we heard voices approaching. They were deep and gruff—orcs without a doubt. My insides started doing somersaults.

This was my plan, sure, but that didn't mean I was excited about it. It's funny, in the real world, the worst I'd ever really considered happening to me was a bar fight like the one I'd had with Kurt. Here, there were things that would dismember me and sell my innards to the highest bidder. Maybe that was what they were planning to do?

They'll probably auction you off to the goblins alive to keep them loyal. Goblins prefer to gut their food themselves. They say the fear flavors the intestines. My guess is they like the taste of diarrhea.

I swallowed hard. Then dry heaved at the thought. Well, I wasn't about to be goblin food.

That's the spirit. Nothing like unmerited confidence.

"Quickly, someone stab me," Curr said.

We all spun on him. The first sound of a voice in hours.

"Huh?" Garvis and I both said.

"Mortally wound me. Only then can I call on Tarton's Rage." He slammed a fist against his chest.

Everyone stared at him, appalled. Except Tevagah. She had her Dagger of Discontent at the ready and was already moving Curr's way.

I stepped between them, stretching my hands as far as they'd go. "No. Stop it. That's insane. He could die."

"We all could die, bard," Tevagah spat. "Move aside and let me try to kill him."

I shook my head. "Absolutely not. I didn't come all this way just to watch my best friend die."

"Best... friend?" Curr said meekly.

"Yes, best friend." I turned to Curr. "I know this all started out with me poorly singing, and you wanting to tear off my arm."

"Ulna," Curr specified. Then he turned to everyone else, pointing to his forearm. "That is this bit right here." His eyes returned to me. "You taught me that, Danny the Bard. I think you are right. We are best friends. And they are our companions."

Your relationship with Curr has improved.

I smiled. When I turned to face the others, only Lilla wore any expression mirroring mine. Garvis glared at us like we were fools. Tevagah had murder in her eyes, a result of the dagger, I hoped.

"We can do this without placing one of our own in mortal danger," I said.

"Well, we'd better get ready," Lilla added. "Because those voices are getting closer."

I clapped once. "Right. Well, Curr, Tevagah, being that you are both so ready for a fight, each of you flank the door."

Tevagah spun her dagger, her eyes boring chasms into my own. I could tell she had no interest in taking orders from a "stupid bard," but she had to be intelligent enough to know that this plan was the best one we had.

"Garvis, quickly," I said, pointing to a ledge just above the door.

Really, it was little more than a loose keystone, allowing him mere inches to gain a foothold, but he was small and agile.

He got in place using Curr as a makeshift ladder.

As for Lilla and me—we were bait, seated directly across from the entranceway.

She sidled up close to me. I took an unsteady breath. The orc voices grew so loud, they must've been on the front porch. I turned to her.

"At least if we die, it'll be in good company," I said.

What a line, you idiot. Exactly what a girl wants to be referred to as. Good company.

Then something happened I never expected in a million billion years. Lilla, Sister of Alyndis, kissed me full-on the lips. With tongue.

You have gained +1 to Speechcraft.

Your Speechcraft is now 18.

Consider my mind blown.

I wish Roxanne was here to play that song.

♫♪♪ *Bom chikka wow wow!* ♪♪♫

52

The door flung open. My eyes, which should have been closed in ecstasy, did too. Still lip-locked with Lilla, I saw the giant imposing figures of three orcs, armed to the teeth, with teeth that were weapons as well.

Orc Berserker x3
Level 20
HP: 389/389

They stopped, eyeing us with an odd expression. It wasn't the distraction I'd expected, but it worked all the same.

In a sudden explosion of action, three things happened. First, Garvis dropped from his position and landed on the shoulders of the middlemost orc. Second, Tevagah's Dagger of Discontent struck out from her position flanking the door on the left side and drove it into the chest of the second orc. And finally, Curr leaped out of hiding and tackled the third to the ground.

Steel blades swiped and stabbed, some of the attacks even landing on Curr's shoulders and arms.

I was shoved as Lilla moved in a seriously impressive display of athleticism. She planted her hands on the ground and spring-boarded forward to smash the heels of her boots into Garvis's orc's face. That effort probably saved the halfling's life. Although the orc had been temporarily surprised by having two thighs squeezing his neck, the little thief simply lacked the strength to do much damage to something so much bigger and stronger than he.

Lilla's double-footed kick sent the orc staggering backward. The back of Garvis's head smacked into the door's crossbeam as the orc stumbled, and down he went. A fall from greater than six feet had him landing hard on the stone floor. To his credit, he rose pretty quickly and made his way out of the building.

Instead of running, like I'd expected him to, he worked in concert with Lilla to ensure the orc was out of the fight. He went low, she went high, and soon the orc was on his back in the middle of the enclosure in front of the tower.

All of this took place in the span of only a few seconds. Then I turned my attention to Tevagah's entanglement.

Her dagger had struck home, but the orc hadn't given up the fight. Orc blood gushed, making the floor wet and slippery. Curr was covered in it, and probably some of his own as well.

Do something!

Screenie's command was successful in snapping me out of my stupor. I ran forward without thinking and kicked Curr's orc in the side of the head.

Anything but that!

First of all, it hurt. Like stubbing my toe on a coffee table made of bricks. But I didn't let that stop me. It couldn't. This was a fight for our lives, and after that kiss, I really wanted to live.

While Curr wrestled with the orc, I kept stomping and kicking. I'm not sure what kind of a monster this makes me, but it felt really good. Even after the orc stopped struggling, I kept going until its sharp nose was flat as an iron, and tusks and teeth were lodged down its throat. Only when realization struck me that Curr had risen and moved to help Tevagah did I stop.

What... the... fuck...?

Orc Berserker Slain!

You have gained +1 to Unarmed Combat, but seriously, wtf.

Your Unarmed Combat is now 7.

That was disturbing...

The fight was over in less than a minute.

Lilla had slit her orc's throat open with his own weapon; Tevagah and Curr had broken their orc's neck; and the one over which I stood was an unrecognizable glob of blood and brains.

"We need to get out of here," Tevagah said. "Grab what you can. Arm yourselves. This fight is not over."

"That was exhilarating," Curr added, spitting blood.

Metal clattered as Garvis stripped the fallen enemies of their weapons. He found a dagger that, in his hand, looked more like a short sword. Curr checked the balance of one of their axes. It was sort of small in comparison to the one he'd always used, but he seemed fine with it.

"For you." Lilla approached me, handing me a sword of my own.

WEAPON OBTAINED:
Orcish Bone Sword (Melee Damage 9-12)

The weight of it nearly toppled me over, but I did my best not to show it. Our eyes met. I don't know what I expected to see there, but whatever it was, I didn't. It was as if, for her, the kiss never even happened. She was all business.

Them's the breaks.

I accepted the sword, and as I opened my mouth to speak, she turned her back on me and started out the door. I stood there for too long a moment, staring at the floor.

That was when I noticed my boots were covered in orc face.

Gross.

Actions have consequences. You really lost it. Personally, I think you should be institutionalized.

Actually, better yet...

TITLE UNLOCKED:
Unhinged.

You have proven yourself to be a bit off your rocker, using brute strength to shatter an orc's skull long after he'd gone on to Ku'lu'lu'bolth (That's the orc afterlife). Additionally, you didn't tire or collapse from the exertion.

You have gained a permanent +5 Strength while in a Duel.

I scraped my feet against the stone, watching the smears of brain matter. My stomach churned. Screenie was right—actions have consequences. And in this case, my actions earned me something I desperately needed: a win.

"Danny, are you coming?" Curr asked.

"Yeah," I said, joining my companions by the open door.

"That will not help us be stealthy," Tevagah said, pointing at my cloak. "Take it off."

Yeah, take it off, Danny. Take it all off!

"But it's cold out," I argued.

"Would you prefer to be cold, or dead?" Tevagah asked.

In response, I tore the cloak off and tossed it aside. It was oddly sad, watching such a hideous thing flutter to the ground. Though I never really liked it, it had been with me nearly as long as I'd been in Aethonia.

ITEM LOST:
Lalair's Elegant Cloak

I sighed. Curr looked over to me, then stomped to where the cloak had fallen. He scooped it up and draped it over my shoulders.

Shaking his head, he said, "You look foolish without a cloak."

ITEM OBTAINED:
Lalair's Elegant Cloak

Make up your mind.

Tevagah glared at him, then blew out a puff of air and stalked out the door.

I looked up at Curr. "Thanks, buddy."

Curr ruffled my hair, nearly snapping my neck. "We should get moving. And try to stay down. She is not wrong. That cloak is as bright as the moon."

OBJECTIVE COMPLETED:
You have escaped orcish prison!

You're on the lam now. Stick to the shadows, Batman.

NEW OBJECTIVE:

Escape the Orc Encampment.

REWARD:
The ability to continue on your quest. Hooray!

We moved outside. Moonlight exposing us wouldn't be an issue. No longer were we outside in the ruins of Alyndis. We were inside a cave. Dark, dank, and cold.

No torches lit our way. In one direction was total darkness. In the other, a reddish hue emanating from somewhere deep down.

Remember: Orcs can see in the dark.

Great.

Tevagah and Lilla chanted in elvish to bring their magical shields to life, and this time it was quiet enough for me to hear. "*Ethu... cicada... denifidi...*" Or something.

"E'thrusiscia de nerridai". Or, "Effervescent protection," in your way less cool language.

I repeated it in my head to try and memorize it. I didn't want to say it yet, but I remembered then that I still had my bracer, and it couldn't hurt to be prepared. Luckily, neither Tevagah nor Lilla had noticed it in the dark, and I used my cloak to keep it that way. "You robbed our dead Sister" wasn't a discussion I was looking forward to.

Their shields' glow was minimal in this oppressive blackness, but it helped us see in our direct vicinity. The caves weren't natural but dug-out tunnels in ant farm. The rock itself had a whitish hue that sparkled when the light touched it—similar to the ruins of Alyndis.

"I don't suppose either of you elves know which is the right way?" Garvis said.

They shook their heads.

"Our people didn't dig these passages," Tevagah said. She knelt and lifted a small skull with sharp teeth and a squat shape. "Goblin. The shaman must have forced them to dig."

"For what?" I asked.

"Many powerful elven sorcerers once used the mountain as a sanctum," Lilla said. "Who knows what lies hidden."

"Treasure?" both Curr and Garvis said at the same time. They glanced at each other, incredulous. It seemed the two of them *did* have something in common.

"Nothing that should be disturbed," Tevagah warned.

Curr strolled off and gave a noisy whiff. "It smells a bit less like orc in that direction." He gestured toward the path with a reddish glow at the end.

"Do you really expect us to follow your nose?" Garvis asked.

"Never underestimate a braug's sense of smell." Curr pointed to his nose.

Screenie, any guidance?

Like the elves said, they didn't make this.

None of it is in my records.

What about a hunch?

My gut says don't go toward the light.

My brain says, without light, the orcs will slaughter you.

"I'm with Curr," I said out loud. "Without light, the orcs can get a better jump on us."

Thanks for the credit...

"Certain death looms either way," Tevagah stated. Nothing like her optimism to get us through tough times. "I will take the lead. Lilla, take the rear."

Don't, I warned Screenie before any words could pop up.

The two elves split up, providing a modicum of light both in front and behind us. Then we began a slow shuffle down the tunnel. Every movement felt like a delicate dance of silence and shadows. It had me feeling oddly poetic.

The air was cool and laden with the scent of moldy stone and forgotten secrets. Every so often, a patch of carved stone peeked into a niche in the cavern. In other spots, half-buried goblin skeletons lay, shreds of flesh still clinging to the bone.

I looked ahead at Tevagah, clad in dark, form-fitting attire that melded seamlessly with the surroundings. I, on the other hand, looked like a puff of cotton candy. I did my best to control my breathing and measure every footfall. The Sisters' feet landed with feather-light precision to avoid disturbing loose debris, while I clambered on like an elephant stomping through the Sahara.

Elves are naturally light on their feet. They may be roughly the same size, but they are significantly lighter weight than wellicks.

If you ever get back with Lilla, try and pick her up. You'll see.

Now is not the time to put that image in my head. But, by the way... I told you she was into me.

She used you to create a distraction.

No. She was into me, couldn't resist, and that wound up creating a distraction.

Any opposing truth was not something I wanted to entertain while we were sneaking around for our lives. We reached a branch in the tunnel. One direction was caved-in, which made the decision easy. The other glowed an even brighter red, and even weirder still, the chill went away. Hot air kissed the sweat on my brow.

"I have a bad feeling about this," I groaned.

Tevagah shushed me.

The echoes of distant voices reached our ears—the rough, guttural speech of the orcish patrollers.

"This way." She hurried us along into a crevice at the next turn.

My heart quickened, and I pressed my back against a crumbling wall even before Tevagah's finger reached her lips. I could almost feel Curr behind me shaking with anticipation of another fight.

The orcs' heavy footsteps resonated through the stone, a reminder of the peril that awaited any false move.

"Let them pass," Tevagah whispered.

At that command, Curr's excitement clearly waned. His face creased in anger, as if someone had just stolen the food from his mouth.

"What is taking them so long?" one of the orcs asked.

"The boss doesn't like waiting," the other agreed.

Their heavy feet stomped past us, kicking up dust. My knuckles squeezed anxiously.

You have gained +1 to Sneaking.

Your Sneaking is now 5.

You're a natural sleuth!

Momentary pride made me feel a bit less horrified, and then, like the great little fool he was, Garvis coughed.

The orcs whipped around.

They didn't even get a word out before Tevagah sprang into

action. Her hate-imbued dagger sliced both of their throats in one smooth, leaping action.

Their loud gargling as they attempted to shout a warning was cut short as Lilla joined her leader, jumping forward and getting her arm around one orc's throat. Tevagah swung her body around the other and did the same, both enemies silently lowered to the ground.

"I greatly enjoyed watching that!" Curr exclaimed. Tevagah's glower quickly silenced him.

"If you cannot be quiet, we will leave you behind," she threatened Garvis.

The halfling's cheeks went red. And not only from the hellish glow of the cavern. I'm not sure if it was embarrassment or fear.

"I'm allergic to dust..." he muttered.

"Move," Tevagah ordered.

The elves returned to their positions, and we pressed on. At the mouth of the tunnel, the source of the reddish glow was answered. The raw, hand-hewn tunnel transformed into a vaulted space with columns along the side. Spouts of molten lava fell around them, filling the gaps in an intricate pattern carved into the floor, forming the same star-constellation insignia the shaman had on his stolen flag.

My fingers brushed against warm, ancient stone as we entered, and I couldn't help but feel the weight of time pressing against me. These elven ruins remained a work of melancholic beauty, almost completely intact except for the faded paintings along the ceiling. Remnants of a civilization—Tevagah and Lilla's civilization—that once thrived in harmony with the natural world. The only ruined portions were slots along the walls that had been broken open. Bones filled spaces in crumbled stone, too large to be goblin.

Tevagah stepped slowly down the center, carefully avoiding the lava-filled troughs.

"They have desecrated these tombs..." she said softly.

"Tombs?" I asked.

"Our people's greatest sorcerers and scholars, honored to spend the eternal sleep amidst the light of the Seven Stars."

What, did you expect elves to be buried above ground?

Well, yeah. They aren't dwarves...

Dwarves send their dead out to sea, Danny. Don't be insensitive with your preconceived notions. The Masked Mountains are home to countless tombs of great and powerful elves. I told you, they believe the stars dripped and formed this mountain. Starlight fells this tomb.

You mean lava...

Tell that to them. Go ahead, insult their faith. I don't want to worsen your relationship with the Sisterhood of Alyndis, but I can.

"Looks like they already took anything of value," Garvis called. I hadn't even realized he'd left our formation to investigate one of the graves.

"Touch nothing, thief!" Tevagah stormed over and grabbed him by the collar.

"Ow, hey! I was just looking!"

She dragged him back to the rest of us.

"I swear, I was just looking," he said to me.

"Sure," I replied.

"It appears this was only a stop along the way." Lilla pointed to another tunnel breaking through the backside of the burial chamber.

"But for what?" Tevagah said.

"I'm okay not knowing that answer," I said. "Right? Anybody?"

Ignored once again.

Tevagah led the group along, and all I could do was follow. She stared straight ahead, avoiding looking at all the desecrated resting places. The strain of her muscles as she did so was evident.

My ears became attuned to every sound as we entered the next dark passage—the churning of lava, the rustle of my own clothing, the faintest whisper of air. It was a symphony of subtleties, and amidst it all, I found myself straining to catch the palest of clues that could hint at any orcs' proximity.

But the next clue wasn't very subtle at all. A horn blew so loudly, it resonated through the cavern. Then, heavy drums made the very earth shake and dust loosened all around us.

"Yig and shog!" Garvis cursed. Then he sneezed twice in rapid succession.

I swore as well. Our escape had been discovered.

53

All I could hear were bellowing horns between intervals of drumming. It reminded me of one time in high school when Chris Taylor pulled the fire alarm, just without the sprinklers. At the time, I knew there was no fire; I knew we weren't in danger. It was a prank, after all. Still, my heart raced like crazy as we were all rushed out onto the school's front lawn.

This time, it was that same feeling, only without the knowledge that we weren't going to burn alive. This time, I was pretty sure we were—or worse.

Worse. Definitely worse. This is Prison Break—orc style.

"It's bad enough you got me into this mess, boyo!" Garvis said, stirring me to the present. "You better not slow us down."

"That's rich, coming from you!" I said. My words sounded more confident than I felt, which wasn't saying much because I barely squeaked them out.

Curr shook my shoulder. "Danny, we must move quickly. Do you need me to carry you?"

"No, I just... Maybe we should go back the other way?"

"Too late for that," Lilla said. "They're coming from that direction."

"Then we delve into the deep," Curr proclaimed. I didn't like how excited he seemed by the notion. Not one bit. But the endless drum of doom approaching spurred me along.

No more creeping along. We raced through the dark passages of a once-great people, zigging and zagging, in and out of more underground burial chambers filled with lava art. It was an archeologist's wet dream. The orcs had clearly been busy digging—or forcing goblins to—for many years.

Soon the sounds of drums and blowing horns were replaced by stomping feet and orcish shouts. They weren't far behind.

I glanced over my shoulder, and when I turned back around, ran face first into Curr's back. It may as well have been a wall. Lilla caught me before I fell all the way to the ground.

I found myself looking up at her soft, pretty, beautiful, amazing... Wait, what was I talking about. Oh yeah, her face. I got lost in it, thinking for the briefest moment that I might get lucky again. Instead, she lifted me upright.

"Why did we stop...?"

My words trailed off as I came around Curr and the answer walloped me in the face in the form of a sweltering wash of air. I thought my eyebrows were going to be singed off.

We'd entered an expansive cavern, the ceiling rising far beyond the shadows. Below our feet was a circular platform at the end of a rocky outcrop, intricately carved by ancient elven artisans. All around us bubbled a vast pool of liquid magma, with no way out except for back the way we'd come.

"*Lilla, the platform. What does it say?*" Tevagah asked in elven, translated by Screenie. I noted the nervousness in her tone. That wasn't good.

Lilla quickly brushed off a section of the floor. "*The Stars watch over us, always,*" she replied.

"How about so we can all understand," Garvis complained.

"It doesn't matter," Tevagah said. "It's just a saying."

"You knife-ears and your sayings!"

"How dare you—"

"Guys!" I shouted and pointed to a rocky outcrop over the wide opening we'd entered through. If we could climb to that, we could reach what looked like another cavern branching off above. Unlike the rest of our route, this towering hollow appeared mostly natural. There were pockets all the way up that we could climb.

You're right. I'm going to put a note in for the boss to add the Climbing Skill to your repertoire.

Wait, what boss?

I don't know, but the note is written!

"There's no way I'm getting up there," Garvis said, echoing my thoughts.

"We try or we fall here," Lilla said.

I was pretty sure she was trying to be encouraging, but the reality that the most likely outcome was to die nearly paralyzed me.

Garvis was right. He wasn't making it up. Neither was I. I wasn't some free-climbing daredevil. I was the kid who made it halfway up the rock wall at Sports Plus, slipped, and dangled from my harness until the heroic instructor could come up and rescue me. There were no harnesses here.

Not for the first time, I wished I had my lute so I could play "Tillith's Last Call" and bolster our group's resolve.

It may not count for much, but it's nice to know you're thinking logically. That's a good idea.

That first outcrop was ten feet up at least, and the surface beneath was smooth as a baby's ass. Okay, maybe not quite—I could see the occasional place a hand or foot might fit. But still, without arms as long and strong as Curr's, it just wasn't happening.

"Climb up me," Curr said.

"Brilliant idea!" Garvis didn't even wait a second before hopping onto the big braug's back and trying to reach his shoulders. A task that was equally as impossible for the halfling as scaling the wall.

"I was not prepared." Curr swatted at him. I went to pull him down.

Turns out, none of it mattered anyway.

A hatchet whizzed by my head and splashed into the lava, where it slowly sank in a dazzling show of embers. I spun to find us staring at a horde of orcs. Twenty or more of them, clad in mismatched bone armor, flashed ferocious teeth.

"End of the road," one said menacingly.

Tevagah and Lilla twirled around at the sound of the voice. Gripped in Tevagah's hand was the Dagger of Discontent.

My hand went reflexively to the lute no longer hanging from my back.

"This is familiar," Garvis sighed. "And to think, there are so many things I didn't get to steal..."

"What do we do?" I asked, frantic.

Curr pounded one fist into his palm. "We fight."

"For once, I agree with the braug," Tevagah said. "I will not be captured again."

"I stand with you, Mother," Lilla said.

I stared at my brave, heroic—minus Garvis—Party as the orcs filled in the entryway to our platform, leaving no way out. Death by tooth and blade, or melted by lava, there were no good choices.

My heart sank.

It was my fault they were all here. I'd bartered with that hag, and all of this came to pass. From finding the lute to her getting me caught, all because I didn't understand her bedside riddles. All my companions were going to die because of me.

Whoa now, go easy on yourself. And that's ME saying this.

Don't do anything rash.

Then an idea came to me. A horrible, desperate, idea.

"Hey, Curr, remember that plan back in the prison?" I whispered to him.

"A number of plans were presented," he replied.

"Your crazy one to call on your Rage."

"Ah, indeed! It would have been effective, but how we escaped hurt less."

"What about now?" I asked softly.

I knew what I was asking. Even in the face of dozens of ravenous, angry orcs, it sounded insane.

Were you not just listening to me? NOTHING RASH...

"It has turned the tide against similar odds for me before," Curr said.

"Should she do it?" I nodded toward Tevagah.

"No, you."

"Me?"

"You."

I glanced up at his big, friendly eyes. His people were renowned for their Rage, and when he fought, it sure seemed that way, but the Curr I knew was the opposite. A little too blunt and overly fond of discussing bodily functions, sure, but he was a big softy.

"Curr, come on," I pled.

"I trust you, Danny the Bard," he said. "There is no time to think. Empty your mind and let Tarton's Rage take hold."

"I'm not a braug."

"You are to me."

Be still my beating heart. Oh, just do it. Show him some love and stab him repeatedly.

My hand trembled as it gripped the orc sword. Fighting killer monsters was one thing, but stabbing a friend? Even with his permission, it felt wrong.

You're in the clear, Danny! #metoo.

I looked up. The orcs formed ranks in the passage. A shadowy mob of ravenous death, ready to engulf us.

"For Alyndis!" Tevagah called out, striking her own chest.

"For Alyndis!" Lilla repeated.

"Screw Alyndis!" Garvis added. "For Garvis!"

Rash, Screenie had said. Not thinking about my actions was what Danny Kendrick did best. If we wanted to survive, I'd have to remember a bit of my old self. That aimless scion of heartbreak, chaos, and unpaid bills.

And so, without thinking twice, I snatched Tevagah's dagger right out of her hand.

WEAPON OBTAINED:
Alyndis Dagger of Discontent (Damage 1-99) [Unique]

In an instant, my mood changed. I was still scared to the point where I was sure whatever I had in my bowels was going to end up in my pants, but now I was also seething, angry, and a plethora of other emotions I didn't truly know how to identify.

Something tells me "discontent" is among those.

Unhappy summed things up, sure.

"What are you doing, bard?" Tevagah demanded.

She didn't dare take her eyes off the orcs to try and steal it back. And I didn't have time to ask her permission.

"My name is *Danny*!" I shouted.

With the dagger in my grip now, this strategy didn't even seem risky. Stabbing someone to near death? How fun. I had to do it. I wanted to do it.

I closed my eyes. "Forgive me, friend."

Whipping around, I plunged the dagger into Curr's chest. To the best of my limited knowledge of a braug's anatomy, assuming it was the same as a human, I avoided his heart.

Curr roared. The orcs stared at us like we were insane.

I was bodily shoved down. My head hit the hard surface of the platform. The dagger clattered along the rock. And blackness started to creep in around the edge of my vision, but I refused to pass out. Not again.

I pushed through the pain and my gaze fell on Curr, whose muscles swelled up three times his normal size like the Incredible Hulk, veins popping everywhere. Curr had entered true Tarton's Rage mode for the first time since I'd met him, and it was unlike anything I'd ever experienced in my life.

ALERT: A member of your Party has been gravely injured.

Ouch! Did you double check for his consent?! Did he sign anything? This seems like a litigation nightmare.

Curr moved like lightning toward the gathered orcs. Blood painted walls and pooled on the platform as he tore off limbs and drove a flurry of fists through chest cavities and stomachs. Orc bodies were flung into the lava. Screams of anguish filled the cavern.

Before I could even react, every enemy present lay dead around him as if a comet had struck.

Then, Curr collapsed to his knees, shrinking to normal size. He clutched a hand to his chest where I'd stabbed him. The silence in that moment was deafening. I could almost hear the heart of the nearest orc ceasing to beat.

"What did you do?" Lilla gasped, her voice startling as much as a thunderclap.

"Curr!" I stood, and pushing everyone aside, I ran to my friend's side.

"That... was... smart," Curr told me. "But... you aim... like... you sing." He chuckled. Some blood leaked out. "Poorly."

I laughed, though it felt forced. "What can I do?"

Tevagah and Lilla rushed over. Tevagah tore her dagger from my hand. "Go back in time and stab him somewhere less lethal!" she shouted at me like she was scolding a child. "We have no means of healing him. He will surely die."

My entire body flushed with heat. "Die? No. He can't die. I just... I did what he..."

"Move!" Lilla demanded. This time, when she put her hands on me, it was definitely not with affection. She basically pushed me aside as she knelt over the wound to study it closer.

Garvis caught me. "Bold move, boyo. It's what he would have wanted."

I shook him off and scrambled to Curr.

Screenie, please. What can I do! There's gotta be something I can do.

Perhaps if you had the lute... On the other hand, you did kill a braug way above your Level, which is pretty cool.

It's not cool! I killed my friend! I thought I was helping!

Then out loud, I repeated, "I thought I was helping!"

Curr labored for breath as blood poured out of his chest like a river. Lilla clutched his hand and placed her other palm over his wound, chanting low in elvish.

"I'm sorry," I said.

Curr's eyes rose to meet mine, and a small smile appeared on his lips. "We are far from Kiel's trading post."

I nodded. "Yeah, buddy."

"You didn't purchase any potions from him by any chance?"

I shook my head. He sighed, which turned into a gurgling cough. "The orcs took mine... Rotten thieves..."

"Hey, don't lump them in with me," Garvis said.

Danny.

I knew Screenie was saying something but couldn't see through welling tears.

"There will be more," Tevagah said. "We can't stay."

"Give them a moment," Lilla said.

"There are no moments in life and death."

DANNY!

"What!" I accidentally screamed out loud. Everyone's gaze snapped toward me.

Check your pockets.

I madly searched around in my pockets and cloak until my fingers clutched a few shriveled pink flowers smushed at the bottom of my pocket that the orcs wouldn't even have bothered to take.

"The flowers!" I tore them free. They were no longer glowing pink. But there they were, the healing flowers Curr had demanded I pick at the start of this adventure.

Oh, thank you, Screenie. Thank you, thank you, thank you!

See? If I were jealous of him, would I have helped you save him?

"You kept my flowers..." Curr groaned, like an ex popping in for one last romp in the hay. I'd have cringed if I weren't so grateful.

I placed them in Lilla's hands. "You can heal, right?" Most of the character profiles Screenie showed me went in one ear and out the other, but Lilla's... I had a photographic memory when it came to hers. Healing Hands, that was one of her Special Abilities.

You paid attention!

ITEM LOST:
Candentis Flos ex Improbi (3)

Lilla's eyes narrowed. "Where did you get these?"

"Can you work quickly with this?" I begged.

"There is no time!" Tevagah warned, scooping up her dagger.

I glared at her, fire raging in my belly. "Then you run!"

Anger contorted her features, but after a moment, she stepped back and held her tongue.

Lilla nodded. "I need water." I looked around frantically. There was no water in sight. Lilla cupped the flowers in her hands. "Everyone, spit in my hands. Quickly." A look of disgust must have shown on my face. "Do it now, or he will surely perish."

I gathered as much spit as I could in my mouth, leaned over and released it into her open palms.

Oh, so this is her kink? Intriguing.

Please, not now.

Fine, fine. I'm just trying to keep things light while your bestest bud bleeds out. But I'm the bad guy.

Lilla and Garvis did the same.

"More," she said.

Tevagah finally joined in. We all spit into Lilla's hands until our mouths were bone dry. With the heat of the lava surrounding us, it evaporated fast. She went to work as fast as she could with the pommel of her orcish weapon to crush the flowers into a paste.

A loud *clang* drew my attention.

While Lilla was busy, Garvis sat on the chest of one of the fallen orcs and was trying to pry metal teeth out of the thing's mouth. I couldn't tell the color in the darkness.

"Really?" I said, aghast. "Right now?"

"It could be precious!"

I could only long-blink at him.

"What?" His eyes glinted with lust. "These guys aren't a threat anymore." He yanked on its mouth.

Laughter rose up, loud and cruel, but it didn't come from any of us. The air grew thick with dread as if I still held the Dagger of Discontent.

Garvis yelped in pain and fell back, clutching his hand. "It bit me!"

I noticed then that the orc's drooping jaw was no longer shut tight. The corpse's eyes began glowing a dark, otherworldly purple. Then, one by one, the dead began to rise.

54

I froze. You know, how one does when dead things come to life all around you. It's not something you get used to right away.

Tevagah, however, remained steady. I supposed sometimes having that blasted dagger in her possession wasn't always bad. Kept her... less excitable.

"Grab any weapon you can use and toss the rest!" she ordered, using her boot to flip a fallen sword into her hand so she wielded two.

"Why not just push them in!" As the orc Garvis was on cracked bones into place to begin its rise, he pushed with all his might, trying to roll it into the lava.

I panicked and dove to grab another sword and be a badass warrior like Tevagah. But between the fighting, the heat, and the nerves, my hands were sweaty as a virgin on prom night. The handle slipped, and I scampered to catch it before the blade skittered off the ledge.

Smooth. That'll impress Lilla.

"I need a few more minutes with him or he'll be lost!" Lilla said, still stooped over Curr.

I rolled back, looking toward her. "Lilla, don't stop, no matter what! We need him..."

I need him, I couldn't help thinking.

Imagine that. Just a few short weeks ago, you were a lonely loser with no friends. Now, here in Aethonia, you've got friends enough to kill!

You're not helping!

Well, maybe next time, you'll consult me on your plan.

You don't waste your deadliest weapon before the Final Boss!

"Tevagah, we can guard him!" I called to her as she darted across the platform, sliding another weapon into the lava so the reanimated orcs couldn't use them.

Garvis' target stopped rolling and grabbed the halfling's ankle. That resulted in curses I'd never imagined as Garvis stabbed at it until its elbow ripped.

I ran to him and whispered, *"E'thrusiscia de nerridai."* Nothing happened.

Roll the Rs, Danny! Remember Spanish 101!

I repeated it, following his instructions, and a magical shield expanded from my elven bracer, oblong in shape and large enough to protect most of my body if I fully crouched.

Lilla's gaze momentarily wandered from Curr, her eyes going wide. I smiled awkwardly and shrugged.

"Tevagah, please!" I implored. "We don't stand a chance without Curr. Tevagah!"

Her attention was lost, facing back toward the burial chambers. Something in her eyes made me turn.

Just beyond the rising dead, I saw the source of their necromantic urging. The orc shaman stepping toward us at a leisurely pace, the bottom of his golden staff scraping across the stone.

OBJECTIVE UPDATED:
Defeat the orc shaman

REWARDS:
An unlikely victory and a [Rare] Title

"You have all proven to be a worthy hunt," he said, his croaking voice chilling me to the core despite the heat. "But cornered prey dies all the same."

He stopped in the archway, leaning on his staff like he hadn't a care in the world. Like we were a minor inconvenience. This time, in addition to his nightmare-inducing getup, he had my lute slung over his oversized shoulder.

Poor Roxanne.

With his gnarly fingers and nails, and her the size of a ukulele to him, she'd never be treated right.

That's what you're worried about right now?

You're the one who taught me about her feelings!

"Hey! Give me back my fucking lute!" I shouted.

The shaman laughed. "I think not. First, I will slaughter your friends. No more chances. Then you will teach me how to unlock its power."

"Never." I shook my head.

"Then I will skin you alive, and perhaps, after I bring you back, you will be more cooperative."

A low growl drew my attention to my right.

Undead Orc Grunt
Level 6
HP: 69/157

I got my newly activated shield up in time to block a downward slash of the orc's claws. Since it was transparent, it still felt like I was going to be struck and so, admittedly, I closed my eyes. Then it sparked with energy as it successfully prevented the attack.

It didn't, however, deflect his weight.

I fell backward—a position I'd found myself in far too often unfortunately. I stabbed forward through the thing's thigh, where its skin and muscles were so dense, the sword got stuck. I did my best to rock the weapon back and forth while the orc's undead teeth snapped wildly at the shield, causing it to flash like strobe lights.

Finally, I abandoned the sword and rolled to the side. I scooped up a stone hammer with a handle made of bone and swung it around, smashing the orc through the temple. Bone crunched as it flipped sideways.

Weapon Lost:
Orcish Bone Sword (Melee Damage 9-12)

Weapon Gained:
Orcish Hammer (Melee Damage 3-13)

Undead Orc Grunt Slain!

You have gained +1 to Melee Weapon Combat.

Your Melee Weapon Combat is now 17.

Behind me, Tevagah bounded like a lioness and plunged her Dagger of Discontent through a risen orc that got close to Curr. She landed, twirled, and unleashed a strong kick into the chest of the orc attacking Garvis, sending it airborne back into the lava.

"Nice one!" I shouted, unable to contain my thrill. "Bring it back from that."

I raced over to Curr and stood side by side with Tevagah, hammer raised.

"You were right, Danny," she said. "Only way out of this is all of us, together. We'll hold them, Lilla. Just get him upright."

Lilla acknowledged her in elvish.

"You cannot resist!" the orc shaman called out. "Your heads will embellish the walls of my new castle. For too many centuries, we orcs have been ignored. Our time has come!"

Another zombie orc rose and charged me from the side. I was about ready to show him what's what when he tripped and slid to a stop at my feet. Glaring down, I spotted Garvis with his dagger and another blade nearly as tall as him in his child-sized hands.

"If they don't got legs, they ain't getting far," he said. For once, he didn't back behind us or anything. I had to hand it to the little fellow: he was tougher than any of us thought.

He jumped and drove both blades downward and through the back of the orc's skull. "If they don't got brains—"

The shaman growled in anger and stepped forward. His unnatural aura shone brighter around him. His eyes were rolled back into his head, showing only pure white beneath spiny brows that jutted out. His twin tusks gleamed a sickly sanguine hue.

"Whatever you are going to say next is wrong," he said as he stretched his staff out sideways. His own blood was all over it and his hand.

Still on the orc's back, Garvis screamed. The orc beneath him radiated with that evil purple glow, and Garvis's blades, hilt deep into orc skull, rose with the shaman's hand. And not just that one. All the orcs we'd killed, both living and recently undead, rose at once.

I shook my head. "They can't die."

The shaman taunted us. "What is dead may never—"

Sounds Alarm: *GRRM Copyright alert!*

What?

Don't worry about it. Focus on the fight!

The orc grabbed Garvis and flung him. He might have taken a one-way trip into the lava if he didn't crash into me. Another came barreling at Tevagah, swinging a war hammer. She gracefully rolled over Lilla's back without interrupting her work. The orc stumbled awkwardly after a lumbering swing through the air, and as Tevagah straightened out, it impaled its own throat on her outstretched blade.

"Get off!" I shoved Garvis off me. He rolled back, grumbling, his shirt lifting over his face as he tumbled.

I popped up as another undead orc lunged at me, its broken teeth gnashing. Trying my best to use the techniques Lilla taught me, I sidestepped and brought my hammer down in what I hoped to be a deadly arc. The blunt weapon smashed through the creature's skull, shattering its head in a shower of black, putrid blood.

The body crumpled to the ground, but it only fell for a second before glowing purple and rising again. This time, with a bashed-in head.

"We have to stop him!" I shouted at anyone listening.

But there was no time. More undead orcs stumbled in our direction, their numbers growing with each passing second. We suddenly found ourselves surrounded.

And that was when I heard it. A battle hymn I'd become all too accustomed to. It was softer and distant, coming from the direction of—

The shaman's back. Roxanne. She remembered me.

"What is that infernal sound?" the shaman yelled.

The burning ache in my muscles diminished. The pit in my chest filled in. And then I felt it, the invigoration Curr did the first time he'd heard the battle hymn. In the corner of my eye, I saw his toes wagging back and forth to the beat, which inspired me even more.

Roxanne's music has super-invigorated your Party!

+5 Bonus to Strength and Courage for Duration of Battle

My grip on my hammer tightened. I swayed with the music. An orc swung a bone sword at me, and I blocked it with my energy shield, except I didn't merely absorb the blow—I pushed into it.

The orc staggered back, and I swung upward with the hammer, catching it on the bottom of the jaw. The orc's feet flew out from under it as it dropped its weapon. The lute unleashed a crescendo of chords.

Undead Orc Berserker Slain!

Another orc swung a club at me, and I ducked under the clumsy attack. On my way back up, I grabbed the sword from the floor, then stabbed up backhanded so the tip of the blade went through its heart. More triumphant chords.

WEAPON OBTAINED:
Orcish Bone Sword (Melee Damage 8-11)

Undead Orc Grunt Slain!

You're really getting the hang of this!

You have gained +1 in Melee Weapon Combat.

Your Melee Weapon Combat is now 18.

Tevagah's dagger was a blur of steel, parrying orc weapons and claws, and cleaving through the undead with precise strikes. Garvis did... something, I'm sure. I could hear him grunting and cursing like a sailor.

It wouldn't matter. For every orc we felled, they just got right back up.

"They keep coming!" I said.

"I hadn't noticed!" Garvis said.

"Don't give ground!" Tevagah ordered. She slipped under the swipe of an orc and slashed it from belly button to gonads in a way that made every part of me feel uncomfortable. Another orc grabbed her by the throat as she rose and heaved her off her feet. She stabbed repeatedly at its arm, saliva spewing all over her face as its inhuman roar rang out.

"Tevagah!" Lilla yelled behind us. She launched her sword, and it pierced the orc's wrist, allowing Tevagah to get free. As she fell, she clutched its handless arm and used the momentum to throw the orc over her back like a WWE superstar. It howled all the way into the lava, where it was silenced.

Even with the music, my muscles wouldn't be able to keep this up. Or Garvis, for that matter. Maybe Tevagah could, but I imagined even elves have their endurance limitations.

I've got a feeling we're about to find that out...

Then I heard movement behind me—something different. Not orcs. Not battle. A familiar grunt.

Sparing a moment and taking my chances looking away from the fight, I witnessed Curr rising to his feet with Lilla's aid. That was how she was able to help Tevagah; she'd done it!

Curr's abdomen was covered in his own blood, but the spot

where I'd stabbed him was now patched by a sloppy glowing pink paste. It looked a little bit like my cloak.

You know what they say. Bros who rock pink together, stick together.

Curr wobbled forward. Each time his boot hit the ground, he winced, but he kept going nonetheless. If the masters at the Fighters Guild could only see him now, they'd be singing a different tune.

He stumbled and dropped to his knee.

Spoke too soon.

The shaman cackled. "Weak. Even the largest of you. Weak."

But Curr wasn't through. Not yet. He rose, gritting his teeth, and let out a growl that harmonized with Roxanne, reaching a volume and level of epicness I didn't think possible.

A boss battle hymn.

The shaman appeared visually uncomfortable as it blasted in his ear. "How is this possible? I claimed it. It cannot answer to you!" He ripped Roxanne off his back and studied it from all angles, distracting him from raising more of the orcs back to life.

Trudging forward, Curr scooped up a war hammer dropped by one of the undead horde. All at once, the undead orcs turned their attention from the rest of us and focused fully on Curr. It was clear they weren't as intelligent in their reanimated forms, but ganging up on the greatest was an age-old strategy.

Clearly shoving aside all his aches and pains—and near-death stuff too—Curr whirled with the hammer in hand and sent one of the witless dead soaring. It flew straight at me, causing me to duck to avoid being battered.

"You get 'em, Curr!" I shouted, but the encouragement was cut off when a fallen orc grabbed my leg. I'm not too manly to admit I yelped. Stamping down with a boot, I managed to knock it free, but being zombie-esque in nature, it didn't do much. The orc crawled toward me, scratching madly at the ground.

It was the one Garvis had dismembered, and evidently, even having no legs didn't stop it.

Lilla rolled over its back, her arms wrenching its neck so violently to the side, it cracked. The beast was momentarily felled. She landed on a knee with her other leg stretched out to the side. Hero pose. And as she looked up, her face caked in grime and sweat, matted with dirty hair, yet still more stunning than ever, she winked.

"Thanks," I muttered softly.

Thanks? That's it? She just saved your best friend, and then you, and you say "thanks" like a toddler who got a lollypop from a grownup?

I... You... Did you see her?

"Stop standing around," she said. She picked up another weapon, then turned to join the fray. What a view...

Danny, this isn't the time to watch her go!

I snapped out of it, then screamed from the bottom of my stomach and charged to join my companions.

"Enough of this!" The shaman slammed his staff down, causing the entire platform to rock and everybody to lose their footing. A crack coruscated down the center, and a chunk broke off, one of his undead orcs with it.

As everyone staggered, it allowed me to get a clear view of the shaman as he clutched the lute's strings in an effort to stop the hymn.

But Roxanne was cold as ice. Its strings vibrated with such force that he tore his hand away, ripped the strap, and sent the lute soaring.

"No!" I yelled. Time seemed to stand still as it flew over us.

Tevagah saw it too. She ran up an orc's chest and used it as a springboard to catapult herself after it. She caught the lute in midair, but my throat closed up. She was headed straight into the lava.

"No!" Lilla shouted. She followed her mother's trajectory, dove, and caught her ankle. But not before Tevagah's top half went in.

We all stood in stunned silence. I expected to watch her be swallowed by liquid death, but radiant sparks shot up from the lava. Her elven shield had repelled death in that instance. It flickered wildly with energy and embers as she lay suspended over the lava, howling in pain from heat I could only imagine. Lilla desperately tried to reel her in.

"Use it, Danny!" Tevagah called out to me, her voice ragged. "A true bard needs no sword."

Your standing with the Sisterhood of Alyndis has improved.

You have earned the trust of Tevagah, Mother of the Sisterhood. Your confidence is soaring. They like you... they really like you!

+10 to Instrument Playing, Singing, and Courage for Duration of Battle.

Who needs a hag's blessing when you have true friends!

I looked down. Roxanne—my lute—lay at my feet. I'd been so distracted by Tevagah's possible doom, I must have missed when she tossed it to me. She was trusting me.

"Take out the shaman and they cannot rise!" Lilla shouted.

"I will hold them!" Curr said.

A true bard needs no sword.

I was just getting the hang of using one too, but maybe she was right. I reached down to pick up my lute. Warmth and energy rushed through me as my fingers closed around its neck.

ITEM OBTAINED:
The Lute of Seven Stars (A.K.A. Roxanne) [Unique]

Let's fucking go! Rock their brains out, Danny.

I brought the instrument to my chest and ran my hand along the fretboard. I gave her a strum. "Good to have you back, Roxanne."

The unmistakable melody to the theme song from Friends, "I'll be There For You," played on its own.

Let's see that Catalog of Songs!

All the usual songs popped up, but there were two new ones I'd unlocked at Level 5 and had yet to play. "Markings of a Fool"... no way that sounded like a smart option.

"A Dance with Thorns." I didn't know what it did, but it was more promising than the other. And gods knew Screenie was never helpful—

Hey!

And so, I trusted in Roxanne. It was another instrumental piece.

Trust... her!? How's this for helpful? Without your little boon from your friends, you wouldn't even be able to play that song. So... there.

Right at the limit of my capabilities. My fingers found the notes, and this time, it was as if two of us were playing the lute. Me, and the lute itself answering with rich tones.

The song sounded like something of a ballet, and as it played, all the swords and weapons in my vicinity rose from the air and began dancing around me as if wielded by ghosts. It was like Tevagah knew what the lute and I could be capable of. Together.

I stared ahead, meeting gazes across the platform with the shaman. Where his snarl would once have frightened me to my core —no longer.

This was my life now, running full-steam into a battle I could surely die in while playing a lute, my bright pink cape flapping behind me, swords twirling all around me.

Curr and Garvis did their best against the wave of undead, allowing me a straight shot. Well, mostly Curr. Garvis sort of hopped around with his dagger, getting in a shot here and there, and then boasting like a tough guy. And orcs who broke off to attack me were swiftly stopped by my shield of blades. Sliced down. Cut. Gashed.

Until I stood face-to-face with the object of nightmares: the towering monstrosity of an orc and his blood magic.

You have gained +1 in Instrument Playing.

Your Instrument Playing is now 22.

Now this is what I call a duel. Trigger your Unhinged state. Let him have it.

"You've hurt my friends for the last time," I said as I picked along to "A Dance with Thorns."

"You think you can stop me?" he asked, sneering menacingly. "I am death."

He grunted, rushed forward, batting aside all attempts by my swirling swords to take him out, and swung his staff down at my head. I shifted back, my ghost-swords converging to parry. Another noisy grunt as he slashed in a wide arc. I ducked, the air whipping my hair as he missed. The dancing swords cut and sliced at him, but he was strong. They were barely nicking him.

Death by one thousand cuts.

I'm not sure I have that long!

He may not have had braug Rage to draw on, but orc rage was impressive in its own right. The oversized brute swung high and low, relentless, not even seeming to tire. All I could do was retreat. I dodged and weaved in time with the song, and my ghost-swords took any opening to try and weaken him.

He kept swinging until my foot hit a corpse and I lurched ever so slightly. Pressing his advantage, he entered the range of my closest blades and swept low. Each of them stabbed through his forearm as he did, but it didn't stop him. My legs went out from under me, and in midair, he walloped me with the gem-encrusted head of his staff.

I don't use that term lightly. The effect of the shaman's attack sent me reeling. My head spun, and I couldn't tell which way was up. I stopped playing and my flying swords clattered to the cave floor.

As the world came back into focus, I saw many things. Lilla had Tevagah back on the edge of the platform and shielded her against an orc assault. Tevagah looked to be in bad shape, half of her face blackened from burns. The undead orcs were all around Curr, scratching at him, grabbing at his legs. He'd be overwhelmed soon. But... no Garvis.

"Death will be a mercy for you, bard."

I turned toward the shaman, who had his staff gripped in both hands. All I could do was smile as he raised the weapon high above his head, ready to pulverize me, which I'm sure really pissed him off.

Because there, through his arms and crouched on top of the ledge over the entryway where earlier he'd claimed he had no shot, was the sneaky little halfling known as Garvis Wittleman.

I brought my lute back to bear and played the intro to "Endless Love," the same song that'd gotten me into this mess with that asshole, Kurt.

"My love, there's only you in my life!" I sang like it was the last

show I'd ever perform. And I'll be honest... I fricken nailed it. *"The only thing that's right!"*

Where did THAT voice come from?!

You have gained +1 in Singing.

Your Singing is now 18.

The shaman's brow furrowed. "The lute's magic can't save you now."

As he prepared to crush me, Garvis jumped off the ledge and landed on his neck.

"Garvis says hello!" the halfling screamed like a maniac as he stabbed the shaman over and over again in the soft skin above its collarbone.

I'm sure in his head that sounded like a badass line...

With the weight of the staff over his head and Garvis unleashing the fury of a halfling on him, it left the shaman stretched out and completely unbalanced. He dropped the staff to try and rip Garvis off.

At the same time, I stopped playing myself and swung Roxanne like a battle axe, smashing her into the side of his head. I say myself, because Roxanne kept the upbeat battle hymn going to pump me up.

The towering orc stumbled to the side, stunned. Garvis toppled off, leaving his dagger stuck in the shaman's neck and spurting blood. I swung again, cracking one of his tusks and causing him to stagger. Once more, but this time, he caught the edge of the lute in his grasp.

"You... will... die," he gasped, squeezing so hard, I could hear Roxanne beginning to crunch. But we were together again, and she played an awful, loud chord that reverberated enough to cause him to lose his grip.

I screamed or I cursed—I'm not sure which. I did something loud as I brought the lute around for one last punishing blow. The shaman slid backward until his head went over the broken portion of the platform. The rest of his body stayed put, but his voice was quickly muffled as the lava engulfed his skull, leaving him headless.

"Revive that, bitch!"

You have gained +1 in Speechcraft.

Your Speechcraft is now 19.

Not the best of catch phrases, but not bad in the heat of the moment. Get it, heat?

You have gained +1 in Melee Weapon Combat.

Your Melee Weapon Combat is now 19.

You have Slain the Orc Shaman (Boss)!

OBJECTIVE COMPLETED:
You beat the shit out of the orc shaman!

Congrats! You are now a Level 6 Bard!

Because of your Skill increases so far, you have improved to Level 6. Everything mean I ever said, I take back. That was badassery at another level. Did you see that? His face literally melted off from your concert! Jack Black would be so proud.

AN UNEXPECTED HERO

With each new Level, your Health, Stamina, and—if you were attuned with any magical abilities—Mana regenerates to 100%. You can also apply +1 to the Attribute of your choosing.

One new song has been added to your Catalog of Songs.

Special Ability Use Restored: [TIME IS OF THE ESSENCE] (Requires The Lute of the Seven Stars Equipped)

[rare] TITLE UNLOCKED: Boss Bitch.

You have gained +10 points to permanently apply to the Attributes of your choosing.

55

Thuds rang all around as each of the zombie orcs crumpled to the ground in useless heaps of tangled limbs. Curr dug himself out of a pile of them, tossing them aside like pieces of cardboard. He was as cut up as the shaman was after my attack, but he was alive.

Another orc had its blade stabbing toward Lilla, but it toppled over like a rag doll and the blade fell from its limp fingers.

There. Now we're even.

What?

That's what you should say to her.
That would come off so suave.

"Did you get him?" Curr asked.

"I got him," Garvis replied, panting. "Bastard never saw it coming."

The halfling was on his hands and knees, trying to gather his breath, and I didn't have the heart to shoot him down.

"You sure did," I said. "You should have seen the look on his face."

Your relationship with Garvis has improved.

His eyes lit up, and then he shook his head in mock-disappointment. "I never will, now. Seriously, boyo, the lava was overkill."

"There is no such thing. A kill is a kill," Curr said. It hadn't been long, but man, I'd missed him. I moved to go and help him get his leg fully free of the heavy orc pile when Lilla called over.

"Danny..." she said, her voice raspy in a way that sounded like she'd been crying.

Suddenly, nothing else mattered. I ran to her—she was cradling Tevagah's head on her lap. The leader of the Sisterhood of Alyndis had her shield arm clutched against her side, scorched beyond belief. Her skin was charred and peeling, with bone showing where it had completely sloughed away. Half her face bubbled with burns from her chin up to halfway across her scalp. The eye on the healthy side of her face remained open, though only a fraction as she groaned in agony, half-conscious.

"Is she okay?" I asked.

Do you not have eyes, Danny? She looks like she just lost the high ground.

"I mean, will she be?" I amended.

"She's the strongest person I've ever known," Lilla replied with a sniffle. "I don't know."

I swallowed the lump in my throat. "She saved Roxanne."

"What?"

"My lute. She saved it. She... trusted me. We have to help her."

Lilla looked up, tears welling in the corners of her eyes. "It's beyond my skills." I went to lay my hand over hers, paused, then found my courage and went for it. She didn't pull away.

"Kiel could help her," Curr said as he lumbered over.

"He's a long way from here," I said.

"I'll carry her."

Lilla nodded. "We can get her outside and the mares will return, I know it. There's nothing faster."

"Did you guys see this thing!" Garvis hollered from across the platform. He crouched over the shaman's staff, mesmerized by the roiling orb at its top. Leave it to him to be scavenging at a time like this.

"Not now!" I yelled.

Then the platform quaked. A screech echoed. It sounded like something coming dislodged.

"What have you done!" Lilla shouted.

"I swear, I didn't touch it!" Garvis backed away slowly, and another quake sent him to his rump. At the same time, I noticed the lava becoming dimmer, as if it were cooling.

Lava doesn't just get cold.

Yeah, and I thought orcs didn't just come back from the dead either.

I peered over the ledge and realized that the lava remained unchanged. Wait, no, it was us. The platform was rising through the cavernous hollow, far enough already that the only way out was below us, and we were stranded.

I craned my neck over the edge, making sure the rest of me was as far back as possible because, you know... heights. There were no gears or pistons below us, just a blueish glow similar to the elven shields, causing us to rise.

Well, you're in an elven city. Magical floating platforms are really to be expected.

"We're floating," I said, incredulous.

"This is very strange," Curr added. I could tell by the way he rocked that he didn't have sea legs, and that was what this felt like. The entire platform tilted from side to side as it ascended.

Lilla held on to Tevagah tight. I held on to her. Garvis even scurried over to Curr and grabbed his leg.

"Get on your knees, you big oaf," he said. "Pretend you're an anchor."

"But I am not in water?"

"Just do it!"

Up we went, until the glow of the lava was gone, and we moved through utter darkness.

Psst, Danny. Is now a good time to ask what you want to do with those sweet Attribute points? You're rich with them.

I don't think now is the time for that.

And what if the orc shaman was just the beginning? Wouldn't you rather be prepared?

It was a fair point. One that I had to consider very possible.

While I liked the idea of being strong, it just didn't feel right. I wasn't Danzig. I was just Danny the sometimes bard who wasn't too bad with a stringed instrument. That meant...

Okay. Three more to Dexterity.

And I had to admit, I was getting pretty good with the ladies. So how about...

Three to Charisma. And three to... what's Constitution again?

Constitution relates to your physical fortitude. Your ability to endure pain, to take damage without going unconscious, to resist the effects of poison, disease, and other physical illnesses, to hold your breath, to travel long distances without rest, and to go without sleep for extended periods.

I thought Dexterity helped me travel long distances?

Sigh. They all work together. Now, make up your mind. We're running out of time.

The air grew still and cold as we got higher. Somehow, Lilla's skin remained warm. It was nice to know that even though I couldn't see her, I could still feel her. Hear her breathing. Whenever Curr and Garvis stopped bickering at least. They couldn't stop jockeying each other for position.

"Danny," Lilla whispered.

"Yeah?" This was it. She was going to kiss me again, and there was no way it was only about causing a distraction because nobody was around. We were rising into blackness, but it felt like heaven.

"Do you mind looking away? Your breath is foul."

HAHAHAHAHAHAHAHAHAHAHAHAHAHAHAHAHAHAHAHAHAHA-HAHAHAHAHAHAHAHAHAHAHAHAHAHAHAHAHAHAHAHAHA!

That was... HAHAHAHAHAHAHAHAHAHAHAHAHAHAHAHAHAHA-HAHAHAHAHAHAHAHA

Oh god... Why couldn't the orcs have just killed me?

"I, yeah... sorry." I looked the other way and feigned a cough into my hand to test it. Didn't seem too bad to me, though, everything in this world stunk worse than what I was used to. Deodorant. I wish I knew how it was made so I could invent it here.

She snickered so low I was almost too focused on myself to hear it.

"Oh, and we're even now," she said.

"What?"

"I saved you back there, then you saved me," she explained. "Even."

"Oh." I laughed nervously, waiting for Screenie to say "I told you so," but I guess he felt bad because he let it go. Damn, I really should have said that first, though. So smooth. "Yeah, I guess you're right."

"You used what I taught you. It was impressive... For a bard."

"So was how you healed Curr... For an elf," I replied.

Okay, first, I told you so. Sorry I'm late. I laughed so hard, I threw up. Second, elves are literally known for healing skills.

Of all the dumb things you've said, Danny, you truly waited until this adventure's climax to top yourself. Bravo. Now, where were we?

Okay, four in Intelligence.

I was hoping you'd say that. You're pretty dumb.

Didn't you just apologize for being mean?

Yeah. Clean slate. Okay.

Your Intelligence is now 9.

Your Dexterity is now 18.

Your Charisma is now 17 (+1).

Perhaps if you'd have made this decision before your last embarrassment, your significantly higher Charisma would have ended in a real kiss.

What? Are you serious? Fine! Put the last one in Charisma!

I'm pretty sure it's too late—

Just do it!

A loud scraping sound buried Screenie's response. I looked up, and a faint light drew closer. The platform slowed down, the edges grinding against rock as it slotted into a perfectly sized opening. After some more hair-raising screeching, we stopped.

"I am not sure whoever designed this intended for it to be so noisy," Curr stated.

"Oh, you think?" Garvis replied.

My eyes quickly adjusted to the soft glow of moonlight. We were inside a domed structure, perfectly symmetrical. Seven oculuses—

Oculi.

Seven oculi were carved into the ceiling, with a series of lenses and advanced apertures set around them, like the inside of a camera. Each one centered upon a bright star.

On one side of the walls stood a set of towering stone doors with the insignia of Alyndis carved across them. On the other was a matching window with a view of the moon over a thick veil of clouds. Then I realized it had grown so cold, I could once again see my own breath.

Like we were at the top of...

"Mount Gheram," Lilla whispered.

We were within some sort of elven observatory at the very peak of the tallest mountain in the range. All around the edge of the room were old scrolls in open cabinets, tables with vials, and other weird equipment like a medieval chemistry lab.

"You took your time," said a withered voice that sounded oddly familiar.

I saw the green glow first. Then, her. Lying on the floor, playing catch with some sort of glass orb, was Phlegm the Hag in all her rotten glory.

56

"**Y**ou!" I spat. I reached for my bone sword, but what Lilla did next stopped me.

She bowed. Like, a full samurai, genuflect bow. On her knees, arms extended, and face to the floor.

Yeah, she did.

"Oracle," Lilla uttered. "How is this possible?"

"The Mother's dagger opens my exile from the outside," Phlegm said. "Betrayal came from within."

She snatched the orb out of the air and stood, all her joints popping. My hand still hovered over the hilt of my sword. Roxanne played a new song on her own. A low, eerie one, like I'd imagine hearing on a boat crossing a swamp.

"She's the oracle?" I asked.

Lilla sat up. Her brow knotted. "Of course, she is."

OBJECTIVE COMPLETED:
You have located the Oracle of Alyndis.

So, about the reward... Tevagah is supposed to pay you, but she's a little incapacitated at the moment.

"Danny, look!" Curr exclaimed. "We have found her without even intending to. What an easy quest."

"You call that easy?" Garvis said. "What do you have, mulch for brains? We all almost died! Twice!"

"Two is not many times."

They bickered, but I ignored them and kept my eyes on the oracle, ready to draw my weapon.

"We faced many perils reaching you," Lilla said. "Our Mother, Tevagah, she... I'm not sure she'll make it. I—"

Phlegm hushed her, sounding more like a concerned parent than the lunatic I'd known her as. "You've done well, young one. The light of the Seven Stars has not yet left her."

"I think this is some big mistake," I cut in. "This can't be the oracle, Lilla."

Her features darkened. "Do not speak of what you don't understand."

At the risk of angering her more, I proceeded. "No, you don't understand. This is the hag I told you all about. The one I made a deal with to get the lute."

"A hag?" Phlegm cackled. "That's what you assumed I was?"

"No, that's... You are..."

Screenie, help me out here. That's what you told me she was.

The Screenie you are looking for is unavailable at the moment. Please leave a message after the beep. BEEP.

"I am no hag," Phlegm said.

She stopped by the headless body of the orc shaman and knelt. Her eyes closed as she laid her hand upon his back and whispered something in elvish, facing down so neither Screenie nor I could tell what.

"But you... you... you made me lose the lute right before I could rescue them," I said. "You speak in crazy riddles and eat gross lamb legs..."

"Better food than I get up here. And *you* forgot the third."

"There it is again! Lilla, can't you see? She's mad!"

Lilla stayed quiet. Phlegm turned her attention from the body to the shaman's staff. Her spindly fingers extended for it.

Finally, I pulled my sword. "Don't you dare pick that up!"

Lilla jumped in front of me, wielding a weapon of her own. The battle hymn started to play softly on my back.

"Put those down, friends!" Curr implored, moving between us. "We are allies."

"I'm with whoever wins," Garvis said.

Phlegm sighed. "Distrust. Hate. Enmity. They defile and corrupt. It happened to him. It can happen to all."

I lowered my weapon as I watched Phlegm grip the staff. What else could I do—try and beat Lilla in a fair fight? I didn't want to fight her. I didn't want to fight anybody.

Phlegm's greenish aura burned bright as she lifted the staff until I could only see her silhouette. Then the light dissipated, and the wrinkly old hag I knew was replaced by a matronly elf. Smooth skin. Silken, silver hair. A strong nose and jaw. Basically, a straight-up MILF.

All the others must have seen the look in my eyes, because they all turned, and their jaws dropped.

"Well, I'll be damned." Garvis combed a hand through his hair. "Good evening to you."

Phlegm held the staff upright in two hands and exhaled slowly. Somehow, it looked like it was the first time she'd breathed in years. Screenie highlighted her.

NAME: *Fa'Lem*
OCCUPATION: *High Sorceress*
RACE: *Elf*
SPECIAL ABILITIES: *???*
WEAPONS: *The Staff of Seven Stars [Unique]*

Fa'Lem. I'd completely misheard all this time.

That's her real name? Why didn't you tell me any of this!

It was all hidden! I swear, this isn't one of those times where it was fun to keep things from you. Even I'm shocked. It's kind of exciting.

"I poured so much of my power into this staff," Fa'Lem said, her voice no longer ragged and muddled by spittle, but elegant and pure. "Without it, I was only a shell of myself. You understand, don't you, Danny?"

Her gorgeous green eyes aimed at my lute. My lute, which performed miracles and had a personality. Her staff had a similar name—*The Staff of Seven Stars*—which I guess meant it too had abilities far beyond most items.

You think she talks to hers?

"I don't understand," I stammered.

"The orcs must have spent centuries digging, trying to reach my exile," she said. "When he broke in and stole it from me, the light of the Seven Stars left me. I became like a specter, ageless but ancient, roaming this plane. And then I found you."

"Me?"

"Him?" Lilla said in disbelief.

"A man unlike others. Lost in his own way, but pure. Worthy of perhaps breaking the cycle that destroyed us. Of saving our people."

"Our people? Danny is not one of us," Lilla said.

That was true, but it still hurt.

"Exactly why it must be him," Fa'Lem said.

"Now I don't understand," Lilla said.

"I definitely do not," Curr added.

"History is told in painted lies," Fa'Lem said. "It fades and layers get added on. Covered. Until it is a new story unto itself, sung by bards who know not the lies. But the truth is, Danny was right. I am not an oracle. I know nothing of the future."

"That's impossible," Lilla said. "It's all in the prophecy. That we should find the Lute of Seven Stars, bring it to you, and deliver our people back to glory."

"A truth, twisted by time," Fa'Lem said. "The instrument delivered may bring redemption in the right hands, not glory."

"Redemption for what?" Lilla asked.

"The fall of Alyndis."

"*His* people caused that." Lilla jabbed a finger at me.

"I did nothing," I argued.

Fa'Lem held up a hand and we both quieted. "We all had our part to play. All this way you have come. I will show you our undoing. Then you will understand."

Fa'Lem raised her staff. The purple orb atop it shone bright, no longer appearing evil, but magnificent. At the same time, the one she'd been playing catch with earlier floated up to the center of the dome, and shafts of moonlight beamed through the oculi into it.

The lenses and apertures all spun into place, focusing the light. Motes of dust around the room swirled and danced together to form an image. It wasn't as clear or filled with vivid color as a 4k TV, but there was a beauty to the simplicity. I could almost sense the emotions.

Someone stood within another domed room at the top of a palace. As the scenery filled in and Mount Gheram materialized, I realized this was the collapsing palace which stood above the orc's encampment.

An aqueduct emerging from a tunnel in the mountain arced across the expanse and into the room. Lava flowed through it, somehow contained by the stone, and filled a basin at the center. Orbs were encrusted around its edge, each of them identical to the one in Fa'Lem's staff, all radiant as if powered by the lava.

The lenses in the observatory shifted loudly again, and the imagery filled in with color.

The person at the basin was a handsome elf male wearing a violet robe stitched with gold. And when I say handsome, I mean it. Like Jude Law, but even more perfect. Skin as smooth as freshly fallen snow, hair like polished obsidian. He may as well have been a sculpture. And he held a familiar instrument. My lute. Only, this one had a magic orb set into the headstock just like the staff's.

I glanced down at Roxanne, and my eyes were drawn to the spot where I'd noticed something missing.

It all seemed innocent until I noticed the pedestals arrayed around the edge of the room. Each bore a chalice filled with what I hoped was wine, but knew was blood. The human—or wellick—skulls set around them sort of gave that away.

An elf woman with a majestic blue dress burst into the room, her staff tapping along the polished floor. "Varun, stop this at once!"

"I told you to stay away," the man replied, not even bothering to look.

"You knew I wouldn't."

"A man can hope."

"Husband." She took his wrist and tried to turn him to face her, but he wouldn't budge. "Please."

"These power-hungry wellicks will not stop, Fa'Lem," he said. "They will take and take until there is nothing left. Every being. Every tree. They'll dominate it all."

"They are still young," the image of Fa'Lem said. "We can show them peace."

"No!" he boomed, pulling away from her. "If we do not stop them, soon even Alyndis will fall. All that we have built. Learned. Will burn."

"So, you would kill them all instead?"

"If that's what it takes." He set Roxanne down, then drew a dagger from the folds of his robe, which I immediately recognized to be the Dagger of Discontent.

"Blood of the blessed." The blade slid across his palm. He didn't even wince as he drew blood. Then he placed the dagger on the rim of the basin and squeezed his hand to let blood trickle into the lava contained therein.

"Light of the Stars," he said.

He then reached for the lute and my mouth went dry.

Roxanne...

He positioned his bloodied fingers over it and began to play. It was a melancholy song. Not off-key but filled with minor notes and sad chords.

"I'm begging you, husband!" Fa'Lem positioned both hands on her staff, as if ready to cast battle magic.

"It's them or us!" he said over his playing.

"That's exactly what's caused this war! We mustn't become like them."

"We cannot be like *them*. Can't you see? We are superior in every way. Blessed with eternity, when all they will ever know is to rot."

Raw magical energy began to swirl around the room, glowing with embers from the pit. The blood from each chalice spiraled upward, coalescing into bars of sheet music in motion, a beautiful ribbon dance of bloody horrors.

"Blood of the enemy," Varun chanted, his voice now echoing with the music. Upon his listing of the third element, the wind grew even more powerful.

"Please, stop!" Fa'Lem yelled. "Don't make me."

Her grip tightened around the staff as she began to chant in elvish. Her features strained. If she was trying to use some sort of magic to stop him, it didn't work. The wind circling the room was so intense, the staff alone seemed to be keeping her from being thrown back.

Varun's playing grew louder. The very earth seemed to be vibrating with bass. Rumbles from the volcanic mountain shook the walls. Visible sound waves emanated from the dome, radiating out across Alyndis—which was as glorious as I'd imagined. But it wasn't the time to marvel.

Fa'Lem struggled against the powerful dark magic, having to use the staff to drag herself forward. By then, the two of them were enveloped in a twister of blood and energy. Varun's eyes were closed, lost in the melody. Something I understood more than most.

Fa'Lem's screams rang out for none to hear as she pushed with all her might. Releasing the staff with one hand, she snatched the Dagger of Discontent and stabbed at the lute. It struck right beside the magical orb, cracking the setting.

"What are you doing!"

Varun's eyes sprang open, flashing yellow, almost orcish, even as the gemstone dislodged and fell to the floor. The whirlwind vacillated in an angry manner, taking on a life of its own—no other way to describe it. He howled in pain and strummed a wrong note, releasing a cataclysmic clap of energy.

"No!"

The dagger and the lute's orb flew in opposite directions far beyond the palace. Cracks split under Varun's feet, causing a swathe of earth and city to sink into the fissure I'd climbed down into earlier.

Fa'Lem's body shot backward with enough force to break through the dome's wall. She soared across the sky, cracking through the surface of the mountain and plunging deep within where sound couldn't pierce. Clutching her staff, her own powers allowed her to survive the impact with a shield not unlike my bracer.

The motes of light forming the scene withered away. Fa'Lem, now in the present, stood at the center of the room, a tear running down her cheek.

Well, that was just depressing. I don't like the truth. Can you reverse time and unlearn it?

"Sometimes I wish I'd stayed here that day," Fa'Lem said, her voice breaking. "That I had not interfered. But then I would be as wrong as him." I watched her gaze flit toward the dead orc shaman.

"I still don't understand," Lilla said. "What was that?"

"You witnessed the fall of Alyndis. It was not wellicks who conquered us. When their first king arrived, we had already fallen, you see."

"That's not true," Lilla argued, anger in her voice.

"Daughter, it's not a grand story of victory worthy of a parade, and so time twisted the story, but it is the truth. I witnessed it with my own eyes. Varun was the greatest of us all. More powerful than you or I could imagine. He weaved song and magic into miracles that transformed Alyndis into a haven for our kind. But when the first wellicks found our paradise, hate transformed *him*.

"All the fighting and the killing... when he couldn't take it anymore, he turned to forbidden magic. Blood magic. He designed a spell that would erase wellicks from Aethonia for good. I tried to stop him, but my efforts only caused the spell to backfire. Every elf in Aethonia was perverted, turned into violent creatures bent on hate and slaughter."

"Orcs," I said softly.

She nodded. "Their minds and memories were twisted. And the only elves who remained were those abroad, women and younglings who'd fled and wanted no part in the war for defending Alyndis. We became scattered, condemned, unable to repopulate... Fallen."

"No," Lilla said, shaking her head. Her cheeks went pale. "No, no, that can't be. They're monsters, they can't be elves. I've killed... so many..."

"Freed so many," Fa'Lem corrected. "For a long time, I thought they remembered nothing. And then *he* found me. Orcs never venture so far up the mountain as to reach this place. Between the frost trolls and golems, there isn't much to find except death and cold. But he made his way up from within, as if he knew my doors were sealed and guarded by ancient magic. As if he knew that the staff—I—would be here."

She knelt again and placed her hand on the orc shaman's back.

"I'm so sorry, my beloved," she said. "There was no other way."

MIND. BLOWN.

57

All right, let's recap what we've learned.

The elves aren't as high and mighty as everyone thinks. Their most powerful sorcerer, Varun, used blood magic to try and kill all wellicks, but it backfired and turned elves into orcs instead. Which means they destroyed themselves.

The oracle, Fa'Lem, which you stupidly thought was Phlegm (LOL) was his wife, another sorceress. She exiled herself here in shame, using the Sisterhood to try and locate the lost lute again. But Varun somehow returned centuries later as an orc, using fragments of memory, and stole her staff to become uber-powerful again.

That's the gist of it. You really had no idea?

No. And now I have a headache.

"Wait, you loved an orc?" Curr said, breaking the silence that had fallen across the room. He sounded like he was going to be sick.

"The orc was her husband, you dolt," Garvis said. "Right? I think?"

Curr scratched his chin. "Hmm, I do not know. Can you tell that story again, hag?"

"By the gods, she isn't a yigging hag!"

Lilla fell to her knees, clutching Tevagah's hand as if she were looking for comfort, but her leader seemed worse than ever, her every breath rattling. Her chest barely rose with her breaths. I wished I could give that comfort to her, but after what she'd just learned, I wasn't sure it was my place.

Au contraire, my friend. Now she knows wellicks didn't slaughter her people! She should like you more.

I don't think it's that simple.

"We brought ruin upon ourselves," Lilla whimpered. Then her face contorted with anger. Anger, which she directed at Fa'Lem. "Why did you keep this to yourself?"

"And break further an already broken people?" Fa'Lem replied calmly.

"And show us that we're on a fool's errand! All this, just to find the instrument of our destruction!" She whipped around to face me. "I should break it in two."

I backed away defensively, swinging Roxanne as far from her as possible. "Whoa, okay. Let's all calm down."

"Calm down?" Lilla rose to her feet and stalked toward me. "Calm. Down?"

"That is what he said," Curr said.

"An instrument is only as great as its player, young one," Fa'Lem said, stepping between us. She had her staff in one hand and didn't look to be aggressive, but it made me question who she would defend if it came down to it—another elf, or me. "I know in his heart my beloved thought he was saving us, but he merely lost his way. And his mistake—"

"Cost us everything!" Lilla roared.

"That's exactly what I've been trying to fix. Varun created the lute eons before what you just witnessed. He designed it only to serve someone worthy of the power he imbued it with—worthy of the man who he was back then, not when he turned to darkness."

And that was when it hit me. One part of Screenie's recap was wrong.

Hey now. Uncool.

"His lute wasn't lost," I said out loud. "It was just waiting for somebody worthy."

A warm smile spread across Fa'Lem's face. "When I felt your presence, I left these walls for the first time in ages. A man unlike any other in this world. A man who didn't run in the face of one so hideous as I'd become, but talked with her like an equal. One who would not judge the peoples of this land based on preconceived hatreds taught by his elders. A man filled with latent potential, waiting to be sculpted, as Alyndis was by my beloved."

Oh please. You're not that great.

Hey! I think she nailed it. That's me. A man filled with latent potential.

You literally aren't like anybody else in this world, because you're not of this world. It's a fricken loophole.

Maybe that's why I'm here. My—

"His purpose," Curr said. His face lit up. He ran to me and shook me by the shoulders so hard, my head spun. "Danny, we have found it! Your purpose! Against all odds, you truly were meant to be a bard!"

His enthusiasm was infectious. I couldn't help but grin. Seeing Lilla wiped it off. Her anger was gone, replaced by abject sadness. I couldn't even imagine. Everything she'd ever known, fought for, was gone in a flash.

Actually, maybe I would know about that. She'd lost her truth, like I'd lost Earth.

She was right. The oracle, or Fa'Lem, or whatever, keeping all this a secret was wrong. Even if she thought she was doing her people a service, it wasn't right. And remembering that aspect of Phlegm made me remember something else.

"Wait," I said, sticking my finger out at her. "You caused me to lose the lute back there. If you wanted me to have it, why would you do that? You almost got us all killed!"

"You weren't worthy then," she said.

"What?"

"You forgot the third."

My chin hit my chest. "Right, the mysterious third."

"The one who can save us cannot be selfish, ungrateful. He cannot condemn. He cannot judge. You met a hag. You received a gift to help you on your journey. And you forgot the third."

"What the hell is the third, Phlegm!" I shouted. I didn't mean to get so angry, but I think everything I'd been through hit me all at once. And Fa'Lem, who'd been proud and stately up until then, shriveled back in the face of my anger in an almost pathetic way.

Being yelled at seemed to paralyze her.

"Danny," Curr said. "Danny the Bard, were you ungrateful?"

"I... what?"

"This wonderful woman took you from a dismal bard, unable to entertain a group of drunken braugs who had spent the better part of a fortnight battling trolls, and turned him into one who does not make me want break his lute. And you did not say 'thank you'?"

"Curr—"

"For her gift. When one receives a gift, it is customary to thank its giver. Everybody knows that."

I turned to Fa'Lem, completely aghast. She didn't appear confused by what he said. She looked...

"Did you almost get us all killed because I didn't say 'thanks'?" I asked.

She swallowed and regained some composure. "You didn't say 'thank you' because you judged an ugly, terrifying creature you believed to be a hag who was only trying to help you."

"No, I didn't say it because it was a trade!" I yelled. "I gave you food, you sent me a magic lute. Bing, bang, boom!"

"My blessing was not part of the bargain. It was a gift."

"How was I supposed to know that?" I groaned audibly. "Oh my god. Thank you, Fa'Lem. Thank you from the bottom of my heart for everything you did for me. There, happy?"

"I am," Curr said."

"It does not matter. It is clear why the lute returned to you, because one of my people trusted you, an outsider, and so you were worthy once more."

I shook my head. That wasn't good enough. After all this, I had to say something. "Or, maybe, you were just wrong. Wrong to keep me in the dark. Wrong to lie to your people. Wrong, just like he was." I gestured to the orc shaman.

Wow. Chill, dude. I'm annoyed too, but that was her husband.

Too soon?

100%.

She didn't respond. Nobody did. I took a measured breath to cool myself off.

"How long were you up here all alone, Fa'Lem?" I asked in my gentlest tone.

She muttered under her breath, then answered, "I've lost count of the centuries."

"Why stay here?"

"Because I failed. I should have seen what he was planning long before it came to pass. My people don't deserve my presence, and I don't deserve theirs."

Can Roxanne play the world's smallest violin?

Now you need to chill.

Sorry, I'm just all amped up. This did not turn out how I expected.

"Well, maybe it's time to change that," I said. It was risky, but I stepped toward her, once, twice, until I was close enough to take her hand.

She winced at the contact. Centuries alone, no wonder she was a kook. Who wouldn't be? Maybe, in the end, she just needed somebody to care.

"You can help her." I nodded toward Tevagah. "Someone who believed in you so much, they're dying for it."

She winced again. "I'm not powerful enough anymore."

"I don't think that's true." I looked deep into her eyes. "You know something? You're the first person who has ever believed in me. Ever. And look at me now. A man with purpose."

I smiled at Curr.

"I'm still not sure what I believe," Garvis grumbled.

Fa'lem backed up slowly and stared down at her hand as I tightened my grip. She closed her eyes and inhaled deep through her nose. In, then out. She then looked at her hand, still clutching her staff, and muttered in elvish. Energy swirled up the length of her staff, gathering at the orb.

A bright burst of light filled the room, then Tevagah gasped for air. Her chest rose and fell like she was no longer on the precipice of death. Her eyes flickered open, and she met gazes with Lilla. Portions of her critically burned skin started to instantly heal.

"Lilla," she rasped.

"Tevagah!" Lilla threw her arms around her leader—her Mother. But as she held her, the healing stopped, and Tevagah fell back unconscious.

"What happened?" Lilla asked, nervous. "Tevagah!"

Fa'lem leaned her full weight onto her staff, exhausted. "Healing her will take time."

"Well, elves live forever, don't they?" I said. "She has plenty of that."

Curr let out a boisterous, single laugh. "She does, indeed! Your sense of humor is improving, Danny."

"I... wasn't trying to be funny..."

Curr laughed again.

Garvis groaned.

Fa'lem looked up at me, one corner of her lips smiling faintly. "Thank you, Danny. I was wrong about so many things, but none more than doubting you."

You have received The Hag's Blessing once more! Though I guess we can't call it that. My bad.

You have received Fa'Lem's Blessing!

+10 Bonus to Dexterity, Charisma, and Intelligence. +10 Bonus to Instrument Playing, Singing, and Speechcraft.

"It's okay," I said. "I've doubted myself plenty."

I never did. Not once.

Bullshit.

"If that is true, then I hope you're ready for what comes next," Fa'Lem said.

I smiled at her until her words sank in. "Wait, *next?*"

58

"All acts in threes," Fa'Lem said. "This is but the first step of your journey. When my transformed husband found me, I realized that maybe I was wrong. That perhaps what he did could be reversed using the very instrument of his creation."

She reached out and touched the neck of my lute, strumming the strings. Fa'lem looked like she was with an old friend. Roxanne didn't fight it like she had with the shaman. In fact, I could feel the rest of the strings vibrating softly on my back.

"Maybe, just maybe, we can transform those that remain back into elves. Enough to rebuild. Enough to stand on our own once more. Enough to redeem our kind."

Danny the Redeemer.
I like the sound of that.

I looked around at my companions. Curr was wide-eyed, eager as always for another adventure. Garvis was barely paying attention anymore. Lilla clung onto Tevagah and stared my way, imploring me with her eyes.

Why does she have to be so damn perfect?

"I know it is a lot of weight to place on one man," Fa'Lem said. "The fate of an entire people. But I believe I found you for a reason. Against all I have seen, I choose to have hope."

"Well, I'm glad you do," I said. "But he was a great wizard or whatever, and I'm just, well, me."

"Yes, but in the end, he stood alone." She looked around at all my companions. "You, clearly, do not."

"You have my axe..." Curr said. "Well, I lost my axe. So, the next one I find!"

Whew, that was getting to be treacherous territory.

"It seems there is no need for the Sisterhood of Alyndis any longer," Lilla said, standing and bowing just her head. "And so, I will stand with you, Danny, in the name of my people."

Did she just bow at me?

Did you like it?

I... don't know...

"You don't have to bow, Lilla," I said, quickly deciding it was weird. I didn't want to be some leader to her. I wanted to date her. And dating your boss is frowned upon, so, I wanted us all on an even playing field.

What a romantic...

You would be too if she kissed you.

That is so offensive to the mouthless.

"Sorry, boyo, but I only work for hire when I get paid," Garvis said. "I'll admit, it has been fun, though. A little too fun."

"Ah, yes. I forget the ways of the new world." Fa'Lem waved her staff, and a large golden chest materialized near us. "Coin paves the path to the future, and you will need it if the future is to be grand. And what was taken by the cursed, re-found."

I stepped toward the chest. Curr brushed me aside and moved ahead. Before either of us reached it, Garvis zipped between us and ran to it like a dog after a tennis ball. I didn't know he could move so fast.

He grabbed the top and tried to open it, but it was too large and heavy. Curr arrived on the scene to crack it the rest of the way. When he looked inside, he pushed Garvis so hard in excitement, the halfling flew halfway across the room.

I swear, a golden beam of light washed over them.

"My axe!" Curr screamed, pulling the great axe from the chest, and clutching it to his chest like a newborn baby.

I finally made it over. Every weapon the orcs had taken was inside, from Garvis' knives to Lilla's bow and quiver. Well, every weapon except for my short sword. I had a feeling that was on purpose. Like Fa'Lem was trying to tell me that the lute was all I needed.

I didn't care. Because beneath all of the items was a layer of gold coins.

You have gained 500 GP. We're rich, biatch!

Garvis sprinted back over and practically dove in, letting the coins trickle through his fingers. I thought he may have even cried. "Don't forget, Danny, you owe me half your take!"

I ignored him and turned back to Lilla, Tevagah, and Fa'Lem. What the hell was wrong with me, caring about them more than gold?

Don't ask me. We're riiiich!

"So, what *is* next, then?" I asked.

Fa'lem used her staff like a walking stick and approached me. "If you remember, in the memory I showed you, the lute held an orb. Much of Varun's power went into it, forged in the starlight of the mountain. If we have any hope of reversing his spell, the Lute of Seven Stars must be fully restored."

Roxanne began playing a new song, and I immediately recognized it. "'Don't Stop Believing'," I said, smiling. "I guess she likes the idea of that."

"She?" Fa'lem leaned in to observe the lute, way too close for comfort even in her less haggy state. "Curious."

"I don't know. It just fits."

"Curious, indeed."

"Where is the orb?" Lilla asked, straight to business. "If it's as lost as the lute was, Danny won't live to find it."

"Hey, I thought we were all on the same team again!" I argued.

"You are mortal," she clarified. "You do not have centuries."

"Oh... right..."

It's not like I didn't know that, but it was the first time anyone said it out loud since I'd met Lilla and developed a crush.

Developed? It was love at first sight. For you anyway.

Was that why she ran so hot and cold with me? If we fell for each other, I'd die, and she'd be left alone for eternity.

Sure, that's the reason. It couldn't possibly be your oh-so-charming personality: Insert Sarcasm Font.

You never know! That must be horrible. To know everybody around you will eventually die and leave you alone.

"You are in luck this time," Fa'Lem said. "The orb was kept as a treasure after the wellick army arrived. It sits in the royal collection of the Pyruunian king. Inside his castle in the capital."

Garvis perked up from admiring the gold. "Did I hear 'royal collection'?"

"We're going to rob a king?" I asked. My jaw may as well have been on the floor.

Oh, hell yeah. Can you say heist time?

Curr clapped me on the back. It'd been a while since he'd done that, and I almost fell onto my face. "Do not fret, Danny. I have robbed a king before. It was simple!" He scratched his chin. "Of course, he was already deceased, and his castle was overrun by marauders."

"Are you frightened, Danny the Bard?" Lilla asked. She brushed my pinky with hers, and I turned to see her wearing a mischievous grin. My heart nearly joined my jaw on the floor.

Wow, okay. Now I sort of get you. She's got it.

"Me?" I replied. "Never."

"Hmm, I can recall many times when you appeared to be frightened like a tiny child," Curr said.

"Fear is what caused this mess," Fa'Lem said. "Conquer it fast, for time is of the essence. With every day that passes, more orcs are slain and cannot be saved." She sank to her knees next to Tevagah and rummaged around near her belt—the Dagger of Discontent appeared in her hand.

She presented it to Lilla on an open palm. "Take my husband's dagger. It will open the way. It's a long way down, so you'd all better get moving. Return to me when you have what is needed. I will watch over Tevagah until you do."

Lilla eyed the dagger with warranted suspicion. Her hand hovered over it, frozen, unwilling to take it.

"I've seen what it did to her." She looked down at Tevagah.

"Varun's black magic corrupted it, but now that he is gone, I feel the darkness has lifted," Fa'Lem said. "Take it. His blade and his instrument, working in harmony, as was always meant to be."

When Lilla hesitated further, Fa'Lem took her hand and moved it to the dagger's hilt and gently closed her fingers around it. Lilla's eyes closed, her expression remaining steady.

Look at us, both with a piece of Varun.

How unbelievably adorable.

Hey, you heard her. Working in harmony.

So, you're saying there's still a chance?

I'm saying there's not, not a chance.

Eloquent...

Lilla drew a deep breath, then her eyes opened, and she nodded. She didn't seem irritated, only focused. Determined. Without a word, she strode to the great stone doors of the observatory and held out the dagger.

It looked like some sort of magic shield dissipated. The air rippled in a way that reminded me of the hot sun on asphalt, and the heavy doors creaked open. Cold air and snow whipped in, tossing her hair back in the most kickass Valkyrie way. Then she looked back at us: a braug mercenary, a thieving halfling, and a man not of her world.

"Well, what are you all waiting for?" she said.

NEW PARTY MEMBER ADDED:
Lilla, Sister of Alyndis (Level 29).

Oh my god. She's officially in.

Should we tell her that she forgot to grab her bow and stuff? That might ruin the badassery of the moment. I don't know. I'm just so excited, I can't feel my toes. I don't have toes. Am I rambling?

Whatever, it's sequel time. Are you ready, Danny?

Are you ready to be even MORE of a hero?

I shrugged. "All right. Let's go rob a king. What could possibly go wrong?"

NEW OBJECTIVE:
Return the Lute of the Seven Stars to its former glory.

REWARD:
A more powerful instrument.

Wow. Have you seen what this thing can do already? Watch out, bad guys!

Curr laughed and clapped me once more on the back. "That is the spirit. I am ready. It has been too long since our last battle."

"We just fought dozens of orcs, literally, like twenty minutes ago," Garvis said.

"Exactly! Already, I am bored."

I chuckled and gave Curr a much weaker clap on the back than he'd done to me. "Never change, my friend."

He shot me a cross glare as he corrected me. "Best friend."

AN UNEXPECTED HERO

Friendly reminder...

CURRENT OBJECTIVE:
Find a way to come clean and tell Curr the truth about where you're from.
Some best friend you are...

Shit! I just haven't found the right time yet. It can wait.

It will have to, because, congrats!

You have reached the end of the first installment of "An Unexpected Hero," by Jaime Castle and Rhett C. Bruno.

The end of what? Jaime Castle? Rhett Bruno? Who the heck are they!

♫♪♪ **We don't talk about Bruno-no-no.** ♪♪♫

Screenieeee!

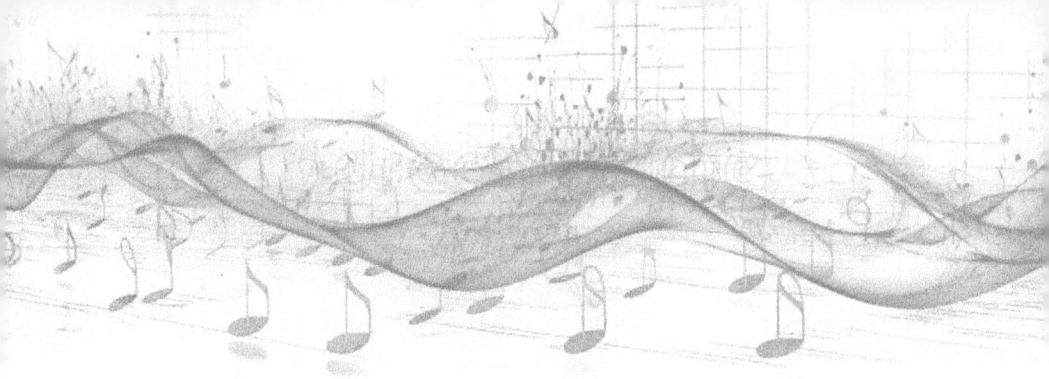

DANNY'S FINAL STATS

NAME: Daniil Kendrick (male)
LEVEL: 6
CLASS: Bard
Health: 125
Stamina: 75
Mana: 0
Defense: 4 (+15)
Attack Damage: 8-11

ATTRIBUTES:
Strength: 12
Constitution: 16
Intelligence: 9 (+10)
Wisdom: 10
Dexterity: 18 (+10)
Charisma: 18 (+11)
Courage: 15
Luck: 33

SKILLS:
Melee Weapon Combat: 19
Ranged Combat: 9
Unarmed Combat: 7
Shields: 3
Singing: 18 (+10)
Instrument Playing: 22 (+10)
Herbalism: 5
Alchemy: 6
Pickpocketing: 9
Bartering: 8
Speechcraft: 19 (+11)
Camping: 2
Sneaking: 5 (-1)
Riding: 2
Crafting:
Smithing:
Leatherworks:
Magic Skills: N/A

SPECIAL ABILITIES:
[Time is of the Essence]

TITLES:
Petty Thief
Wraith Whisperer
Vermin's Bane
Protector of Pikeman's Trail
Womanizer
Get the Orc Outta Here!
Survivalist
Unhinged
Boss Bitch

INVENTORY:
The Lute of Seven Stars [Unique]
Dented Chain Mail Hauberk
Basic Pants
Basic Tunic
Boots
Lalair's Elegant Cloak
Elvish Silver Bracer [Enchanted]
Orcish Bone Sword (Melee Damage 8-11)
Gold: 526

Jaime Castle hails from the great nation of Texas where he lives with his wife and two children. A self-proclaimed comic book nerd and artist, he spends what little free time he can muster with his art tablet.

Jaime is a #1 Audible Bestseller, Audible Originals author (Dead Acre, The Luna Missile Crisis) and co-created and co-authored The Buried Goddess Saga, including the IPPY award-winning Web of Eyes.

All books below are available on eBook, Print, and Audiobook

FANTASY:
The Buried Goddess Saga:
Web of Eyes | Winds of War | Will of Fire
Way of Gods | War of Men | Word of Truth

Dragonblood Assassin:
Black Talon | Red Claw | Silver Spines | Golden Flames

RHETT C. BRUNO & JAIME CASTLE

Black Badge (Western Fantasy):
Dead Acre | Cold As Hell | Vein Pursuits | Ace in the Hole

Jeff the Game Master (LitRPG):
Manufacturing Magic | Manipulating Magic
Mastering Magic

An Unexpected Hero (LitRPG):
Book 1

Raptors (Superheroes):
Sidekick | Superteam |Scions
Baron Steele | Mega-Mech Apocalypse

Harrier (Superheroes):
Justice | The Trench | Invasion

SCIENCE FICTION:
The Luna Missile Crisis | This Long Vigil

Rogue Stars:
Purgatory | Divine Intervention | Reclamation

Find out more at www.jaimecastle.com
https://www.facebook.com/authorjaimecastle
Follow me on Amazon!

Rhett C Bruno is the USA Today and Washington Post Bestselling & Nebula Award Nominated Author of 'The Circuit Saga', 'Children of Titan Series', 'Buried Goddess Saga', 'Vicarious', 'The Roach', and 'The Luna Missile Crisis' (Audible Originals); among other works.

He has been writing since before he can remember, scribbling down what he thought were epic stories when he was young to show to his friends and family. He is currently a full-time author and publisher living in Delaware with his wife, daughter, and dog Raven.

Find out more here: http://rhettbruno.com/

Also, please consider subscribing to his newsletter for exclusive access to updates about his work and the opportunity to receive limited content and ARCs.

Subscribe Here: http://rhettbruno.com/newsletter

Together, they own www.aethonbooks.com